Coco's Secret

NIAMH GREENE

PENGUIN BOOKS

PENGUIN BOOKS

Published by the Penguin Group
Penguin Books Ltd, 80 Strand, London WC2R 0RL, England
Penguin Group (USA) Inc., 375 Hudson Street, New York, New York 10014, USA
Penguin Group (Canada), 90 Eglinton Avenue East, Suite 700, Toronto, Ontario, Canada M4P 2Y3
(a division of Pearson Penguin Canada Inc.)
Penguin Ireland, 25 St Stephen's Green, Dublin 2, Ireland
(a division of Penguin Books Ltd)
Penguin Group (Australia), 707 Collins Street, Melbourne, Victoria 3008, Australia
(a division of Pearson Australia Group Pty Ltd)
Penguin Books India Pvt Ltd, 11 Community Centre, Panchsheel Park, New Delhi – 110 017, India
Penguin Group (NZ), 67 Apollo Drive, Rosedale, Auckland 0632, New Zealand
(a division of Pearson New Zealand Ltd)
Penguin Books (South Africa) (Pty) Ltd, Block D, Rosebank Office Park,
181 Jan Smuts Avenue, Parktown North, Gauteng 2193, South Africa

Penguin Books Ltd, Registered Offices: 80 Strand, London WC2R 0RL, England

www.penguin.com

First published 2013
001

Typeset in 12.5/14.75pt Garamond MT Std by Palimpsest Book Production Ltd,
Falkirk, Stirlingshire
Printed in Great Britain by Clays Ltd, St Ives plc

A CIP catalogue record for this book is available from the British Library

ISBN: 978-0-241-95198-9

PENGUIN BOOKS

Coco's Secret

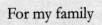
For my family

'A girl should be two things: who
and what she wants.'

Coco Chanel

Paris, November 1993

Sarah jiggled the key in the lock, twisting it this way and that, to no avail. The door was stuck and it simply wasn't budging. She had spoken to the landlady about it half a dozen times already, but Madame Bouche had merely shrugged and smiled enigmatically every time, as if the upkeep of her own boarding house was somehow none of her affair. There were lots of things about the small Parisian hotel that weren't entirely satisfactory, Sarah thought, but it was relatively clean and the views of the city were incredible, and that made up for most of them.

She set down the box of antique trinkets she'd purchased in the market that morning and put her shoulder to the door. She leaned the full weight of her body against it and, with a creaking sigh, it finally gave way and swung open. She smiled with pleasure as she scooped up the cardboard box once more and stepped into the small, always chilly bedroom that was her temporary home in the City of Light. She'd found more than a few pieces that would sell very well back in the shop in Dronmore, she was sure. She could already imagine how her father would love the silly little cuckoo clock she'd unearthed – he'd probably want to keep it for himself. She could understand that – she already wanted to keep the sweet costume jewellery she'd bought at one of the stalls. But thinking like that would defeat the whole purpose of her trip: she was in France to buy stock for Swan's Antiques, not on a personal shopping expedition, even if some of what she found was irresistible. Like the pearls, for instance. Sarah rifled through the box and spied the gorgeous string of pearls peeping up at her. They really were very beautiful ... It would be hard to let them go and allow someone else to buy them. But, then, she already had one strand so she didn't need another. She had to stop this habit of getting so attached to objects: it was detrimental to profits.

Shrugging off her coat and unwinding her scarf from her neck, Sarah spotted an envelope that lay address side up on the doormat, the unmistakable Irish stamp in the corner. She picked it up and turned it over, immediately seeing the Swan's Antiques logo on the reverse flap. It was from Dronmore.

Putting the box of trinkets to one side, she clasped the envelope to her chest and crossed to where a battered cane chair stood by the tall shuttered windows. She sat down, tucked a blanket around her legs to ward off the cold and looked out across the city. The cracked pane was frosted with cold, tiny drips of condensation gathering in the corners, but in the distance she could see the Eiffel Tower rising out of the mist. It lifted her spirits, just as it did every morning. Then she turned over the envelope – her eye on her mother's looped handwriting and the Irish words for Dublin stamped in the corner 'Baile Átha Cliath'. Sometimes home seemed so far away she wasn't sure it was even home any more. She slid the letter out of its slim envelope.

My darling Sarah,

I thought I'd write and say hello before we see you next week. It's snowing here today – the street is so pretty with everything coated in white. Your dad is a bit grumpy about it. He says it stops people getting to us here in the shop, but I think it adds to that lovely Christmassy magic. Coco adores it, of course. She and her school pal Cat Reilly have had such fun sliding up and down the pavements outside. We can't wait for you to get home for Christmas, darling, Coco especially. She's been such an enormous help in the shop – you'd be so proud of her. She even came up with the theme for the Christmas window all by herself. She gathered together all the clocks we had on the shop floor and arranged them in a sort of Alice in Wonderland montage – it's just gorgeous. Your dad couldn't believe how clever she was – she has such a great eye, everyone says so. Your dad says she's a mini-Sarah, but more obedient!

Coco is the reason I'm writing, really, if I'm honest. But you probably saw through me already, didn't you? It's just that now she's almost thirteen, I think she needs you in her life more, Sarah. It's such a funny age – don't you remember how it felt to be a teenager? All those hormones are flying about and everything is so uncertain and confusing. It seems like only yesterday that you were that age yourself. I can hardly believe you're a grown woman now. Anyway, we love having Coco here with us, we always have, but I do think she needs you now, more than ever. She doesn't complain, but your dad and I can see that she misses you terribly all the same. I know you love to travel and you don't like being tied down to boring old Dronmore, but maybe the time is right to stay put with us for a while, for Coco's sake. Promise me you'll think about it, will you? The mother-and-daughter bond is so important, as you and I both know. Now is the time to cement it, before it's too late.

I'd better get on – there's so much to do before you get home. Your dad has grand plans for your bedroom. Just wait and see!

Lots of love,
Mum

PS Here's a photo of Coco in the snow – her expression is so exactly like yours at that age. Can you see it?

Sarah held the photograph at arm's length. Coco was standing on the path outside Swan's Antiques, dressed in a red wool coat with a multicoloured striped scarf wound around her neck. In the background, Sarah could see the display of clocks in the window, fairy lights entwined among them, twinkling in the half-light. Coco was staring straight into the lens, laughing at whoever was taking the shot. The tip of her nose and her cheeks were pink and snowflakes adorned her black beret – the one Sarah had sent her two weeks ago, as a consolation for not being there herself. Coco was going to be taller and broader than she was, but the similarity around the eyes was uncanny. They couldn't be mistaken for anything other than mother and daughter.

Where had all the time gone? Could almost thirteen years have passed so quickly? And what of her mother's gently worded suggestion about staying put at home? She had always told herself – and everyone else – that she had to travel far and wide to source unique and interesting stock for Swan's, but was that really the truth? Yes, Swan's was known for its unusual antiques, but it would probably do just as well without her flitting all over Europe, gathering things as she went. If she were honest with herself, she knew that two or three short trips a year would probably be enough to keep the shop ticking over. They all knew that. But the thought of going back for good, to settle down, made Sarah's chest tighten. She loved her parents and her daughter with all her heart and soul, but she'd never been very good at living a conventional life. That was why she'd left Coco behind in Ireland, to give her some sort of stability. Being on the road was no good for a child, and it wasn't as if Coco's father was around to help. But the idea that Coco might believe she didn't care was terrible.

Sarah studied the letter again. Reading between the lines, she felt her mother might be saying that Coco was perhaps feeling abandoned and unloved.

An enormous wave of guilt washed over her as she gazed down at the street below, where pedestrians were making their way along the frosty cobbles. In truth, her mother's words were pushing at an open door – Sarah had known in her heart that a change was coming, was needed, really. Her mind was constantly being tugged in the direction of Dronmore and Coco. She had been putting off the inevitable: things had to change, for her daughter's sake. Her own parents had always been there for her through thick and thin. When she had arrived back from one of her trips, pregnant and with no man to show for it, they hadn't judged her. Instead, they had stood staunchly by her side, even when half of the town was busy gossiping about it, while the other half had pretended they weren't. She wanted to be there for Coco in the same way, give her the same sort of unconditional love, and if that meant going back for good, then that was what she would do.

She would learn to adjust. Yes, it might kill her to be tied down to the small town in which she'd grown up, where everyone knew your business before you knew it yourself, but she would do it if she had to, if Coco needed her.

Sarah looked at the photograph of her daughter again and smiled. It might not be so awful, of course. Maybe when she returned this time, it would be different – maybe she would appreciate her roots more instead of feeling they were strangling her. Her natural optimism buoyed her as she reached for a pen. She would write to Coco right now, tell her the good news, reassure her that she loved her more than words could say and would always be there for her, no matter what.

She wrote quickly, deep in thought, pausing now and again to glance out of the window or fiddle with the string of pearls she always wore at her throat.

My darling Coco,

I just wanted to write and tell you how much I love you. That's pretty soppy, I know, but it's true. I can't wait to spend Christmas with you all in Dronmore. In fact, I'm planning to stay on, if you'll have me. Travelling is fun, but I miss you too much to be away any more. I know I probably don't remember to say it as often as I should, but I hope you know that I couldn't be prouder of you. You were a little gift into my life and I cherish you. I can't wait to see you soon.

Lots of love,
Mum

Sarah rooted out an envelope from the drawer, addressed it with a flourish and sealed it. There was so much to get done before she went home. Her mind whirred with all the jobs she had to tick off before she could head back for good. She knew exactly what she would give Coco for Christmas – the gorgeous pearls she'd found that morning. She should have thought of it before – now they would both have a string. Yes, they were just costume jewels but Coco would love them all the same, and when she was older Sarah would buy her some real ones, like her namesake, Coco Chanel, used to wear. She'd get her a genuine Chanel bag, too, some day, just as she'd promised, to match her special name. People had laughed when she had named her baby girl after her idol, but Sarah had never regretted it. It suited her daughter down to the ground and Sarah knew she was destined for great things – just like Coco Chanel.

She grabbed her coat and left the room, pulling the door shut behind her, then dashed downstairs and onto the street. There was no time to waste. Now that she had made up her mind, she wanted to post the letter straight away. She ran across the icy cobbles, clutching the precious letter, her mind full of Coco's smiling eyes. This was the right thing to do: she could feel it in every fibre of her being. She flew past the tiny *boulangerie* on the corner, where she bought her baguette every morning, and across the street, determined to catch the morning post. If she did, Coco would get the letter in a day or two – Sarah could see her daughter's excited reaction in her mind's eye.

She was midway across the street when she heard the shout.

A cyclist she had failed to notice was swerving wildly to avoid her. Sarah screamed and leaped out of his way, but from the corner of her eye she saw a flash of white, bearing down on her. There was a terrible sound, a splintering screech that ripped through the air, through her senses, through her. As the metal crunched against her body, her mouth formed a single word: Coco. But it was too late. Everything was too late.

In the police report after the accident, the old baker on the corner of the street sadly recounted how the lovely Irish woman, who always wore pearls, had dashed across the road, not seeing the van as it careered towards her. It had all happened so quickly, so out of the blue. The poor *mademoiselle* hadn't stood a chance. He thought she had been holding something, a letter perhaps, but he couldn't be sure because it had fluttered away on the icy city breeze, and he had never seen it again.

I

The girl behind the desk at Maloney's Auction Rooms doesn't bother to look up as I approach. 'Name?' she demands, pen poised to write down my details so she can give me a bidding number and move on to the next person in the long queue that snakes behind me. She has the bored-rigid air of someone who's been working here for donkey's years and has lost the will to live, even though I know for a fact she's only been here five weeks, tops.

'Coco Swan,' I reply quietly. There's a beat and then she raises her head from the sheet of names and numbers in front of her so she can look at me properly, running her eyes from my face to my body, slowly taking in every detail. She skims over my favourite skinny navy scarf that's now more than a little well washed and knobbly, past the striped maroon-and-cream sweater that's gone baggy at the elbows, down to my worn jeans and the scuffed brown ankle boots I'm never without. She's not impressed by what she sees – I can tell that by the slight curl of her perfect Cupid's bow mouth.

'Coco?' she repeats. 'What – like Coco Chanel?'

'Ah, no, like Coco the Clown,' I joke, then laugh, half expecting her to join in. It's my fail-safe reply to this question, used hundreds of times before to deflect people from the chasm of difference between my name and how I look.

The girl stares uncomprehendingly at me, her grey eyes unblinking. Either she has no sense of humour or she doesn't get the joke. Maybe both.

'Just kidding.' I sigh. 'Yes, like Coco Chanel.'

'Why are you called that?' she asks, her gaze settling on my nose for just a fraction longer than necessary, just long enough to let me know that she's clocked the body part that's been the bane of my life since I was a gangly, spotty-faced teenager.

I feel the woman behind me leaning in closer to hear my reply to this pressing question. That's the problem with having a name like Coco, of course. People expect you to be glamorous and exotic, wear a little black dress and smoke foreign cigarettes. They definitely do not expect you to be tall and a little hefty of shoulder, with uninteresting hair, a wonky nose that sort of veers sideways and a personal style that can only be described as shabby chic, but without the chic.

'My mother loved France . . .' I say, embarrassed, as always, by this honest explanation '. . . and, em, Coco Chanel.'

'But you look *nothing* like her,' the girl says.

I know she's not referring to my mother now, because Mum's been dead for almost twenty years and this girl can't be more than that herself.

'Nothing *at all* like her,' she goes on, with heavy emphasis. 'I know because I saw that movie last week.'

'Oooh, yes! I saw it too,' the woman behind me pipes up, clearly unable to contain herself. 'You really *don't* look anything like her, do you?'

There's a slight air of accusation in her voice, as if this

is somehow my fault and I've let them all down by not living up to my name. I tug at my scarf, suddenly feeling a little restricted. 'No, I know I don't,' I admit, 'but I don't think that's why Mum . . .' I trail off. Sometimes I really wish that Mum had named me something nice and ordinary – like Jo or Clare. Something non-committal and open-ended, a name that doesn't make any promises. The problem is that I just don't care about clothes or makeup or any of the glam stuff. If my mother had known that, she could have saved me the embarrassment and all these pointless conversations. But Mum was never one for making straightforward decisions about anything – and I've had to learn to deal with a name I can never live up to.

The woman behind me has moved right next to me now, so close I can smell the faint whiff of stale cigarette smoke on her breath. There are deep, puckered lines around her mouth, and her pink lipstick is sort of bleeding away from her lips, like it wants to escape.

'God, that film was terrible depressing altogether, wasn't it?' she says, to the girl behind the desk. 'She had a sad life, Coco Chanel. Never married, of course.'

They both look at me, and the implication that the same fate awaits me hangs in the air between us.

'I'll just, er, give you my details,' I say to the girl. All I want is a bidding number, for God's sake. I don't need an examination of my life by two complete strangers. I haven't the guts to say so, though, even if I wish I had.

'She never went anywhere without a cigarette,' the woman with the bleeding lipstick is now informing everyone in earshot. 'It was part of the look back in those days, wasn't it? Now you can't smoke anywhere – they'd lock you up and throw away the key if you tried.' She sighs heavily, eyeing the No Smoking sign that hangs on the wall as if she wants to wrench it down with her bare hands and rip it to shreds.

Finally, the girl loses interest and slides the bidding number across the scratched desk to me. As I move away, happy to escape, my phone buzzes with a text from my best friend, Cat.

> Don't forget to keep an eye
> out for more of those mirrors!
> Give hell to anyone who dares
> bid against you! x

Cat is trying to do up her family's hotel on a tight budget and I'm helping her. I've already sourced an oversized gilt mirror for the foyer and am on the hunt for more, as well as other bits and pieces to spruce up the place. I text back quickly to tell her I'm on it, then start to weave through the aisles, my eyes flicking over the piles of stuff on display.

I have about ten minutes to look around before the auction starts and I want to use my time wisely by making a list of possible purchases. As well as stuff for the hotel, I already know the type of thing I want for the shop – definitely no large pieces of furniture. They never sell, which is a pity because I can see at least a dozen gorgeous old wardrobes lined up along one wall, like awkward wallflowers waiting to be asked onto the dance-floor. I can guarantee no one will want them. People like fitted furniture now, not free-standing hulks of mahogany. If Swan's Antiques had the space, though, I'd take them all. I absolutely love old wardrobes. It's the unknowable possibility they represent: who owned them? What sort of clothes once hung in there? Glamorous sequined ballgowns? Beaded 1920s flapper dresses? My imagination always runs riot when I see an empty old wardrobe.

I tear myself away from them reluctantly. Today I'm going to stick to the plan, no veering off course. I turn back to my catalogue as I wander, examining each page and double-checking which things might work. I look around the packed auction room and try to focus. There's so much to see: worn, faded rugs unfurled on the floor, china piled high in glass cases, books jammed into boxes, tables, desks and chairs in every sort of wood imaginable. Everywhere I look people are picking things up, turning them over, sniffing them, looking for signs of moth, woodworm or water damage, all intent on their own possible purchases. The competition will be stiff today. I've already spotted half a dozen other professional traders, too, all of whom will be after the same things. It might go my way, it might not, but then, that's what makes auctions so exciting. The main thing is not to get carried away, not to let my heart rule my head. Don't buy anything you can't sell on: that's the golden rule my grandmother drummed into me from a very young age. Ruth, as she prefers to be called because she thinks it's less ageing, is an expert, and everything I know about the antiques business I learned from her.

Right on cue, I spot her across the room, flirting outrageously with everyone in her path, as she always does, charming everyone she encounters. She doesn't even have to work at making everyone fall a little in love with her.

She just has 'it' – whatever 'it' is – in spades, and everyone adores her. It doesn't matter if they're young or old, male or female, rich or poor, Ruth makes a connection with them and they never forget her. I really wish I had 'it' too, but the charm gene seems to have skipped my generation. Instead I got the wonky nose, the broad shoulders and the social awkwardness.

I watch as Ruth chats animatedly to Hugo Maloney, the proprietor and auctioneer, fiddling with a stray corkscrew curl and winding it around her ear as she talks. He's utterly captivated. I notice, not for the first time, how men look at her, and how attractive she really is. She's almost seventy but her smile is wide, her dark eyes sparkle, her skin is still luminous and her mass of unruly silver ringlets is piled higgledy-piggledy on top of her head, showing off the elegant curve of her neck.

'Now, Hugo,' I hear her chide gently, 'don't go trying to pull any fast ones on me today – remember, I'm a loyal customer.' Then she lays a hand on his arm, throws her head back and peals with laughter at his response. Hugo – an otherwise ruthless businessman, who stands for no nonsense in his auction house – is gazing at her with open admiration. He's always had a soft spot for Ruth, and she's very aware of it.

I know exactly what she's playing at, of course, and Hugo probably does too. She's trying to charm him before the auction starts, hoping he might throw a few decent lots her way, bring the hammer down a little quicker than he technically ought to in her favour. He doesn't take his eyes off her as she sashays away from him and over to me where, with a small, satisfied sigh, she takes a seat.

'You do know that you're the biggest floozy I've ever seen?' I say, sitting beside her.

She giggles in a very non-OAP way and winks at me. 'Ah, well, like I keep telling you, Coco, age is just a number and there's never a good reason to stop having fun. Now, have you seen anything you like? Any nice jewellery?'

Even though I'm a tomboy at heart, I have a real soft spot for old costume jewellery. Ruth says Mum was the same – she was never parted from her favourite pearls apparently. We still have them at Swan's now, in a frosted-glass cabinet. I wear them sometimes, for special occasions.

'No jewellery, but I think lot two twenty-one looks interesting,' I reply quietly. No point in drawing every-one's attention to it. The walls can have ears in here.

'Lot two twenty-one . . . the wash-stand?' Ruth is peer-ing at the catalogue, flipping through the pages, all the while keeping a beady eye on everyone else in case she misses anyone she knows or sees a possible rival.

'Yeah. There's so much junk on top of it, boxes of books and stuff, I'm not sure many people have noticed it has a marble top. We could get a bargain.'

'Well spotted, Coco,' she says, grinning at me. 'You have an eagle eye.'

'Yeah, but so do a lot of other people here,' I reply. 'Including Perry Smythe.'

Perry is a small-time antiques dealer, who has a very irritating habit of outbidding me regularly at auctions up and down the country – it's almost as if he senses when I really, really want something and swoops in at the very last second to snatch it from me, just when I think I've got it sewn up. If I didn't know better, I'd say he did it on purpose, just to aggravate me, but Perry's so proper and such a gentleman I'd have great trouble proving it.

'Ah, yes, good old Perry. I think he's lost weight, don't you?' Ruth says, eyeing him as he approaches us from across the room. He's dressed in a three-piece tweed suit, Church's brogues on his feet.

'Don't even think about it,' I warn her.

'What?' she replies, all wide-eyed innocence.

'Ruth! Coco! How are you?' Perry is upon us before I can reply.

Ruth jumps up to greet him, kissing him warmly on both cheeks. 'Perry, darling. How handsome you look,' she purrs.

'Hi, Perry,' I say, squinting at the catalogue in his hands – has he marked anything I want? But he swiftly – and quite deliberately – shoves it into his pocket, wily old fox that he is.

'You both look smashing, as always, ladies,' he says grandly, in his cut-glass English accent, even though he's from a small town in Cavan. The story is that his parents were English gentry and Perry was sent to boarding school from the age of four – hence the old-school manners and accent to match.

'As do you, Perry, as do you,' Ruth says, smiling warmly. 'Have you lost weight? You're so trim!'

Perry pats his stomach, almost automatically, and gives a proud smile. 'Nineteen pounds. I'm on the caveman diet,' he says.

'The caveman diet?' Ruth repeats, her eyes trained on his. 'What's that?'

'Well, it means I only consume what our ancestors would have, Ruth,' he explains earnestly. 'I can eat meat, vegetables, food in its natural state, nothing processed – that's the key to success.'

'I have to say, it's really working – you look wonderful,' Ruth says.

'Thank you.' He blushes. 'But I need to lose some more,' he says, and pats his stomach again.

'Don't be silly! You're positively fading away,' Ruth exclaims. 'But maybe I should try it – I'm getting a little plump.' She pinches an imaginary spare tyre and grimaces.

'You don't need to, Ruth,' Perry says gallantly. 'You're as slim as you always were, as beautiful as . . .' He goes mute, like he knows he's said too much, and there's a short silence as he tries to decide what to say next. 'And, ah, Coco. How are you?' He turns to me.

'Oh, I'm fine. Still gorging on all the processed foods I can get my hands on, unfortunately,' I reply, straight-faced, unable to resist the urge to tease him.

'Oh, I see.' He coughs a little nervously, unsure whether I'm joking or not. 'And, um, how's that fellow of yours? The farmer? Tom, isn't it? Terribly nice chap.'

I can almost feel Ruth's breath in my right ear as she inhales sharply. 'Perry, Tom is –'

'It's OK, Ruth,' I interrupt. 'No one's dead, it's no big deal.'

Perry is looking from me to Ruth, confusion all over his now svelte face. The diet really *is* working – I can see the shadows of cheekbones for the first time since I've known him.

'Tom emigrated to New Zealand last month, Perry,' I

say calmly. 'He's going to manage a cattle ranch over there. It's a great opportunity.'

'Oh. I see.' Perry looks from Ruth to me once more, clearly unsure how to react to this news. 'And, um, are you going to follow him?'

There's another intake of breath in my right ear. Poor Ruth. She's taking this worse than I am. She loved Tom.

'No, I'm not,' I say firmly. 'I'm happy where I am.'

Again Perry looks from Ruth to me, his mind clearly working overtime. I can almost see the mental cogs grinding: if Tom is over there and I'm over here, that means . . .

'We've broken up, Perry,' I say, putting him out of his misery.

'Ah, I see.' He twists his still meaty hands. Clearly the caveman diet has some work to do in this regard. 'Sorry, Coco.'

'That's OK. I'm fine,' I reply, surprised by how cheerful I sound. But, then, everything about Tom leaving has surprised me. Right up until the very last second I think he was convinced I'd go with him. We'd been together for eight years so he and everyone else had expected me to go, or at least to declare that I'd wait for him in case he came back. When I broke up with him instead, it took everyone in town by surprise. Even me, at first.

'How are the family, Perry?' Ruth asks, changing the subject.

'Wonderful, thank you, Ruth. Did you know my first great-grandchild is on the way?'

'How fabulous!' Ruth claps her hands together. 'A new baby!'

I feel myself bristle, clocking their sideways glances.

18

Everyone thinks I've missed the baby-making boat now that Tom has left. No one has said as much, but they don't need to, I know what they're thinking: thirty-two years old and she's thrown away a good man right when her biological alarm is about to go off. But maybe I don't want to have a baby. I wouldn't have a clue how to be a mum, that's for sure.

Around us, people are choosing their seats in the lines of chairs set out in neat rows. The chairs are for sale too, some of them in better shape than others.

'Is that how you really feel?' Ruth asks, once Perry has shuffled away in his lace-up leather brogues and we've perched on a pair of faded, slightly smelly Queen Annes. 'Or were you just putting on a good face for Perry?'

'It's how I really feel,' I reply, a little irritated. 'I keep telling you, don't I?'

Ruth has been checking my emotional temperature almost every hour on the hour since Tom's plane took to the air. I know she's acting out of love and concern for me but, my God, it's tiresome. Sometimes I'm tempted to fake a nervous breakdown just to reassure her.

'You don't miss him?' she presses on.

'No, not really. I mean, I know I should, but I don't.'

'I do,' she says, almost to herself.

'I think you miss the idea of him.'

'It's not that, Coco. He was a nice boy, he always was, and you were good together.'

She's right, in a way – we *were* quite good together. We rubbed along nicely, as they say. And if he was still here, we'd probably still be together. But he's not: he's as good as a million miles away. And no matter how hard he tried to persuade me to join him, to start a new life over there, it was never going to happen. I like my life here. Besides, when your boyfriend tells you he's moving halfway round the world and your first reaction is relief, it can't be a good sign.

I can feel Ruth staring intently at me, like she's trying to read my innermost thoughts. She's done the same thing since I was a teenager and everyone was worried about me after Mum died. She's the personification of kindness, but she also loves to talk about emotions, and her full-on, unblinking gaze is usually the first warning sign that a 'talk' is looming. The truth is, I don't like to talk about feelings as much as Ruth does. I didn't when I was a teenager and I don't now. A little bit of chit-chat around the topic is OK, a bit of vague skirting around the issue, but a full-blown post-mortem of my emotional landscape now that Tom's gone? No, thanks.

I concentrate very hard on the podium, where Hugo is settling into his seat behind the tall, narrow desk from which he'll conduct the auction. I have to say something to head her off at the pass or the staring will continue – and that will put me right off my game.

'Maybe we were good together,' I concede, 'but can you see me on a ranch in the middle of nowhere? It would never have worked – you know I hate cattle. They're so . . . smelly.' I laugh to let her know that this is my idea of a little joke.

'But you could have tried it, Coco. You could have given it a go. You still could. I don't want you to think that you have to stay here to take care of me. I'm absolutely –'

'I keep telling you, I don't feel I have to stay here to take care of you. I know you're perfectly fine, Ruth. Now, can we move on, please?'

Lord, why can't everyone just drop it? Sometimes it feels as if Ruth never stops going on about Tom leaving and neither does Cat. She thinks I should have gone and tried it out too. Neither of them knows what I do: that it would never have worked. And it's not like I'm heartbroken. Yes, Tom was a nice guy and I liked him, loved him once. I still like him and wish him well. But he'll be fine. In no time at all he'll meet a nice girl over there and they'll get married and raise little cattle-hustling kids in cute cowboy hats. That's not for me. And the fact that I'm not bothered about him meeting someone else proves we weren't right together, no matter how good it looked on paper.

'OK,' Ruth murmurs, sighing a little. 'But I don't think I'll ever understand how you can be so cut and dried about it.'

'Maybe that's just the way I am,' I reply. 'Now, can we please forget about Tom and focus on getting what we want for the shop?'

Thankfully, Hugo is clearing his throat. The auction is officially under way.

'Good morning, ladies and gentlemen. Let's get started, shall we?' he says, talking at a rapid-fire pace. Hugo won't waste time – he wants to get on with it. 'The first lot we have today is this magnificent sideboard.' He gestures to his right, where two sweaty-faced men are dragging out a massive dark wood sideboard so everyone can get a good look at it, if they didn't manage to beforehand. 'It's in perfect condition,' he says. 'Now who'll give me one hundred euro?'

Hugo surveys the room, his eyes darting this way and that to make sure he's not missing a bid. Some people will be quite open about their interest in an item, holding their allocated bidding number aloft, but others will simply incline their head or raise a finger. Right now, however, it looks as if no one is remotely interested. People are always hesitant to be the first to jump into the water: they'll wait until Hugo pares back his asking price.

'Seventy-five euro? Seventy-five, anyone?'

Nothing. Hugo sighs and shifts in his seat behind the desk, as if he knows this is going to be a long day, that he'll have to cajole and prod people into action.

'Come on, ladies and gentlemen. Surely someone will give me seventy-five euro for this solid mahogany piece? It's an absolute steal at that price!'

Nothing.

'Fifty, then?' He's fighting to keep the desperation from his voice and then his eye moves to the back of the room – someone has finally bid and, although he tries to hide it, Hugo's relief is almost palpable.

'Fifty euro to yourself, sir, thank you. Fifty-five?'

Someone else raises a hand.

'Fifty-five to the lady in the front. Sixty?'

And so it goes, the price ping-ponging back and forth between two bidders, until he gets to a hundred and ten euro and it stalls.

'A hundred and ten? Are we all done at one hundred and ten euro?' Hugo's face is impassive, but I can tell he's quietly pleased. There's a beat of silence as people wait to see if the other bidder will make a comeback. When he doesn't, Hugo bangs his gavel with force on the desk.

'Sold!' he cries. The victorious bidder in the front row raises her number and Hugo's assistant, sitting beside him, makes a note of it on the laptop in front of her. Then, like lightning, he's on to the next thing on the list. Hugo doesn't wait around and, with more than a thousand items to get through, he can't afford to.

Nothing in this first tranche of lots interests me – I still have a while to wait. But it's never boring in an auction room because there's always so much going on. Maybe that's why so many people who have no intention of ever bidding on anything come along. I sneak a look to my left. At the end of the row a middle-aged woman in a beige raincoat sits on the edge of a wooden kitchen seat, a catalogue in her hand, her pen poised to record the sale price of every item. She's a regular at this auction, I see her every time I come, yet she never buys anything. She never even bids. She just sits there, taking down all the prices. It's bizarre, but she's not alone. Other people here will be doing exactly the same thing – maybe curiosity, boredom or even eccentricity drives them. Who really knows?

An hour later, I've bought a hat-stand, some pretty vintage china, so much in vogue these days, and a small clock that needs repair. Next up is the wash-stand with the marble top. I know it would definitely sell in the shop – it's scratched in places and needs some work but people love this sort of French style and I could even give it a wash of colour.

'Next is this lovely wash-stand. It's a part lot, along with some boxes of assorted odds and ends,' Hugo says, as the two men drag the piece and all the boxes on top to the front of the room. Ruth nudges me discreetly and I nod.

I don't need reminding – I've been waiting for this. 'Who'll give me seventy euro?' Hugo says.

I sit perfectly still. Seventy euro is far too much for an opening bid and fortunately it looks as if everyone else thinks so too – there's no other interest in the room.

'Fifty then?' Hugo asks hopefully, to silence. 'Thirty?'

Thirty euro would be a steal. I raise my number and Hugo flashes me a look. 'I have thirty. Now, who'll give me forty?'

I hold my breath, hoping against hope that no one else will bid – if I get it for thirty euro, plus agent's commission, it'll be the deal of the century.

'Come on now,' Hugo says, not giving up yet. 'The marble top alone is worth three times that!'

Ruth groans quietly beside me and my heart sinks. Now that he's alerted people that there's marble involved, the price will soar. Sure enough, there's a flurry of activity behind me and within seconds the wash-stand is at seventy euro – and it's Perry's bid. Of course it is, but I'll be damned if I let him outbid me. Last time he stole a gorgeous walnut side table from me at the very last minute. I'm not going to let that happen again.

Hugo looks at me. 'Eighty?'

I nod. Eighty is still OK. Just about.

'Ninety to the gentleman.'

Dammit. Perry is still bidding. Almost automatically I raise my hand to bid again. It's at a hundred now and Ruth nudges me. She wants me to pull out, I know, but I can't bear to see Perry get what I want – again.

He goes to a hundred and ten, I go to a hundred and twenty and suddenly people are sitting up and taking notice. A bidding war like this, even though it's for little enough money, always gets a buzz going. Perry returns the bid – it's at a hundred and thirty now. Hugo looks at me – the ball is in my court.

'Is it worth it, Coco?' Ruth whispers to me. She always tells me the key to success at auction is knowing when to quit – just like gambling. I should pull out – it's too steep at that price. But something inside me tells me not to let Perry win – not today.

'I know what I'm doing,' I whisper out of the side of my mouth, nodding to Hugo once more. I'm still in this game – and I'm in it to win.

Hugo raises one eyebrow at me – enjoying the heat of the chase.

'One hundred and forty euro to the feisty lady. Sir?' He looks at Perry, somewhere behind me, and I hold my breath. Step away, Perry. *Step away.*

There's a moment's pause and then, in a whoosh, Hugo brings the hammer down and the wash-stand is mine.

'*Yeees!*' I whoop quietly.

'That was pricey.' Ruth whistles.

'Don't worry – I already have a customer in mind for it,' I lie.

'You do?'

'Yep. And there are some nice bits and pieces in the boxes too. We'll definitely make on them.'

'Like what?' Ruth snorts. She knows, just as I do, that those odds-and-ends boxes are usually filled with rubbish. The truth is, I doubt there's anything good in them – probably just old newspapers, mouldy books and cracked pottery all fit for the bin.

'Just wait and see, O ye of little faith,' I murmur. 'Now, please stop talking – you're distracting me.'

'OK, Miss Know-it-all,' she whispers back, nudging me good-naturedly. 'I look forward to seeing what those end-of-the-rainbow boxes have in store for us – maybe they'll make our fortune!'

'Ha, ha, you're hilarious,' I reply, trying to be deadpan, but grinning now. I can't help it. I've been rumbled – trust Ruth to know I'm bluffing. The woman never misses a trick.

2

It's just gone nine a.m. the next day when I turn the battered Swan's Antiques sign to 'Open'. Pulling up the cream muslin blind that drapes prettily across the doorway, I take a quick look up and down the street. Once a thriving market town, Dronmore has become far quieter since the bypass was built almost a decade ago. It's now more a suburb of the capital than anything else, but thankfully it hasn't lost its small-town feel.

This morning it seems as if half the locals are still asleep or running late because the only real activity out there is the sparrows, pecking hopefully at the ground around the street's monument to fallen 1916 heroes. Directly opposite Swan's, even the white shutters of the butcher's are still closed, which is very unlike the proprietor, Karl. He runs his shop like clockwork – opening at eight fifty-eight every morning and not a moment after. Ruth says it's because of his German heritage – his mother was a Berliner, not that you'd know it: he speaks with a thick Dublin accent because his father was a Ballymuner, from the north side of the city.

'Germans can be so uptight, can't they?' Ruth says, every time we see Karl carefully arranging the racks of lamb in his window to show them off at the best possible angle.

'You can't say that, Ruth,' I always tell her.

'Why? It's true.'

'Yes, but it's also a cliché.'

'Aha! But clichés are clichés for a reason, Coco. Karl *is* uptight. He needs to loosen up a bit. I mean, he's only fifty-five, for goodness' sake. He should take that Harley-Davidson of his out a bit more, tear up the streets. What's the point in having such a fabulous motorbike if he hardly ever uses it?'

Ruth says it like she sees it – it's her *modus operandi*. Mind you, Karl doesn't seem to mind – not even when she tells him to his face that he should live a little, which she often does when she pops across to buy some of his award-winning sausages.

As I look across at his window now, I can't help wondering if he's taken her advice. Maybe he's gone out for an early-morning ride on the bike. Of course, the other possibility is that he's had a dreadful accident and is lying somewhere unable to call for help, but that's just my unhelpful imagination working overtime. Karl is hale and hearty and very much alive – and I'm sure he's safe and sound.

Next door to Karl's shop, the TV repair place is closed too. But Victor, the guy who runs it, keeps really odd hours. The sign that reads, 'We have had to close due to unforeseen circumstances,' hangs limply in the window almost every day now. Mostly the 'unforeseen circumstances' are the very predictable circumstances that Victor is in the bookie's – he's been inclined to spend a lot of time there since his wife left him last year.

Only Peter and Nora from the Coffee Dock across the

way seem to be up and running this morning. From here, I can see Nora arguing animatedly with Peter. She's a tiny woman, not even five foot tall, and he towers over her at six foot four, yet she practically terrorizes him. Poor Peter – he has the hang-dog look of resignation on his face that he always wears when Nora's losing the plot, which she does quite a lot. He probably got the bread order wrong again or forgot to pick up teabags from the cash-and-carry. If Karl is unnaturally organized, Peter is his complete opposite.

As the 'Open' sign sways in Swan's doorway, I turn and admire my favourite place in the world. Every morning I take a moment to stand and breathe in the sweetest aroma I know: old things. Almost every inch of the small shop is piled high with vintage objects I love – some of which I've even grown up with. In one corner sits the grand walnut dresser, here since I was a child, its gleaming brass handles polished with care. Beside it are the mahogany library steps I never want to sell because I like to fantasize that one day I'll have a library of my own and will balance on them, straining to reach my exquisite collection of old paperbacks. An old birdcage sits alongside the steps as well as a deep red Chinese vase with an iridescent pearl finish that glistens in sunlight. Every crevice is packed with all sorts of trinkets, from the minuscule jet beads that lie in porcelain trays, patiently waiting for the right person to pluck them from obscurity and take them home to make a wonderful neckpiece, to the enormous deer antlers from which old pocket watches hang on their chains.

The walls are covered with gilt mirrors and yellowing

pictures in a mixture of frames, and from the ceiling hang candelabras, vintage light fixtures and rackety old chandeliers. Against the walls, wobbly painted bookcases lean precariously against each other, crammed with hardbacks of every description, looking like they might topple over at any second. Half a dozen brass bedheads are propped in a row, vintage nightgowns draped prettily across them. Two old dressers are crammed with delicate crockery and fragile figurines, and next to them is the frosted-glass cabinet where Mum's beloved pearls are on permanent display. And everywhere there are fairy lights. My absolute favourite time is towards the end of the day when they are twinkling and I can imagine what all of these objects have witnessed, where they've been, what lives they've had before they came to me. With one glance I can almost picture the back story of certain pieces, the relationships that played out around them, the loves and losses they saw. They are more than just things. They're snatches of time, pieces of history, each with its own unique story to tell.

I love every square inch of this place. This shop and the small flat upstairs, where I've lived on and off since I was a child, feel like the heart of me and have done since I was a little girl. I know I live in a small town, I know everything might be familiar and boringly reliable here, but I still get a rush of happiness every morning when I turn the sign around and open the door to the day's possibilities. Cat teases me no end about my passionate love affair with Swan's, but I don't feel I'm missing out on anything. Yes, I've had to move back into the flat since Tom left, but Ruth and I are getting used to that and we'll succeed. Cat would say that a single woman my age should have a swanky apartment and a buzzing social life to match, but that's just not me. Of course, behind her teasing, I know she'd miss me like crazy if I did take off and do all those things. We're still as close as we were when we were kids.

My tummy growls and I realize I'm hungry. I go into the tiny kitchenette behind the counter at the back of the shop and flick on the kettle, then root around in the cupboard for something to nibble on. I could just go back upstairs to the flat and have a proper breakfast, of course, but that would require a little too much effort. A stale biscuit will do for now. When Ruth comes downstairs, maybe I'll pop over to the Coffee Dock and treat us to a takeaway brunch.

'Is there any milk in here?' a deep voice says behind me, as I'm opening the half-eaten packet of digestives. I gasp in shock and swing round. A half-naked man is standing in the doorway, his little pot belly hanging over a pair of too-tight Homer Simpson briefs. It takes me a second or two to register that it's Karl. Karl the butcher. From across the street. Our Karl. Our butcher.

'Jesus Christ! Karl!'

'Sorry, Coco, did I scare ya?' he replies, grinning at me like it really doesn't matter that there's only the tiniest piece of worn fabric between me and his man bits and that it's almost impossible not to stare.

'Eh, just a bit.' I gulp, dragging my eyes up his body, past many alarming tattoos on his upper arms and his hairy chest, to his face. I had no idea Karl had tattoos –

but, then, I'm used to seeing him decently clad in his butcher's apron, not cartoon underwear.

Does this mean . . . can this mean that Karl and Ruth are actually *having sex*? My brain searches frantically for another explanation – any other explanation. Maybe he had to evacuate his flat in the middle of the night. Was there a fire? Perhaps Ruth put him up because there was some kind of emergency. It's exactly the type of thing she'd do – help someone out if they were in trouble. She wouldn't think twice.

'Ruth wants a cuppa but there's no milk upstairs.' He reaches across me to get a mug for her and I get another serious close-up of his nether regions, briefs straining around the picture of Homer's bald head as he stretches.

OK. If he's bringing her a cup of tea wearing nothing but a wisp of fabric round his bum, then he and Ruth are clearly on more than nodding terms. They're definitely doing it.

'You didn't know I was here,' he says, sounding unfazed by the situation.

'Something like that,' I squeak.

Ruth and Karl have always been friendly – yes, I knew that. But not this friendly. Not sleeping over, shagging-each-other-senseless friendly. When did all this happen?

'Sorry if I gave you a shock,' he says, plonking a teabag into the mug.

'That's OK,' I say. 'I just didn't know that you and Ruth, that Ruth and you . . .' Words fail me. Utterly.

'That I'm her toy-boy?' he says, with a grin, then bursts out laughing at his own joke. 'Yeah, she's keeping it quiet for now.' He opens the fridge and reaches in for a carton of milk. It hits me that he knows his way around – this isn't the first time he's been here.

'I see,' I mutter. The dark horse, I want to say. How did she manage to keep it from me?

'Ah, Jaysis, is that the time already?' Karl says, glancing at the clock. 'I have to get going. The meat won't look after itself.'

'I suppose not,' I say.

'I'm late. I'm never late.'

'Yes. I know.'

'You can blame your grandmother.' He sighs. 'She says I need to relax in me kaks. But it doesn't come natural.'

I glance down involuntarily at his Homer Simpson briefs and stifle a horrified giggle.

'So. See ya,' he says, disappearing with Ruth's tea.

'Yep. See ya,' I call, as cheerily as I can. Just hopefully not in those briefs ever again.

A few minutes later I'm perched on the stool behind the shop counter, trying to steady my nerves. Karl had already left through the side door that opens out onto the patio, and I pretended I didn't see him go: I'm presuming that if he didn't leave by the front entrance, he didn't want to be noticed. From the patio, he would have had to scale the wall, loop back up the lane and go around to the street to get back to his place. Maybe that's what he's been doing all along.

I'm just thinking I should have laced my coffee with brandy to deal with the after-shock when Ruth appears, a great big dirty grin on her face. She's wearing a bright blue wool shift top over her favourite black jersey pants. Pinned to her bosom is an antique rose-gold brooch with a small red garnet, and her curly silver hair is down around her shoulders. She's practically glowing.

'Morning, my love! Isn't it a glorious day?'

'Yeah,' I reply, biting my lip and not wanting to meet her eye. From the state of Karl earlier, God knows what the two of them were doing upstairs while I've been down here. Worse, who knows what they were getting up to last night when I was right across the landing from them? I can't bear to think about it, but now I have a very disturbing visual in my head that I can't shake.

'Look at that sunshine!' She peers out of the side door, to where the tiny patio is bathed in the pale autumn sunlight. 'Will we take some coffee outdoors – what do you think? We'll hear anyone if they come in. We have to make the most of such a beautiful day.'

She's made a pot of coffee and is outside in moments, sitting at the painted wrought-iron table and chairs that I bought for a song at a car-boot sale a few years back, her face lifted to the weak sun. I follow and sit opposite her. She's right – even though the days are getting chilly now, it's still lovely out here. It's a tiny space, but beautifully kept. It used to be Granddad's favourite spot. He'd spend hours out here, fiddling with clocks he was trying to fix. He wasn't much of a gardener, but he didn't have to be in this small space. He just loved being outdoors, tinkering with his beloved clocks, listening to the water gurgling in the tiny stone fountain by the ivy-clad red-brick wall. He always said its trickling sounded so peaceful.

In the silence between us now, I listen to the water and wonder what Ruth is going to say about Karl. I have to hand it to her – she's certainly playing it cool.

'So, are you all set for your class?' she asks.

'Just about,' I say, sipping the coffee she pours for me, feeling it warm my insides. My up-cycling class is the highlight of my week. I've been running it for two years now, teaching people how to bring battered old pieces back to life. Today I'm looking forward to starting a brand-new project with my regulars: renovating old chests of drawers.

'Is something wrong, darling?' Ruth says, looking across the table at me. 'You seem a little distracted.'

'Well, I guess meeting the butcher in his underpants in the kitchen wasn't exactly how I imagined starting my day.' It's out of my mouth before I can stop it.

There's a millisecond before she replies. 'Ah, yes. Karl insisted on making me a cup of tea. He's sweet.'

'He said you insisted he make you one.' Thinking about it now, Ruth had probably sent him downstairs on purpose so that I would find out about them. That way she wouldn't have to tell me herself. I wouldn't put it past her.

'Did he?' she tinkles. 'Silly man! Anyway, I'm sorry if you were unprepared. Maybe I should have warned you, now that you're back.'

'How? By leaving a sock on your door knob to let me know you have company?'

She pauses to consider this for a moment.

'Ruth, I was joking.'

'It might have worked, though – at least you'd have had some notice.'

'This wasn't his first night here, I take it?' I ask.

'Not exactly.' She blushes, just a little.

'And how come I never knew about it?'

'Well, we haven't been publicizing it. Besides, usually when he's been here you've been . . . at Tom's.'

She's right. Before Tom went to New Zealand, he and I lived together in his bungalow on the outskirts of town. He and his brothers had built it with their own bare hands, or so his mother loved to tell me every time I met her – as if she was determined to remind me that I would never have a claim on the place. When he left I just moved back to the flat above the shop. I guess I have sort of invaded Ruth's privacy. We've worked together in Swan's for years, but her evenings have always been her own. I suppose she's not used to having me under her feet all the time, poking my nose into her private life. And I'm not used to seeing her private life so up close and personal. Clearly, we both have some major readjusting to do.

'You could have told me,' I say.

'I wasn't sure you'd approve. I mean, you adored your grandfather and Karl is my first since . . .'

'Ruth!' I shoot her a warning look.

'What I'm trying to say is that I hope you don't think I'm being disrespectful to Granddad.' Her eyes are misty as she blinks back tears.

'Of course not,' I reply, reaching for her hand across the table. 'No one expects you to mourn for ever.'

'I don't know about that.' She smiles weakly as she dabs at her lashes with a hanky from her pocket. 'Sometimes I think Anna would like to see me wear widow's weeds until I drop dead myself. For God's sake, don't let anything slip in front of her, OK?'

Anna is Ruth's sister, my great-aunt. They're so different that it's hard to believe they're related. Where Ruth is a free spirit and full of irrepressible *joie de vivre*, Anna is a closed book – conventional and more than a little judgemental. She's a widow, too – her husband died years ago – and spends most of her time doing parish work. I'm not sure what that entails, but it seems to keep her extremely busy. She and Ruth love each other, of that there's no doubt, but they rub each other up the wrong way constantly. Ruth is young at heart; Anna was born middle-aged.

'I don't think Granddad would have minded you and Karl getting it on,' I say, to lighten the mood. It's true, too. He adored Ruth and would have wanted her to be happy. Besides, he's been dead almost four years now and I know she's been incredibly lonely since he passed away. She deserves some happiness, especially after nursing him through Parkinson's for so many years.

'Yes, well, he always liked Karl,' Ruth goes on. 'He admired his meat.' She gives a little chuckle at this completely inappropriate joke and we both burst out laughing.

'He's not exactly your type, though, is he?' I ask.

'Because he's so much younger than me, do you mean?'

'Well, sort of. And he's a bit of a rough diamond.'

Granddad was a gentleman – an antiques dealer who drove a vintage car, read Joyce and wore a tweed waistcoat. Karl's a butcher with tattoos – and he has a dirty

37

great motorbike. Not only that, but he's about fifteen years younger than Ruth. He's not exactly what I would see as her type.

'He's surprisingly tender, actually,' Ruth replies. 'You wouldn't think it to look at him . . .'

From her face I can guess what she's talking about. 'Oh, God, I don't want the details.' I put my hands over my ears.

'Coco, relax. Karl and I aren't serious – we're just friends.'

'You're far more than friends by the look of things,' I mutter. 'Not that I want to know.'

'Well, maybe more than friends,' she muses. 'We're probably what your generation call FBs.' For a split second I don't get what she's talking about. FBs? What's that? Then realization hits. Oh, my God, she cannot mean . . . *fuck buddies*, can she?

'Yes, we like each other a lot, but it's not as if we're in some sort of exclusive relationship. We meet when we want to. We have an . . . understanding.'

'I can't believe I'm having this conversation with my own grandmother.' I shake my head. 'You shouldn't even know what an FB is, for God's sake. And, by the way, the polite expression is "friends with benefits". FWB.' I can't even bear to say the other version out loud.

'FWB? What's an FWB?' an imperious voice suddenly says. I turn to see Anna peering at us from the side doorway. I look at Ruth, horrified. We never heard her come in – so much for listening out for customers.

Ruth grins cheekily at me – like she couldn't care less if Anna overheard us. 'Will I tell her, Coco?' she asks, as

Anna walks out onto the patio, looking from me to Ruth. She's wearing a black wool coat, buttoned up to the collar, a black scarf at her neck and black leather gloves. Black has been her uniform since her husband died when I was only little. She's like a professional widow. Like Ruth, her hair is silver, but it's cropped short and close to her head. She's striking, like her sister, but very severe in appearance. Ruth exudes warmth and openness.

'Tell me what?' she asks.

'What an FWB is. Would you really like to know?'

Sweet Jesus. I can't believe we're having this conversation. It's not even ten a.m.

'Is it really that interesting?' Anna says, picking invisible fluff off her coat sleeve as she stands before us. She is the type of woman who vacuums her way out of her house. Disorder has no place in her life.

'An FWB is a . . . furniture . . . washing . . . broom,' I say limply, grasping the first idea that pops into my head and regretting it instantly. Why, oh, why did I have to use a lie related to housekeeping? Anna is looking at me full of interest now. Housekeeping and religion are her twin passions.

'What does that do?' she asks me seriously.

'Yes,' Ruth says, smirking, 'what does an FWB actually do, Coco?'

I could murder her. 'Well, it's just a new-fangled yoke I saw . . . somewhere. It's meant to be a broom filled with liquid that can clean your furniture without the elbow grease, but I'd say it's a swizz.' I can't look either of them in the eye. This is completely ridiculous.

Anna looks unimpressed. 'I'm an elbow-grease woman

myself,' she says stoutly, 'and I hope to God I always will be. FWB is not for me.'

Ruth looks dangerously close to bursting out laughing, and I'm not too far behind her. If Anna knew the true meaning she'd keel over, rosary beads in her hands.

'Now,' Anna says, and turns to me, sucking air between her teeth as she does. I prepare myself immediately. She always does that sucking-air thing before she asks something big — it's like a red warning flag.

'Coco.' Her eyes search my face.

'Yes?'

'How are you, pet?' she asks.

'I'm grand.'

'Are you? Are you really?'

'Yes. Honestly.' I shift a little under her fixed stare.

'But what about poor Tom?'

'What about him?'

'His mother said he's fierce lonely over there.' Significant pause. 'In New Zealand.' She says the last bit like I've somehow forgotten where Tom has gone, even though he left just a few weeks ago.

'Did she?' I glance at Ruth, who's not laughing any more. Her eyes have narrowed and she's watching Anna closely, obviously wondering, like me, where this is going.

'Yes. I met her yesterday in the graveyard. Poor woman — her heart is scalded without him.'

'Doesn't she have three other sons to keep her company?' Ruth asks, and I throw her a grateful look. Ruth may think I made a mistake turning down Tom, but she's not about to let Anna know that.

'Ah, yes, but Tom was her *baby*.' Anna sighs. 'It's very hard to lose your baby. And, of course, she knows what will happen next . . .'

I concentrate on looking past Anna, to the water feature that Granddad loved so much.

'He'll meet some nice native girl over there and then he'll never come back.'

'Leave it, Anna,' Ruth says, and I see her looking at me in concern.

'It's OK. She's right,' I say, smiling at them. 'He probably will meet someone else – I hope he does, to be honest.'

I can tell by their expressions that Anna and Ruth are shocked that I've said this. I sounded cold, like I don't care about him, but the opposite is true. I know I hurt Tom deeply by not going with him but I also know that, with time, he'll see I made the right decision. It was his pride that was hurt more than anything else. He'll get over me faster than he thinks.

'Coco, I didn't mean to upset you,' Anna backtracks. She doesn't do it on purpose, not really. At least she hasn't mentioned the biological-clock thing, although she's probably itching to.

'Well, why didn't you keep your big trap shut, then?' Ruth says tightly.

'I was only saying –'

'Look, *I*'m fine and Tom will be too,' I say. 'We probably should have broken up years ago. It's for the best.'

'Oh.' Anna's voice is small.

'Are you happy now?' Ruth asks, staring hard at her sister.

'Well, I just thought . . .'

'You never do think. That's the trouble,' Ruth replies.

'I don't know what you mean, Ruth!' Anna blusters. 'That's an outrageous thing to say!'

'Oh, get off your high horse, you silly woman.'

'I only came in to ask poor Coco how she was! But I'll go – I know when I'm not wanted.' Anna's neck is red and blotchy – as it always is when she's taken offence. If I don't pour oil on this little spat, it could go on for weeks.

'I know you were only looking out for me, Anna. I appreciate it,' I say, keen to make peace.

Her face softens. 'Yes, well. Thank you, Coco – I'm glad *you* realize that I was only trying to help.' She glares at her sister, who glares right back.

'Will I make us all some more coffee?' I suggest. 'This pot is gone a little cold.'

Ruth caves first. 'Oh, go on, Anna,' she says, sighing. 'Sit down and enjoy the sunshine with us. It might improve your mood.'

'There's nothing wrong with my mood,' Anna retorts huffily. 'At least, there wasn't until I came in here.'

'Build a bridge and get over it, will you, sis? Now, have a coffee.'

'No, thank you,' she says, but with less ice now. 'I'm actually on my way to see Father Pat – I'd better get on.'

'What about? The parish committee?' Ruth asks.

'I couldn't say,' Anna says darkly, as if parish business is more important than an MI5 undercover operation.

'I heard Peggy Lacey is a shoo-in to be the new chair-woman,' Ruth goes on, a wicked gleam in her eye that her sister misses. 'She's very efficient, isn't she?'

'She most certainly is not a shoo-in,' Anna replies, her whole body stiffening. 'And she's far from efficient.'

'Oh, I see,' Ruth says innocently. 'How did I get that impression?'

'I don't know,' Anna's tone is haughty, 'but it's not true.'

'Hmm . . . Maybe it was because I heard that Father Pat loved her flowers last week – at that ecumenical service.'

'He did not.' Anna glares at her again. But behind her eyes I see a flicker of panic, as if she's doubting herself.

'Really? Well, maybe Stella Doyle was wrong – she told me he said they were . . . refreshing.'

'That woman!' Anna exclaims. Then she readjusts her handbag on her shoulder and takes off without a backward glance, clearly on a mission to set something straight. Anna is fiercely competitive and hearing that Father Pat may have preferred anyone's flower arrangements to the ones she spends hours creating would be like a bucketful of rock salt on a wound to her. She certainly won't take it lying down.

'Ruth. That was unfair.' I laugh, as I gather our coffee things and head back inside, where the bell is still jangling plaintively from Anna's exit.

'Maybe,' Ruth says, with a devilish grin as she follows. 'But I can't help it. She's so easy to wind up.'

'If you really want to wind her up, maybe you should tell her about you and Karl,' I say.

'All in good time, my dear. All in good time. Now I have to do a little tidying upstairs. Will you be all right down here on your own?'

'I'll manage,' I say, smiling at her. 'I just want to get organized for the class, but it won't take long.'

'They really are a committed bunch, aren't they?' she muses. 'I don't think any of them has ever missed a session since you began.'

'They obviously know a good teacher when they see one,' I joke, and she laughs loudly.

'Usually self-praise is no praise,' she says, 'but in this case, you're right.' Then she kisses my cheek, her distinctive musky perfume enveloping me for a moment before she disappears upstairs.

3

It's almost eleven o'clock by the time I've set up everything in the small room off the main shop floor where I hold my classes. Sandpaper, paint stripper, old cloths and turpentine – everything my regulars will need is laid out neatly for them at separate work stations. They know to come wearing old clothes. I glance up at the clock, expecting the first of them to arrive any second, when the shop bell dings and Cat comes in. As usual, my best friend looks supremely glamorous, all petite, feminine curves and impossibly glossy hair.

Cat likes to tell people that we met on our first day at primary school – but that's not technically true. We met on the second. I know this for sure because on the first day I sat beside Siobhan Kelly. Siobhan – or Smelly Kelly as I liked to call her in revenge – drew all over my brand-new copybook with her green crayon and I've never forgotten how devastated I was. I was the poster child for colouring within the lines and I hated the mess that Siobhan created with a passion. On the second day I met Cat in the playground, she shared her skipping rope with me and we've been best friends ever since. Even back then, when everyone used to call us Little and Large, because of the difference in our height, she was always neat and well groomed and I was always scruffy. Nothing's changed.

Today, Cat is wearing a fitted black and grey pinstripe

suit and a crisp white blouse, with a simple gold chain glittering at her neck. The suit jacket nips in at the waist, showing off her enviable curves and the skirt sits just below her knee, highlighting her shapely legs. As usual, she's wearing killer heels. She never goes anywhere without them, claiming she needs them to make up for her short stature, being five foot nothing in her socks. She practically wears heels with pyjamas, but I don't know how she does it because she's forever running all over the place, even more so since she took over the family hotel last year when her father retired.

So far, she's been doing an amazing job at the Central. The hotel is going from strength to strength, even if Cat's had to deal with some tricky staff issues on the way. Some of the employees have been there for years and don't want things to change so they've been making her life difficult because she's desperate to move the hotel into the twenty-first century. From the chef not wanting to amend the decades-old restaurant menu to the receptionist sulking about the décor change in the lobby because her favourite, and very tatty, chair had to go, Cat has been fighting a lot of fires. Not only that, but she's been working all hours at weddings, christenings and other functions, as well as juggling her home life – and with three sons to take care of, that's not a piece of cake. Luckily her husband, David, a lecturer at the local technical college, is a sweetheart and really supportive.

'Hiya,' she says now, dumping her oversized designer bag on the counter and shoving her massive sunglasses on top of her blow-dried blonde locks. Her eyes are huge in her perfectly made-up face, their violet colour accentuated by a thick coat of mascara and a smudge of grey eyeliner. Cat can transform herself in seconds with just a flick of eyeliner and she's spent years trying to teach me how to do the same. Unfortunately, any sort of eye makeup makes me look like a man in drag, and no matter what she says to convince me otherwise, I can't buy into it.

'Hiya,' I say, grinning at her. 'Where are you off to?'

'I just had a meeting with the accountant.' She makes a face. 'I'm on my way back to the hotel.'

'Everything OK?' I ask.

'Yeah, fine. The tight bastard won't give me a penny to repaint the exterior walls, but I'll get around it.' Cat's not in the habit of letting small details get in her way. She may be small, but she's fierce. 'So, how are you?' she asks. 'Have you been moving stuff about in here again?' She looks around the shop.

'Er, yeah, I guess I have,' I admit, a little sheepishly.

'Do you ever stop?' She laughs.

'Not if I can help it.' I laugh too. 'It's one of my favourite pastimes.'

'That sweater's cute,' she says, shifting from observing the shop to observing me.

'This?' I pull at my old sweater. Compared to Cat, I'm a total mess. My hair is scraped back into a ponytail, I don't have a scrap of makeup on and I'm wearing a tatty old jumper, jeans and the usual ankle boots.

'Yeah, it's very biker chic. If you pulled it down, off your shoulder, and let your bra strap show, it'd be really sexy.' She reaches across the counter and starts to tug at my collar.

'Er, there are two chances of that ever happening! Slim and none!' I slap her hands away. Cat's always trying to get me to glam up a bit, but it's never going to work. Glamour comes easy to her – with her teeny-tiny waist and hour-glass curves, she's a real pin-up. I could never look like her in a million years, not even if a crack team of top stylists burst through the door and had their wicked way with me. My inner geekiness would always shine through.

'What about that bra and pants set I gave you for your birthday?' she demands. 'The burgundy lace one. It would look really hot under that sweater. You should show some more skin, Coco – you have a great figure. You don't have to be so old-fashioned about it.'

'Yeah, maybe,' I reply, avoiding her eye. Cat doesn't know I swapped the lingerie set for a thermal vest and a pair of walking socks, and I'm not about to tell her. The best thing to do is distract her. 'So, how are the boys?'

'Mental, as always,' she says, with a sigh. 'You know it's the twins' birthday this week?'

'I can't believe they're five already.' The time seems to have flown since they were newborns keeping Cat and David up all night. Now they're in 'big school', as they love to announce to anyone who'll listen.

'I know.' She sighs. 'It's all gone by in such a blur. The poor kids'll probably end up on the psychiatrist's couch when they're older. Sometimes I think I don't spend half enough time with them.'

'You're a great mum! Stop beating yourself up,' I say, trying to reassure her. 'The twins will be fine.'

'I don't know about that – they're getting really wild,

Coco. They ran rampant through the restaurant yesterday, made a complete show of me. I was mortified.'

'They're only kids, Cat. Give yourself a break.'

'Yeah, but you know what Liam's like. He has a right poker up his arse. I'm just waiting for him to say they should be barred from the premises.'

I snort with laughter. Liam Doyle is the long-serving bar and restaurant manager, but he behaves as if he's single-handedly running the Dorchester. He prowls around, looking for reasons to criticize Cat because in his book no one will ever replace her father, except perhaps him.

'I'm serious,' she protests. 'I'm trying to make the hotel more child-friendly, but he thinks kids should be seen and not heard. I mean, we're not living in the dark ages. Not that the twins are helping my case, of course.'

'What did they do?' I say, almost afraid to ask. Patrick and Michael are full of beans, and that's putting it mildly. They're really cute, but they're also incredibly hyperactive and never sit still for a second. Their antics are legendary in the hotel and beyond.

'They unscrewed the tops of the salt cellars again.' She sighs. 'Father Pat emptied an entire pot into his parsnip soup – lid and all.'

'Oh, no!' I can't help laughing.

'Oh, yes. And then I had to listen to Liam lecture me about respect. Honestly. Father Pat didn't even mind – we had a good laugh about it.'

'Listen, ignore Liam. He's a tosser,' I say.

'Easier said than done.' She groans. 'I swear that man will drive me to an early grave. That's if Mark doesn't get me there first.' She sighs again, heavily this time.

Mark is Cat and David's fifteen-year-old son. She had him when she was only eighteen, 'out of wedlock', as the town never tired of pointing out at the time. She and David weren't exactly the flavour of the month when that happened. In fact, her usually very tolerant parents sort of freaked out when she told them – which was why she ended up living with me, Ruth and Granddad at Swan's for a while before Mark was born and she and David moved in together. Cat's always told me how grateful she was to us back then – which is silly because she'd do the same for me if I ever needed help. Besides, we used to have such fun, talking deep into the night about what her baby would be like and what she'd do if he was unfortunate enough to get David's nose, which is even worse than mine, if that's possible. Luckily, Mark got his mother's good looks and his dad's even temper. At least it used to be even until he hit puberty and turned into a walking bag of fluctuating hormones. Cat and he have had lots of spats recently, just the usual mother versus teenager stuff, I think, but it's really been getting her down. She's said more than once that she feels he's backing away from her more and more and she can't get through to him. I keep telling her it's just a phase and that we all went through it at that age, but it doesn't seem to be helping.

'What's happened now?' I ask, worried that there's been a really bad row.

'Well –'

The bell jangles once more and we look up to see Harry Smith and Lucinda Dee, two of my class regulars, walk through the door.

'Oh, crap,' Cat mutters, out of the corner of her mouth.

'I'd better go. I don't want Harry cornering me about that damn anniversary party he wants to throw for his wife. He expects me to do it for half nothing. Will you pop over later?'

'Sure,' I say. 'I have to tell you what happened to me this morning. Believe me, you'll be shocked.' I can't wait to tell Cat about Ruth and Karl. I know Ruth wants to keep it quiet, but Cat won't tell anyone. Besides, I'll burst if I don't talk about it.

Cat arches her eyebrow. 'Sounds intriguing,' she says. 'See you then.' She shoves her oversized sunglasses back on and hurries out.

An hour later, my motley crew of regulars is finishing off a session of sanding and preparing their furniture for painting, chatting happily among themselves.

'I think I'll do mine a nice apple green,' Lucinda remarks, standing back to admire the chest of drawers she's carefully sanded.

'That'll be lovely,' I say. 'Any stencils or motifs this time?'

Lucinda, a trim woman in her sixties, loves to motif everything and her pieces usually feature découpage in some form. Her last up-cycled piece – a battered old trunk – was completely transformed when she covered it with overlapping floral cut-outs, then varnished it. She lined the interior with vintage newspapers she had collected over the years and it now sits in pride of place in her sitting room.

'Oh, I'm sure I'll manage a few here or there.' She chuckles.

'Oh, God, not more flowers.' Harry Smith groans the-atrically from across the way, grinning at her over his half-moon glasses. Harry, sixty going on sixteen, is a pur-ist. He likes to strip everything back to basics, then French polish where he can, revealing the beauty of the wood. For this reason, almost everything he works on is the best mahogany.

'Oh, shut up, you old fart, or I'll motif you!' Lucinda says good-naturedly. She has a wicked sense of humour, and they love nothing better than baiting each other.

'Where do you think you'll put it, Lucinda?' I ask. She always has a plan for her pieces – she can visualize how they're going to turn out and where in her home she's going to put them.

'My bedroom,' she says confidently.

'Don't tell me it's going to be your knicker chest?' Harry guffaws.

'You're a dirty old man, Harry Smith,' Lucinda replies primly, but her mouth is twitching with repressed laugh-ter.

'Now, now, don't make me get my ruler out,' I say, put-ting on my best teacher voice.

'Promises, promises,' Harry says, winking at me.

'For God's sake, man, get your coat on and go home to your wife,' Lucinda says.

At this, people start muttering about the time, down tools and start to shrug on coats. Another class is over and it's time to leave.

'Right everyone, see you next week,' I say. 'Don't be late!'

'As if!' some call, as they go.

I'm still smiling as the last straggler leaves. They really are such a great bunch, a proper mix of characters, and they all get along together so well. Their banter would lift anyone's spirits. And, as well as the fun of the class, up-cycling shabby old bits and pieces is so rewarding. There's nothing more satisfying than knowing I can help someone rescue a piece of furniture that no one else wants, give it a new lease of life and a brand-new home. I get a real buzz from it every single time.

Left to my own devices now in the silence of the shop, I consider what to do next. I decide to sort the last of the boxes of bric-à-brac that came with the marble wash-stand I bought at the auction. I've already gone through almost all of them and was gutted to discover nothing but rubbish – dusty old books that no one will want, and chipped china figurines that will never sell. I've put all these pieces aside for my classes – you never know when they'll come in handy – but I'm still disappointed that there was nothing really good in there after I parted with more than a hundred euro.

Ruth appears, just as I'm rifling through the last box. 'So, what have you got in that box of goodies of yours? Anything interesting?' she asks, peering over my shoulder.

'I don't think so,' I say, with a sigh. 'Just the usual old rubbish, really. You were right.'

As well as being disappointed, I feel a little foolish now that I was so gung-ho about getting this stuff because Perry was bidding against me. Although I know I'll probably make a small profit on the wash-stand, I still paid over the odds and we both know it.

'That's a pity,' she says lightly.

Ruth never rubs it in when I make a purchasing error – she's extremely gracious like that. When I first started buying for the shop I messed up many times, but she never admonished me.

'It's silly, but I always kind of hope that one day I'll stumble across some priceless artefact in one of these things,' I admit.

'Like they do on *Antiques Roadshow*?'

'Yeah, it's stupid, really.'

'No, it's not,' she says kindly, reassuring me. 'That's part of the magic of buying at auction – sometimes you just don't know what you're going to get.'

'Well, I should have known that I wouldn't get anything good in these,' I say. 'I won't be able to give some of this stuff away.'

I've pulled out more odds and ends – a couple of old lighters, mismatched cutlery and dog-eared books – but there's been nothing that I could sell. All that's left now is a pile of musty old music magazines.

I plunge my hand beneath the magazines, just to make sure I haven't missed anything. I feel something right at the very bottom and pull it to the surface. It's a cream-coloured dust bag.

'Oh, is there a handbag in there?' Ruth asks, her voice rising in interest as I gently pull off the cover and reveal a small, black quilted handbag.

'Just a knock-off Chanel.' I sigh. 'Oh, well. Another one for the charity bin.' This isn't the first cheap bag I've found in this type of lot – people chuck all sorts in when they're getting rid of stuff. Some folk can use an auction as a sort of rubbish tip.

'Oh, my God.' Ruth's face is suddenly a little pale.

'What's wrong?' I ask, concerned. 'Are you OK?'

'That bag . . .'

'What about it?'

She's staring at it as if she's seen a ghost, her eyes wide. 'I think . . . I think it's a Chanel 2.55.'

'Yeah, right.' I laugh. 'It's a fake, Ruth. Someone probably bought it at one of those street-corner stalls in New York. And it's not even a good one – it doesn't have the double-C lock.' It's a cheap replica, that's all. These things are ten a penny. I'll be lucky to get a fiver for it.

'But that's the thing, Coco! The earliest versions had a Mademoiselle lock, remember? Just like this one! It was called that because –'

'– Chanel never married,' I finish, almost automatically.

I hold the bag away from me, looking at it with fresh eyes, examining the sturdy lock she speaks of. She's right – it does look like a Mademoiselle lock. And on closer inspection, the bag is exquisitely made, not shabby at the seams like reproductions are. My heart begins to hammer in my chest. Could it be genuine?

I know the story of the famous 2.55 almost by rote because Mum used to tell me it when I was little. The first bags were handmade in Coco Chanel's Paris salon on rue Cambon. They were reissued in the 1980s by Karl Lagerfeld, in tribute to her. But this bag isn't a reissue, I know that much. It's far older – it could even be an original. But how has it ended up with so much worthless junk? No one accidentally leaves a vintage Chanel handbag in a box full of tatty books and shabby trinkets. It just doesn't happen.

'Open it,' Ruth urges, her voice shaky. 'Carefully now.'

I ease the lock open, my hands trembling, and peep inside. 'Oh,' I gasp, my heart skipping a beat when I see that the interior is the famous shade of maroon – the colour of the uniform that Chanel wore as a child in the orphanage where she was raised. As well as the original lock, this is another sign that it's real. I can barely breathe.

Ruth is agog as she peers inside. 'Look – it has the secret interior pocket that Chanel created for love letters,' she whispers reverently. 'It even has the raised CC on the inside flap.'

I allow my fingers to graze the interior of the bag. The stitching and the zip detail are sublime. The quilting is superb and perfectly symmetrical – another good indicator. I hold the bag close to my face, breathing it in, and instantly I can smell a distinct if faded lavender aroma, mingled with the particular scent that all old things share. 'You don't really think . . . I mean, the chances . . . It's one in a zillion, like the lottery.'

'I know,' she says. 'But I think you might just have hit the jackpot, Coco. Quick, try it on, for goodness' sake.'

Almost in a daze, I loop the gilt chain handles over my shoulder and examine my reflection in the antique mirror on the wall in front of me. I may be scruffy and covered in paint spatters but suddenly it doesn't matter because all I can see is the bag. It's like a magnet, drawing my eyes towards it. The weight of it on my shoulder, the feel of it under my arm . . . It's undeniable. Ruth is right – it's real.

I feel as if I'm dreaming as she chatters excitedly beside me, her voice sounding very far away. It's a Chanel handbag. *A vintage Chanel handbag*. This is amazing! Yes, sure, sometimes you can strike it lucky at auction – and when that happens it's fantastic – but to find a rare Chanel bag in a box of old knick-knacks is a once-in-a-lifetime thing. I could make a fortune on this – vintage Chanel must be worth at least a few thousand euro. What a profit! If I find the right buyer, who knows what I'll make? People out there collect Chanel, and someone may be willing to pay way over the odds to get their hands on this.

I slide the bag off my shoulder and hold it carefully, still unable to believe this stroke of good luck. How amazing that I should have stumbled across it, and what an incredible return for such a small investment. Suddenly my desire to outbid Perry seems like a work of genius. The only pity is I have to sell it. I'd kill for a bag like this. It wouldn't go with anything in my wardrobe, of course – everything I own is far too ordinary to set it off properly – but just holding it makes me giddy with desire, as if by slinging it over my shoulder I've somehow been transformed into a far more exotic creature than I am, more worthy of my name even. Then it strikes me. I don't *have* to sell it, do I? I mean, yes, I should, because I could make a mint on it and the shop could certainly do with the extra revenue. But the other option would be to . . . keep it for myself.

Suddenly I'm imagining myself in all sorts of handbag-related scenarios: walking down the street, the bag swinging seductively on its gilt chain handles as I go; in a restaurant, reaching inside the bag for my purse. I'd have to replace that, of course: if I had a real Chanel handbag, I couldn't be doing with the Hello Kitty purse that Cat bought me as a joke for my twenty-first birthday. I'm thirty-two now, in my grown-up decade. If I had a grown-up bag like this, then I'd need a grown-up purse too. I stroke the beautiful bag again and let myself dream. I could never afford something as beautiful as this – not if I saved for a lifetime. And now I have one, right in front of me. In a way, it's almost like this bag has found me – like it was meant for me. After all, Mum always said I should have a Chanel bag of my own to match my name. When I was little she told me she'd get me one. And here it is – like a gift from Heaven.

'I wonder who it belonged to,' Ruth says, taking it from me, putting it over her shoulder and checking herself out in the mirror. 'It really is gorgeous – it's in mint condition.'

There's a moment's silence as we look at each other and I know what she's thinking: that this is a mistake, that no one gets rid of a bag like this on purpose. It's far too valuable.

'You think I should give it back, don't you?' My euphoria vanishes.

'I didn't say that.' Her gaze drops to the floor.

'You think it, though.'

'I just wonder how it got into that box, that's all.'

'That's not my problem,' I say mulishly.

'I know that. Here, take it from me before I run away with it.' She's smiling at me, but I can't shake the uncomfortable sensation that she disapproves because there's a question mark hanging over the bag's provenance. OK, so we have no idea how or why it ended up in a box of worthless trinkets, but should we be concerned with that? Why shouldn't I just accept this as a very happy accident?

Ruth is still looking at me. 'Tell you what, how about we have a coffee? I'll go and put the kettle on, will I?' she asks.

'OK,' I say, but I'm not really listening. Now that the bag is back in my hands, I'm too busy admiring it to concentrate on anything else. I don't want to give it back and I don't see why I should have to. Whoever it belonged to or wherever it came from, it's with me now. And a very big part of me wants to keep it.

4

As I stride through the lobby of the Central Hotel, the Chanel handbag stowed safely in my battered leather satchel, I'm struck again by how much the place has improved since Cat took over from her father last year. The exterior may still be a little shabby and in need of a lick of paint, but in here it looks properly stylish. It's already getting much better reviews on TripAdvisor, with tourists calling it charming and unique, which is definitely down to the improvements Cat has made.

She always had a really strong vision of how the hotel should look and feel. The problem was, it was completely at odds with her father's view. His idea of what a hotel should be like was stuck in the 1970s, the decade that taste forgot. She wanted opulent chic, with a boutique-hotel atmosphere, and since his retirement, that's exactly what she's created. Instead of the draughty, old-fashioned entrance hall of years gone by, the lobby is cosy and instantly welcoming. The silk drapes at the windows are thick and luxurious, and their oyster colour works beautifully with the polished parquet floor and the sage walls. The golden velvet sofas with their burgundy scatter cushions add warmth and comfort. When the fire is burning in the high, wide grate, and the elegant floor lamps are diffusing soft light, the effect is gorgeous, far removed from the awful brown and orange swirly patterned carpet and the grubby magnolia-painted wallpaper that used to be there.

I helped Cat with the redecorating and in return she has hung a small framed note about Swan's at the front desk, thanking us and recommending the shop to her customers. Her very tight budget certainly made the transformation a challenge, but I found the right stuff for her eventually. The lamps were a real bargain, as was the massive gilt-framed mirror that dominates one wall. I got it for a great price because it was so oversized that it wouldn't suit anywhere smaller. Cat would love another like it, but that sort of mirror is not easy to find – not that I'm giving up. Cat says I'm like a blood-hound when I want to be and she's right, especially when it comes to antiques. The Central has become a second Swan's to me and everywhere I go I'm looking for more things that will suit its spaces and help to realize its potential.

I make my way into the hotel bar, into which Cat has also breathed new life, with smart leather banquettes and low lighting. It remains the favourite meeting place of Dronmore's residents, even if some of the older crowd like to purse their lips at the fancy new style. Over the years this bar has witnessed the aftermath of weddings, funerals and christenings, as well as lovers' quarrels, gentlemen's agreements and the odd infamous exchange of fisticuffs. If these walls could talk, they'd have a hell of a lot to say!

'Hello, Coco.'

I snap out of my daydream. Liam Doyle, bar and restaurant manager, has appeared in front of me. As usual, he's wearing a too-tight shirt under his black suit and his plump, florid face is puce, like that of a schoolboy who's been caught doing something he shouldn't.

'Hi, Liam,' I say, flinching a little, as I always do when he appears suddenly out of nowhere. Something about him makes my skin crawl.

'Looking for Herself, are you?' he asks, smirking.

'Er, yes, I am,' I reply.

'There she is, then.' He jerks his head to a corner seat, where Cat is talking to a young couple.

'A wedding.' Liam sniffs. 'Want to get married right here they do, instead of in the church. I never heard the like.'

'Lots of couples do that now, Liam,' I reply. 'It's getting very common, actually.' He really is a pious, self-righteous prat. No wonder Cat can't stand him.

'Well, I hold no truck with that sort of carry-on. And we certainly shouldn't be entertaining the notion of accommodating them.'

Out of the corner of my eye I see Cat wave goodbye to the couple and gesture at me to come over. In a second, Liam is gone from my side, vanishing as fast as he appeared.

'Hiya,' Cat says, as I reach her. 'Drink? I'm finished for the day, thank God.'

'I'd love one,' I admit, sliding into the booth opposite her.

Cat calls to the young bartender and soon we're both

sipping a large glass of Pinot Grigio. 'Jesus, I need that.' She sighs happily.

'Tough day?' I ask.

'Aw, just the usual. Fighting fires, you know how it is!'

'Liam isn't too happy that you might be starting civil ceremonies,' I report, glancing over my shoulder to make sure he's not somehow listening.

She rolls her eyes. 'He'll have to get used to it. It's the way forward, no matter what he thinks.'

'You're a hard nut!' I tell her.

'You have to be in this game. Besides, I'm the mother of three boys – no one scares me!'

'Speaking of whom – spill. We were interrupted earlier.'

'Ha! Where do you want me to start?' She groans.

'Trouble in Paradise?'

'Well, the twins are gone into excitement overdrive about their party – which, by the way, still isn't properly organized. And Mark's being a total nightmare.'

'What's happened?'

'I dunno, but he's acting like he hates me,' she says miserably.

'He doesn't hate you,' I reassure her.

'I dunno about that, Coco. He won't listen to a word I say. And every time I try to talk to him he bites my head off. It's like he's had some sort of personality transplant. Even David thinks so.'

'Aw, it's just teenage stuff,' I say.

'I'm so worried about him. I mean, what if he's like this for the rest of his life, battling with us, day and night? I don't know if I can cope with it any more.' Cat shakes her head and takes another slug of her wine.

'It's just a phase he's going through,' I say, hoping I don't sound patronizing. 'You've always been great and you will be again. He just has to go against you for a while, before he comes back.'

'I don't know . . . I can't seem to do anything right these days.'

'Maybe he just needs some space,' I suggest.

'I give him space, for God's sake!' she snaps irritably. I hold her eyes for a couple of seconds. 'Sorry, I guess I'm just worried about him, Coco.'

'Listen, he's growing up, figuring things out. Plus his hormones are raging. It's bound to get a bit tense, isn't it?'

'Well, I'm going to get some books and read up on it,' she says, her face set in determination.

'Do you think that'll help?' I ask.

'It can't hurt. I need to do something. I mean, we weren't like that at his age, were we?' she says.

'I can't remember – it's a long time ago.' I laugh ruefully.

'Yeah! Imagine – we left school fifteen years ago. It's mad. I've been thinking, actually, maybe we should organize a reunion. We never did anything for the tenth anniversary.'

'You can count me out,' I say. 'Anyway, don't you have enough on your plate?'

'Ah, come on, it might be fun to see everyone again! Well, except that cow Monica Molloy. Did I tell you she tried to friend me on Facebook?'

'She did not!' I gasp.

'She did too! The nerve of her, as if I'd ever be a friend of hers after what she said about me.'

Monica was a former classmate of ours and she had delighted in calling Cat awful names when she fell pregnant with Mark. Not only that, but she'd tried to get off with David too. She's on our ultimate hit list of all the people we'd inflict painful deaths on if we ever got the chance. Monica is right up there with the nun who made us run round the basketball courts ten times for not knowing our Irish grammar and the midwife who thought giving Cat pain relief when she was in labour wouldn't be a good idea. The list features quite a diverse cross-section of society, come to think of it.

'Cow-face Monica lives in New York now,' Cat mutters, her eyes narrowing as she takes another sip of her wine.

'How do you know that?' I ask. Before this, we hadn't heard from Monica Molloy in years – since we left school and everyone scattered to the four winds.

'I Googled her, of course,' she replies, grinning at me. 'You should try it. It's amazing what you can find out about people. I ended up Googling half our Leaving Cert year.'

'You didn't.'

'I did. Some of them are really successful now. Laura Mangan is global director for corporate affairs in some bank in New York, and Snots O'Brien is a bigwig in London.'

'Oh, my God – Louise O'Brien! I'd forgotten about her! Why did we call her that again?' I rack my brains and try to remember.

'Because of Jon Jo "Snots" Maguire, of course.'

'Oh, yeah! Jon Jo. I forgot about him too!' I laugh.

Jon Jo 'Snots' Maguire had a nose that never stopped running. He was gross but Louise never seemed to mind – they were glued to each other's faces during fifth and sixth year. Jon Jo inherited the family farm a while ago, all three hundred acres of it. I can't help wondering if Louise is sorry now that she finally dumped him when she left to go to college in Dublin.

'Imagine . . . They've all travelled the world and the two of us stayed right here in little old Dronmore . . .' For a second, Cat looks melancholy.

'You don't regret that, do you?' I ask.

She looks at me, and that touch of sadness is still there. 'Not really, I suppose,' she says, but she doesn't sound very convincing. 'But don't you ever wonder what other life you could have led?'

'I can't say I do,' I tell her, shrugging.

'Coco Swan,' she says, shaking her head, 'I've never met anyone so attached to their own past.'

I blush a little, hearing the implied criticism. 'Come off it. There's nothing wrong with loving where you're from, is there?'

Cat smiles at me. 'You always were sweetly crazy,' she says.

'Well, you were always just plain crazy,' I shoot back, making her laugh. It's good to see her laughing – she seems to have so much responsibility now and it's weighing her down.

'Right, that's enough about my children and my regrets

and everything else – what about you? What's happening?'

'Well, I *do* have some news actually . . .' I've been holding off telling her about the bag I found because she needed to let off steam about Mark, but I'm dying to tell her now.

'I knew it!' Her eyes light up excitedly. 'You're getting back with Tom, aren't you? I told David. I said to him, "She'll rethink things"! He thought I was off the mark, but I just had a feeling that –'

'Are you joking, Cat?' There's an awkward silence as she realizes how far off the mark she is.

'Oh, so you're not?' Her face falls, her mouth turning down at the corners like a cartoon character's.

'No, of course not. Why would you think that?' I can't keep the chill out of my voice.

'You said you had news. I suppose I just sort of presumed . . .' Her eyes flick away from mine.

'Well, you presumed wrong.'

'Sorry. I thought you might have had a change of heart, that's all.'

'Why would I?' I ask, crosser than ever.

'Well, people do,' she says. 'I mean, lots of couples break up and then get back together.'

'Not us,' I say firmly.

'But . . . don't you miss him, Coco?' she asks, her eyes searching my face. She's looking for little signs that I'm lying to her about how I really feel. Cat reckons she can suss a lie in ten seconds flat – she says it's all in the body language.

'A little, of course,' I reply honestly. 'But it was over long before he went, you know that.'

Cat was always fond of Tom, in a distracted sort of way. We never really socialized much as a foursome, although he and David would happily have the odd companionable pint together.

'But he was a really nice guy. And he was mad about you,' she says. 'He was a good catch.'

'He was a nice guy, you're right, but it had run its course. I told you that already.'

'But what if breaking up was a mistake?'

'It wasn't.'

'What about . . . kids?'

I feel the hackles rise on the back of my neck. I'm getting a bit tired of people implying that I'm going to be a barren spinster for the rest of my days. 'What about them?'

'Tom would have been a great dad,' she says. 'He would have taken to it like a duck to water. Sometimes, I think that –'

'Cat,' I interrupt her little fantasy, 'I have never said I want children. Have you ever in all our years as friends heard me say otherwise?'

She twists the stem of her glass in her fingers, then blurts out, 'It's just sometimes it seems like –' She stops abruptly.

'Seems like what?' I demand.

'Nothing. It's none of my business. I'll keep out of it.'

'Oh, for God's sake, just spit it out. My patience is wearing a bit thin here.'

'OK. Don't be pissed off when I say this, but sometimes I think you're afraid to step out of your comfort zone.'

'No, I'm not.'

'Aren't you? Think about it, Coco. Tom was a perfectly nice guy and he adored you. I know moving halfway round the world was a scary prospect, but it might have been a great adventure. You can't hide in that shop for ever.'

'I'm not *hiding* in the shop.'

'Aren't you?' She eyeballs me, and for some reason I can't hold her stare.

'I don't want to talk about it any more,' I say, feeling my cheeks flame. Cat may be my oldest friend, but sometimes she oversteps the mark.

'OK.' She sighs. 'If that's the way you want it. I just hope you won't regret it, that's all.' She picks up the bottle and tops up our glasses. 'Let's start again,' she says, smiling at me. 'What's your news?'

I reach into my satchel to take out the bag, although I can't help feeling that the big reveal has been a little spoiled by all this talk about Tom. When I pull the elegant 2.55 out of its protective bag, though, Cat's reaction is gratifyingly dramatic.

'Wow!' she gasps, wide-eyed, like a character in a pantomime. 'Jesus! Is that real?'

'We're pretty sure it is, yeah,' I reply, relishing her shock. 'I bought it a few days ago at an auction. It was at the bottom of a box of odds and ends. We're almost certain it's vintage Chanel.'

'Oh, my God! How cool is that! I'd kill for one of

those!' I laugh and she grabs my arm. 'Seriously,' she says. 'I would literally kill for one, so you just be careful on the way home. You might be mysteriously clubbed over the back of the head and wake up empty-handed.'

'Well, I'm not sure I'm going to keep it,' I say.

'What? Why not?' she asks.

'I feel guilty.' I sigh. 'Or Ruth is making me feel guilty.'

'Guilty?' Cat says. 'Are you crazy? Why would you feel guilty?'

I wish I didn't feel guilty, but I do. I may have found a real Chanel handbag and that may be the sort of thing that dreams are made of – or my sort of dreams anyway – but I know I can't just keep and enjoy it. What if someone somewhere is looking for it frantically and mourning its loss?

'Well, obviously it got into that box by mistake,' I say, turning it over and over in my hands. It really is an exquisitely beautiful object.

'Well, yeah, obviously. But so what?' she replies.

'I don't know if I can live with the idea that someone is missing it.'

'Jesus, Coco, you're a businesswoman. You can't be getting involved in other people's lives like this – it makes no sense. I mean, who knows where the bag came from? But that's not your problem!'

'Ruth thinks it is.'

'That's just silly. You're not responsible for what other people do with their stuff.'

'But what if someone's looking for it?'

'If they were, they'd have come knocking on the auctioneer's door, wouldn't they? They'd have tried to track it down by now, surely.'

She may be right. It's been a few days since the auction, after all, and Hugo keeps records of all purchasers.

'Maybe,' I reply, doubtfully.

'I say keep it for yourself,' she says, taking it from me again and holding it up. 'It's just gorgeous – you should have had a bag like this years ago. We always said you needed a Coco Chanel bag to match your name, didn't we? You want to know what I think this is? This is Fate, Coco. And you can't deny Fate, can you?'

I think about how I felt when I had the bag slung over my shoulder – that it was Fate. But keeping it may be the wrong thing to do.

'Yeah, it could be Fate, I guess. Or someone else's bad luck,' I say.

'Nah, screw that. It's Fate. This bag has your name on it – it's meant for you. I say enjoy it!'

'You would!' I laugh.

'God, one day I'm going to treat myself to one of these babies. How old do you think it is?' She holds the bag at arm's length.

'Well, the first ones were made in February 1955 – that's why they're called the 2.55. We think this could be one of the earliest versions – it might even be a prototype. We looked it up in some of the old books about Chanel that Mum had.'

'Wow, that's insane!'

'Yeah, and did you see the secret compartment inside? Chanel created that to hold her love letters – or that's what they say.'

'Oh, God – that's so romantic, isn't it? I mean, who writes love letters any more? I can't remember the last

71

time David even sent me a lovey-dovey text! As for a full-on sex text, well, I'm still waiting.'

'Cat!' I say, giggling. 'Isn't it far from sex texts you were raised?'

As we're talking, I'm showing the interior of the bag to her, when I spot that the zip of the love-letter compartment is slightly open. I try to close it, but as I do I feel something shift under the fabric. I look at it closely.

'What is it?' Cat asks.

'There's something in here. I didn't notice it before . . .'

I ease my finger into the pocket, feel a piece of paper and gently coax it out. It's thin, almost see-through, and it's been folded many times. No wonder I missed it earlier – it's almost feather light.

'Is it a letter?' Cat whispers. 'I don't believe it. What does it say?'

I unfold the piece of paper slowly and carefully.

'Hurry up and read it, for God's sake!' she urges me.

'I'm not sure I should. Maybe it's private.'

'Don't be so stupid!' Cat says. 'You have to read it – if you won't then I will. Give it to me.'

'No.' I clasp it to my chest. 'I found it so I'm going to read it, if anyone is.'

'Go on, then – what are you waiting for? A sign? Jesus, it could be a proper love letter!' She can't sit still for excitement and I'm afraid she's going to tear the fragile paper out of my hands.

'All right, all right, give me a second.' I take a deep breath and start to read the large, firm handwriting.

November 1956

My darling,

From the very first moment I saw you, I knew without a shadow of a doubt that you were the love of my life. I looked into your beautiful blue eyes, so tender and expressive, and my heart was lost to yours for ever. It was as if we had met many moons ago, as if we were two souls who had known each other in a different life. Our time together has been so very precious, my darling, and all too brief. As I write, my heart is breaking, for today we will be parted. This letter is my way of saying goodbye.

Please know that, with every fibre of my being, I want to be with you, hold you close in my arms and never let you go, but I cannot. Know that I will never forget you, for you are my heart. How can I forget my own heart?

I pray that one day, somehow, we will be reunited and that I will hold your hand again in mine.

For ever yours x

'Oh, my God!' Cat exclaims. 'Star-crossed lovers. How tragic!'

'There's no signature.' I turn the letter over, but there's nothing on the back either.

'Whoever owned this bag must have been some woman to inspire a letter like that,' Cat goes on. 'You can feel the passion in his words, can't you? It's so sad.'

'I wonder why he had to leave her.' I turn the letter over again, searching for clues. But there's nothing. How long has it been in the bag? It's impossible to say. There's nothing to go on, no sign as to who wrote it – just those few short, painful sentences.

'Look how old and yellow the paper is,' Cat says. 'It's been in there for years, maybe since it was written. She must have carried it everywhere with her. I wonder if we're the first people to read it since she did.'

'What should I do with it?' I wonder, dumbfounded. 'It's so . . . personal.'

Cat has a faraway look in her eye. 'Do you think they were ever reconciled? I wonder if he came back for her.'

My mind is working overtime. The letter is so heartfelt and moving but I feel a little strange that we're stepping into these people's lives. It's like reading someone's private diary entry – you know you shouldn't but you're just compelled to.

'God, people were so romantic back then, weren't they?' she goes on. 'Just like in the movies. Most men's idea of romance now is letting you hold the remote control.'

I giggle – she's right. There's something undeniably old-fashioned about the sentiments – that sort of romance doesn't exist any more, or if it does I've never experienced it.

'What are you thinking now?' Cat makes a face at me.

'What do you mean?' I already know what she's implying.

'You can never hide what you feel, Coco Swan. It's written all over your face! You're feeling even guiltier now, aren't you?'

I look at her, then back at the bag in my hands. 'Maybe,' I admit.

'Look, just because you found the letter, it doesn't mean

74

you shouldn't keep the bag, OK? It doesn't mean anything!'

I nod, but inside I'm disagreeing with her. What if my
finding the bag – the letter – does mean something? What
if it means far more than I ever imagined?

5

The following morning, Ruth is sitting opposite me in the shop and the letter I found in the handbag is lying on the counter between us. After I left Cat, I rushed home, bursting to tell Ruth about it, but all I found was a note telling me she wasn't going to be back and that I could get her on her mobile if I needed her. No explanation as to where she was going – although I assume she was with Karl, getting up to . . . whatever they get up to. I had to restrain myself from calling her and demanding her immediate return so I could tell her what I'd found.

'So, what do you think?' I ask her now, taking a sip of tea from my favourite vintage teacup, the cream one with the pretty rose pattern.

'I'm still a little shell-shocked by it all,' she says.

'I know! It's mad, isn't it? I mean, first I find the bag at the bottom of a box of rubbish – and now this . . . I can't get my head around it.'

'I have to say I've never come across anything like it before in all my years working in the business,' Ruth says. 'Yes, you find things, old photographs that you wonder about, inscriptions in books that make you think. I remember one time I even found a really valuable diamond earring – just one – in the pocket of an old fur coat we got in. But this is . . . this is different.'

'I wonder why he had to leave her,' I muse. 'Was there

a war somewhere in 1956? Maybe he was a soldier and had to go overseas to fight.'

'Well, the Suez crisis was around then, so it's possible, I suppose,' Ruth says thoughtfully. 'I guess we'll never know now . . .'

'And she kept the letter in the bag all that time . . . she must have loved him very much,' I say.

A silence hangs heavily between us – the unsaid in the air. What am I going to do with these things? Can I keep the bag and ignore what I found inside? Would that be ethical? For some reason, I find myself thinking about Mum again. What would she have made of all this? For her, finding a Chanel bag would have been a dream come true. I can almost hear her voice in my head, promising to get me one some day. Is it too silly to think that she somehow sent this one to me? Is it too outlandish to believe that finding this bag could be some sort of message from her?

'I feel really strange about all this,' I say at last.

'Of course you do, darling,' Ruth says. 'It's only natural that it's stirred up a lot of questions – first you find the bag and now the letter, too. It's a lot to take in.'

'What do you think I should do?' I say.

'What do *you* think you should do?'

'I should track down whoever this bag belongs to and give it back to her.'

The words are out of my mouth before my brain has even processed what I'm saying. I need to find the bag's owner. I've no idea how it got into a box of worthless junk, but it can't have been on purpose. It was obviously included in the auction by mistake. Besides, now that I've found such a personal and heartfelt letter inside, I can't just do nothing. The letter meant so much to some woman that she carried it in her bag for decades. It would be cruel to ignore that fact. If Mum is trying to send me a message, I'm not entirely sure what it is. But maybe if I find the previous owner, everything will become clearer. It sounds a bit mad, but I can't help feeling there's something to this theory.

'Good girl.' Ruth smiles at me.

'You think I'm right?' I ask.

'Yes, Coco, I do. You should follow your instinct. It's the only thing to do. I only wished I'd stuck to that rule during my own life . . .' She frowns and looks away.

'What do you mean?'

'Oh, it's just that I often think if I'd insisted your grand-dad go to the consultant earlier, like my gut told me to, he might not have . . .'

'That's silly. You can't blame yourself because Grand-dad got sick.'

She smiles at me, but I see the real sadness and regret in her eyes. 'Yes, I know. I just mean that following what your gut tells you is never wrong. Besides, you know you'll never be able to enjoy the bag now that you've thought about it like this. If you held onto it, you'd hold onto the guilt too. It would be pointless now.'

'I might learn to live with it,' I say, smiling at her. The thought of handing back such a beautiful heirloom makes my heart break a little.

'I doubt it, sweetie.'

'I wish I didn't have the guilt gene.' I sigh. 'It passed Mum by – how come I had to inherit it?'

78

There's a beat of silence between us again as we consider the truth of this. Mum didn't believe in guilt. She was a free spirit, not restrained by society's conventions. That was why when she fell pregnant with me, after months away, she felt no shame in coming back to her small home town.

The way Ruth tells it, she showed up one day, when they hadn't seen her for about six months, with a massive baby bump and a suitcase in her hand. Ruth and Granddad were shocked speechless, of course, because Mum hadn't prepared them. She was instantly the talk of the town, but she wasn't bothered. She never felt the need to explain herself to anyone. Instead she settled back into her old room above the shop, the room where I was born. Her only explanation to Ruth was that I had been conceived in love, the result, she said, of a passionate fling with a gorgeous Frenchman. There's no way of knowing the truth, though, because she died before I could ask her. I might have been the result of a one-night stand for all I know. Either way, Ruth always says it was love at first sight for Mum when I was born, but there's no way of knowing how true that is either. If she loved me so much, why was she happy to spend so much time away from me?

All I really know for sure is that Mum didn't care what other people thought. She couldn't have cared less. After I was born, she just kept living her life as she wanted to – flitting back and forth to her beloved France, searching for treasures for the shop. Sourcing unusual finds for Swan's was her passion and she was happy to leave me in Dronmore, sometimes for weeks on end, while she trawled antiques markets and sent home her finds. I didn't like or understand it at the time, and I'm not sure I do now. But that's the way Mum was. Life was one big adventure to her and chasing across Europe was her idea of Heaven. Her beloved France claimed her in the end, though. She was knocked down and killed on a Paris street when I wasn't even thirteen, and I was robbed of my mother for ever. Ruth claims that before she died Mum was planning to move home for good, to spend more time with me. But there's no way of knowing the truth of that either – Mum never said anything about it to me.

Looking at Ruth again, I push the thought of Mum's death away, like I always do, to a place in my mind where I don't have to deal with it. It stays in the shadows along with the angry thought that if she had really loved me she wouldn't have left me in the first place – that she would have been happy here in the shop with us, not having madcap adventures and chasing rainbows.

'Your mum would have loved that bag,' Ruth says softly now, snapping me back to the present.

'Yeah,' I agree. 'She sure would.' Even though Mum adored anything Chanel and often said she was going to get me a bag one day, she never had one of her own.

'I remember when she told me she wanted to call you Coco –' Ruth goes on.

'– and you told her that she was nuts.' I laugh. I've heard this story countless times.

'And she said you needed a big name because you were going to do big things,' Ruth corrects me.

'If only she'd known how wrong she was about that,' I say.

'Coco!' Ruth looks at me sternly. 'You are going to do big things – have some faith in yourself.'

'Well, I haven't managed very much so far, have I?' I'm only half joking. Even though I'm very content where I am, the truth is that I've been living in the same small town since I was a child and I work with my grandmother. I'm not exactly setting the world alight. What Cat said about hiding, being afraid to step out of my comfort zone, flits into my mind. Was she right?

Ruth is looking at me strangely now and I realize I may have hurt her feelings. She's been so good to me. It can't have been easy coping with the death of her own daughter, then having to care for a teenager and an ailing husband. Plus she welcomed me back with open arms when Tom left, even if I was imposing on her privacy – and her secret affair with a toy-boy.

'You've managed quite a lot actually,' she says now, her eyes bright, 'and I think you're going to do lots more. I know you're going to surprise yourself in lots of unexpected ways, Coco Swan, mark my words.'

I smile gratefully at her for letting me off the hook, as she always does when I feel a little sorry for myself. Ruth doesn't do self-pity – she has the most get-up-and-go of anyone I know. That's another Swan attribute that seems to have passed me by – the get-up-and-go gene.

'I wonder what Mum would have done with this?' I pat the bag once more.

'I know exactly what she would have done,' Ruth says. 'She would definitely have tried to track down the owner. And she would have been hoping for the most dramatic conclusion possible!'

I laugh wryly. She's right. Mum loved a good story, I know that much.

'I don't want to say goodbye to it,' I say, giving the bag another sad little rub. It really is so beautiful and I'd love to keep it. But I can't. Especially now.

'I know, pet, but it's the right thing to do,' Ruth says. 'That letter must mean a lot to whoever owns that bag – they deserve to have it back.'

'I'll talk to Hugo this afternoon,' I say.

'Good girl, seize the day!' Ruth says. 'I bet he won't be pleased, though.'

'I bet he won't.' He'll be livid when he finds out he missed a real Chanel handbag – he could have made a much bigger commission for himself.

'Oh, he's a pussy cat at heart. You just have to charm him a little. Work with what you've got, Coco – I keep telling you. Dust off your feminine wiles and give them an airing!'

She sounds like Cat. Sometimes I think the two of them are just desperate to get together and force me into a little black dress and heels.

'Yeah, right,' I say. 'The problem is I missed out on that gene too!'

Later that afternoon I'm standing in Maloney's Auction Rooms, having explained the story to Hugo. Just as we predicted, he's not a happy man.

'You found a *Chanel* bag in those boxes?' he says, his jaw dropping. 'For fuck's sake!'

He's furious, just as we predicted. Knowing what he

knows now, he would probably have sent the bag to Dublin to be included in a specialist sale – maybe even London.

'It was just pure luck, Hugo,' I say, feeling uncomfortable all over again. It's not like I deliberately pulled the wool over his eyes, but I still can't help feeling a little guilty.

'And you're sure it's real?' he asks, not bothering to disguise his annoyance. A pink blush of vexation has worked its way up his portly neck to his jowls and is still travelling.

'Pretty sure, yes,' I reply.

'I don't fucking believe this! *Danielle!* Danielle, get out here!' In answer to his bellowing, a young girl lopes out of the office, in no great hurry it has to be said. It's the one who gave me my bidding number that day – and told me I didn't look anything like Coco Chanel. Today her hair is piled on top of her head in a messy topknot style that looks effortless but probably took an age to perfect. She's wearing a baggy black acrylic jumper, and her reed-thin legs are clad in Aztec-patterned leggings and scruffy fake Ugg boots.

'Did you call me?' she asks Hugo, the same bored-rigid expression on her face that I remember from auction day.

'Yes, I bloody well did.' Hugo is now flaming red in the face with rage, his nostrils quivering. 'Did you go through everything in the boxes before the auction, like I told you to?'

She looks blankly at him. 'What boxes?'

Hugo takes a deep breath, obviously trying very hard

not to clip her round the ear. 'The boxes that came in with the marble-top wash-stand.'

'Yeah, I looked in them,' she replies cagily.

'Well, if you looked in them properly, how in God's good name did you miss this?'

He gestures to the bag in my hand and the girl's jaw drops. 'Is that real?' she splutters, her blue eyes widening. Despite her appearance, she obviously loves her fashion – she recognized it immediately. I'm guessing she's the type who spends an entire wage packet on Louboutins, then lives on crisps for a month.

'Yes, it bloody is real,' he yells at her. 'And if I'd known that was in there, can you tell me what I would have done with it?'

The girl looks at me, then him, then me again but says nothing.

'I'll tell you, will I? I would have made a profit. A very nice profit, thank you very much!'

'Sorry,' she mutters, her eyes still glued to the bag.

'So you should be,' he retorts. 'Don't let it happen again.'

'Do you have to give it back?' she asks me. I can see her mind ticking over – she's thinking that if I do she may have a shot at getting her hands on it.

'No, she bloody doesn't!' Hugo roars. 'She bought it fair and square, thanks to you!'

'Oh. Right.'

The girl skulks away and Hugo gives a massive sigh. 'God, she's hopeless. Absolutely hopeless. My sister's daughter – hasn't a clue.' He shakes his head despairingly.

'Maybe she'll improve,' I suggest.

'I doubt it. Her mother's the same – a right screw-up, she is. But that's another story.' He sighs again. 'Anyway, you want to know who this belonged to, do you?' He gestures to the bag.

'Yes.'

'Why?'

'What?' I look at him, confused.

'Why? Why do you want to know? You got it fair and square, much as it kills me to admit it. It was pure luck, like you say. Why do you care who it used to belong to? It's nothing to do with you.'

'But it must have got in there by mistake, Hugo,' I say.

'So? Don't tell me you're going to give it back! Are you nuts?'

'It just doesn't seem right to keep it,' I mutter. I'm still trying to decide if I should mention the letter or not. It's such a personal thing – it seems wrong to tell everyone about it.

'You can't be soft in this business, Coco, you know that,' he says impatiently. 'You gotta get tougher or people will walk all over you. Take me, for instance.' He pokes himself in the chest.

'What about you?'

'If people thought I was a walkover, they'd take advantage. It's human nature. That's why I try never to give an inch.'

'But someone might be looking for this bag, Hugo – it shouldn't have been in that box, we both know that. I don't feel right keeping it – it's bad karma.'

'No, they're not.' He shakes his head. 'No one is looking for it.'

'How do you know?'

'Because the old dear that bag belonged to is six feet under, Coco. Kicked the bucket a few months ago, I heard.'

'Oh.' I feel flat all of a sudden. The woman who owned this bag is dead – I hadn't been expecting that.

'Yeah. What was she called again?' His forehead creases as he thinks. 'Tatty something . . .'

Tatty. So that was her name. I try to imagine her. Where did she live? What did she look like? Was she ever reunited with the lover who wrote her that heartbreaking letter?

Hugo is still talking. 'She was very well-to-do apparently, but she had no family. Dermot Browne organized the sale of her stuff – prick that he is.'

'Who's Dermot Browne?' I ask.

'Her city slicker of a solicitor. Robbing bastard. Made a song and dance about my commission. God, this business . . . there has to be an easier way to make money.' He sighs heavily again.

I've never heard of Dermot Browne, but clearly there's no love lost between him and Hugo.

'So she had no relations at all?'

'That's what he said. Bastard kept all her good stuff in Dublin, of course. We only got a few bits and pieces that the big shots turned up their noses at.'

'Right, so it was an estate sale – everything went in one go after she died?'

'Yeah. We're the poor country cousins down here,' he goes on, with real bitterness in his voice. 'Not good enough to sell her collectibles, apparently. Well, good luck

86

to those boyos in Dublin, that's what I say. Looks like they missed a trick when they overlooked that bag, though – serves 'em right.' He chuckles then, like he's getting a little kick out of the situation, even though he lost out too. 'Funny thing is, all the profits from the sale are going to charity. What a bloody waste.'

'Charity?' I ask. 'Why did she do that?'

'She didn't have any kids so she decided to donate all the proceeds, that's what Browne said. It's mad what people do.'

'Yeah – mad,' I echo.

I clutch the bag a little closer to my side, feeling I need to protect what's inside. So Tatty died alone, with no family to speak of. What became of her lost love? It looks like I'm not going to find out now.

'As a matter of interest, do you know what charity it was?' I ask.

'Haven't a clue,' he says offhandedly. 'That'd be confidential.'

'I see.' I'm a bit deflated that he doesn't know any more – the trail has gone cold.

'So . . . how's Ruth keeping?' Hugo asks.

'She's good,' I reply, trying to think what to do next. Should I try to contact this Dermot Browne? Should I just forget about the whole thing and keep the bag? No one else need ever know what I found inside, after all. I did the right thing – I came back here and tried to reunite the bag with its owner. But if the lady it belonged to has passed away that changes everything, doesn't it? Maybe Cat is right – maybe I should try to forget I ever saw the letter and get on with simply enjoying my stroke of good fortune at finding the bag. I'd love to do that – but something about it still doesn't feel right. In my mind I can almost hear Mum telling me to keep going, investigate more.

'Ruth's an amazing woman,' Hugo says, giving a little whistle. 'Amazing.'

'Yep, she is,' I say absently. I'd almost forgotten that Hugo is another of her admirers.

'How long is your granddad gone now?'

'Almost four years.'

'Four years . . .' His voice trails away. 'He was a gentleman, your granddad.'

'Yeah, I know.' Granddad *was* an old-fashioned gent. He had beautiful manners and wouldn't have hurt a fly. My heart aches when I think of how the Parkinson's robbed him – and us – of so much.

'Loved the clocks, didn't he? I lost count of the number I sold him over the years. I remember one grandfather clock he just had to have – beat off four other bidders to get it, he did.'

'We still have it in the shop.' The beautiful oak clock stands behind our counter, marking the time in melodious chimes every hour on the hour.

'You do?' He looks surprised and I know why: that clock could easily fetch high four figures if we sold it.

'Yeah, Ruth says she'll never sell it. You know how it is.' The grandfather clock is one of her most treasured possessions – and one of mine. Every day I look at it and think of Granddad.

'Yes, I know.' He clears his throat. 'So, are you going to keep it, then?' He jerks his head towards the bag.

'I don't know,' I reply truthfully. 'Will you give me that solicitor's number? I might give him a ring and dig a little more.'

In a split second I make up my mind. I can't just let it drop – I have to find out more. I feel almost compelled to and I can't explain why.

Hugo frowns. 'All right, but for God's sake, don't tell him about the bag. He'd probably hop straight into that Mercedes of his, drive down here and try to get it back.'

'I won't. I'll make up some excuse, don't worry.' I'm sure I'll think of something.

'Here it is.' He scrolls through his phone and gives me the number. 'Kind of ironic, though, isn't it?' he says, as I finish in-putting it into my phone.

'Why's that?'

'Well, you're called Coco and the bag is by Coco Chanel. Maybe it's Fate that you found it – I mean, it practically has your name stamped on it, like.'

That's what Cat said, and it was what I thought at first – that the bag was destined for me. But everything has been changed by what I found inside.

'Maybe,' I say. 'But –'

'Hugo!' The girl appears from the office, a phone at her ear.

'What is it, Danielle?' he shouts back, grumpy again.

'You know that wardrobe we sold last week?'

'Which one?' He throws his eyes to Heaven.

'Er, the really big one? I have the customer on the phone and he says he's got it home but now he can't get it through the front door.'

'That's not my damn problem!' Hugo growls. 'Can't people measure the bloody furniture before they buy it?'

The girl shrugs and holds out the phone to him. It's his problem to solve, not hers.

'Oh, for Christ's sake. Sorry, Coco. See you again some time. Tell Ruth I said hello.'

'OK. Thanks, Hugo.'

With a final curt nod to me, he stalks away, muttering under his breath, leaving me holding the bag, its secret letter almost beating like a pulse inside.

I can't give up now. I'm going to have to find out more – and Dermot Browne may be the man who has the answers.

6

This has to be my worst decision – ever.

'I want a giraffe!'

'I want a python!'

'I want an iguana!'

I'm in a function room at the Central Hotel, surrounded by what seems like hundreds of screaming five-year-olds, attempting to blow up what feels like the millionth balloon of the day. I can't believe I agreed to step in and be the clown when the entertainer Cat had lined up for the twins' party cancelled.

'Please, Coco,' she'd begged, when she'd called me in a complete panic. 'I have a professional photographer booked to take shots of the party for the new hotel brochure. I want to show everyone what we can do – I *have* to have a clown there.'

'But I wouldn't have a clue what to do,' I had pleaded, desperate to get out of it.

'You don't need to, I swear. I'll get the costume, all you have to do is blow up a few balloons, maybe tell a few jokes. *Pleeeeease.*'

Of course I gave in. And now my temples are pounding and my scalp is itching so badly under the orange wig I'm wearing that all I want to do is rip it off and stick my head under a hosepipe.

'OK,' I say, to the assembled crowd of shouting kids, gritting my teeth as I smile. 'Who's next?'

'*Meeeee!*' they scream at once, a sea of pudgy little faces, all wanting their own way. They're so demanding, and they don't want simple sausage dogs, oh, no, they're all about rare animals and extinct species. I take a deep breath and try to refocus. I'll do a few more balloons and then I'll move on to face-painting. There's only another hour or so left before their parents will be back to pick them up. But, God, it's hot. The clown suit is stuck to my back, the multi-coloured polyester slick against my skin. I feel like I'm roasting alive. And the bloody photographer isn't even here yet. There's no escape.

'I was here first!' A chubby little boy pushes his way to the front, folding his arms across his Ben 10-clad chest and sticking out his lower lip.

'You were not!' a freckle-faced little girl in a Dora the Explorer sweatshirt roars.

'Was too!' he yells back.

In a split second, they're nose to nose, like two bulldogs about to do battle.

'Now, kids,' I say calmly, 'there's no need to fight. Everyone will get a turn.' Jesus, you'd need to be in the United Nations to deal with this lot. Is this what motherhood is really like? Because if it is, I'm definitely not cut out for it.

'I *was* here first!' the little boy insists again.

'No, you *weren't*!' the little girl squeals and then, right in my line of vision, leans over and clamps her teeth into his arm with gusto.

There's a collective gasp among the other kids, followed by a second of silence. Then the little boy starts to scream at the top of his lungs. The little girl stands back, shakes her pigtails and looks very happy with herself.

Shit.

'There, there,' I say, rubbing the top of the boy's head ineffectually. 'It's OK.'

'She bit me!' he wails, his sobs gaining in volume and intensity.

'I know she did, and that wasn't very nice. You need to apologize, young lady,' I say sternly to her.

'No!' She sticks out her chin and eyeballs me. The little boy is almost blue in the face from screaming now and I have no clue what to do. There's no blood, but the bite mark is clearly visible on his arm. There's going to be one hell of a bruise. This sort of scenario was not part of the job description.

'Would you like to see a card trick?' I ask, feeling a little desperate. 'Or I could paint your face! How about Spider-man – that'd be cool, wouldn't it?' Basically I'm willing to try anything to stop him screaming the place down.

Across the room, I can see Cat doling out crisps and drinks to another crowd of braying kids. She glances at me in alarm and hurries over.

'Everything OK?' she says, hunkering down to comfort the sobbing child.

'She bit me!' the little boy wails.

'*Whaaaat?* Coco? What happened?' Cat's expression is one of pure shock.

'Not *me*,' I say, trying not to laugh at the horror on her face. 'That little demon over there.' I point to where the freckle-faced biter is now trying to swing another little girl around the room by her hair. Clearly she has major anger issues.

Cat stoops to give the wailing child a quick cuddle, then hands him a Rice Krispie bun, which he promptly drops on the floor and grinds into the carpet before running off.

'Jesus, this is a nightmare,' she says, wiping her hand across her brow. 'The photographer is late. He's not going to get any decent shots at this rate – they're all too wild. What a disaster.'

I feel really sorry for her. It's so stressful trying to cope with all these kids – fights are breaking out every five minutes and she's already cleaned up two pukers. It's not exactly the fun environment she was hoping to capture for a brochure, more like mini savages on a rampage.

'Er, are you positive that you want to make these parties a regular event?' I ask. 'It's a lot of work, isn't it?'

'Yeah, but the kids'-party market is still really big. If I can get word out that we throw a great event here, we might be able to compete with those indoor playgrounds. We'd be something new – mums are always looking for the next great thing.'

'I guess . . .' I reply doubtfully.

Around us, kids are swinging out of each other. Cat's husband, David, is in a corner, trapped, as children throw themselves at him like cruise missiles.

'My father says it's a terrible idea, of course,' Cat goes on, bending down to try to clean the Rice Krispie bun off the carpet. 'He thinks kids should be seen and not heard, like Liam does.'

'He might have a point,' I say wryly.

'Not these days,' she replies. 'The hotel has to be

kid-friendly. The family market is the most important one for us – and we have to stand out.'

Out of the corner of my eye, I see Liam Doyle peer round the door. A look of utter contempt crosses his face before he disappears again. I decide not to mention his spying to Cat, though – she didn't spot him and she has enough to be getting on with.

'Jesus,' she says now. 'I spent half the night making those stupid buns. I have Krispies in places you don't want to know about.'

'Well, I can officially give them ten out of ten.' I grin at her as I nibble at one and she laughs hollowly.

'At least the twins are having a great time. Thanks, Coco – you're a star for doing this. I owe you one.'

'You certainly do, but it's fun,' I lie.

'No, it's not.' She sighs. 'It's a nightmare, let's face it. And, of course, my darling teenager's gone AWOL.'

I look around the room. She's right – there's no sign of Mark. He was definitely here earlier – he even laughed at my costume when I waddled in. I couldn't help thinking when I saw him, a young man of almost six foot, his dark fringe low over eyes that are the exact same shade of violet as Cat's, his faded blue jeans slung low around his skinny hips, that he's grown up so fast. He seems to have made the transition from boy to man almost overnight and I can't help feeling sad about that. He used to come running into my arms and smother my face with sticky kisses. Now he barely says hi. It's just a phase he's going through – I know that – but it's so strange. It's like Cat told me – they used to be really close but now she feels there's an acre of space between them, as if he's built some sort of invisible wall around himself.

Suddenly Cat's eyes fill with tears.

'Hey, are you OK?' I ask, concerned.

'Yeah, I'm fine.' She quickly wipes the tears away, flicking glances left and right to make sure no one saw. 'I'm being silly.'

'I'm sure Mark will be back soon,' I say.

'Do you think? I don't even know where he went – drinking in the park with his friends probably.'

'Cat!' I'm shocked by her tone.

'What? He might be for all I know. He never tells me anything any more. I have no clue what's going on in his life, and apparently that's just the way he wants it.'

'It'll be OK,' I say, trying to console her. 'We were like that when we were fifteen, all moody and disobedient.'

'Were we?'

'Of course we were! We were worse, probably. Don't you remember raiding your mother's drinks cabinet?'

She laughs then and some of the stress on her face falls away. 'Yeah, I suppose I do.'

'You were a real pro,' I remind her.

'I used to fill the vodka bottle back up with water. God, I was a bit of a brat.'

'Totally. You were a really bad influence on me!' I giggle. 'Do you remember that time you drank half a flagon of cider and threw up all over Monica Molloy?'

'No wonder she always hated me.' She giggles too. 'I ruined her best Levi's.'

'They were rank on her anyway.'

'Yeah, stone wash, yuk!'

We burst out laughing.

'See? It's not so bad,' I say. 'Mark is just going through a teenage thing – he'll come out the other side, just like we did, and you'll both look back and laugh, I swear.'

'I hope you're right,' she says. 'We used to be so close. Sometimes I think he resents the twins. I mean, it was just the three of us for so long that maybe he feels pushed out.'

'No, he doesn't. He loves them. That's plain to see.'

'If he loves them so much, he should have stayed at their party,' she grumbles. Then she composes herself. 'Right, I'd better go and see if I can round up that bloody photographer.'

As she moves away, my phone rings in my clown costume pocket. It takes a bit of rummaging around to find it and when I do it's not a number I recognize.

'Hello?'

A child is tugging at the leg of my baggy costume and I put my finger to my lips to shush him. He sticks out his tongue at me, then scampers away. Talk about ungrateful – I've already made three complicated dinosaurs for him. You'd think he'd cut me a bit of slack.

'Is that Coco Swan?' a voice says in my ear, and I try to concentrate.

'Yes, it is.'

I'm only half paying attention. In the corner a fight has broken out over the piñata and three kids are already crying. One has a river of thick green snot running from his nose to his top lip. It's not a pretty sight. I should probably step in and distract them with some magic. I'm just about to tell the caller that I'll ring them later when the man speaks again.

'This is Dermot Browne. You left a message with my secretary?' he says.

It's Tatty's solicitor! I can barely believe that he's actually returned my call. He's still speaking, but I can hardly hear what he's saying.

'Can you hang on for one sec?' I ask. I slide the exit door across and slip outside, crunching across the gravel, making my way towards the deliveries entrance at the side of the hotel.

'Hi, sorry about that,' I say. 'It was a little noisy in there.'

'Uh-huh. So, what can I help you with?' His tone is clipped, as if he couldn't care less about any of my excuses and just wants me to get to the point and off the phone sharpish.

'I was calling about Tatty –' I begin.

'Tatty Moynihan?' he interrupts, as if I'm not talking fast enough for him.

Tatty Moynihan – that must be her. He can hardly have two clients called Tatty, can he?

'Er, yes, Tatty Moynihan,' I say, chancing my arm, trying to hold my nerve.

'What about her?' he asks gruffly.

'She was . . . she was a friend of my grandmother. We only heard that she died recently and I was told you dealt with her affairs.' The lie comes easily.

'She passed away a few months ago,' he replies brusquely.

'Yes, er, so I was just wondering if you had an address for her family, so we could send them a card. My grandmother lost touch with Tatty, you see . . .'

'Uh-huh. Well, Miss Swan, Tatty didn't have family. She

98

lived alone for her final years and was cared for by a nurse in her own home. That house has been sold, though, along with everything else.'

'Oh, I see. Well, do you have any contact details for the nurse, then? Granny is really quite keen to get in touch with someone and I don't want to disappoint her.'

There's a pause before he replies and I hold my breath. He could just tell me to get lost – solicitors definitely aren't in the habit of handing out confidential information over the phone.

'Yes, I suppose I might do . . . Hold on,' he says at last. There's rustling in the background and within a minute or so he's back on the line. 'Here it is. The nurse's name was Mary Moore. She lives on Kylemore Way.' He recites the exact address and I make a mental note of it. I have a vague idea of where it is – by the canal in Dublin.

'Great, thanks. And do you have a phone number for her by any –'

'Goodbye.' There's a rattle in my ear and I realize he's hung up on me.

Damn. Her phone number would have been good. Still, I suppose that's easy enough to get now that I have her name and address. If I can track her down, maybe I'll find out if Tatty was ever reunited with her lost love. I know I'm being silly, but I can't help getting excited – I'm dying to know if the parted lovers ever saw each other again. Who knows what this Mary Moore will be able to tell me?

I slip the phone back into my pocket and take a deep breath of the afternoon air. It's so stuffy in that function room that just being outside is a relief. Just as I'm about to

99

go back inside, a sudden movement opposite catches my eye. Directly across the road from the hotel, down a narrow side-street beside Doherty's chemist, I see Mark talking to another teenager. So that's where he got to – he's out skiving with his friends. Cat will be relieved when I tell her I saw him and that he was just chatting to his mates, not off drinking. I'm just about to call over to him when the second teenager turns. I see his pinched face and my heart drops. It's Sean O'Malley, the biggest troublemaker in the town. He's only a year or two older than Mark, but he's already been on the wrong side of the law for drugs offences. Why on earth is Mark talking to him?

As I watch, the two part ways and I nip back inside before Mark sees me. I don't want him to think I was spying on him. Cat will hit the roof when she finds out, though – she's already banned Sean from the hotel's monthly teenage disco for smuggling in alcohol. She'll kill Mark if she finds out he's friendly with that holy terror; it'll make things much worse between them. This is bad news.

Readjusting my clown suit, I slip back into the function room, perturbed by what I saw. But there's no time to ponder on it because the photographer has finally arrived and is lining up the kids, trying to get them to smile in unison for the camera.

'Coco!' Cat screeches, when she sees me. 'I've been looking everywhere for you – we need you in this shot.'

Fixing a grin to my face, I decide for now to keep to myself what I saw. Maybe I can have a quiet word with Mark later, persuade him that hanging out with Sean is a very bad idea. Either way, now is definitely not the time to say anything to Cat. I do my best to grin for the shots, trying to look zanily cheerful for the photographer and cajoling the kids into posing with me. Mercifully, it's all over quite quickly, and the parents arrive to take their exhausted children home, not a minute too soon.

'Thank God, that's over,' Cat says, as the last of the mums and kids wave goodbye. 'I'm shattered.'

'It all came together in the end, though, didn't it?' I ask, peeling off the orange wig and shaking my hair free. It's a huge relief to have it off my head. Now that everyone has left, including the twins, who've gone home with David, I can relax.

'Yeah, thanks to you.' She beams at me. 'The brochure photos will look quite decent.' She's so happy and relieved that the party is over and was a success, despite everything, that I can't bring myself to tell her about Mark. Maybe there's some reasonable explanation for him to have been talking to that thug, although I can't think what it could be. Still, I'm reluctant to get him into even more trouble than he already is. I decide to hold my tongue, talk to Mark later and see if we can figure out this thing between us. Cat's hassled enough, trying to cope with everything that's on her plate. I'll talk to him before I do anything else – ask him what was going on. Hopefully I'm worrying about nothing.

'So, how are Ruth and her toy-boy?' Cat asks, flopping into a chair and pouring us both a well-deserved glass of wine from a bottle she had hidden behind a table. 'Imagine! She's taken a lover!'

We both snigger – the episode in *Sex and the City* when Carrie tells everyone she's 'taking a lover' is one of our favourites.

'Don't ask,' I say, flopping down opposite her. 'I think they're at it like rabbits.'

'I still can't believe she's bonking the butcher.'

'Believe it.'

'And she says they're FBs, like –'

'Don't say it out loud, Cat, I might self-combust.'

'Good on her, that's what I say. You're never too old for sexual relations, I guess.'

Cat and I always call sex 'sexual relations' – it's a throwback to our convent education when the nuns had to teach us about the ways of the world. Cat used to pride herself on asking Sister Ignata about orgasms and blowjobs in the Religious Education class. She could keep a perfectly straight face, too. Poor Sister Ignata – no wonder she took early retirement. I think it was the time Cat asked if you could have sex during your period that sent her over the edge.

'Hey, guess what? Tatty's solicitor called me.' I still can't believe I have a new lead. Just thinking about it gives me goose-bumps.

'He did?'

'Yeah. I left a message for him after I got his number from Hugo, but I didn't think he'd get back to me. And guess what else?'

'What?'

'He gave me the name of the nurse who looked after her before she died – she's called Mary Moore and she lives in Dublin.'

'And?' Cat eases off her high heels with a sigh, leans back in her chair and closes her eyes.

'I might contact her, see if I can find out more.'

Cat opens one eye. 'Why?'

'Because I'm curious, that's why.'

She opens them both. 'Yeah, but if Tatty is dead, what can you achieve by going on a wild-goose chase? I told you, Coco, you have nothing to feel guilty about.'

'You were the very one who thought the letter was the most romantic thing you ever saw,' I point out.

'Well, it was,' she says. 'But I just don't know what you can get out of trying to find out more. I mean, no one's looking for the bag, are they? It might sound callous, but if it was me, I'd just keep it.'

'But you're a different kettle of fish from me!' I joke, then duck as she throws a shoe at me.

'Oi!' she says, laughing. 'Seriously, though, Coco, I know the letter you found is really sad and everything, but do you think chasing a ghost like this is a good idea?'

'You don't think so?' I ask.

'Well,' she says, 'what are you looking for really? I mean, what do you want to achieve?'

'Hark at you, Businesswoman of the Year. Not everything can be accounted for on a graph or a spreadsheet, you know.' The truth is, I don't exactly know why I want to find out more. But something inside me is telling me this is the right thing to do. *It's what Mum would have wanted.* The thought pops unbidden into my mind, and not for the first time. Ruth said Mum would have tracked down the story behind the bag, tracked down the drama. It's probably a crazy idea, but there's still a part of me that thinks Mum wants me to do the same. I just can't get it out of my head.

'I suppose I am a bit clinical,' Cat muses. 'Sometimes I think this hotel has sucked the spontaneity out of me.'

'I'm not exactly the spontaneous type myself,' I say. 'So, if I'm honest, I don't know why I'm so keen to follow it up. I just am.'

I don't want to admit to Cat my theory about Mum just yet. If it sounds crazy in my head, it'll sound twice as crazy if I say it out loud.

'Well, I'm right behind you,' she says. 'But be careful, OK? You're not responsible for this – it's not your job to solve this mystery. The man who wrote that letter is probably dead, too, you do realize that, right?'

I can feel the heat of her gaze on me. 'Yeah, of course,' I mutter. 'I'm just curious, that's all.'

'OK.' She shrugs, smiling at me. 'Well, here's to you. Thanks for doing such a fab job today. Are you interested in a full-time gig by any chance?'

'I'd rather drink formaldehyde, spiked with toenail clippings,' I reply seriously. Then we crack up laughing as she leans across to clink her glass against mine.

7

'Howarya, Coco.'

I'm in the kitchen, rinsing my plate of toast crumbs, when I hear the deep male voice behind me. It's Karl. This time, he's got on more than his briefs, but only barely. He's wearing Ruth's tiny pink silk kimono, pulled tight around his little pot belly.

'Oh, hi, Karl,' I say, feeling instantly mortified.

'How are things?' he asks, smiling at me. 'Haven't seen you about much lately.'

'Er, yeah, I'm fine, thanks,' I say, not meeting his eye.

The truth is, ever since that morning when I met Karl in his underwear, I've been actively avoiding him. He's a really nice guy, but I just can't get the image out of my head of him and Ruth engaging in . . . 'sexual relations'. Ruth is happier than I've seen her since Granddad died, which is fantastic, but she and Karl seem such an odd match. I can't get to grips with it, try as I might.

'I just want to make Ruth a cuppa,' he explains, pushing the silk kimono sleeves up his hairy arms and simultaneously reaching across to switch on the kettle, all business.

'Er, yes,' I reply. 'I was finished in here anyway.'

'You don't have to leave, you know,' he says, as I begin to back out. His cheeks are a touch pink and I realize that he might be a little embarrassed by the situation too. It's all very awkward.

'Well, I'll just finish my coffee then,' I say weakly, sitting back down. Poor Karl – I don't want to seem rude. I'd better try to make small-talk, at least.

He smiles broadly at me, and I feel another stab of guilt. It's not his fault I've moved back in here. He was used to complete privacy before – I've probably ruined his and Ruth's party.

'So. Ruth tells me you found some handbag,' he says, kicking off the chit-chat.

'Yes, that's right. A vintage Chanel. It was a real stroke of luck,' I say, relieved we have something safe to talk about. Fair play to him.

'I'll say. Those yokes are collectors' items, aren't they?'

'Well, yes, they are,' I reply. 'Finding one was a million to one.'

'And a letter too, I hear.' He reaches up into the cupboard and I get an eyeful of very hairy upper thigh and a bum cheek. He's not wearing anything under the kimono, I realize that now. I swallow hard and try to forget this piece of information.

'Yes, a really sad letter.'

'And you're going to try to find out more, Ruth says.'

'Well, I don't know how much more I can find out, to be honest. The woman who owned the bag has passed away so I've hit a dead end, really.'

'Yeah, Ruth told me. But you got another lead, didn't ya? Some nurse?'

He measures a half-spoon of sugar into the cup of tea he's made for Ruth and stirs carefully, as if he wants it to be absolutely perfect for her.

'Yes, I did.' I smile at him. The poor man is trying

desperately to have a normal conversation with me – it's really sweet. 'I got her address and everything, but when I tried to look up her number I discovered she's not listed.'

'Aw, no, that's a bummer.' His face falls. 'Where does she live exactly?'

I give him the address in Kylemore Way and his face lights up. 'Aw, Jaysis, I know it well!' he says. 'That's down by the canal. Lovely old community it is – salt-of-the-earth folk down there.' He leans back against the counter and folds his arms thoughtfully. 'You should go and see her,' he announces. 'See what else you can find out.'

'Er, I don't think so,' I say. 'I wouldn't have the guts.'

''Course ya would!' he says. 'What do you have to lose?'

'What's going on in here?' Ruth's tousled head appears around the door. Her curls are askew, her eyes still sleepy.

'I have your cuppa here, pet,' Karl says, smiling kindly at her. 'I was just bringing it up to you.'

'You were taking your time,' she teases him. She yawns widely, then plonks herself down and plants both elbows on the kitchen table.

'Will I make you some toast?' he asks, all considerate attention, fussing around her.

She waves him away good-naturedly. 'No, I'm grand, honestly. Now, tell me, what were you two gabbling on about?'

'Well, I was telling Coco here that she should visit that nurse, you know, the one she found. She lives down by the canal,' Karl says.

'But I don't think it's such a good idea –' I begin.

'Why?' Ruth's eyes are sharp. 'Have you given up trying to find out more?'

'I never said that. But maybe I should just leave well enough alone.' I've been thinking more and more about what Cat said and maybe she's right. What can I gain from pursuing this story? Maybe I should just keep the bag and forget about the letter.

'Rubbish!' Ruth says excitedly. 'You can't give up now – you found that bag for a reason. Karl's right – you should talk to this Mary Moore woman and see what else you can find out.'

'She might be able to fill in some gaps,' Karl says.

'It's so intriguing, isn't it?' Ruth sighs. 'I mean, who was Tatty Moynihan? What did she do for a living? Where did she live?'

'And why did she leave everything to charity?' Karl adds.

As they talk, a dozen different scenarios run through my mind. I'd love to go and see the nurse, find out more about Tatty and try to piece the story together, but I'm nervous.

'What would I even say to her?' I ask, interrupting Ruth and Karl. 'I mean, she'd think I was some sort of lunatic if I just turned up out of the blue, asking all sorts of questions.'

Ruth's face scrunches up in thought. Then, with a little yelp, she pokes her finger in the air. 'I have it! We need to bring that rosewood table to the French polisher, don't we? His workshop is near the canal. You can tell her you were just passing and thought you'd make a few enquiries while you were in the area. That'd take the weirdness out of it. And it'd be the truth.'

'And then what? Ask her what she knows about the letter?' I ask.

'Yes!' Ruth says.

'Ruth, this isn't some *Famous Five* mystery,' I reply, unable to stifle a giggle at her enthusiasm. I used to love those stories when I was younger: Ruth read them to me over and over again when Mum was away in France and she and Granddad were looking after me.

'I know it's not. It's more like a *Nancy Drew* – and you're Nancy,' she says, her eyes glittering. She's enthralled by the story of the mysterious letter in the bag, almost more than I am, if that's possible.

'Come with me, then, if you're so eager to find out more,' I say.

But she shakes her head. 'No. Two strangers turning up on the woman's doorstep would be far too much for her to cope with. It could frighten her off. Couldn't it, Karl?'

'You could sit in the car and wait?' Karl suggests.

'I can't – I have to stay here and watch the shop,' she says. 'Anna is calling in here this morning.'

Out of the corner of my eye, I see Karl flinch a little at the name. Clearly my great-aunt makes him nervous.

'How do you know she is?' I ask. Anna never usually announces when she's planning to make a visit – she just pops in, almost as if she's trying to catch us unawares doing something we shouldn't.

'I woke up with a feeling of doom,' Ruth says. 'She'll be here before eleven, mark my words.'

'You don't really know that,' I say, grinning at her.

'Oh, I do. My feeling of doom is rarely wrong. Besides, Peggy Lacey was elected chair of the parish committee last night, so she'll definitely be on the warpath – and that path, as you well know, leads straight past our front door. Now, are you going to go and see this nurse or not?'

'I don't know,' I reply, still unsure.

'Go on, Coco!' Karl says, egging me on. 'Grab the bull by the horns!'

'Yeah, go on, love – aren't you dying to hear more of the story?' Ruth says.

'If you're not, I am,' Karl says.

'You're an old romantic, Karl,' Ruth says, laughing up at him. 'Who would have guessed it?'

'So what if I am?' He smiles back loftily. 'Even butchers can have romance in their souls, you know.'

'Oh, for goodness' sake,' I say, laughing. 'OK, then, I'll go. But if it goes horribly wrong I'll blame you two.'

8

Kylemore Way is a row of crammed-together red-brick terraced houses opposite the canal, all with a small patch of neat garden at the front. As I stand outside number ten, I feel distinctly uneasy. Now that I'm here, it seems a completely mad jaunt. If Ruth and Karl hadn't persuaded me it was a good idea, I'd still be nice and safe at home, which is exactly where I want to be. I knock on the door, hoping no one will answer. Then I can go home, look Ruth in the eye and tell her honestly that I tried my best but didn't get anywhere. I really am a bit scared now: all my bravado when I lied to Dermot Browne to get this information seems to have deserted me. I'm almost turning on my heel to make my escape when the door swings open.

'Yes?'

The plump, middle-aged woman who answers is wearing a striped red-and-black apron wrapped round her thick waist and has flecks of flour in her dark hair. Her face is lightly tanned, her sleeves are rolled up to the elbows and at her red-Croc-shod feet are three white-and-brown Jack Russells, all of which are now yapping at me in a very unfriendly way.

It's now or never.

'Hello – er, are you Mary Moore?' I ask tentatively, watching out of the corner of my eye as the smallest dog bares his sharp little teeth and growls. What is it that people say about terriers? That once they latch onto you they won't let go?

'Who wants to know?' She rubs her floury hands on her apron, and stares openly at me. She's a tough cookie – that's obvious straight away – and my stomach lurches. How stupid could I have been to turn up here unannounced? I should have written her a letter and let her answer it in her own good time.

'Er, my name is Coco Swan. I –'

'Are you from the council? Is this about the household charge? Because if it is, you can get lost. I'll go to jail before I pay it.' Her feet are apart, hands on hips, chin jutting forward defiantly.

'No, no, it's not about anything like that,' I reply quickly, feeling even more nervous now. She certainly knows how to go on the defensive – what's that saying? 'The best form of offence is defence'? 'I'm not from the council. I just wanted to ask you about Tatty Moynihan.'

'You knew Tatty?' Her green eyes narrow as she looks me up and down from head to toe. I can tell she believes this is highly unlikely.

'Not exactly,' I say. 'But I know that you were her nurse before she passed away and I wanted to ask –'

'And how do you know that?' She's regarding me with very deep suspicion.

'Well, er, I spoke to Dermot Browne, her solicitor. He gave me your address.'

Her eyes narrow even more. 'Oh, did he now?' she says acidly. 'Well, hasn't he a nerve?'

Crap. This is all going horribly wrong. Instead of getting her on-side, I'm making a complete mess of explaining myself – she's going to tell me to get lost any second. 'Well, it wasn't exactly his fault. I sort of got it out of him. You see, I badly wanted to track down anyone who knew Tatty. I found something that I think belonged to her, and I wanted to find out more about it.' The words are tumbling out of my mouth now. I'm desperate for her not to close the door on me before I can explain myself properly.

'Something belonging to her? What is it?'

'Well, it's a long story and it's sort of . . . complicated. I was hoping we might be able to have a chat and I could tell you more about it.'

As I stand there, she looks me up and down again, clearly trying to decide whether I'm some sort of scam artist or not. The dogs, no longer yapping, are now sniffing at my feet, giving the odd guttural growl. I can't help thinking they might be about to cock their legs on my shoes to mark their territory so I concentrate on looking friendly and honest.

'You're not trying to sell me anything?' she says.

'No, not at all,' I reply.

'Or convert me to anything? Because I don't believe in all that mumbo-jumbo.'

'No. I just want to ask you about Tatty, that's all. It won't take long, I promise. I would have phoned ahead but I couldn't find a number for you. And then I happened to be close by on business so I thought I'd just knock. I know it must seem odd.'

I'm sticking closely to the story Ruth came up with, and it seems that it might be working because, from her expression, she's now considering letting me across her threshold.

'Well, I suppose you'd better come in, then,' she says reluctantly. 'You're not a serial killer, I take it?'

'Definitely not.'

'Good. Because I'd have to set the dogs on you if you were.'

Right on cue, the three dogs start yapping fiercely at me again as she ushers me in and I'm not convinced she's joking – from the look of them, they could easily savage me if they wanted to, especially the smallest one: he seems absolutely vicious.

I follow her down a narrow hallway, glancing around in admiration. From the outside the tiny terraced house looks pretty ordinary, but its interior is nothing like I would have expected. The hallway walls are painted a pure, brilliant white, and dark wooden African masks hang in a line, interspersed with watercolours of desert landscapes. Underfoot, there's a red wool runner that may be Moroccan in origin, and the ceiling has been covered with tiny, colourful mosaic tiles. The effect is pretty breathtaking.

I step into the kitchen that runs across the back of the house and am surprised all over again by the charming room – in here, it's wonderfully bright and deceptively spacious. Over the scrubbed kitchen table there is a massive woven wall hanging that depicts an African mother cradling a child tenderly in her arms. The floor is bleached wood and the units are free-standing, all painted a pale ochre. More Moroccan rugs are scattered everywhere. Either Mary Moore has travelled extensively or her friends and family have.

'Sit down,' she instructs, and for a split second I'm not sure if she's talking to me or the dogs. It's only when she jerks her head towards a chair at the table that I know for sure she meant me.

I sit, keeping one eye on the dogs, which are circling the room, sniffing the floor. 'You have a lovely home,' I say. 'It looks like you've travelled quite a bit.'

'I nursed overseas for years, yes,' she says briskly.

'Where? Africa?'

'Among other places.' She purses her lips, as if determined not to give away any more. 'I just need to put these in the oven – bear with me for a second.'

I watch as she slides a tray dotted with blobs of gloopy mixture into the oven and try to think of something else to say before I ask her about the bag. If I can defrost the atmosphere a notch it might help, but she's certainly not making it easy for me.

'You like to bake?' I ask. Baking is a nice neutral subject, surely.

'Not really,' she replies matter-of-factly, stopping my attempt at chit-chat in its tracks. She takes off her apron and washes her hands at the deep Belfast sink. 'But I work at an old folks' home now – have done since Tatty died – and most of the residents like scones so I bring them some when I'm on nights.' She dries her hands thoroughly on a tea towel, then sits down opposite me. All three dogs have finished their rambling and are lying at her feet.

I notice there's no offer of tea. This isn't going to be

easy. She's watching me carefully now, waiting for me to speak. It's time to get to the point.

'I'll tell you why I'm here, shall I?' I smile at her.

She doesn't return it. 'If you would.'

'Er, I run an antiques shop with my grandmother and I found this bag recently in a box of stuff I bought to sell in the shop. I think it was Tatty's.' I take out the Chanel bag from where it's been nestling in my leather satchel and show it to her.

She looks at it, bemused. 'You're here because of this?'

'Em, yes, I am.'

'Well, I can't help you, I'm afraid. I'm sure Tatty had lots of bags. I don't know if this was hers or not.'

'You never saw her with it?' I say, instantly deflated. My theory that Tatty carried this bag everywhere with her is crumbling and I'm childishly disappointed.

'I can't say I did. Mind you, we were indoors almost all of the time – she wouldn't have had much occasion to use it, even if it was hers. Where did you say you found it?'

'I bought it at an auction – it was in a box along with some other stuff.'

She shakes her head then, and gives a sigh. 'I still can't get my head round that business – all her things scattered to the four winds.'

'I heard everything belonging to her was sold off,' I say.

Mary nods and leans down to rub a dog's ears. 'I didn't think it was right but, then, that was the way she said she wanted it. Only a fool would argue with someone's last wishes.'

'And she left everything to charity?' I ask tentatively,

afraid to push her for too much detail, but keen to know more.

'Yeah. She organized everything with her solicitor beforehand. Right prick he was.'

I stifle a giggle – clearly she and Hugo have a shared opinion of stuffy Dermot Browne.

Mary leans down to pat another dog and the three snuggle in closer to her stout legs, snuffling softly.

'Did you work with her for long?' I ask.

'About ten months – she'd been very independent up till then, lived alone all her life, never married or had children. She was a rich woman, though. Mind you, you'd need to be to pay the rates the agency charges,' she adds darkly. 'Highway robbery, if you ask me.'

'I wonder where she got her money from,' I say aloud. This is something I've been thinking about. I'm not surprised to hear that Tatty was a woman of means – she had some valuable possessions and could afford to pay agency rates for a companion in her final months – but how had she made her money? That's still a mystery.

'I never asked her,' Mary Moore replies, a little tartly. 'That was her business, not mine.'

'And she had no one else to help her? No relatives?'

'No. She contacted the agency after she had a fall. She interviewed me herself – she'd already met half a dozen others. I was the last on her list.'

Something in the way she says this sparks my curiosity. What was it about Mary Moore that Tatty liked? Why did she choose this woman above the others to care for her?

'Did she interview you at home?' I ask, hoping she'll

describe where Tatty lived and give me more insight into her life. Now she seems to be lost in memories and her guard is down. That's to my advantage because I get the feeling she's not usually so free with the information she discloses.

'Yes. I'll never forget it.' She gives a rueful laugh. 'She lived in a beautiful Georgian house, off Merrion Square. I'd never seen anything like it before.'

'It sounds impressive.' I know that houses in that area are pretty exclusive, most of them three-storey mansions.

'Yes, it was. Totally unsuitable for someone who was convalescing, of course, what with all the stairs. And I told her that too.'

'At the interview? That was courageous of you!'

She laughs then, and leans forward to rub the dogs once more. 'That's what she said – that I had balls. God, that made me chuckle! Tatty had a marvellous sense of humour.'

'But she had no family of her own? No one at all?' I ask. I don't want to mention the letter I found in Tatty's handbag, not yet.

Mary fixes her green eyes on me. 'Not that I ever met, no,' she replies. 'There were no visitors when I was there. But that's what happens all the time – people forget about the old. They become invisible.'

She looks away and I can tell that, despite her tough demeanour, this makes her sad. If she works in an old folks' home, she knows more than most about the elderly and how they can be sidelined when age and illness set in. A picture of Ruth pops into my head, although she's far from your average old-age pensioner.

But she's hale and hearty — if her health was failing, things might be very different and the thought makes me shiver.

It sounds as if Tatty Moynihan was quite isolated and alone. No family, no visitors. What can have happened to cut her off from the world like that? And whatever happened to the lover who wrote her the letter?

Suddenly Mary leans closer to me, suspicion back on her tanned face.

'Why do you want to know all this? What's it got to do with you?' she asks. 'You're asking a lot of questions about Tatty just because you found a bag that might have belonged to her once. What is it you're really after?'

I know immediately that I have to confide why I'm here. Otherwise I'll be out on my ear, the dogs nipping at my heels. In an instant I decide to tell her the truth. She's not like the solicitor, Dermot Browne, who sounded as if he couldn't have cared less about the old lady as long as his bill was paid. OK, I doubt Tatty confided in Mary about her old love, but from what I can gather she seems to have kept much of her life from others. But it's obvious from the way Mary is talking about Tatty that she cared deeply for her. They had a relationship that transcended money or any professional arrangement. They were friends. Showing her the letter won't be a betrayal.

I take a deep breath. 'I found a letter. In the bag,' I reply.

'A letter? What sort of letter?' Her tanned forehead wrinkles in surprise.

'A letter from an old lover of hers. Here, read it for yourself.'

I slide it across the table and watch as she reads it, her hand to her throat.

'Oh,' is all she says. But there's deep sorrow in her voice. She's been affected by the letter just as much as I have, I can tell.

'I know this will probably sound crazy, but after I found it I just felt a sort of . . . connection to Tatty. That's why I've been trying to find out more about her. I rang Dermot Browne and he led me to you, but to be honest, I'm not even sure what I'm looking for.'

Mary Moore regards me thoughtfully. 'Well, in my experience,' she says slowly, 'someone who's looking for something and doesn't know what it is has usually lost something along the way and is trying to make up for it.' She stares at me so hard I can feel a blush creeping up from my chest to my face. 'So, Coco Swan, the question is, what have you lost?'

I look at her, unsure how to reply or what to say. But, unnervingly, an image of Mum pops into my head. 'I don't know what you mean,' I say. 'I'm just curious, that's all.'

'Hmm . . .' She smiles at me, then glances at the oven as it pings to say the scones are done. 'Tell you what, let's have a cuppa, shall we?'

Half an hour later, Mary Moore and I are chatting like old friends. I've already had two of her delicious scones, dripping with melted butter and homemade jam, and I'm munching my way through a third, still warm from the oven.

'From what you say, it sounds like Tatty was very elegant,' I say, through a mouthful of crumbs.

'She was,' Mary replies. 'She had a way with her. She
was very particular about her appearance, even though
she was housebound.'

'Was she?'

'Oh, yes. She would have me do her hair and her
makeup right till the end. She had the most incredible
bone structure – she must have been a real beauty in her
day. Her cheekbones would have cut glass. You know who
she reminded me of? That red-haired actress from *The
Quiet Man* and *Miracle on 34th Street*. What's her name?'

'Maureen O'Hara?'

'Yes! She was exactly like her. She loved music too, and
she had a beautiful voice.'

'She sang?'

'All the time. The oldies but goodies, she called them. I
used to tell her that she should apply for *The X Factor*!'
Mary chuckles at the memory.

'What did she say to that?'

'Oh, she laughed it off. Always smiling, even when she
started going downhill. And she was such a lady. I should
know. I've worked for plenty who weren't.'

The way that Mary is describing Tatty to me, so vividly,
I can almost see her in my mind's eye. I feel a little sad that
I'll never meet her.

'I wonder why she never married or had kids,' I say,
sighing a little. Tatty sounds like an amazing character so
how did she end up all alone at the end of her life, save for
hired help?

'Lots of people end up alone, Coco. It's not so unusual,' Mary replies. A wistful expression crosses her face and then disappears.

She's right, of course. Not everyone finds someone special. Maybe Tatty was never reunited with the mystery man. Maybe Mary herself hasn't anyone special in her life. Thinking about it, neither do I right now. Who's to say I ever will again? The thought makes me feel a little odd and unsettled.

I watch Mary divide a scone between the dogs. Once they've snaffled it all, she gently pushes them away. They retreat to the corner of the room where a large worn tartan dog bed is wedged between a pine dresser and the fridge. They scramble in, twisting and turning until they get comfortable, a bundle of fur and wet noses.

'I can't help wondering about the man who wrote Tatty the letter,' I go on. 'What happened to him? He clearly meant a lot to her, if she kept his note all this time.'

Mary looks down at the letter again, still lying on the table between us, like a message from another time. 'I don't know,' she says, puzzled. 'She never said anything about him to me, not even towards the end. That's when people confide things that are on their minds. I often know there's not much time left when people ask for others who have passed on before them. But she never mentioned this man.'

'You were with her when she died?' I ask.

'Yes. She was in pretty good health before her fall so that helped for a while afterwards, but she got frail quite quickly. I was there six months before she had to use the wheelchair almost all the time. And then she got pneumonia . . .' Her voice trails away. In the silence, I can hear the dogs snoring softly, asleep already.

'I'm sorry, Mary. You were obviously very fond of her.'

'Yes, I was.' She lifts her head and looks sadly at me. 'I know I was supposed to be taking care of her, but sometimes it felt like the other way around.'

'It did? Why?'

She pauses for a long time. 'She was just that type of person,' she explains. 'We had a . . . What was the word you used? A connection. You don't have them with every patient, but Tatty was different.'

'It's weird that I feel it too even though I'm never going to meet her. It's a bit mad, isn't it?'

'Not really,' Mary says, shrugging. 'You feel what you feel. The question is, what are you going to do with the letter now?'

'I don't know.'

'Well, what do you *feel*? Don't stop to think about it, just tell me. Say whatever comes off the top of your head.'

'I feel I need to follow where it leads me.' That's the truth of it – I don't know why I feel obliged to find out more, I just do. I can't explain it but it's as if something, or someone, is pushing me forward. Yes, Ruth and Karl have encouraged me to pursue it, but that's not it, not entirely at least. Something about the bag and the letter has captured my imagination. And I can't shake the feeling, now more than ever, that it has to do with Mum.

'Go on, don't stop,' Mary says, pouring me another cup of tea.

'Well . . . look, this will sound insane, but my mum

loved Chanel. She had these pearls, just like Coco's, that she never took off.'

'That's why she called you Coco?'

'Yeah.' I roll my eyes, a little embarrassed as always by this explanation. 'Anyway, she died when I was almost thirteen, before I really got to know her properly. I can't help feeling that . . . she's sent this bag to me for a reason.'

'Like she's whispering in your ear?' Mary asks.

'Exactly! It's nuts, isn't it?'

'No, it's not,' Mary says. 'I've seen enough in my lifetime not to dismiss anything. Everything is possible, Coco. You should follow your heart, see where it leads you.'

'But I don't really see where it *can* lead me,' I reply, frowning a little. 'I mean, Tatty's gone and there's no way to find out who she loved, is there? And even if this man was alive and I managed to find him, what could actually come of it?'

'I guess you'd have to cross that bridge when you got to it,' Mary says.

Then a thought strikes me. 'Maybe, if he was alive, I could give him the letter and it would make him happy, bring a smile to his face. It could give him a wonderful memory, remind him of Tatty and let him relive a special moment from his past.'

It sounds a bit lame, even to my ears.

But Mary doesn't seem to think so. Her face suddenly breaks into a broad smile. 'Ah, I think I have it now. You're just an incurable romantic,' she says.

'No, it's not that,' I protest. 'It's just, you know . . .'

'It's just,' Mary finishes for me, 'that you think life can

have magic moments, and you want to deliver one to this anonymous old boy who loved Tatty.' She raises her eyebrows. 'Could it be that you're looking for love yourself, by any chance?'

Her bluntness is unnerving. And she's wrong, of course. I'm not looking for love. I'm perfectly happy the way I am.

'Well, Tatty certainly had you pegged,' I say.

'How's that?'

'You've got balls, all right.'

The two of us burst out laughing.

'Aha! But am I right?' she teases. 'Or have you already found the love of your life?'

'I recently split up with someone, actually, so technically I'm young, free and single.'

Mary's face falls, as if she's afraid she may have offended me. 'Oh, I'm sorry, Coco. I didn't mean to speak out of turn.'

'It's OK, honestly,' I say. 'I broke up with him – it was the right thing to do. We were more friends than anything else.'

'No passion?' She makes a funny face.

'Not too much, no.' I laugh ruefully. Tom and I never had the overwhelming passion that other people seem to. Cat and David couldn't keep their hands off each other at the beginning. They still have that spark. But I've never had it with anyone.

'Well, maybe there's a passionate affair just around the corner,' she says.

'I doubt it,' I reply.

'Why do you say that?'

'Well, I think you're either that sort of girl or you're not. And I'm not.'

'I don't know about that. I wouldn't go pigeonholing yourself too soon. You seem pretty passionate about this bag and the letter.'

'That's different.' I chuckle.

'How so?'

'Well . . . to be passionate in love you sort of have to let yourself go, don't you?'

'And you don't do that?'

'Er, no, I guess I don't.'

'Well, maybe that's something you can learn to do. You know, take more risks.'

'Maybe.'

'I think so. I wouldn't write passion off just yet.'

We smile at each other.

'Mary, why is it sometimes easier to talk to a stranger than it is to talk to family or friends?' I can't believe I've had such a meaningful conversation with a woman I barely know. It's very unlike me.

'I've no idea,' she replies, grinning at me. 'That's life, I guess. But a trouble shared is a trouble halved. I do believe that.'

'Thanks for talking to me, Mary,' I say, reaching across to hug her. 'I'd better get going, but I'll leave you my number in case you remember anything that might help me to find this man.'

'You know, there *was* someone she used to talk about,' Mary says suddenly. 'I don't know if it would be relevant, though.'

'Go on.'

'She had a friend in England – they used to write to each other now and again. There was even talk of a visit, but Tatty kept putting her off. She wanted to keep everyone at arm's length when she got very frail. She was so proud – she didn't want anyone's pity.'

My heart rises in hope. Maybe this is another lead. 'Where in England was she from?'

'London. Tatty lived there once, when she was much younger. I got the impression that she left Ireland after some argument with her parents, although she never really spelled that out.'

'Can you remember the friend's name?'

'Yes, she was called Bonnie Bradbury. The name always stuck with me – she's an actress actually, still working too, although she must be in her seventies, I'd say.'

'I've never heard of her.'

'She's not famous but she does stage work, I know that. The letters were always full of talk about some theatre . . . Now, what was it called?' Her forehead crinkles in concentration. 'The Parlour! That's it. It's in Farringdon.'

'Thanks so much, Mary. I might look her up, see if she can tell me any more.'

'Oh, do!' Mary says, squeezing me tight as we part at the door. 'The poor woman, I always felt badly about her. Tatty left very strict instructions about the funeral, you see – she didn't want anyone there. Poor Bonnie didn't find out she'd passed away until it was too late to come.'

'Oh, really?'

She nods sadly. 'Yes. She wanted it the way she wanted it – that was Tatty. Anyhow, let me know what you find out, won't you? Now that I know about this mysterious letter, I can't help wanting to know more myself.'

I wave goodbye to Mary at the gate and jump into the car. But I don't head straight for the motorway and home. Instead I drive up the canal and towards Merrion Square. As I pass the beautiful Georgian buildings, warm lights flickering from their tall windows, I imagine Tatty bounding up the steps towards her own front door, the Chanel bag under her arm. And in my ear I can hear Mum, like Mary said, telling me to keep going.

9

All the members of my up-cycling class are working happily on their projects in the small room off the shop. There's a real buzz of contented activity in the air, heavily scented with the different paints and glues that people are using to bring their shabby pieces of furniture back to life. As I walk from one person to the next, offering advice or encouragement, I'm thinking of what I learned from Mary Moore about Tatty.

When I got back from the city, Ruth and I looked up Bonnie Bradbury online. The website for the Parlour Theatre described a small, community-based outfit near Farringdon. There were some fuzzy group photos and mentions of roles that Bonnie Bradbury had played in recent productions, but no more information about her. 'Coco, you're miles away today!' I hear someone say, and come to.

It's Lucinda Dee, grinning at me, and I realize she's right – I *was* miles away, daydreaming about Tatty. 'Sorry, Lucinda, what were you saying?'

'I said I don't know if this looks right. What do you think?'

She steps back from her freshly painted chest of drawers and considers the particular shade of apple green she's applied, her forehead crinkling with indecision. The black-and-white checked headscarf she sometimes wears for class is flecked with green and so are her faded work dungarees. I really recommend the dress-down approach: you can't immerse yourself fully in a project if you're wearing good clothes. You have to be comfortable and not afraid to make a mess. Maybe that's another reason why I'm so content here – I can wear my scruffiest clothes and feel completely at ease.

'I like it,' I reply truthfully. I try to be honest with everyone in the class. They all have their own taste, of course, so variations on a theme can be vastly different, but if I think something looks wrong, I say so.

'I don't know, there's something about it that just doesn't sit right with me,' she says. 'Is the colour a little too flashy? Maybe I should have mixed some more white into the green, made it more muted . . .' She cocks her head to one side and places her hands on her hips, surveying her work.

'Well, if you had chosen a quality article, like mine, you wouldn't have that problem,' perfectionist Harry Smith remarks from the corner of the room, where he's lovingly applying oil to his mahogany piece.

'Oh, shut up,' Lucinda replies good-humouredly. 'At least mine's not boring.'

'Yes . . . at least it's not that,' he says, smirking at her in an antagonistic manner.

Lucinda picks up her paintbrush and pretends to threaten him with it.

'Now, now, settle down,' I say, laughing. The two of them are forever at each other's throats, even though, deep down, they're very fond of each other.

I turn to Lucinda. 'You know what? I don't think the

handles are right. That could be what's throwing you. Cream ones would look much better with the green. I have some in the shop, I'm almost sure.'

'Oh, yes! I see what you mean,' she says, her face breaking into a wide smile. 'It'd look much better if I replaced them. Thank you, Coco!'

'Let me go have a look. I'll be back in a tick.' I make my way into the shop and pull out the large cardboard box from under the counter where I keep all the bits and pieces I never throw out. There's a set of handles in here somewhere. I remember unscrewing them from an old dresser a few months back.

Just as I spot them, wedged under an industrial roll of tape, the shop bell goes and I look up in time to see Cat come in. Today, she's wearing a beautifully cut pale grey trouser suit, with a pair of small diamond earrings, a sheer cream top and very high black patent heels. Her hair is swept up in a loose chignon. Her violet eyes have been highlighted with gold eyeliner and her skin is as flawless as ever. When she shoves her oversized sunglasses to the top of her head I see the only thing that's slightly off about her appearance: she has shadows beneath her eyes. She can't disguise the tiredness, even with her expertly applied concealer.

'Hiya,' I say, pleased she's dropped in. I haven't had a chance to talk to her about my visit to Mary Moore yet and can't wait to tell her every detail.

'Hiya,' she replies glumly.

'You don't sound very cheery. What's up?'

'Oh, nothing. Just the usual nine-carat crap that is my life.'

'What's happened?'

'Where do you want me to begin?' She grimaces. 'I've just had another massive row with the chef for starters.'

'Still no moving him on the menu, then?'

The dispute about changing the restaurant menu has been steadily gaining momentum – and neither Cat nor the Central's chef has been willing to budge an inch.

'No. He just won't let go of the damn chicken or beef. Jesus, shoot me now!'

'Some people like chicken and beef, though,' I venture. 'It's not that bad.'

'It's not that feckin' good either,' she says. 'The hotel needs to be dragged into the twenty-first century. We're still serving the same crap we had at our Debs dance, Coco! And that was a zillion years ago.'

'I like chicken,' I say, 'and I'm not a zillion years old, excuse me.' She may have a point, though: the hotel did serve something similar at our school graduation ball, which seems aeons ago.

'Well, I think we should start being more adventurous,' she says, mutinously. 'Try new things.'

'Like what?'

'I don't know! Anything! Sushi!'

'You want to serve sushi in the restaurant? I'm not sure how that would go down,' I joke.

'Yeah, I'd probably be run out of town if I tried. It'd be pitchforks at dawn.' She rolls her eyes.

'Maybe you could start an Asian night,' I suggest. 'Just once a week.'

'Huh! Chef won't even do spring rolls. I haven't a chance. And my father agrees with him. He says we need to "remember our market". Sometimes I feel like I'm banging my head off a brick wall. Am I in charge or not?'

'Maybe your dad has a point, though,' I say. 'The locals know what they like.'

'Well, I think people need something different,' she says. 'No one wanted me to refurbish either, but they all like it now.'

'Hey, take it easy there, Tonto. I was only trying to help,' I say.

'Sorry, Coco. I'm like a bag of cats today.' She sighs heavily. 'I had a row with Mark too.'

I wince a little when I hear Mark's name. Ever since I saw him talking to Sean O'Malley I've been meaning to chat to him, but Tatty's bag and the letter have distracted me. 'What happened?' I ask.

'He's been late for dinner every day this week, and his school grades are in the toilet. I just can't get through to him.'

'And what do you think it's all about?' I ask, almost afraid of her answer. I feel terrible that I haven't made time to ask Mark if anything's wrong. Maybe I should just tell Cat what I saw. But with the mood she's in, she might just hit the roof altogether. I could make it a million times worse, all for nothing. Mark talking to Sean might have been a coincidence, nothing to do with the way he's been behaving recently. I need to find out more before I go telling tales.

'Well, I've been reading up on it, and apparently his behaviour is part of him trying to detach from me.'

'Detach from you? That sounds weird.'

'Yeah, it does, but it makes sense, I suppose. He's

almost a man. It's natural that he's cutting the apron strings, rebelling and trying to find his own identity. That's what the books say.'

I'm tempted to say it sounds like a load of bullshit, but I feel I can't. I have no kids of my own: who am I to give advice?

'Right,' I say. 'I suppose the experts know best. I'm sure you'll sort it out.'

'I don't know if I will. It's like he's decided to hate me, like he's flicked some switch and hit the despise-your-mother button.'

'Well, if he has, I'm sure he'll switch back just as quickly. All teenagers go through this sort of thing – it's a rite of passage.'

'What if he doesn't, though, Coco?' she says, her eyes despairing.

'I'm pretty sure you just have to hang on in there,' I reply. 'He'll get through this phase and come out the other side. Then you'll both look back and laugh.'

'I hope you're right,' she says grimly.

'I am,' I say, and smile at her.

Just then, Lucinda pops her head round the door. 'Oh, Cat, I didn't know you were here.'

'Hi, Lucinda, sorry to monopolize the teacher!' Cat says brightly, quickly hiding her concern.

Lucinda laughs. 'Not at all – I'm sorry to interrupt you two. I just wanted those handles, Coco, if you have them.'

'They're right here.' I pass them to her. 'I'll be back in a couple of minutes – tell the others I haven't run out on them.'

'Take your time, Coco – I can manage that bunch if

they step out of line!' She disappears back to her chest of drawers.

I turn to Cat. 'Don't worry about Mark. We'll all look back and laugh, I swear.'

'You think?'

'Of course! I'm already planning his twenty-first party. I'm going to make a really embarrassing speech about him being a moody teenager. He'll probably have a girlfriend by then – it'll mortify him.'

'Actually, David reckons there might be a girl on the scene already,' Cat says.

A light-bulb goes on in my head. *That* could explain why he's being so moody. Maybe him talking to Sean means nothing. 'Well, there you go. Girl trouble could explain why he's so up and down.'

'Maybe. It's impossible to know when I can't get a word out of him. He's practically monosyllabic. It's freaking me out.'

'What? That he might have a girlfriend?'

'Yeah.' She nods. 'If he's dating someone, that means he might be having sex!'

'Ah, no, he's way too young for that!'

'He's fifteen, Coco.'

'God.'

'Yeah. God,' she replies mournfully. 'I mean, I'm not grown-up enough to deal with this stuff.'

We both laugh weakly.

'Jesus,' Cat says eventually, 'I don't know why I'm laughing – this is serious stuff.'

'Don't worry,' I say. 'Mark'll be fine. He's a sensible kid. I'm sure he's making good choices.'

'Like I did?' I know she's referring to her teenage pregnancy. Despite all her success she can't forget everything she went through during that difficult time. It's shaped her as a person, much like Mum's death and the aftermath have shaped me.

'Stop beating yourself up,' I say. 'That was then, and this is now.'

'All I know is that I can't wait for him to go to Spain on the school tour – we need a break from each other.' Her eyes fill with tears.

'Hey, come on.' I feel terrible that she's getting upset.

'I'm sorry.' She snuffles. 'It's just that I feel so awful for admitting that out loud. I used to hate being apart from him and now I'm looking forward to him leaving. Isn't that terrible? I never thought things would end up like this, us at loggerheads all the time.' She tries to compose herself.

'Look, Cat, I think you need a night out. Why don't you and David arrange to go on a date night and I'll come over and mind the twins?'

Her eyes light up. 'Really? I'd love that so much – you have no idea.'

'No problem. You can always ask me.'

She hugs me quickly. 'Thanks, Coco. I really appreciate it. I'm sorry to keep offloading on you.'

'Don't worry about it,' I say. 'You know you can always pop in and have a chat, anytime.'

'Actually, there's another reason I'm here,' she says, clearing her throat and looking even more serious.

'Jeepers, what now?'

'It's about Tom.' She pauses dramatically before she goes on. 'I met his mother in the supermarket.'

'You lucky thing.' I make a face. Tom's mother was never my number-one fan. I always got the feeling she disapproved of my background – child of a single mother, father unknown. My pedigree isn't exactly sterling.

'Coco, I hope you're not going to be upset, but she told me something I should tell you before anyone else does.' She pauses again. 'Tom's going out with someone. A New Zealander.'

'Oh, right.'

I poke around a little inside, trying to figure out how this makes me feel. I'm not surprised by the news, of course not. I'd been expecting it. But still.

'Are you OK?' Her eyes are searching my face.

'Yes, totally.' I realize, with a rush of relief, that it's the truth. 'Why wouldn't I be?'

'Well, because it's a bit flipping quick, isn't it?' she says crossly.

'I broke it off with him, remember?' I remind her. 'I can't exactly be upset. That would be hypocritical, to say the least.'

'Well, he could at least have had the good manners to pretend to be broken-hearted for a while longer,' she puffs, outraged.

Cat's always been a bit protective of me. I'm not sure why – maybe it's because she was the popular, beautiful one at school. I know people always thought I hung onto her coat-tails, even if she never made me feel that way.

'Actually . . . I'm glad he's found someone new,' I say.

'You're glad?' Cat repeats, staring at me as if I've completely lost the plot.

'Yeah. It makes me feel less guilty. If he's moved on, it means he's over me.'

'Not necessarily.'

'Yes necessarily,' I say.

'Just because he's having sexual relations with another woman doesn't mean he's over you, Coco.'

'I think it means exactly that,' I say. 'He's over me. Chapter closed. We can move on.'

'And what about you?'

'What about me?'

'When are you going to move on to someone else?'

'Please. It's far too early to think about that.'

'It wasn't too early for him. I always thought you two were the perfect match. None of this makes sense.'

'Look, Cat, I'm perfectly happy, OK?'

'OK. Well, I'll say no more.' She sighs then, a great big sigh that comes from her toes. 'What do I know, sure? Men are a mystery to me.'

'Er, you have nothing but men in your life.'

'Yes, I'm surrounded by them. And I still know nothing. Go figure.'

I glance over my shoulder, conscious that Lucinda and the rest of the class must be wondering where I am. 'I'd better go back to my class,' I say. 'God knows what they're getting up to. They're like a bunch of teenagers in there.'

'Don't say that, for God's sake,' she says, rolling her eyes. 'Call me later, OK? I want to hear about your trip to the Big Smoke. Did you find out any more about the bag?'

'I did actually,' I reply. 'I'll fill you in later.'

'Great. I can live through you vicariously.' Then, with the briefest of smiles, she's gone.

As I make my way back to my class, an image of Tom pops into my head. It's difficult to imagine him with someone else, but I'm glad for him. He's not the type to want to be alone. It's hard to believe that I'm not more upset by the news, really, but I'm so preoccupied with Tatty's story that I'm finding it hard to concentrate on anything else.

Tom wasn't my true love – I know that. Mostly he felt like a good friend, sometimes even like an annoying brother. When I look back now, I think I went out with him because he was there and he was . . . non-threatening. That doesn't cover me with glory, I know, but Tom was gentle, quietly spoken and predictable – a man of routine and morals. He was safe.

I walk to the door and lean against the frame, watching my class at work, some chatting, others concentrating. They're all either married or widowed. Sometimes I feel like the only salmon in town – swimming upstream, wilfully going against the current. I smile to myself. I must tell that to Cat – the only salmon in town – give her a laugh. The upshot is I'm pleased for Tom, yes, but I've also got a feeling I can't put my finger on – not disappointment, exactly, but maybe . . . a little loneliness. Love and marriage. What do you do if you're thirty-two and you don't do them?

10

I can hardly believe it's almost October already and time for another window display. I'm not sure how the tradition of a new display on the first of every month started, but it's become a Swan's custom. I began doing the windows every now and then when I was growing up, and soon realized that I loved coming up with unique ideas to make them show-stoppers. Over the years, my displays have become quite famous and lots of locals make it their business to walk by or pop in on the first of the month, just to see what I've done.

Ruth sometimes worries that expectations are now a little too high and that it might become more of a chore for me than anything else, but I don't feel like that. I love working behind the sheet that I hang across the window so no one can see in until it's perfect. Working almost in a twilight world, not watching the clock, just concentrating on creating something beautiful is still absorbing, great fun and very satisfying.

I sit back on my hunkers now and survey what I've done so far. I'm trying to create a winter wonderland to celebrate the arrival of the colder weather. I draped a large sheet of crisp white fabric as a backdrop. Next, I stacked some old wooden jewellery boxes, packing each one with white satin, then arranging some pieces, allowing a few strands of white-gold necklaces to peek out, giving customers a tantalizing glimpse of what's inside. Beside those I've placed a kneeling prayer chair that I've had upholstered in a pure white linen. I can't imagine anyone uses these to pray any more, but they still look pretty in a bedroom. Beside the chair I've piled a selection of decades-old leatherbound books, their pages open to reveal the words inside. On top of these I've placed some little wooden birds, to reflect the sparrows that always gather at the foot of the monument outside. I've given the birds a silver wash of paint and sprinkled some iridescent glitter over everything to give the scene a proper frosty air. I pause now to admire the effect.

I'm really pleased with how it looks so far, almost exactly as I'd hoped. I love it when that happens – when the vision I have in my head comes together. I still have a few more things to perfect before I can unveil it, though – it's not complete yet. I need a stunning centre-piece to pull everything together – an arrangement of some massive church candles may work well, perhaps displayed on top of the wooden children's sledge we have in the shop. That would give the window a really old-fashioned, almost magical feel. Right now, though, I'm ready for a break.

Standing to stretch my legs, I peep over the sheet. Across the road Karl is talking animatedly to a customer – probably explaining the difference between various cuts of meat. He can get very excited about that sort of thing. Next door, Victor's TV repairs is still shut. Poor Victor – he definitely has a gambling problem. He's been trying to hide it from everyone, but even I can see that he's never out of the bookie's now. Next to his shabby premises, Nora from the Coffee Dock is sweeping the path, her face set in a grim expression. Clearly things between her and Peter aren't improving.

I jump when there's a sudden knock at the window. It's Ruth, wrapped up in a bright red Puffa jacket, grinning widely at me.

'Can I have a look?' she calls, as she opens the shop door and steps inside, a whoosh of chilly air following her. The weather really had taken quite a wintry turn.

'Not yet,' I reply.

'Oh, come on . . . Just a peep?'

'Nope. You'll have to wait till I'm done, like everyone else.'

'Spoilsport.' She chuckles, unwinding her scarf, then shrugging off her Puffa jacket, revealing her tight black Lycra gym gear underneath.

I wonder, as I often do, how she manages to look so damn good for a woman of almost seventy. Hopefully, I've inherited some of her genes. Her body is still slim and firm and her skin is glowing.

'Oh, it's cold.' She whistles, rubbing her hands together. 'I'm freezing my tits off!'

'Ruth!'

'What? Isn't that what everyone says these days?' She laughs mischievously.

'Everyone might, but I'm not sure you should.'

'I like to get down with the kids, Coco! Why else do you think I took up Zumba?'

'How's it going?' I ask.

Ruth started at the classes a few weeks ago to keep fit. It's exactly the sort of not-for-an-OAP thing she likes to do.

'Really good! Robbie said I'm a marvel!' She giggles.

'Ah, the gorgeous Robbie!'

It's a running joke that Ruth has a massive crush on her twenty-two-year-old instructor, who has rock-hard abs and buns of steel. She doesn't even deny it any more.

'He took me for coffee afterwards. I think I'm in there – Karl had better watch out.'

'You're incorrigible!' I guffaw.

'I try.' She laughs. 'Did anything interesting happen while I was gone?'

'Well, Carmel Ronan was in earlier.'

Carmel is the town snob, who deigns to visit the shop every six months or so and drives a very hard bargain.

Ruth throws her eyes to Heaven. 'God, she's a rat-bag. I don't suppose she bought anything?'

'She did actually – those two awful ashtrays we got last year.'

'You're kidding me!' Ruth's jaw drops. 'I've been trying to get rid of them for months.'

'I know you have. She gave me almost the full asking price too.'

'I might have to sit down.' Ruth shakes her head at the improbability of it all. 'Carmel must be getting soft.'

'I think she was having an off day, all right,' I say. 'She only argued with me for a couple of minutes.'

'What can she possibly want with those ashtrays anyway? She doesn't smoke.'

'Maybe they're for guests,' I say. 'Although I'm not sure she gets many of those.' Carmel has two grown-up children who both moved to the States after college and very rarely come back to town. Her husband died years ago and she never seems to have any friends to stay. Everyone knows this as despite the general dislike of her, or maybe because of it, people still keep a beady eye on the comings and goings at her massive house.

'Poor woman, I feel sorry for her, really,' Ruth goes on.

'You're very forgiving,' I say, arching a brow at her. The last time Ruth had an encounter with Carmel she was still giving out about her days later. Carmel had marched into the shop and demanded to return a vase, saying she'd discovered it was chipped when she got it home. Ruth knew it had been in perfect condition when it left the shop because she'd made sure to check, knowing what Carmel was like. Still, other than calling Carmel a liar, she had no choice but to refund her. It took Ruth ages to get over that incident – she's not one to hold a grudge, but Carmel is one person who gets under her skin in a bad way.

'Well, you know what, I think she's lonely. That's why she pretends to be so hard,' she says now. 'She hasn't got anyone in her life and that's a huge hole. Imagine sitting up there in that mansion night after night all alone – what must she get up to?'

'You're very understanding today, Ruth,' I say, taken aback by her change of heart towards her sworn enemy.

'Maybe I can afford to be. I have my lovely shop, I have my friends and, most of all, I have you. What more could a woman ask for?'

She grins at me, but I detect the shadow of sadness, as always. She still misses Mum and Granddad. She tries hard to get on with her life, throwing herself into new things and keeping active, but part of her will never recover from their deaths. Although I can't help thinking that her dating Karl is a very big step in the right direction, even if she claims it's just a fun distraction.

'So. You've been busy,' she says now.

'Yes. I might just do the floor next, while I'm on a roll,' I say, as I haul out the bucket and mop from the cleaning cupboard.

'You washed it the other day,' she points out, as I survey the mop and wonder if it needs replacing.

'Did I? Well, no harm in doing it again.'

'Cleanliness is next to godliness, eh?'

'You don't believe in God, Ruth.'

'Good thing, too – if I did, I might just end up in Hell for what I'm doing with Karl.' She glances out of the door and gives her beau a flirtatious little wave. Even from here, I can see him smile from ear to ear as he catches her eye – she really has him right where she wants him: in the palm of her hand.

'That's way too much information.' I grimace. 'Are you trying to traumatize me?'

I'm glad that Ruth seems happy, but I can't help wondering how Anna is going to feel about this when she finds out – which she will. This is a small town: word will leak out sooner or later if it hasn't already and I have an inkling that my great-aunt will strongly disapprove.

'Sorry. So, anyway, you're not the only one who's been busy,' she says airily.

There's something about the way she speaks that makes me sit up and take notice immediately. 'Really? What's going on?' I ask.

Her eyes flick back to my face, her expression now

extremely guilty. 'If I tell you, promise me you won't kill me?'

'What have you done?' I say, and groan.

'Well, you know how we looked up the Parlour Theatre's website?'

'Yes?'

'I called them.'

'You didn't!' I'm shocked by her solo run, but undeniably excited too.

'I did.' She's sheepish now. 'I just couldn't resist it. But I didn't get very far.'

'What do you mean?'

'Well, the nice man who answered told me that Bonnie *was* in the theatre, rehearsing for some new play that's going to be staged next month, but that she couldn't speak to me.'

'You actually asked to speak to her?' I say, incredulous.

'I did. Only to see if she was there, though, I was going to hang up. But it didn't matter in the end because it turns out she's hard of hearing, and she finds it difficult to talk on the phone.'

'What are you like, Ruth!' I say, half annoyed with her, half admiring her boldness.

'I'm sorry, darling, I was just trying to do a little groundwork for you,' she says, knowing she's totally getting away with it. 'So, the good news is you can reach her there. The bad news is, it might take more than a phone call. But I've already thought of a way around that.'

'Now why doesn't that surprise me?' I laugh.

'Yes!' she replies, her eyes glittering with excitement.

'Let's go to London. Then you can talk to her in person!'

'You're not serious?'

'Why not? I've been threatening to go to the markets over there for stock, you know that. We can kill two birds with one stone.'

My heart lifts with excitement. I'd love to talk to Bonnie, see what she knows about Tatty and the letter. But would I have the nerve? 'I don't know. Maybe I should just leave it,' I say, unsure.

'Leave it?' she squeals, appalled. 'You can't do that! It's just getting interesting!'

'Don't get carried away, Ruth,' I warn. She has a tendency to put the cart before the horse.

'I'm not getting carried away – but you can't give up now. Don't you want to know more? I can't get this story out of my head! I mean, who was Tatty really?' Ruth goes on, evidently trying to pique my curiosity to get me to agree. 'How did she end up so alone at the end of her days? Was she waiting all that time for the love of her life to come back to her? Did she die of a broken heart?'

'But, Ruth, London is –'

'London? Who's going to London?'

Ruth and I stare at each other in horror when we hear the voice behind us.

It's Anna. How long has she been standing there? How much has she heard? It's impossible to say. Blast her and those rubber-soled shoes she buys in the nursing-supplies shop.

'Anna!' Ruth whirls to face her. 'For Christ's sake – are

you trying to give me a cardiac arrest? It's so creepy the way you sneak up on people like that!'

'I didn't sneak up on anyone. I walked through the door – is that a crime?'

'Hi, Anna,' I say brightly, still thrown by her arrival but eager to see off any bickering between the two sisters. 'How are you?'

'I've been better,' she grumbles, but doesn't elaborate. 'What's all this about London?'

I shoot Ruth a warning glance. I still haven't told Anna about Tatty's handbag or the letter because I had a feeling she might just dismiss it. Anna isn't the most romantic of souls. She never dated another man after her husband, Colin, died – it was like she just gave up on love. I'm not sure she'd understand my interest in Tatty's story.

'I'm going over to the markets,' Ruth says airily.

'Why?' Anna asks, almost suspiciously.

'Why not?' Ruth replies. 'Life doesn't revolve around this small town, you know.'

'There's nothing wrong with this town,' Anna shoots back, on the defensive immediately.

'You're right. It's not the town. It's the small-minded people who live here,' Ruth says, teasing her sister.

'To whom are you referring?' Anna says, her eyes narrowing, not seeing the funny side.

'No one. She's referring to no one,' I interrupt. Honestly, these two old-age pensioners sometimes act like toddlers around each other.

'No, come on, Ruth, tell me. Are you saying I'm small-minded?' Anna does not intend to let it go.

Ruth shrugs. 'You said it, not me.'

Two dark red spots have appeared on Anna's pale cheeks. She's not seeing the funny side. 'And what? You're such a free spirit, is that it?' she says.

'Why don't I make us all a nice cup of tea?' I suggest.

'Well, at least I'm not as tightly wound as some people,' Ruth retorts smartly.

'Why? Because you think that making a complete fool of yourself once a week by jumping round a dance hall with people a third your age is *cool*? Is that it?'

I cringe at her criticism of the Zumba class. Ruth has been enjoying it so much.

'I knew it!' Ruth crows. 'I knew it embarrassed you. That's sad!'

'Just because I don't think Zumba is a suitable pastime for a woman of your age doesn't make me sad,' Anna retorts.

'You should try it – it's fun. It might loosen you up a little,' Ruth observes.

'I don't need any loosening up, thank you very much. And I certainly don't intend to throw myself around like some teenager. It's . . . unseemly.'

'Unseemly for a widow, you mean?' Suddenly Ruth is no longer laughing. Her voice is cold.

'I didn't say that.' Anna's gaze drops.

'You didn't have to. Would you prefer me to stay indoors mourning for the rest of my life? Maybe I should just sit by the fire and wait to die.' Ruth's eyes are dark pools of anger now.

'You're being ridiculous, honestly.' Anna is clearly trying to backtrack, knowing she's overstepped the mark.

The air reverberates with tension as the two women stare at each other.

'Hey, what do you think of this?' I say, gesturing to the antique sledge I'm considering putting in my window display, trying to veer them off the collision course they're on. 'I might put it in the window as part of the monthly reveal. What do you think?'

Anna gives it a cursory glance. 'It'll look very well, I'm sure, Coco,' she says, smiling tightly at me. 'You're a talented girl.'

'Thanks,' I rattle on. 'This month's window is going to be extra special. I can't wait to . . . '

But Anna isn't listening to me. She's looking at me oddly, head cocked to one side, a sympathetic expression on her face. Now I'm regretting breaking up their fight because her attention is fully on me, instead of Ruth, and I can see her mind ticking over. Oh, no, she's going to ask me about Tom. She's heard all about it. Crap. This is definitely not the way I wanted Ruth to find out. Even though it's been a few days since Cat told me he's seeing someone else, I still haven't found the right time to break the news to her. She thought Tom and I were good together. Hearing that he's moved on so quickly might upset her and that's the last thing I want.

'You heard about Tom, I suppose? Getting . . . involved with some girl in New Zealand?' Anna asks. Just like that. Good thing I had already heard because the way she's just dropped the bomb wasn't exactly subtle.

Out of the corner of my eye I see Ruth's jaw drop. 'What?' she squeaks.

'Yes. He's doing a line with some local girl over there.'

Anna tuts loudly, as if she thoroughly disapproves of this development.

'You knew about this, Coco?' Ruth asks me, her gaze on my face now.

'Yeah, Cat told me a few days ago . . .' I reply vaguely, not meeting her eye. She's annoyed I didn't confide in her, I can tell.

'It's all very quick. I don't think his mother is best pleased,' Anna goes on.

'Isn't she?' I ask. 'It didn't seem that way when she almost tore a ligament catapulting herself over a corn-flakes mountain to tell Cat in the supermarket.'

'Well, she's putting on her best face, of course, but how could she be happy, really? She knows nothing about the girl . . . about her family. How would she, Tom being so far away? And she's no way of finding out either. That girl could be anyone.'

'I'm sure she's perfectly nice,' I say. 'Tom wouldn't go out with someone who wasn't.'

'Hmm . . .' Anna sounds doubtful. 'Maybe. I'm not too sure about those New Zealanders, though. There's something . . . odd about them.'

'Anna, you can't say that!' Ruth pipes up.

'Why can't I? I'm entitled to my opinion, aren't I?'

'Not when it's a ridiculous one,' Ruth grunts under her breath. Ironically, Ruth is capable of making similar sweeping generalizations, like she used to about Karl and his German heritage, but I don't think now is the time to mention that the sisters may have more in common than they realize.

Anna turns to me, doing the head-cocking thing again.

'You're upset, aren't you, Coco?' she coos. Her eyes search my face for signs of distress. She's convinced I'm heartbroken to hear this news.

'No, of course not! Why would I be?' I reply.

'Coco.' Anna leans across and clasps my hands in hers. 'You don't need to hide your pain from me.'

'I'm not.'

'Of course you are. I mean, who knows when you'll meet someone new? It could take years. It might never happen.'

I look at her, wondering if she ever regrets not meeting anyone else after Colin died. She never mentions being lonely or wanting any sort of companionship. But, then, she almost wears her widowhood as a badge of honour, as if she's proud to be alone. She doesn't see herself as less whole because she has no kids or because she's spent most of her life alone – so why does she seem to see me like that?

'Anna, for God's sake, shut up,' Ruth snaps.

'What?' Anna says. 'It's true. I read an article in last week's newspaper about a woman who split up with her boyfriend because she thought she could do better, and she's still single ten years on! She was very bitter about it. He married someone else a year later and they had three kids and yet there she was, still on the shelf after all that time. She said that if she could do it all again, she would stay with him, even if he was only her Mr Make Do. That's what she called the fellow she left – her Mr Make Do. Turns out he was her Mr Right all along. And do you know what else she said? She said that if you're still single by the time you're forty, you'll be single for life – those are the statistics.'

She pauses and takes a great big breath. In the silence I can hear my heart pounding in my ears.

'Anna, you are the greatest pain in the arse I've ever met,' Ruth growls, as I'm trying to digest the fact that I may die alone, having walked away from my Mr Make Do, who was possibly my Mr Right all along.

'I know what you think of me, thank you,' Anna says primly. 'You tell me often enough. But my point is, giving up on someone because you think someone better will come along doesn't always work out.'

There's a deafening silence in the room as they both look at me.

'I'm completely fine about Tom meeting someone else,' I tell them wearily, sure they're not going to believe it anyway. 'I know you think I'm going to be a barren spinster, left on the shelf for the rest of my life –'

'I don't,' they say in unison, looking at each other, stricken.

'Yes, you do. But if I am, then it's got to be better than being with someone who isn't right for me. Tom was nice but he wasn't . . .'

'The One?' Ruth finishes.

'Well, I don't like that phrase but, yes, I suppose that's what I mean.'

'I see,' Ruth says. 'Well, then, you made the right decision, didn't she, Anna?'

'I suppose so,' Anna replies reluctantly, still not looking convinced.

Ruth clears her throat. 'So, as I was saying before you so rudely interrupted us, sister dear, a break in London would do you good, Coco. I've already looked up the

153

flights and we can get a really good deal if we go on Thursday.'

'This Thursday?' I squeak. 'But that's far too soon!'

'Why?' Ruth asks.

'Well, because . . . I've got loads on here. I have to finish the window and I need to sort out stuff for my class . . .'

Ruth's eyebrows are almost in her hair. 'Nonsense. A few nights away won't do you any harm at all. Isn't that right, Anna?'

Anna is thinking it over. Agreeing with her sister would be a milestone in itself and I can tell she knows this too. 'Yes, it would,' she says, nodding. 'You should go.'

I'm so shocked that they're actually in agreement about something that I'm almost lost for words. 'But what about the shop?' I ask.

Even as I ask this, I can see Anna's mind working overtime, what she's thinking. Crap! She's going to –

'I'll mind the shop for you!' she announces.

'We couldn't ask you to do that.' Ruth is trying to hide her horror at the idea with a veil of good manners – manners that are killing her to fake. She was so busy trying to work her charms on me that she hadn't spotted the possibility that Anna would volunteer to step in.

'Why not? Don't you trust me?' Anna asks, a steely glint in her eye as she throws down her gauntlet.

'Er, of course we trust you. It's not that. It's just . . .' Ruth is trapped.

'Well, then. It's settled.' Anna rubs her hands together. 'I'm quite looking forward to it. I can give the place a proper clean.'

'It doesn't need one!' Ruth protests.

'Of course it does.' Anna clucks. 'Now, don't you two worry about a thing. Off to London with you. I'll have this place running like clockwork by the time ye get back.'

She bustles off to put on the kettle and Ruth and I are left standing in her jet stream.

'What have I done?' Ruth moans.

'You've got no one to blame but yourself,' I reply, laughing.

'God knows what she'll get up to when we're gone. I dread to think.'

'It won't be that bad.'

'Yes, it will. It'll be worse. Don't you remember the last time – when we went to Kerry?'

'That time we went to see Granddad's cousins?'

The three of us had driven for hours across country in Granddad's Aston Martin to see some far-flung relations who lived outside Killarney. We kept stopping on the way to have roadside picnics and get ice-cream. Granddad loved his 99s – he taught me to push all the ice-cream down into the cone with my tongue so I could savour every last mouthful. That was one of the best holidays of my life: we stayed on a farm in the middle of nowhere and I got to help milk the cows in the mornings. I can still remember the stink of the farmyard. I thought I'd never get used to it, but I did. I even started to quite like it. I named all the hens and even the pigs.

'Yeah – we were only gone for a week,' Ruth says now. 'But by the time we got back she'd reorganized the whole damn shop.'

'I don't remember that part,' I say.

'Maybe you've blocked the trauma from your mind,' Ruth says darkly. 'She'd polished every surface, moved every piece of stock around. Granddad and I couldn't find anything – and we couldn't get rid of the smell of bleach for days afterwards.'

'She must have thought she was helping.' I giggle, suddenly struck by the comedy of the situation.

'We can do without her sort of help,' Ruth mutters.

'Maybe I should stay at home,' I say. I'm dying to talk to Bonnie, but the prospect fills me with butterflies too.

'No!' Ruth protests quickly. 'No, we're going. Anna won't try anything this time. I'll make sure of that.'

'Ruth . . .' I say warningly, as Anna appears, carrying a tray with tea things.

'Don't worry,' she whispers. 'She'll behave. Or I won't be responsible for my actions.'

'It's a bargain at that price, darlin'!' the man behind the stall calls to me as I pick up a small metal tankard and examine it.

I'm in Portobello Road, the most famous market in London, and as I've wandered up and down the street, traders have been assuring me that everything I touch is the deal of the century. This guy, whose stall is packed with all sorts of odds and ends, is no different.

'I don't know about that!' I smile, cradling the tankard as I search it for hairline cracks. It's a sweet piece, but not worth anywhere close to his asking price of fifty pounds.

'That's a perfect specimen, that is,' he goes on. 'Mid-nineteenth century.'

'Or a knock-off made in China?' I say, with a grin. I'm teasing now – the tankard isn't fake, I know that, but he's delusional if he thinks it's worth more than a fiver.

'China?' he gasps, then clasps his hands to his heart, as if he's about to keel over with shock. 'Do I look like a bloke who'd be selling rubbish, love?'

'That's exactly what you look like!' the guy on the stall beside him calls. 'He's a proper diamond geezer, love! Forget him and come and see what I've got for you!'

'Don't listen to him.' The dealer tuts. 'Right mummy's boy you are, Frank!' he shouts to his neighbour, who laughs uproariously at this, then twists the top off a flask and pours himself a steaming mug of tea.

'Brass monkeys today,' he says, winking at me.

He's right. It's absolutely freezing, my favourite sort of day when the sky is a perfect blue and the air is crisp and cold, so you can see your breath.

The stallholder is talking to me again. 'Now, what sort of thing you after, love?'

'I'm just looking,' I reply, picking up a small heart-shaped ceramic trinket box and turning it over in my hands. This is sweet, but Ruth and I have already bought enough. I don't need any more, but I can't stop myself looking. My love of old things is like an addiction I can't control.

'You Irish, darlin'?' the trader asks, a smile splitting his ruddy cheeks, showing his small even teeth, sparkling white in his weather-beaten face. I can't help thinking of Del Boy – he's even wearing a flat cap and a sheepskin coat to ward off the cold. Talk about a cliché!

'Guilty.' I smile back.

'I could tell – that gorgeous Irish accent gets me every time.'

Further along, his neighbour is pretending to play a romantic tune on a violin. 'He's a right 'un, he is,' he calls to me as he sways, making a see-sawing motion with an invisible bow.

'Now that is a lovely piece,' the dealer goes on, ignoring his neighbour. 'You have a great eye – look lovely on your mantelpiece that would.'

I turn the little box over, feeling its weight under my fingers. 'Maybe,' I reply. He's a persistent, if charming, salesman.

'Tell you what, special price for you, my darlin', just because I can't never resist that beautiful Irish accent. A Lady Godiva and it's yours.'

Good thing I used to love *Only Fools and Horses* when I was younger – I know he means a fiver. This guy is getting more like Del Boy every minute.

'I'll give you four.' I grin. It would make a really nice gift for Cat – it might cheer her up. We chatted before I left for London and things haven't improved much between her and Mark. To make matters worse, the hotel chef is now threatening to walk out. A little present like this will remind her that I'm there for her if she needs to talk. I make a vow to myself to tackle Mark as soon as I get back and see if I can help smooth things over.

'Go on, then, you chancer. I ain't never been to Ireland,' the trader goes on, wrapping the box in some of the newspaper that's stacked at his feet.

'They wouldn't let him in,' his neighbour catcalls.

'Shut it, you muppet!' He hands me the trinket box, now tucked in newspaper and a plastic bag. It can go with the other bits and pieces Ruth picked up this morning in the cavern of wonders that is Alfie's Antique Market in Marylebone. The car boot will be stuffed for the trip back.

'Anyfink else I can do for you, darlin'?' the trader asks me now. 'I have some nice copper measuring jugs, came in yesterday. Proper quality they are.'

'No, that's OK, thanks,' I say, handing over a five-pound note.

I glance at my watch. I have half an hour to get to the Parlour Theatre near Farringdon station and I don't want to be late.

'All right, darlin'," he replies, his eyes moving past me, darting this way and that to spot the next potential customer in the crowd.

'Thank you,' I say, tucking my change into my coat pocket.

'Thank you, my darlin'." But he's not looking at me now – he's working his charm on someone else, hoping to make another sale. It's his stock in trade – he seduces each and every customer who comes his way.

I walk to the far end of the market soaking up the atmosphere as I go, my hat pulled down low over my ears. There's something quite magical about this place. The narrow street is crammed with stalls, everyone selling their wares, calling out to each other and their customers. I can't help thinking as I mingle with the crowd, everyone pink-cheeked from the cold, that Tatty might have walked this way too. Perhaps she stopped and browsed at market stalls as I did, all the while carrying the very same bag that is now secured safely in my satchel. I almost feel as if I'm walking in her footsteps.

I breathe in the scent of freshly brewed coffee that floats on the frosty air, mingling with the peculiar scent of old things. If I had more time, I'd have a good root around all the stalls, with a coffee in my hand, but if I don't leave now I might miss my chance of speaking to Bonnie Bradbury. Rehearsals run all afternoon – that's what Ruth was told when she called. I might only have one chance and I have to grab it with both hands.

Half an hour and a ride on one of London's famous red buses later, I round a corner and there on the left-hand

side of the road is the Parlour Theatre. It's a shabby building, paint peeling off the walls, dog-eared posters
advertising long-finished shows fluttering in the breeze. I
don't recognize any of the acts that are billed. I don't
know what I was expecting – something a little more
upmarket, maybe – but the Parlour Theatre looks like a
Z-list venue.

I pause outside the door to take a deep breath. I wish
Ruth was with me, but again, just like when I went to
meet Mary Moore, she refused to come. She said I'd be
better off alone and, anyway, she had an important errand
to run; I could fill her in on all the details later. When I
asked what the mysterious errand was, she tapped her
nose and said that a policeman wouldn't ask her that, so I
left it. Ruth has her secrets – and that's the way she likes
to keep it. She and Karl seem to be going from strength
to strength – they're spending a lot of time together,
that's for sure. Maybe she's gone to get him a present.
Perhaps she spotted something at Alfie's Antique Market
this morning and decided to go back for it. She might
have been too embarrassed to say.

I glance at my watch again. It's now or never. I push
open the door and step inside.

I can hear the shouting before I see anyone.

'What are you bloody playing at?' a male voice yells
angrily.

'It wasn't my fault! You missed your cue!' a female voice
bellows back.

'Only because you fluffed your bloody lines! You need
to turn up your damn hearing aid, Bonnie!'

I stand in the foyer, unsure of what to do. If I push

through the set of doors in front of me, I'll be in the theatre proper – and it sounds as if the rehearsal is not exactly working out in there. Suddenly the double doors fly open and an elderly lady appears, a younger woman at her side.

'I can't work like this,' the older one declares, eyes flashing, clearly annoyed. 'He's just a young pretender.'

'Let's take a break,' her companion soothes. 'Then we can try again. I'll see you in ten, OK? And he's right, you know – you do need to adjust your hearing aid.' The younger woman turns and goes back through the doors, her dark ponytail swinging behind her.

It's her! It's Bonnie Bradbury in the flesh.

She hasn't noticed me yet so I can stare at her all I want. She's tall, almost as tall as me, wearing a flowing multicoloured top to her knees with fitted black trousers underneath that stop just above her ankles, which are still slim and shapely. The most striking thing about her, though, is her hair – it's pure silver, flowing down her back in a sheet of shimmering light. Her face is lined, yes, but her cheekbones are high. I can see that she must have been a great beauty in her time – she's still extremely attractive. In fact, she reminds me of Ruth – they're cut from the same cloth.

I'm trying to gather the courage to introduce myself, when she turns and sees me watching her. Her back straightens, as if she's pulling herself up to her full height. 'Can I help you?' she asks.

'Er, hello,' I say. 'My name is Coco Swan.'

'Who?'

'Coco Swan. I was wondering if I could have a word.'

162

As I talk there's an alarming buzzing in the sound system and Bonnie clutches her ear, wincing. 'I swear they do that on purpose to aggravate me,' she says. 'Let's go to my dressing room to chat – we'll have some peace and quiet there. Come on.'

Without another word, she takes off through another door and down a narrow corridor, with me trailing in her wake. We're in her tiny dressing room and she's lighting a menthol cigarette before she speaks again. I've never been in a proper theatre dressing room before and it's nothing like I imagined it would be. It's absolutely tiny – and instead of a mirror running the length of one wall, surrounded by glamorous light-bulbs, like in the movies, there's a small, cracked specimen propped on a chair in a corner. The red carpet on the floor is shabby and worn at the seams and there's a slimy damp patch on the wall. A dehumidifier runs noisily in another corner. Around me, dozens of photographs line the walls, showing past productions. The edges curl on most of them and the images are blurred, grainy with time – or possibly smoke.

Bonnie lowers herself onto a small two-seater floral sofa that's wedged into the space between an overflowing bin and a rack of empty hangers. She pats the seat beside her to indicate that I should sit. It's a really strange sensation to be squashed up against her in such a tiny space, but I do it because I don't want to offend her.

'I'm not allowed to smoke in here, of course,' she says, inhaling deeply and then exhaling with a satisfied sigh. 'But rules are made to be broken – don't you think?'

'Er, yes,' I reply. I certainly can't disagree with her. In

fact, I get the impression she's the sort of formidable woman people rarely disagree with, full stop.

'So, my dear, what can I do for you? And speak up, will you? I'm half deaf these days,' she says, flicking her cigarette expertly into the ashtray that's perched on the sofa between us. There are half a dozen butts in it already, each kissed by her bright orange lipstick.

'Well, I came to talk to you,' I say.

She looks surprised, and a little confused, at this. 'Was I expecting you?'

'Er, no, you weren't.'

'So, you're not a journalist, then?'

I shake my head and she sighs. 'I should be so lucky. Trying to get a review in this town is impossible now. Not like the good old days – they used to beat my door down then. I had hacks queuing up around the block to talk to me.' She looks off into the middle distance, as if remembering a golden era, before she focuses on me again. 'So, you're not a journalist. Well, what are you then? A fan?' Her voice rises in hope.

'Not exactly.'

She sighs again, then takes a deep drag of her cigarette. 'Thought not. I don't get many of them now either. My day has passed.'

'I'm sure it hasn't.'

'Oh, yes, believe me, it has. My one consolation is that I still have good legs, for what they're worth. Voted Legs of the Year three years in a row back in the sixties.'

I decide to dive in and tell her why I'm there. I was plain-spoken about my quest with Mary, which worked well, even if it went against the grain, so I'll press on now.

'I wanted to talk to you about Tatty Moynihan. You were friends, weren't you?' I ask.

She pauses, her face softening at the mention of Tatty's name. 'You knew her?'

'Not exactly,' I say. 'The thing is . . .'

I start to explain, but Bonnie isn't really listening. Instead, she seems to be lost in thought again.

'Such a beautiful person,' she says quietly, as if to herself. 'Heart of gold she had. There we are together, look.'

She gestures to a black-and-white photograph on the wall and I jump to my feet to take a better look. Two beautiful young women stand arm in arm, beaming into the camera. I recognize Bonnie instantly – those high cheekbones are unmistakable, even if the hair is dark in the picture. And beside her, eyes dancing with life and good humour, is Tatty. I examine her every feature and realize that she's almost exactly as I'd imagined she would be. Mary was right – she does look like Maureen O'Hara. Her nose and jawline are strong, her hair in waves about her face. But it's her expression that stands out: she looks so full of life that it's hard to believe that she simply doesn't exist any more. I can practically feel her energy coming at me in waves. It's as if this photo was taken yesterday, even though it's yellowed at the edges underneath the glass frame.

It almost takes my breath away to see her for the first time. This is her – the woman who once owned the iconic Chanel bag that I found at the bottom of a box of junk.

'I miss her,' Bonnie says sadly, extinguishing her cigarette, then immediately sliding out another and lighting it. 'The larks we used to have, oh, boy!'

Even from the old photo I can see the friendship that existed between the women. Their body language speaks volumes as they lean on each other, holding each other tight, like close friends do. As if she comes back from where her memories have taken her, Bonnie straightens.

'Who are you again, did you say?' she asks. 'Start at the beginning.'

'My name is Coco Swan,' I reply. 'I'm from a small town in Ireland called Dronmore – I have an antiques shop there.'

'Uh-huh. And how does this relate to Tatty? Or to me?' she asks, puzzled.

I'm just about to answer her when the younger woman I saw earlier pops her head around the door. 'For God's sake,' she says crossly. 'How many times do I have to tell you? You cannot smoke in here. Which part of that don't you understand?'

Bonnie rolls her eyes at me, then smiles sweetly at the woman as she grinds out the fag. 'Sorry, sweetie,' she says. 'I forgot. It's probably my age.'

'Age, my arse,' the woman replies irritably. 'You're as sharp as a tack. Now, everyone is waiting for you, so if you'd like to grace us with your presence, it would be much appreciated.'

Bonnie stands and gives a sigh. 'Sorry, Coco Swan,' she says theatrically. 'I have to go. Time is money in this game, I'm afraid.'

'But, Bonnie, I haven't told you the rest,' I say, panicked at the thought of losing her when I've just found her. 'And I have so much to ask you!'

'Well, you'll just have to come back,' she says. 'Tomorrow at the same time? I'll meet you here.'

She smiles at me, pats my cheek and then she's off, telling me to let myself out.

As I gather my things to leave, frustrated and disappointed that I haven't found out more, the photo of Bonnie and Tatty catches my eye. It's probably my imagination, but it's as if Tatty is smiling straight at me from the battered frame.

'Well, Tatty,' I say, 'it looks like your secret's safe for another while.'

I know that it's definitely my imagination this time, but something in her expression makes me feel that she hears me loud and clear.

Ruth and I are curled up on the softest, squishiest sofas in front of a roaring fire at the Chancery Park Hotel. Outside, the chill of the night has drawn in, covering the city with a blanket of darkness. The bustle of traffic is a distant drone beyond the windows, light from cabs and buses flashing occasionally through the curtains. I've been telling her everything about my meeting with the enigmatic Bonnie and she's as intrigued as I am to know more.

'I bet you can't wait to see her again tomorrow,' she comments now, taking a sip from her glass of red wine, then giving a tiny sigh of satisfaction.

'I can't!' I reply, hugging myself with excitement. I'm dying to discover more about Tatty and her life and whether Bonnie knows anything about the mysterious letter and her lost love. The story has just swept me away.

'You're glad we came, then?' she asks, arching a brow.

'You were right to force my hand, I admit it,' I reply.

'Me? Force your hand?' she says, smiling innocently at me. 'As if I'd ever do that!'

'Yeah, right!' I laugh. 'You had it all planned out – don't try to deny it. I've never seen anyone book flights so fast.'

'I believe in grabbing the bull by the horns. And I think you're learning to do that as well. You barely put up a fight!'

'Maybe I am,' I muse. Just a few weeks ago, I never

would have believed I'd be playing detective like this. But I am, and it's turning out to be a whole lot of fun. 'So, what did you get up to this afternoon?' I ask. I'm not sure if it's the cosy fire or the alcohol, but I feel utterly content here. I make a mental note to tell Cat about the hotel's cosy ambience. The tall pillar candles that dot the space are really atmospheric – they'd work brilliantly in the Central too.

'Oh, not much,' she says. 'This and that.'

Ruth has been really vague on the details of the important errand she had to run this afternoon, keeping it very much to herself. I decide to press her on it.

'Were you getting something for the shop?' I ask, curling my legs under me and settling back against the soft cushions.

'No,' she replies. 'Hey, will we order some bar food? I'm quite peckish.'

'Were you getting something for Karl, then?' I ask, not letting her off the hook.

'No, nothing like that,' she replies, evidently trying to change the subject. 'See if you can catch the barman's eye, will you? We could order some nibbles.'

'Ruth! Why won't you tell me what you were doing?' I ask. 'What's with all the secrecy?'

Something about the way she looks at me stops me in my tracks. Her expression is serious, as if she has something extremely important on her mind.

'What is it?' I ask, a tremor in my voice. Suddenly I have a horrible doom-laden feeling that something's wrong. Maybe she's sick. Maybe she went to see a doctor. For all I know, she might have been to see a Harley Street specialist for an ailment she hasn't confided in me about. It would be just like her to keep the worry to herself so as not to burden me.

'I suppose I'd better tell you. I do need some advice,' she says at last.

My heart is in my mouth. From feeling so warm and content in front of the fire, I now feel ice cold and very worried. 'Jesus, Ruth, you're scaring me. You're not sick, are you?'

'Who – me?' She shakes her head. 'No, of course not. I'm as strong as an old ox.'

'Thank God for that.' I exhale. 'So what is it, then?'

'I went to visit someone. Someone who *is* sick. Dying, in fact.'

'Who?'

'A man I used to know, years ago. He's in a hospice in St Albans. He hasn't got long left.'

'You went all the way to St Albans? Isn't that miles away?'

'It's only half an hour by train. I promised him I'd visit, you see, and I didn't want to break the promise.'

'But why didn't you tell me? I could have come with you, if you were going to visit a friend.'

She lifts her head. 'He's not a friend,' she says clearly.

'Who is he, then? A relative?'

She swirls the wine in her glass. 'In a manner of speaking.'

This is all a bit cloak-and-dagger for me. 'Ruth, spit it out, will you? It's like trying to get blood from a stone!'

She pauses, as if she's trying to find the right words. 'I went to see Colin. Anna's husband.'

I'm stunned into silence. This makes no sense. Anna's husband died years ago, in an accident in England.

'He's not dead, you see,' Ruth goes on, looking into the fire. 'That's just what Anna told everyone when he left her.'

I put my glass on the table because I'm half afraid I'm going to drop it. 'You are joking?'

She shakes her head. 'I'm deadly serious.'

'Sorry, Ruth, but I'm struggling to keep up here. You're saying that Anna told everyone her husband was dead but all this time he was living over here?'

She sighs. 'Yes. She had this crazy notion that it would be better to tell the entire town he had been killed, instead of admitting the truth.'

'Which was?' I can't get my head around this – why would she do such a thing?

'That he left her for a woman he met when he was working over here. He's been living in St Albans for the past forty-odd years.'

I pick up my glass and take a massive slug. This is mad. My great-aunt has effectively been living a lie for decades. 'I can't believe it,' I say. 'So Anna's been pretending to be a grieving widow all this time?'

Ruth nods. 'Yes. She always said she would be too ashamed to admit to what had really happened. Telling everyone this lie was easier for her.'

'But people split up all the time! We're not living in the dark ages.'

Ruth sighs once more. 'You know what Anna's like, Coco. Appearances are very important to her. Sometimes I think they're more important to her than anything else.'

'But she had such strong opinions about me and Tom!' I say. 'Why would she say all that stuff about me being left on my own for the rest of my life when she's chosen to be alone all this time and lie to everyone about the reason?'

'Aw, well,' Ruth says. 'That's easy. She loves you, Coco. She doesn't want you to experience the pain that she did – she wants you to have a happy ending.'

'This is nuts.' I'm trying to process what Ruth's just told me. 'And no one else knows this story? No one's ever suspected the truth?'

'Well, Colin didn't have any family in Dronmore – he was English, remember? Anna told everyone he was killed in a car accident when he was visiting his family in Surrey and was buried there. Everyone believed her.'

'But you knew all along?'

'Yes – your granddad did too.' She pauses. 'And your mum.'

'*Mum* knew?'

'Yes. She overheard Anna and me arguing about it one day. I thought it was a crazy way to live . . . I hated all the lies, the covering up.'

'Why did you agree to it?' I ask.

'Because she's my sister and she asked me to.' She smiles wanly. 'Family is family, Coco.'

'And did he keep in touch with you all along?' I can't believe the tangled web of untruth that Anna has created to hide the simple fact that Colin left her. I mean, he was the bad guy – she could have told the truth about what had happened and lapped up the sympathy.

'No. I got a letter from him, a few weeks ago, telling me

he was very ill and wanted to talk to me. For a long time, I didn't know what to do, how to respond . . .'

'And then you decided to visit him?'

'Yes.' She nods. 'I thought this trip could kill two birds with one stone, so to speak. You could see Bonnie Bradbury and I could see Colin.'

'Wow,' I say.

We both lapse into silence for a second or two, watching the flames lick in the grate.

'So, what on earth did he want?' I ask. 'After all this time.'

'He wants her forgiveness,' Ruth replies. 'He's dying and he wants to be at peace with her.'

'Jesus!' I say. 'And you're supposed to act as the go-between?'

She shrugs. 'I guess I am. I was fond of Colin. He never meant to hurt Anna. She doesn't see it that way, naturally.'

'Of course not. What does he want you to do? Ask her to contact him?'

She shakes her head. 'No, thankfully. I was afraid he was going to ask me that, but he knows she'd never agree to it, not even now. It's something else.' Ruth rummages in her bag and produces a small box. 'He wants me to give this to her,' she says, putting it on the low coffee-table between us.

'What is it?' I'm half afraid to open it.

'It's the pocket watch Anna gave him on the morning of their wedding. He's carried it with him every day since. That's what he said.'

'And he wants to return it to her?' I'm puzzled by this.

'Yes, as a sort of apology, I suppose. This is his way of

trying to tell her he's sorry for the pain he caused. He said she'd know what it meant.'

'Phew.' I whistle. 'I can't believe that there's been such a secret in the family for so long. I'm astounded.'

'I guess all families are like that, though,' she says, with a small smile. 'Everyone has their secrets. Colin even told me today that your mum had visited him once. I never knew that.'

'Really?'

'Yes. I have no idea how she tracked him down, but she did. He said that she was on her way back from France and just arrived on his doorstep.'

I laugh at this — it's so typically Mum, appearing out of nowhere when you least expected it. Ruth joins in and somehow we both dissolve into nervous giggles. It's all so crazy, sort of gallows funny.

'Can you imagine?' she says, hiccuping with laughter. 'He got the fright of his life, he said. Of course, he hadn't a clue who she was at first, but once she'd explained, he thought she was there to castrate him!'

'That's hilarious!' I wheeze, imagining Mum turning up out of the blue. He must have had the shock of his life.

'They ended up spending the afternoon together, having a drink and talking. He's never forgotten it.'

'Oh, Ruth, that's priceless,' I say.

'Isn't it? That was your mother. Full of surprises. I can't believe she never told me.'

'I can,' I muse. 'There was plenty she kept to herself.' Like exactly who my father was, for example. But I don't say that aloud. Instead, I open the box, pick up the old watch and examine it closely. On the back is an engraving, with Colin's initials and a date.

'Their wedding date,' Ruth explains, before I have to ask.

'Ouch,' I say, wincing. Will giving this to Anna just remind her of the pain she suffered all those years ago? Will it stir up emotions she's tried for years to suppress? 'What are you going to do now?' I ask Ruth. 'Are you going to give it to her?'

'I have to, don't I?' Ruth says glumly, looking into her glass. 'I don't have any choice. She's not going to like it, though, and I'll be the one in the firing line.'

'I'll come with you,' I say, not entirely sure where the offer came from. Telling Anna this news isn't going to be pretty, but Ruth needs support and I want to give it to her.

Ruth's eyes light up. 'Would you?'

'Of course,' I reply. 'You can do the talking but I'll be there for moral support. It won't be so bad when there's the two of us.'

I'm trying to sound braver than I feel. Anna can be a little terrifying when she's cornered and this scenario will definitely make her feel trapped.

Ruth reaches across the table to squeeze my hand. 'Thanks, darling. I really appreciate that.'

'No problem. Of course, I might be the one hiding under the table.'

She grins. 'I don't think so. You might think you're only a little mouse, but you're beginning to be as brave as a lion.'

'I'm not too sure about that,' I say, 'but I'm trying. Now, let's have another drink. We deserve it.'

'There's a thought,' Ruth says. 'Maybe we should get Anna drunk before we tell her. It might help.'

'I don't think I've ever seen her even tipsy.' Anna is far too buttoned up to lose control in any way.

'Yeah, she even uses non-alcoholic sherry in her bloody trifles,' Ruth replies grimly. 'No wonder they taste so bad.'

She looks at me and we dissolve into helpless laughter once more.

13

'So, now you can start again from the beginning,' Bonnie says, lighting up one of her menthol cigarettes and inhaling deeply. 'Tell me why you want to know about Tatty.'

It's the next afternoon and I'm back in Bonnie's shabby, cramped dressing room at the theatre, so excited to hear what she has to say that I can hardly contain myself. I've spent the morning with Ruth, rehearsing how we're going to tell Anna about Colin, but I push that out of my mind. This is my big chance and I can't afford to be distracted. I'll worry about Anna later.

'OK. Well, the thing is, I bought something at an auction recently and it used to belong to Tatty. This bag.' I take the Chanel bag from my satchel and hand it to Bonnie.

Immediately, her eyes fill with tears. 'Oh. This was her favourite,' she says, so softly I can barely hear her.

'Really?' I ask, thrilled that she's recognized it. Mary Moore hadn't, and I would have been so disappointed if the same had been true of Bonnie.

'Oh, yes. It meant a great deal to her because of . . .' Bonnie jerks her head up to look at me, then physically composes herself as if she doesn't want to tell me any more just yet. 'But I'm getting ahead of myself. You need to explain a little more first. Why did you track me down? It seems like an awful lot of trouble to go to just because you found an old lady's bag?'

'Well, there was something inside. A letter.'

'Duke's letter,' she says, almost to herself. 'Of course.'

Duke! So that's his name. It's thrilling to know that at last. 'You know about him?' I ask, almost breathless with excitement.

'Oh, yes. Tatty carried that letter with her everywhere.' Bonnie looks away, her eyes glittering, and I can't take my eyes from her face – there's so much expression and emotion there, as if seeing this bag has brought treasured memories flooding back. She clearly knows the whole story behind the letter and I almost have to sit on my hands to stop myself shaking it out of her.

'What happened? Can you tell me?' I ask.

'Why do you want to know so badly?' she asks. 'I still don't understand.'

I'm unsure how to answer. The truth – that I think it's a sign from my dead mother – will sound ludicrous but, then, any watered-down lie will sound suspicious. I look at Bonnie and just know that if I don't tell her the truth she won't talk to me. So, like I did with Mary Moore, I take a deep breath and plunge in with a bit of straightforward honesty.

'OK, well, the truth is, I guess . . . I feel I must have found this bag for a reason. I mean, it appeared out of nowhere, at the bottom of a box of junk, and then the letter . . . It intrigued me.'

'You think someone somewhere was trying to send you a message, is that it?' Bonnie asks, her bright eyes trained on my face.

I'm startled by her ability to read me so well. How can she possibly know that? Is it so obvious? 'Well, yes.

Exactly that. I've never found anything like this before. It seemed . . . important.'

'Yes. I get that. But who do you think is trying to send you a message? Tatty?' She's leaning towards me, her expression intense.

'No,' I say. 'Well, not quite.'

'Who then?' she probes.

I know that what I say will sound outlandish to this woman. 'Well, this will sound silly, but my mum – she died when I was young – loved Coco Chanel. It's why she called me Coco.'

'Aha, of course . . . so when you found a Chanel bag –'

'– it kind of seemed like some sort of sign from her. And then I found the letter and I just felt that –'

'– you had to pursue it? Like it was Fate?'

I look at her, square in the face. 'Yes.'

She pauses, as if she's making up her mind about me in some way. Minutes seem to tick by before she speaks again. I'm almost holding my breath for all that time.

'Tatty believed in Fate, too,' she says at last. 'She believed in signs and superstitions.'

'She did?' I ask, almost afraid to exhale.

'You'll find most theatre folk do. It's in our blood in an extraordinary sort of way. And she was even more extraordinary than most. I'll tell you about the letter, Coco, but let me tell you about her first.'

'Please do.' I can hardly wait.

'I first met her in 1957. She was fresh off the boat from Ireland. We waitressed together in a greasy spoon in the East End. Fast friends in no time, we were.'

'Go on,' I encourage her. Hearing about this part of

Tatty's life is already fascinating. How did she go from working in a greasy spoon to living in a grand mansion in an affluent part of Dublin?

'They worked us like dogs, but the tips were good and we'd go to dances after dark. Oh, the larks we had! Tatty was a marvellous dancer.'

'Was she?' A picture of her jiving the night away flits into my mind's eye. I can imagine her kicking up her heels and having fun.

'Oh, yes – she had rhythm. She was a wonderful singer too. That was why she started the group. I was only the back-up, really – she was the star.'

'You sang together?' I remember Mary saying that Bonnie loved music, but I hadn't known that she'd sung professionally.

'Oh, yes! We called ourselves the Chanelles.'

'The Chanelles?'

'Yes – it was a play on words. Tatty just loved Coco Chanel, you see.' She glances sideways at me as I absorb this nugget. Coco Chanel weaves her way through this story like thread through fabric – she's everywhere I look.

'That's us when we first started out,' Bonnie says, pointing to the black-and-white photo on the wall. 'We were working in a place called the Candy Club then, singing together every night. The money was terrible, of course, the crowd sometimes worse, but we loved it.'

'What sorts of things did you sing?' I ask, enthralled.

'Oh, the music of the day, all-time favourites, that sort of thing. Tatty loved jazz. She had the most beautiful voice for it, really melancholy, you know. But we mostly did crowd-pleasers.'

I can just picture them, singing in smoky clubs together, too beautiful and spirited for their own good. Breaking hearts and falling in love with abandon.

'Yes, it was so much fun . . .' she muses. 'Tatty could have been a star – she even made a demo recording once – but she gave it up when she went back to Ireland. That was when I went into the theatre. I couldn't sing without her.'

'Why did she go back?' I ask. Did it have something to do with the mysterious Duke? Maybe he came back for her and they were reunited. That sort of ending to her story would be incredibly romantic. It's definitely the one I'm hoping for.

'Well, her parents died in a house fire. They were very wealthy people and Tatty inherited everything – their stock portfolios and the rest. She went back to Ireland to sort it all out. She always said she'd come back one day, but the years passed and she never did.'

'And what about Duke?'

Bonnie glances at her reflection in the small, cracked mirror that's still propped on the chair in the corner, smoothing her silver hair before she answers.

'Tatty didn't want to give him up, I know that. But she didn't have any choice,' she says finally.

'Where did he go? Was he sent to war?'

'War?' she asks, her expression puzzled.

'I was thinking maybe he was a soldier. Was that why they had to part?'

Bonnie is looking at me very strangely now. 'What are you talking about, Coco?' she says.

'In the letter he said that he had to leave, as if he had no choice. They were like star-crossed lovers.'

Bonnie's eyes are wide. 'You think that the letter was from Tatty's *lover*?' she asks hoarsely.

'Well, yes, of course, this Duke. He must have written it to her before he left. I'm just dying to know where he went, why they had to be apart.'

Bonnie shakes her head from side to side, a regretful look on her face. 'Oh, but, my dear, you've got the wrong end of the stick,' she says. 'Duke wasn't her lover.'

'He wasn't?'

'No. He was her child.'

'Her *child*? *What*? But that doesn't make any sense . . .' My head is starting to spin as phrases from the letter float through my mind. *From the very first moment I saw you, I knew without a shadow of a doubt that you were the love of my life . . . Our time together has been so very precious . . . and all too brief . . . my heart is breaking, for today we will be parted . . . I pray that one day . . . we will be reunited and that I will hold your hand again in mine . . .*

My God, it hadn't even occurred to me that that was a possibility. Suddenly I'm aware that tears are gathering in my eyes. The emotion in the letter has taken on a new hue now. It's almost unbearable to think about.

'It's true, Coco,' Bonnie says, clearly grief-stricken herself. 'That letter was written by Tatty – and addressed to the baby she had to give up when she was only a girl.'

'Tatty had a baby she gave up for adoption?' I repeat, my voice sounding very far away. I can't believe it.

'Yes,' Bonnie answers sadly. 'It almost broke her heart to do it. But she had no choice.'

My hands are trembling slightly. How had I got it so wrong? I'd just presumed that the letter had been from a lover . . . We all had. It had seemed so obvious that none of us ever thought to question it. Even Mary Moore hadn't recognized Tatty's handwriting – but when she'd first met her, Tatty had been a frail old woman: her writing could have changed a lot from when she was young and vibrant.

'But . . . why did she give him up?' I ask. 'Why didn't she keep him?'

Bonnie sighs sadly. 'Things were very different back then, Coco. Young women who became pregnant in Ireland in the fifties really had no choice – there was no such thing as single mothers. Almost all of them would have had to give up their babies, often against their will.'

'That's barbaric,' I say, my heart breaking for the young Tatty.

'You're right. It was,' she says. 'But back then girls who had babies before they were married were social lepers – they were second-class citizens. They were lucky if they didn't end up in those laundries.'

'I saw that film, *The Magdalene Sisters*. It was stomach-turning.' I hadn't been able to sleep afterwards, haunted by images of those poor girls slaving in horrendous conditions.

Bonnie nods, her expression bleak. 'They were dreadful institutions,' she says bitterly. 'It was forced labour, really – so cruel. And society just turned a blind eye . . .'

'At least she didn't end up in one,' I say. 'She came here – she was able to start a new life.'

'Yes. Although she was never able to forget the old one, I know that. She lived with the pain every day.'

'Is that why she kept the letter with her?' I ask unsteadily.

'Yes. She wrote that letter to her baby the morning she was forced to give him away. She wanted it to go with him to his new home, for him to read when he got to the right age, but the nuns who ran the mother-and-baby home wouldn't allow it. They refused to give the letter to the adoptive parents.'

'But that's awful,' I gasp. 'Did they have the right to do that?'

'Rights never came into it.' Bonnie's voice hardens. 'They knew best, or so they said. There would be no contact between mother and child – it was strictly forbidden.'

'So she wasn't told where Duke was going?'

'No. In those days there was no further contact with the adoptive family, you see, like there may be today. Once a woman handed over her child, that was it. She never saw that baby again, unless the child tracked her down when they grew up. And that can be mighty tricky to do. A lot of people out there have no idea where they came from and they'll never know because the records simply don't exist. It's a downright disgrace.'

'So who knows how many mothers and babies had to endure the same anguish as Tatty?' I muse.

'That's right, my love. Tatty was unique but, sadly, her story isn't.'

I can't imagine what it must have been like to have to hand over your baby unwillingly and walk away, never to see your child again or know how she or he was doing. Mum was a single mother – what if she had been forced to give me away? Where would I be? I wouldn't even know Ruth probably. I wouldn't know any of my blood family. I can't begin to think what it would have been like, how different my life might have been if I'd been born a few decades earlier.

I look at the letter in my hand. 'It's so awful, isn't it?' I say, feeling tears prick the back of my eyes again. 'This letter was the only link she had to her baby . . .'

'It was, and she kept it with her always. She used to say that if Duke ever found her, she would show it to him. She wanted him to know that she hadn't given him up lightly. It was just that she'd had no choice.'

All this time I'd thought the letter was from a lover to Tatty when it was a raw and lonely love letter to her baby. The baby she'd had to give up. A wave of sadness washes over me. This is nothing like how I wanted the story to go. 'It's heartbreaking,' I whisper.

'She didn't even have a photograph of him,' Bonnie goes on, 'but she often used to say that she didn't need one. His face was imprinted on her heart.'

In the gloomy beat of silence that follows, something occurs to me. What about Duke's father? Where was he in all this? 'What about her boyfriend?' I ask. 'Couldn't they have got married?'

'Well, yes. But he was already married – so that would have been a problem,' Bonnie says, her voice cold and hard now.

'Oh.'

So Tatty was having an affair with a married man when she fell pregnant – that really was taboo back then. No wonder she fled to London afterwards – she was trying to escape from what sounds like a desperately sad, traumatic history and start afresh.

'Yes, he was married good and proper. Said he was

going to leave his wife, same old story,' Bonnie goes on. 'He gave her this, actually.' She pats the Chanel bag, her eyes misting. As she does so, it almost feels as if its history is coming alive. It represented the love that Tatty had for the father of her baby. No wonder she kept the letter in it. It seems more precious than ever now.

'They went to Paris for a weekend, early in 1956,' she continues, 'and he got it for her there. It was one of the first bags that Coco Chanel ever made, a prototype.'

So we were right! This is one of the original 2.55s.

Bonnie is still talking. 'She couldn't believe it when she got to meet Coco – she had idolized her for so long.'

'Tatty *met* Chanel?'

'Yes, that weekend. Her married man was a friend of a friend of Chanel's, you see – they even had supper with her when they were there. Tatty loved to tell that story.'

'They *dined* with Coco Chanel?' I ask. 'That's incredible!'

'Isn't it just? They went to her salon on the rue Cambon and had a picnic at midnight – olives, cheese and baguette, Tatty said. And lots of red wine. She always said it was one of the best weekends of her life – the weekend Duke was conceived.'

I can barely breathe for excitement. There's so much to this story, more than I could ever have imagined. Tatty and her lover met Coco Chanel and ate with her in the legendary salon. It's amazing. And for their child to have been conceived at the same time . . .

'What happened then?' I ask. Clearly it had all fallen apart.

'Well, after Tatty found out she was pregnant, everything changed, of course – the bottom dropped out of her world. Her married lover didn't want to know her any more. Suddenly she was more of an inconvenience than anything else. He disappeared off the face of the Earth, the toe-rag.' Her voice is bitter – as if Tatty had confided the true extent of her pain to her and she can remember it vividly.

'That was incredibly unfair,' I say, anger bubbling up inside me. Tatty had to pay a heavy price for an unwise love affair – she was the one who lost everything while others sat in judgement on her.

'That was the way the world turned back then. Tatty was at fault – the woman always was.'

Glancing across at the photo on the wall of Tatty laughing with Bonnie, I see nothing in her face of the pain she must have experienced. If there was sadness in her past, you couldn't tell it from that photograph – the two women seem to be having the time of their lives.

'What did she do next?' I ask.

'Well, her parents were scandalized by her fall from grace, as they saw it. They bundled her off to a mother-and-baby home in the Irish Midlands so no one would know. They were terrified people would find out.'

'Tatty must have been so scared.'

'She was, and that's a fact. They were never reconciled, not even after baby Duke was born. Even though she'd done as they'd asked and given him up, they couldn't forgive her, or she them for making her go through with it. Instead she came to London and tried to move on.'

'Poor Tatty.'

Bonnie lights another cigarette and inhales deeply. 'Yes, poor thing. Part of her never really got over it. The trauma of losing Duke stayed with her for ever. Even though she only had him with her for eight hours.'

Fresh tears spring to my eyes. *Eight hours?* 'Why did she call him Duke?'

'She named him after Duke Ellington – "In A Sentimental Mood" was their song, you see, her and her lover's. She even asked the nuns if the adoptive parents could keep that name, although of course she never knew if they respected her wishes . . . The nuns weren't exactly the warm and fuzzy type. They wouldn't even take the letter, remember.'

'It must have been an impossible situation to get over.'

'She tried her best, she soldiered on. Her way of coping was never to speak about Duke – except on his birthday. She would allow herself to cry on that day – the tenth of November. Every other day of the year she just pushed it down inside. It was the only way she could get by.'

A silence falls between us as we think about what it must have taken to keep going after such a huge loss and heartbreak.

'And the bag?' I ask.

'She kept that with her always. That and the letter were her links to her baby – and her only connection to his father, I suppose. I don't think she ever stopped loving him, despite everything. For her, no one else compared to him. He was the love of her life. I think that was why she never married.'

'You two were very close, weren't you?' I can see the love Bonnie had for Tatty shining from her every pore.

'Yes, we were. I owe her everything. It's as simple as that.'

'What do you mean?'

'Well, Tatty was the one who helped me cope when *I* got pregnant in less than ideal circumstances. She supported me through thick and thin, helped out in every way she could after my good-for-nothing boyfriend left me high and dry. If it hadn't been for Tatty . . . well, who knows what would have happened?'

'She took you under her wing?'

'Yes. She was determined the same thing wouldn't happen to me – that I wouldn't lose my baby.'

'And could it have?'

'I was lost myself, I know that. I didn't know what to do, who to turn to. Tatty was my rock. Times had changed since she had had Duke back in Ireland but there was still a taboo about being a single parent, even in London. If she hadn't looked out for us, who knows what could have happened. She insisted we live with her until we got on our feet. She had almost nothing then but she was willing to share it with us.'

This reminds me of what Mary Moore said about Tatty – how she felt taken care of by her. No wonder she had left all her things to some charity: she was that sort of giving person.

'It sounds like she was a really good friend.'

'She was. We kept in touch over the years. I wanted to go and see her at the end, but she kept putting me off. Eventually I put two and two together – she didn't want to see me. I had to respect that, although it was hard, I won't lie to you.'

'Her nurse says she forbade everyone to come to her funeral.'

Bonnie nods. 'I didn't even hear that she'd passed over for weeks afterwards. I felt terrible I'd missed it all. But that was the way she wanted it, I knew. Just like she wanted to auction all of her things. It's understandable, I suppose. Who could she have left everything to? She had no family.'

'Do you think she was ever happy again, Bonnie?' I can't bear to think that Tatty had spent the rest of her life mourning the son she was never allowed to know.

Bonnie pauses before she answers. 'She learned to cope,' she says at last. 'She never reconciled with her parents, like I said, but she believed her inheritance was their way of making amends. She drew great comfort from that. She was a canny investor too. She lived very comfortably on the proceeds for the rest of her life. She had good times. She had her music. She had lots of admirers. I think she was happy in a way, although there was a hole in her heart that could never be filled. Losing Duke left its mark.'

'Did she ever try to find him?' I ask.

'She wanted to – I know that. She used to talk about it after a drink or two, how she'd go back to the nuns, force them to give her more information. But she never did. I think part of her didn't want to intrude on his life – in case he didn't even know about her. But she was waiting, hoping, for him to make the first move . . .'

'I wonder where he is now. Or if he even knew he was adopted.'

'Who knows?' She shrugs. 'He could be anywhere, I guess. It's too late to do anything about it now.'

'But there must be some way of finding out more,'

I say. 'There has to be. Can you remember any other details?'

She taps the long line of ash from her cigarette against the ashtray. 'The mother-and-baby home was called St Jude's, I know that much. It was in Westmeath, I think. And he was born on the tenth of November 1956. That's all I know for sure.'

'I wonder if that's enough . . .'

'To what? Track him down?' she asks, eyes wide.

'Maybe,' I say. 'Do you think I should?' I'm desperate for her opinion. I have this information, but I don't know what to do next. Bonnie was one of Tatty's closest friends and allies so she must know what she would have wanted me to do with this letter, which was so precious to her.

'I can't tell you what to do, Coco,' she says sadly. 'I wish I could, but unfortunately life isn't like it is on the stage. It's far more complicated. And sometimes there's no clear end to a story.'

'But you must have some idea what I should do. Some advice to give me. Please, Bonnie.' I'm almost begging now, but I can't help it. I need some direction, some idea what to do next, if anything.

She surveys me for a second. 'You said you think that finding the bag was some sort of message from your mother. Is that right?'

'Yes,' I reply. 'This bag – it's the one she always wanted me to have, as a sort of namesake.'

'And what message do you think your mother was trying to give you?' she asks. 'What would she have been trying to tell you by sending this bag to you, do you think?'

'I don't know,' I reply.

'Well, maybe you need to figure that out,' she says kindly.

Before I can ask her to elaborate, the woman who was with her in the foyer the day before, the one who reprimanded her for smoking, sticks her head around the dressing-room door. She catches sight of me but doesn't say hello. 'How many times do I have to tell you? You can't smoke in here, Mum.'

Mum? This woman is Bonnie's daughter?

'Oh, for goodness' sake,' Bonnie mutters mulishly. 'It's not like they're even real cigarettes.'

'Try telling that to Health and Safety,' the woman says crossly and promptly disappears.

'Kids.' Bonnie rolls her eyes. 'Think they know everything.'

'That's your daughter? Is she an actress too?' I ask.

'God, no.' She laughs. 'She's the stage manager – a right bossy madam, has been since the day she was born. Tatty used to call her Little Miss Bossy Boots.' She smiles fondly as she remembers those days, now long gone. 'Now, I'm sorry, my dear, but I really do have to go – they'll have my guts for garters if I'm late back to rehearsal.'

She hauls herself to her feet, checking her reflection in the cracked mirror again as she does so. She dabs her eyes a little, takes a deep breath and straightens her back once more. 'Keep in touch, won't you?' she says, hugging me.

'I will, I promise,' I say. 'Thanks for taking the time to talk to me, Bonnie.'

'You're welcome, Coco,' she says. 'Thanks for taking me back in time. I'm glad it was you.' She holds me at arm's length and beams at me.

'Glad it was me? What do you mean?' I ask her.

'Who found Tatty's bag, of course. I think you're right. It was sent to you for a reason. All you have to do is figure out what it is.'

And, with another brief embrace, she's gone, leaving me to think about what I should do next. I feel drained after the emotional story she told me. Drained and very confused. Should I try to trace Duke? Give him his mother's letter? Would it even be possible, with so little to go on? And would he welcome the knowledge, or hate me for complicating his life?

I rummage in my satchel and retrieve my dog-eared notebook. Creasing open a page, I write what I know:

NAME: DUKE MOYNIHAN
DOB: 10 NOVEMBER 1956
PLACE OF BIRTH: ST JUDE'S MOTHER-
AND-BABY HOME, CO. WESTMEATH

Is it enough? I doubt it very much. Unless there's more in that box of bric-à-brac — something I missed maybe, another clue that will help me. Snapping my notebook shut I turn to Tatty's photo one last time.

'OK, Tatty,' I say. 'If you want me to keep going, I will.' Then I look Heavenward. 'I hope you're watching, Mum. You're certainly not making things easy.'

14

'We're never going to get rid of the smell of bloody Jeyes Fluid,' Ruth grumbles. 'You do realize that, right?'

'It's not too bad,' I say, trying to appease her. 'I can barely notice it, I swear.'

We're back in Swan's and, despite what I'm saying to Ruth, the whiff of extra-strength cleaning product is so strong it could knock out a horse. I'm starting to think that might be Anna's housekeeping motto, actually – she certainly seems to believe that nothing is clean unless it stinks of bleach and could fell a large animal. She could give the two women from *How Clean Is Your House?* a serious run for their money – in fact, she could probably have her own TV show if the urge took her.

We didn't notice the pong too much last night because when we arrived back from London we were so exhausted we just went straight upstairs to bed. But this morning it's all too evident. Anna has had her wicked way in here and everything has been scrubbed to within an inch of its life. And things have been moved around too. Not everything is where it used to be, not by a long shot.

'I woke twice during the night with this horrible feeling that I was being asphyxiated,' Ruth says now. 'I thought I was having a bad dream. But it was this.' She sweeps her arms wide. 'The toxic fumes must have been creeping up the stairs – it's a wonder we didn't both choke to death in our sleep.'

'Tell you what, I'll light a scented candle, will I?' I say, digging around under the counter for the matches. 'That might help.'

'It'll take more than a candle to get rid of the stink in here,' Ruth mutters. She's really on edge this morning and I know why: she has to face Anna and tell her about Colin. She's dreading it. She's not the only one.

Being back in Dronmore is an anticlimax in more ways than one. The first thing I did this morning was trawl through the box where I'd found Tatty's handbag, in case there was anything else that might help my search. But there was nothing, no other clues. It was really disappointing – and now we have Anna to face. The thought of it is giving me stomach cramps.

'Why don't you go and say hello to Karl, get some fresh air? It looks like he missed you,' I suggest. Ruth needs to take her mind off things and Karl could be the perfect distraction.

We both look to where he is now leaning on his broom outside the butcher's, looking directly across the road at us and smiling widely, as if he's trying to catch Ruth's eye.

She gives him a distracted wave, then turns back to me. 'No, I won't rest until I talk to Anna. I'm going to ask her to meet us for lunch in the hotel today. Somewhere neutral would be best to break the news, I think.'

'So soon?' I gulp, thinking with dread about what lies ahead. Ruth isn't one for procrastinating, something I, on the other hand, am very comfortable with.

'Yes, it's best to get it over with,' she says briskly. 'Get it all out in the open.'

She disappears upstairs as the shop bell jangles and Cat and Mark walk in. Cat's face is like thunder and Mark doesn't seem much happier.

It looks like nothing's improved between them. Again, I feel a stab of pure guilt that I haven't made time for Mark since the twins' birthday party. If it had been Ruth, she would have jumped in and resolved it as soon as she could. 'Hi, guys!' I say. 'What are you doing here, Mark? No school today?'

'No, Coco, there is school today,' Cat almost snarls. 'But my darling son here has been suspended, so he can't go. Instead he gets to trail around after me – as if I don't have enough to do without him making things even more difficult.'

Cat glares at Mark and he looks at the floor, saying nothing, his dark fringe flopping over his forehead and concealing his eyes.

'What happened?' I'm almost afraid to ask. This is definitely not good news.

'Well, Mark apparently thought it would be funny to get into a fight on the plane on the way back from the school trip to Spain,' she says. 'He's lucky he's not in some Mediterranean prison right now.'

'That's a total exaggeration, Mum,' Mark mutters, raising his head just a fraction so I can see his face. He looks exhausted: his skin is waxy and pale.

'Is it?' Cat rounds on him, clearly incensed. 'Mid-flight punch-ups are taken very seriously these days, Mark – people have been imprisoned for less.'

Mark's face closes, as if he's fed up with trying to explain things to her. He looks at the floor again.

'So he's suspended?' I ask.

'Yes. He's off school for the week. Then there'll be a disciplinary meeting. Let's just hope he doesn't get himself expelled.'

Mark moves away and sits down on a stool by the wall, shoving in his iPod earphones.

'They won't expel him, will they?' I say quietly to Cat, horrified at the thought. 'It's not that bad, surely.'

'Who knows?' She sighs. 'They could. David is up the walls about it. He wants to ground him for the rest of the year.'

'But what happened? How did the fight start?' I ask.

'We still haven't managed to get to the bottom of it,' Cat says wearily. 'The other boy involved said something. That's all Mark will tell us. He won't say what it was. The thing is, though, the teacher seems to think Mark started it.'

'That's really unlike him, Cat,' I say, sneaking a quick glance at Mark. His head is still bowed, his hands clasped in his lap. There's something sad and downcast about him that's very unsettling.

'I know,' she says, sighing again. 'I just can't get through to him, Coco. I'm at my wit's end.'

'Maybe I could help,' I say, an idea taking shape in my mind.

'What do you mean?' She glances over her shoulder in his direction to make sure he's not listening. But I know he can't be because I can hear the beat of his music from where I'm standing.

'Would he talk to me, do you think?' I say.

Cat shrugs. 'I don't know – maybe,' she says doubtfully.

'Well, how about he comes to one of my up-cycling classes?' I say. 'I'm having an extra session tonight to make up for the lost one while I was in London. I could try to get the truth out of him.'

The idea has only just come to me, but it's not a bad one. The class could be the perfect way for me to get Mark on his own and try to find out what's going on. I don't want to mention the troublemaker Sean O'Malley to Cat just yet, but at least this way I'm being proactive, not just resting on my laurels and doing nothing. If I find out something concrete, I can tell her and we can act on it.

Cat looks at me, then at Mark, thoughtfully. 'Yeah . . . You know what? That might just work.'

'I'll get him busy and then I can try to get to the bottom of what's going on.'

'He might confide in you,' she says, hope in her voice.

'Exactly!' I say. 'You'd be surprised what people can tell you when they're immersed in work. It's like being a hairdresser – their clients tell them all sorts of personal stuff. If I can find out what's going on with him, we can take it from there. It's worth a shot.'

'Thanks a million, Coco. If you can get anything out of him it'd be great. We're so worried.' She smiles at me, but I can see the anxiety in her eyes.

'No problem.' I wink at her. 'Now, how will I break it to him that he's going to be the newest member of the most exclusive club in town?'

'How about I say he has to come as a punishment? To keep him out of trouble?' Cat suggests.

'Hey!' I laugh and she grimaces.

'Sorry, but it needs to sound plausible or he'll suspect we're up to something.'

'You're right,' I agree. I turn to call to Mark, but then I remember something and lean towards Cat again. 'One other thing – myself and Ruth will be in the hotel later, for lunch with Anna.'

'Do you want me to reserve a booth?' she asks.

'No. Ruth already did that. It's just . . . would you mind steering clear of us if you see us?'

'Sure,' Cat says immediately, but she looks puzzled. 'Can I ask why?'

'I'll explain later, but it's to do with stuff that happened in London. We have an . . . awkward conversation ahead of us and it would be easier if there are no interruptions.'

'I'll keep out of your hair. But you have to put me out of my misery as soon as possible and fill me in on things, promise?'

'I promise. Now, about your son . . .' I turn to him and raise my voice. 'Hey, Mark?'

He pulls out one earphone. 'Yeah?'

'You're going to come to my up-cycling class tonight. Isn't that great?'

His face falls. 'You're kidding!'

Cat puts her hands on her hips. 'No, we're not kidding,' she says sternly. 'And say thanks to Coco for helping to keep you out of trouble.'

I fix a smile on my face as he looks from her to me, still speechless. 'But I don't want to,' he says.

'Why not?' Cat demands, her eyes glinting dangerously at him.

'Because I don't want to spend time with a bunch of randoms and wrinklies.' He shoots me a glance. 'No offence, Coco.'

'None taken,' I say. 'But why don't you give it a go, Mark? It's fun, I swear.' I really want to talk to him when Cat isn't around and this is my chance. But he's shaking his head from side to side, like there's going to be no persuading him.

Cat's not taking no for an answer, though. 'You are going to Coco's class, young man, and that's that. No more discussion. Now, let's go. I'm already late for a meeting, thanks to you.'

'But, Mum –'

'No buts. Move it.'

Mark peels himself off the stool slowly, his mouth set in a line. He's disgusted that he has to come to my class. I can only hope that when he gets here he might enjoy it and open up with me a little.

'Mark, I have an old coffee-table that you can start on,' I call, determined to muster a bit of enthusiasm for tonight. 'Any ideas for what you might do with it?'

'I dunno,' he says. 'Maybe I could nail myself to it.'

'If you don't like it, you shouldn't have got suspended, should you?' Cat says, winking at me behind his back.

'I'll drop him home afterwards,' I say, as they leave.

She shoots me a smile. 'You're an angel. And I'm dying to hear every juicy detail about London.'

'I can't wait to tell you all about it,' I say. I'm looking forward to Cat's take on recent events – she's always a wise owl about such things so she'll give me good advice about what to do next.

'It sounds like there's plenty to tell.' She cocks her head to one side.

'That's one way of putting it!'

'I'll have the kettle on,' she says.

'No, open a bottle of wine,' I reply. 'I have a feeling I might need a drink before today is over.'

'That makes two of us!' she calls, grinning conspiratorially at me over her shoulder before the door closes behind them.

Ruth and I are already sitting in a booth in the Central Hotel bar when Anna strides in. She's dressed in black as usual, and it strikes me as she approaches us that her appearance is completely fake – she's been wearing mourning outfits for years, but she's not a widow. It's all so bizarre. Her whole life and social standing in this town are based on a fabrication. How has she managed to keep it up for so long?

Beside me, I can feel Ruth's nervousness seeping out of her and I squeeze her hand to give us both a little courage. If it were up to me, I would have put this off for a bit. I detest confrontation.

'I can't stay long,' Anna announces breathlessly, as she sits down opposite us, carefully spreading out her coat underneath her as she does so. 'I need to talk to Father Pat about the Service of Light. There's so much to do – there aren't enough hours in the day.'

I glance at Ruth. She wanted us to meet somewhere neutral, where she could tell Anna about Colin. The hotel seemed like a good idea, but now that we're here, I'm not so sure. There's no chance that anyone could overhear us as we're in a private corner, but what if Anna reacts badly? What if she has a complete meltdown?

'Would you like a drink, Anna?' I ask, knowing full well she'll refuse alcohol, but chancing it anyway.

'Just a tonic water, thank you, Coco,' she replies.

'Nothing stronger?' I wonder hopefully.

'In the middle of the day? Of course not.' She's shocked that I've even asked.

I obediently get the tonic water for her and sit down opposite her again.

'So, what's all the mystery?' she asks, glancing at her wrist watch. 'If you want to tell me about your trip to London, can it wait? I really don't have time for lunch. I don't want to keep Father Pat waiting.'

Ruth and I exchange a glance. I can tell by the determined look in her eye that she's going to plunge right in. My stomach does a very large flip-flop.

'Anna,' Ruth begins, 'there's something I have to tell you and there's no easy way to say it.'

'Ah, I see where this is going,' she says, cutting off her sister's prepared monologue.

'You do?' Ruth asks, flabbergasted.

'Yes – and honestly, Ruth,' she rolls her eyes, 'you're completely overreacting.'

Ruth looks as taken aback as I feel. Does Anna already know? How can that be possible? 'You know?' she says, glancing at me, her eyes wide. Can Colin have contacted her already?

'Of course,' she replies primly. 'You're cross because I've moved some stuff in the shop – but, believe me, you'll thank me for it. I've started a much better system now – you just need to get used to it. There's a place for everything and everything has its place. I can explain it all to you.'

Oh, God, she thinks we're talking about the cleaning frenzy she had.

'Anna,' Ruth's voice is strangled, 'that's not what I want to talk to you about.'

'It isn't?' Anna raises one quizzical eyebrow.

'No,' Ruth says.

'So, are you saying that you actually agree that the re-arranging I did is an improvement?' she asks triumphantly. 'I knew it! I said to myself –'

'Anna!' Ruth snaps. 'Please listen. It's about Colin.'

Anna pales at the very mention of his name, her cheeks suddenly grey beneath her oyster-coloured face powder. The wind has been well and truly knocked out of her and my heart breaks as I see the shock registering on her face. Ruth is ploughing on, desperate to get it out as quickly as she can before she loses her nerve.

'He wrote to me some time ago so I visited him when we were in London. He's very sick, Anna. In fact, he's dying.'

'He's already dead, remember?' she replies slowly, almost robotically, her voice like ice.

'Anna, please listen,' Ruth begs. 'He wanted me to give you something. A message.'

Ruth scoops the watch that Colin gave her from her bag and places it on the table between us. For a split second, I see Anna's expression soften, before it hardens again, more than before. 'Is this a joke?' she asks, through gritted teeth.

'No,' Ruth replies helplessly. 'I'm sorry. I didn't know what to do.'

'So you did this?'

'She was only trying to help, Anna. Don't shoot the messenger,' I pipe up, wanting to protect Ruth. She throws me a grateful look.

Anna glares at me. 'Keep out of this, Coco,' she snaps. 'You never should have known anything about it.'

'Just listen to me for a second, Anna,' Ruth begs. 'I thought you should know. He wants your forgiveness – it's his dying wish.'

Anna's reply, when it comes, chills me. 'He can't die soon enough as far as I'm concerned,' she says slowly, deliberately. 'And when he does, I hope he rots in Hell. Now, we are never to talk about this again. Do you both understand?'

Ruth and I nod dumbly.

'Keep that, or send it back,' she says, pointing to the watch. 'It means nothing to me.'

'But, Anna –' Ruth begins.

'I think you've done enough, don't you?' she says, holding up her hand to stop Ruth continuing. 'Now I have to meet Father Pat.' She gathers up her bag and strides away before we can utter another word.

'Oh, God, that was a disaster,' Ruth says, sighing heavily as we watch her leave, shoulders back, head held high. No one would ever know we had just told her that the husband she's been pretending for years was dead is still alive and wants her forgiveness before he meets his Maker. No one would believe it.

'You did what you could, Ruth,' I reply. 'It was very brave of you.'

'Did you see her face, though? She'll never forgive me for interfering.'

'You weren't interfering,' I reply. 'You were trying to help.'

'She doesn't see it that way,' she says regretfully. 'She thinks I betrayed her by going to see him.'

'You were trying to do the right thing. Once she gets over the shock she'll see that.' I'm not sure if this is true, certainly not from the way she reacted to the news, but I have to give Ruth some sort of lifeline. I can only hope Anna will come to realize that her sister was only trying to help.

Ruth picks up the watch and puts it back in her bag. 'I hope so,' she says, shaking her head sadly. 'I really hope so. But I have a horrible feeling that this is one can of worms I should never have opened.'

15

'Nice to meet you, Mark. It's good to have some young blood in here with us oldies,' Harry Smith says, pumping Mark's hand enthusiastically.

'Just ask if you need anything, young man, don't be shy. And ignore Harry – he's a plonker.' Lucinda Dee hugs him warmly.

'Thanks,' Mark says, stepping back and smiling shyly at everyone in the class as, one by one, they welcome him to the up-cycling group. Even though I haven't spelled out why Mark has joined us out of the blue, they seem to know instinctively that he's nervous and needs a warm welcome. I could hug every one of them for being so kind.

'Now, don't mind this lot, Mark,' I say jokily. 'If they try to bully you, they'll have me to answer to.'

'Bully him?' Harry says. 'Why would you think that, Coco?'

'Because she knows what you're capable of, you old fart,' Lucinda replies, and the whole group dissolves into laughter.

'So you'd better watch out,' I say, wagging a finger at him.

'You're a right old mother hen,' Lucinda remarks fondly, smiling at me.

'Am I?' I'm surprised. I never thought I had any maternal

instinct whatsoever, but I certainly feel protective of Mark. I want to help him – in fact, I'm desperate to.

'Oh, yes, you are.' She clucks knowledgeably. 'You remind me so much of your mum sometimes. She's so like her, isn't she, Harry?'

'Just the same.' Harry agrees wholeheartedly with her for once. 'A carbon copy.'

The idea that they think I'm anything like Mum is sweet. Maybe I did pick up something from her after all. I've certainly been thinking about her a lot since I found Tatty's bag. Although, since lunchtime, it's been hard to think about anything other than Ruth and Anna. Ruth's been really downhearted all afternoon and spent most of it resting in the flat upstairs, which is very unlike her. This has really taken its toll on her and it's cast a dark shadow over me, too. I hate to think that Anna is so upset, and that Ruth is too. Maybe we never should have given Colin's message to Anna.

I try to push those thoughts out of my mind and focus on Mark. He has to be my priority right now. I so want to help him and Cat.

'Right, come with me,' I say, leading Mark to where I've set up his work station. The old coffee-table is waiting for him and I'm hoping he'll be able to think of some creative way to transform it.

'What am I supposed to do with it?' he asks dubiously, as we survey the table together.

'That's up to you,' I reply. 'But first you'll have to strip it right back, get rid of all the varnish and paint so you have a clean slate to work on.'

'That sounds like a lot of work,' he says.

'For a strapping lad like you?' I scoff. 'No chance. Start by sanding it down – you know how to do that, yeah?'

'Suppose,' he agrees half-heartedly.

'Well, then, what are you waiting for? Hurry up and get cracking. Everything you need is here. Any questions, just ask. OK?'

With a grin, I leave him to it, crossing my fingers as I walk away. This class could be the perfect way for us to reconnect and get back the old closeness we used to have.

I spend the next hour advising, cajoling and refereeing the group as they work on their various projects. Things are going well, and everyone is making progress. But I keep away from Mark, making sure to give him space. I don't want him to feel crowded, especially not his first time. He doesn't ask me for help, but I keep a close eye on him as he works on the table. To my surprise and delight, he seems totally engrossed in its transformation. As the last of my regulars leave at the end of the class, calling their goodbyes as they go, I go back to him. He's on his hunkers, his sweatshirt rolled up at the sleeves, still sanding back the wood. He's made brilliant headway – the old coffee-table already looks much better than it did to begin with.

'Well, did you have any ideas about what to do with it?' I ask him.

'I sort of did, but it's probably stupid,' he says, standing and stretching out his back.

'Go on.'

'What if I made the table into a sort of play station for the twins? It's the perfect height for them. I could paint roads, so they can drive their toy cars around. I could even build a little garage on top.' He looks at me sheepishly, almost embarrassed by his own idea, and I force myself not to throw my arms around him and embarrass him even more. This is the Mark I know and love, thoughtful and sweet, looking out for his kid brothers.

'That's a fantastic idea,' I say.

'Really?' His eyes light up. 'Maybe I could give it to them for Christmas.'

'Absolutely. I have all the acrylic paints you'll need – it'll look amazing. The boys will be thrilled.'

'Thanks, Coco.' He smiles bashfully at me. 'This class is great. I wasn't expecting it to be any . . .'

'Good?' I say, finishing his sentence for him. 'Well, I'm glad I can still surprise you.'

'I never even knew you did it. How do you advertise it? Twitter?'

'Er, no. I'm a bit of a technophobe, you know that.'

'Aw, come on, Coco, everyone's on Twitter.'

'Are they? Is it good?' I ask.

'Well, it used to be cool – now it's just another way for people to sell you stuff, which is a bit lame, but I guess that's probably why you should be on there.'

I know nothing about Twitter or how people use it, but I decide to keep that nugget of information to myself.

'Right, I get you. You spend a lot of time on-line, do you?'

Cat has often told me that interrupting him when he's on the computer can lead to serious battles. She's wary about the Internet, and all the dangers associated with it, even though she and David have put security measures in place to stop the boys stumbling across anything disturbing. Still, I know you can never be too careful – computers can get all sorts of viruses, and if teenage boys want to find something on-line they probably can, security measures or not.

'Yeah, well, porn can be pretty addictive,' he says sarcastically. 'You can be on there for hours before you know it.'

'Oi! You're not too old for me to clip you around the ear, young man.' I laugh. He clearly knew full well what I was thinking.

'Isn't that what all you adults reckon? That we spend our lives looking at porn?' he asks innocently.

No,' I reply, feeling myself start to blush. 'I dunno why you'd think that.'

'Yeah, right.' He guffaws.

'Stop winding me up!' I say. 'It's not fair – I'm too old for it now.'

'I keep forgetting you're ancient, sorry,' he says, laughing once more.

'Don't be so cheeky. Actually, I was thinking of improving our website for the shop,' I say, suddenly inspired. 'Would you be interested in helping me out? I'd pay you.'

His face brightens and I give myself a mental pat on the back. Technology is the way to the boy's heart.

'Are you serious?' he says, his eyes gleaming beneath his floppy fringe.

'Absolutely. It needs a total revamp – here, let me show you.'

I lead him over to the ancient computer and click into Swan's Antiques' very basic website.

'OK, so you're just holding the domain name, more or less,' he says, his face scrunching as he looks at the page on the screen.

'What do you mean?' I ask.

'I mean, there's nothing on here except the shop's address and telephone number. How many hits have you had in the last month?'

'I haven't a clue,' I admit. 'How am I supposed to know that?'

'You don't keep track of your hits?' he asks, clearly baffled.

'Er, no.'

'What about your Facebook page? What kind of traffic does that have?'

'Er, we don't have a Facebook page,' I say. I'm a little ashamed of this, it has to be said. Unlike Cat, who keeps up to date with everyone on Facebook, I've never even looked at it.

'You're joking me!' He's horrified by this revelation.

'Is that very bad?' It must be – he looks positively shocked.

'*Everyone* has a Facebook page, Coco – it's, like, a basic. Even Mum has one.'

He says it like she's a dinosaur who can barely keep up instead of a successful businesswoman.

'Yeah, I know. She uses it to keep track of all the losers we went to school with,' I say, not thinking before I speak.

'You went to school with losers?' he asks, his eyebrows shooting up.

'Yeah, well, not all of them were. Some. And I wasn't exactly flavour of the month back then,' I add.

'How come?'

'I was tall. I stood out a bit. I got some stick.'

'Well, Mum's tiny – did she get stick too?'

'Your mum was always way more popular than me. Everyone loved her.'

'Why?'

'They just did – she was cool, like you are.'

'Are you sucking up to me?' he asks, cocking his head to one side and grinning impishly at me, reminding me of a teenage Cat.

I laugh in response. 'Maybe a little,' I admit. 'I want you to work on the website, after all.'

'Well, before I tackle it, you really need to get a Facebook page. It'll only take a second. You don't want to be a total loser,' he says, laughing.

With a few clicks, Swan's has a new Facebook page, complete with logo. He made it look so easy that I feel ashamed of myself for not having tackled it before.

'Thanks a million, that's amazeballs,' I say.

Beside me, Mark rolls his eyes. 'Aw, God, Coco, you can't say things like that – you're way too old! Now, you have to keep this page updated to get a buzz going, OK? You need to start building up "Likes".'

'Oh, God.' I groan. 'Am I going to feel like I'm being judged all the time? That freaks me out.'

'Well, you are, a bit,' he says. 'That's the way it works. But it's easy. All you have to do is post something every day to let your customers know what's going on – like take photos of new stock and stick them on there. It'll build pretty quickly. You could do a few giveaways to improve your profile – that's what everyone does.'

'I have to admit something, Mark,' I say, cringing, 'I actually don't know how to post a photo on-line.'

'God, Coco, how can you not know this stuff?' he says, laughing again. 'I mean, it's like you're some sort of throwback to the seventies.'

'I guess I just stuck my head in the sand about technology,' I reply. 'Ruth is probably better than me.'

'That wouldn't be hard.'

'Ouch. Direct hit!' I wince.

'Sorry. Look, I'll show you how to post photos – don't worry, it's easy. I've got some great ideas for your website, too. Facebook is OK to raise brand awareness, but people need the option of buying your stuff on-line.'

'I've been meaning to do that for ages.' It's just one more thing I've been putting on the back burner, procrastinating about.

'Yeah, well, it's the only way to go, and it'll help the business to grow,' he says and, again, he looks and sounds exactly like his mother. Cat has the same sort of spark, the same sort of can-do attitude. It's just that Mark is quieter about it.

'You're a bit of a whiz on the old computer, Mark,' I say admiringly. 'You put me to shame.'

He smiles shyly at me. I can still remember him when he was the twins' age and I used to babysit for him. Now he's guiding me round the Internet like a pro. Talk about role reversal.

'Yeah, well, I've got to help the oldies – it's my civic duty.' He sniggers and we both burst out laughing again.

Mark and I are having great fun and I feel closer to him than I have done in months. This is what we need to do more of – this sort of goofing around. I feel guilty that I neglected him when Tom and I were together. It's like he's gone from being a little kid to an adult in the blink of an eye and I seem to have missed most of it. Well, not any more. From now on my godson and I are going to spend proper quality time together every week.

'I'll share your page on mine so Swan's gets a few Likes, OK? It'll help get you started,' he says. He clicks onto his own Facebook page and then, in the blink of an eye, his expression changes.

'What is it?' I ask, straining to see what's made him go so pale.

'Nothing,' he snaps, clicking off the page quickly.

'Has something you don't like been posted on there?'

'No.' He shakes his head. 'It's fine.'

'Mark, what's going on?' I ask. 'You can tell me, you know.' There, I've said it.

Immediately, his expression grows much warier. 'What are you talking about?'

'Well, you seem . . .' I search for the right words. 'You're not yourself recently.'

'Coco, you're not going to give me a lecture, are you? Cos I get enough of those at home.'

'No, I'm not, I swear. But I know you've been under some sort of stress recently and I might know why.'

He observes me from beneath his long lashes. 'Go on.'

'I saw you talking to Sean O'Malley, the day of the twins' party.'

'You were spying on me?' His eyes widen in shock.

'No, of course not. I was taking a call outside and I just happened to see the two of you speaking. But he's not the type of guy you should be hanging around with. He's trouble.'

'Coco, no offence, but I don't think it's any of your business who I speak to,' he says, angry now.

'It's not, I agree. But I want you to know that if there's anything you'd like to talk about, I'm here – OK?' I say carefully. I don't want to spook him, but maybe, just maybe, he might want to confide in me.

'Like what?' His voice is warier now.

'Well, if something's going on in school . . .'

'Who told you that?' He springs away from me.

'No one. But you were suspended – and that's not like you.'

'I don't want to talk about it, OK?' His body language has totally changed: his eyebrows are knotted together, his mouth downturned and his arms folded tightly across his chest.

'OK, sure,' I say. I back down immediately, not wanting to destroy the tenuous connection between us by pursuing this. There's an awkward pause as I try to think of what to say, something that won't put him on the defensive any more than he is now. Clearly I hit a nerve, but he's not going to divulge anything, not yet anyway.

'Can you take me home? You have to chaperone me, right?' he says, bitterness in his tone now.

'It's not chaperoning,' I explain. 'I just offered. I'd like to see your mum anyway.' It sounds feeble, even to me.

'Whatever,' he says, walking away from me. I could kick myself: the connection has definitely been lost and I have no one to blame but myself.

*

Twenty minutes later, I'm trudging up the path to Cat and David's house behind Mark, wondering how it all ended on such a disastrous note. He unlocks the door, then stomps straight upstairs, grunting goodbye without even turning around. Despondent, I make my way into the kitchen where Cat is sitting at the table, poring over what looks like the hotel accounts. Her hair is piled on top of her head, a pencil stuck through the middle, and she's wearing an expression of intense concentration.

'How did it go?' she says anxiously, leaping up when she sees me.

'Hello to you too,' I reply.

'Sorry. Hello. How did it go?'

'Good. I think he enjoyed it. He had some brilliant ideas – he's really creative.' This isn't a lie – he was enjoying it until I screwed it all up by pushing him too hard.

'That's great. Did he say anything?' she asks hopefully.

'Not really,' I confess. 'We were getting on brilliantly, but when I tried to get him to open up, the shutters came down.'

'Shit,' she says, giving a massive sigh as she reaches for the bottle of wine I told her to have to hand, unscrews the cap and pours us both a glass.

'I think he wanted to tell me what's going on, but he just can't bring himself to.'

'I still can't believe he doesn't want to talk to me any more. He used to tell me everything,' she says.

'And he will again,' I reply, to reassure her. 'We'll sort it out, don't worry. I won't give up.' I'm already thinking about how I can get him to open up to me.

'Hark at you,' she says, smiling wanly. 'You're getting very determined in your old age.'

'Maybe I am,' I reply, grinning back at her. 'I think I'm coming into my own.'

'You'll be wearing little black dresses and matching underwear yet.'

'Well, I don't know about that,' I reply, kicking off my trusty brown boots and revealing a pair of holey old socks. 'But I might have found a bit of courage.'

'Like the Lion in *The Wizard of Oz*?' she says, and laughs.

'Yes, just like him.' I giggle. 'Now, let's put Mark on the back burner for a bit, OK? I have a lot to tell you about London and I need you to put on your wise-owl advice hat.'

'Oh, God, give me every last dirty detail,' she says eagerly. 'I could do with some cheering up.'

'OK,' I say, 'but I have to warn you, you're in for some shocks!'

16

'What a miserable day.' Ruth sighs as she looks out of the window, where the rain is coming down in thick, grey sheets, pelting so hard that it's difficult to see Karl's shop across the street.

'It's a proper duvet day,' I say, wishing with all my heart that I could go back to bed. The idea of snuggling under the covers, just this once, is very appealing.

'No one will venture out in that weather,' Ruth says. 'We're going to have a very quiet morning.'

Just as she says that, the door flings open, almost coming off its hinges in the howling wind, and a figure steps inside, an umbrella held low over her head.

'Anna!' I exclaim, as she steps across the threshold. 'You're soaking.'

The umbrella doesn't seem to have done much to protect her from the elements: she's dripping from head to toe.

'I'm fine,' she says, as a puddle forms at her feet on the shop floor.

Ruth is around the counter in seconds, tugging off her sister's soaking coat. 'Are you crazy?' she says. 'You'll get your death in this weather! Father Pat isn't worth the flu, Anna.'

'Actually, I didn't come out for him,' she says, allowing Ruth to remove her coat. 'I wanted to see you two.'

Ruth and I glance at each other as Anna steps out of

her wet shoes and accepts the cardigan Ruth takes off and gives to her.

'You did?' Ruth asks, her expression strained.

'Yes.' She takes a deep, shaky breath. 'I've been thinking about it and I know that I owe you both an apology. I'm sorry.'

This is greeted by a shocked silence as Ruth and I try to get over hearing those words from Anna's lips.

'No, you don't.' Ruth finds her voice first, but Anna already has her hand in the air.

'Let me finish, Ruth,' she says. 'You were only trying to help, I realize that, but hearing about him out of the blue was a bit of a shock. That's why I reacted the way I did.'

'We completely understand,' I say, crossing the room and taking her hand. Anna can seem like she's as tough as old boots but she's not really.

She smiles at me. 'I'm sure you had a shock too, Coco. After all, you thought he was dead.'

'Well, yes,' I admit. 'It is a bit strange – that story wasn't exactly what I'd expected to hear.'

'You must think I'm a very foolish old woman,' she laments, 'especially after everything I said to you about Tom . . .'

'No, I don't,' I say gently. 'I know you were only looking out for me. And as for Colin, you did what you felt you had to at the time. That's all any of us can do.'

'I just thought it was easier all round to tell people he'd been killed,' she says. 'It was a simple explanation and it worked – no one ever questioned it. That's what I wanted – no questions. I was so ashamed, you see.' Her eyes fill with tears that she tries to blink away.

I've never seen Anna like this, so vulnerable and . . . human.

Ruth is silent, her face twisting as she searches for the right words, and Anna turns to her. 'You thought I was wrong all these years, of course,' she says sorrowfully.

'I didn't think you had anything to be ashamed about,' Ruth says kindly. 'Marriages break down all the time. It wasn't your fault.'

'Maybe, maybe not,' Anna says sadly. 'There are two sides to every story.'

'No way,' I disagree hotly. 'He cheated on you!'

Anna flinches as I say this. 'Well, yes, that's true,' she says. 'But sometimes I think I drove him to it.'

'That's crazy talk,' Ruth says.

'No, listen to me. It's true, Ruth, you know it is. All that baby business – it got too much for him in the end.'

Ruth doesn't reply.

'What baby business?' I look from one sister to the other, confused. What is she talking about?

Anna turns to me and takes another deep breath. 'I was pregnant when Colin and I were married, Coco. More than once.' More tears glitter in her eyes now, and one falls onto her cheek. She brushes it away.

'What happened?' I whisper.

'I lost them all. I never got past sixteen weeks. The doctors couldn't tell me why. There was no reason for it.' Her voice is hollow, numb.

'Oh, Anna, I'm so sorry.' I take her hand again.

'It's silly, really, after all this time, but the pain never goes away.'

Ruth is by her side now too, gripping her other hand fiercely.

Anna takes another very deep breath and composes herself. 'Anyhow, I pushed Colin a lot to try again. I put him under a lot of pressure. It was too much.'

'You think that's why he went?' I ask, appalled. How could he leave her at a time like this? He should have been there to comfort and protect her when she was so miserable, not in a different country with another woman. Part of me wants to give him a piece of my mind for being so thoughtless and unfeeling. He broke her heart, that's plain to see.

Anna nods, struggling to find the right words to express herself. 'Situations like that can either make or break a couple,' she says at last. 'It tore us apart.'

'And you could never go back,' Ruth says sadly.

'No. I could never forgive him for giving up on me like that. That's what hurt the most. I can't go back, not even now,' she says. I can see the pain etched into the lines on her face. No wonder she's always been a little distant, more formal than her sister. She's had a lot of loss and anguish in her life, but while Ruth clung tightly to those who loved her when Mum and Granddad passed away, Anna dealt with it very differently. She turned inwards, building a wall around herself to protect herself from more pain.

'I probably should have ignored his letter,' Ruth murmurs. 'I never should have gone to see him.'

'I understand why you did, Ruth,' Anna says, 'but I can't forgive him. I know it's not Christian and you probably think it's very hypocritical of me.'

'I'm not judging you, Anna, and I'm not going to try to influence you either,' Ruth says. 'But I will say this. Maybe you should consider forgiving him in your heart if not in your head. What's the point of carrying the pain with you every day? Let it go – if not for him, for yourself.'

'Maybe,' Anna replies doubtfully. 'I'll think about it.' There's a small silence between us before she pipes up again, her voice stronger now: 'So was that the real reason you went all the way to London, then? To see my "dead" husband?' She smiles wanly at us.

'Actually, there was something else too,' I say hesitantly. I'm not sure if the timing is right, what with all she just told me about her miscarriages, but I want to tell her Tatty's story. I want to be honest with her, as she has been with us. I hope the story doesn't hurt her, remind her even more of what she's lost.

Anna looks at me quizzically as she dabs her eyes. Ruth nods at me, giving me the OK to go ahead.

'A while back I found a letter in a bag I bought at auction,' I explain. 'This Chanel bag.' I take it out and hand it to her. 'After lots of investigating, I now know that it was written by a mother to the son she gave up for adoption back in 1956.' I wait for her reaction – maybe this is too close to the bone for her.

'Go on,' she says, her expression unreadable as she examines the bag.

'Well, she never got the chance to give the letter to him so she kept it with her until she died. I've been trying to find out as much as I can.'

'You've been Nancy Drewing?' She smiles at me, tears glittering in her eyes, and I know she's letting me know it's all right to continue. The relief on Ruth's face is clear. She'd been as anxious as I was to hold off telling Anna this story and now I know why. But Anna has surprised us both with her reaction.

'Yes, she has!' Ruth says, linking Anna happily.

'Just like her mother,' Anna adds, and my heart gives a little leap that this might be true. Mum was irresponsible in many ways, but she was also brave and big-hearted.

'That's the thing, Anna,' I say. 'I feel that I found this bag for a reason.'

'Of course you did. Your mum always wanted one of those for you,' she says. 'She was saving up for it. She said it was going to be your coming-of-age bag.'

'Did she?' I'm a little shell-shocked – I've never heard that part before. Finding the bag means even more to me now because it *has* been my coming-of-age bag – it's helped me to be braver than I've ever been before.

'Oh, yes, she said it more than once,' Anna says. 'We used to have such lovely chats, your mother and I. I often suspected she knew about Colin . . .'

I glance at Ruth and she gives a tiny shake of her head. Telling Anna that Mum did know about Colin might be a step too far, too much for her to hear right now.

'So, Anna, we're wondering what we should do next,' Ruth says.

'You mean you want to track down this son – this man? Is that it?' Anna asks, as if a spark has been lit within her. She's not concentrating on Colin any more because Tatty's story has captured her imagination, just like it's captured everyone else's.

'Maybe. I don't know if it would be possible,' I say.

'What do you know so far?' she says.

'I know he was born at a mother-and-baby home in Westmeath, but that's about it,' I say, taking out my notebook and reading out the information I wrote down so carefully in London. 'It was called St Jude's.'

'I know that place!' Anna exclaims. 'My old friend Sister Dolores was in that convent.'

'No way. Are you serious?'

'Yes – it was one of the better homes, too, not like those dreadful laundries,' Anna goes on. 'They did some good work – helped out girls who were in trouble and couples who wanted to adopt. At one point I thought they might be able to help . . .' Her voice trails away and then she clears her throat.

'So, where is Sister Dolores now?' Ruth asks eagerly.

'She's still there, actually,' Anna replies. 'They're one of the very few convents left. Almost all the other nuns in the country live in purpose-built bungalows now.'

'Maybe you should pay her a visit, Coco,' Ruth says. 'She might know something. It wouldn't take that long to get up there.'

'That's not a bad idea,' Anna remarks, her eyes lighting up. 'I haven't seen Dolores in donkey's years. Can I come?'

I'm flabbergasted. Anna rarely leaves the town, unless it's for a funeral in the next parish. It's most unlike her to volunteer to go on a road trip on the spur of the moment. Or very unlike the Anna I've known all my life. Apparently there's a very different character underneath the widow caricature.

'Great idea!' Ruth is already heading off to find her coat. 'Let's go now. We can close the shop – the weather's so bad no one will be in anyway. It's the perfect day to go – what do you say?'

'Right now? This minute?' My head's spinning.

'Why not?' Ruth says. 'What do you think, Anna? Are you on for a road trip?'

'I'm game,' she agrees. 'As long as I get to sit in the front. And Coco has to drive. I'm not going anywhere if you're driving, Ruth.'

'What's that supposed to mean?' Ruth demands.

'Nothing. Just that you're the worst driver in the country,' Anna replies.

I smile to myself as they head out of the door, bickering as they go. If they're fighting, things are almost back to normal. Or as normal as they can be, considering I'm apparently on another wild-goose chase to find out more about Tatty, accompanied by two squabbling old ladies. I grab the Chanel bag and tuck it into my satchel before I follow them. If we're going to see where Duke was born, I have to bring my lucky talisman with me.

Two and a half hours later, we're following Anna's old friend Sister Dolores down a wide black-and-white tiled corridor. A smooth-faced nun who's dressed in a modest navy skirt and sweater, Sister Dolores's short salt-and-pepper hair is uncovered and she wears a silver cross at her throat. I notice that she has on the same sort of soft-soled nursing shoes that Anna favours. She's very light on her feet, with a spring in her step that belies her years.

As we follow her I glance around, soaking up as much detail as I can.

There's no one else about, although Anna did say that

the nuns' community had shrunk to almost nothing now that vocations are practically non-existent. It must have been so different when Tatty was here, banished when her parents found out she was pregnant. How was she feeling as she walked along this corridor? Scared and lonely, no doubt. The history of the place isn't lost on me, even if the cream walls and religious pictures seem pretty harmless now. This stone building was witness to plenty of sorrow in its past. I remember that in a different time Mum might have ended up here when she was pregnant with me. The very idea makes me shudder.

'It's wonderful to see you after so much time,' Sister Dolores says, inviting us to sit down as we enter her cosy office. It's stopped raining and weak sunlight streams in through the solitary stained-glass window, making pretty, multicoloured patterns on a large beige rug. The same sort of religious pictures that adorn the corridors hang on the bland cream walls. In the middle of the room is a large wooden desk, behind which stands a massive rosewood cupboard. Anna, Ruth and I sit on a leather sofa, cheek by jowl, and Sister Dolores settles herself at the desk.

'You too,' Anna says warmly. 'You haven't aged a bit.'

'That's the nuns' skin secret,' she confides. 'No sun damage – we don't get outside much.'

She and Anna go off into fits of laughter together at this joke.

'You were always a tonic,' Anna says.

'A sense of humour is important in this job,' Sister Dolores replies. 'Not that Mother Superior would necessarily agree with me.'

'She's still a handful, then?' Anna enquires.

Sister Dolores sighs. 'Something like that. But we're all God's children. At least, that's what I keep reminding myself.'

The two of them go off into fits of laughter again. All this time I'd thought Anna was a pious holy Joe but here she is laughing about her religion. It's a whole other side to her, which I love. Now that I know the truth about her past, I can empathize with her a whole lot more.

'Now, we'd better get down to business. I know you're a busy woman,' Anna says, placing her handbag carefully on the floor and clasping her hands in her lap.

'I didn't think this was just a social visit,' Sister Dolores replies, leaning towards us across the table, ears pricked, a smile playing on her lips. 'What's going on?'

'Well, the thing is, Coco is trying to track down a child who was born here in the fifties.'

'Ah, I see. Now there's a hot potato if ever there was one,' Sister Dolores says ruefully, shaking her head.

'There's no way to do that?' Ruth asks.

'Well, it depends. We have records for some, but not for others . . .' The nun frowns, a few little wrinkles appearing on her otherwise smooth forehead.

This was what Bonnie was talking about – the secret adoptions, for which no records were kept. If Duke was given away like that, there's no chance I'll ever find him. I'll never solve the mystery.

'And if you did happen to have a record of his birth?' Anna prompts.

'Well, naturally that would be of a confidential nature.' Sister Dolores stares at her, unblinking. 'I couldn't divulge any details.'

'I understand,' Anna replies, nodding. 'Of course, it probably wouldn't hurt just to check.'

There's a short pause. It's as if the two women are having a whole other conversation, like they have some sort of unspoken understanding.

'You're right, it wouldn't,' Sister Dolores agrees amiably. 'No harm in checking. Now, what was the child's name, Coco?'

My heart is hammering in my chest. 'He was called Duke at birth, on the tenth of November 1956,' I say. 'His mother's name was Moynihan, Tatty Moynihan.'

Sister Dolores moves towards the large rosewood cupboard directly behind her and twists open the lock with a small key. The door opens to reveal several large red ledgers. She pulls a few from the pile, places them on the table in the centre of the room, humming and hahing as she does so. One in particular seems to draw her attention and she examines a few pages carefully. As I watch her, I realize I'm holding my breath; beside me, so are Anna and Ruth. Minutes, like hours, seem to tick by until she raises her head again and looks straight at Anna.

'I need to use the lavatory, Anna,' she says abruptly. 'I'll be back in a moment.'

The minute she's out of the door, Anna and Ruth are on their feet.

'What are you doing?' I gasp, as they pounce on the ledger.

'She's giving us the chance to look,' Anna says.

'Are you sure?' I glance over my shoulder, certain she'll reappear at any second and we'll be done for. Those soft-soled shoes are a curse.

'I'm positive,' Anna replies. 'Sister Dolores has always been a bit of a renegade – she's trying to help us, believe me. Now, find the name, quick!'

Anna is running her finger down the page, searching for Duke or Tatty's names among the scrawled writing. Beside her, Ruth is muttering names and addresses out loud.

But I've already spotted it – the name simply jumped out of the page at me, as if it was waiting to be found. *Baby boy, 10 November 1956, mother Tatty Moynihan.* On the opposite page there's another set of names with an address. *Luke and Eileen Flynn, Glacken.*

'There it is,' I say, my voice hoarse with excitement. 'That's him.'

'Glacken?' Ruth says. 'That's only an hour from Dronmore! I can't believe he was so close by.'

'There's no time for that now, Ruth.' Anna scribbles down the details and whips her notepad back into her handbag, snapping it shut. 'Quick! Sit down – she's coming!'

She spins us back across the room and we plonk ourselves on the sofa, like naughty schoolgirls, just as the door opens and Sister Dolores reappears. She stands in front of us, clasping her hands together solemnly, as if she's about to recite a decade of the rosary. You would never know from the innocent look on her face that she's colluding with us in this. Butter wouldn't melt in her mouth. 'Sorry I couldn't be of more help, ladies,' she says gravely, her eyes flicking to the ledger on the table.

'Never mind, Sister,' Anna replies, just as solemnly. 'It was lovely to see you anyway.'

'You too, Anna. I'll keep you all in my prayers.' There's a flicker of a smile between them.

'That's very kind of you,' Ruth says, and I murmur my agreement. Thanks to this renegade nun, I now have the next piece of the puzzle. I could hug her. I could lift her off her shuffle-soled feet and spin her round the room until we're both sick. I have to sit on my hands to stop myself punching the air.

'We'd better be off,' Anna goes on, calm as you like, and we all stand to leave.

'Me too,' Sister Dolores says regretfully. 'Those chapel pews won't polish themselves, ha ha.'

We all laugh nervously, and then we're out of the door and back in the car in a flash. Ruth and Anna cheer as I pull away from the convent.

'I can't believe it,' I say, indicating to go left at the gate. 'I can't believe we have an address for him. I think I'm in shock.'

'And I'm in shock that you pulled this off, Anna. You're as bold as brass,' Ruth says admiringly. 'I wouldn't have thought you had it in you.'

'Maybe there's more to me than meets the eye,' Anna crows. 'Now, the question is, Coco, when are you going to Glacken?'

'You have to go there now!' Ruth whoops. 'It's in the stars!'

'Definitely,' Anna proclaims.

'You two are a very bad influence,' I say, laughing. They're behaving like big kids today, and it's hilarious.

'Yes, and isn't it just bloody great?' Ruth says. I watch in the rear-view mirror as she wraps her arms around Anna and squeezes her tight, the two of them collapsing into laughter.

17

'Oh, my God! I so wish I was coming too!' Cat squeals into my earpiece, the next morning, as I drive.

'You don't think I'm nuts?' I ask nervously, shifting gears.

'I didn't say that!' She laughs.

'I'm bricking it,' I admit.

'You'll be great,' she says. 'Who knows what you'll find out? Ring me later and tell me everything, OK? I have to go – the twins are shoving Cheerios up their noses as we speak.'

'Er, can I cancel that babysitting gig tonight?' I joke. I'd finally persuaded Cat to go on that date night with David and allow me to mind the boys.

'Over my dead body, Sunshine. That gig's on lockdown and you can't get out of it.'

I'm still laughing as I hang up. I can't believe I'm actually going to Glacken to search for Duke. The countryside passes in a blur as I drive by frosted trees and hedgerows, cattle in the fields, their breath making icy clouds in the air.

'You'd be proud of me, Mum,' I say, as I grip the wheel. This is exactly what she would have done if she was still here. Driving into the unknown like this reminds me of when I was little and she'd creep into my bedroom to surprise me when she got back from one of her trips.

'Let's go on an adventure,' she'd whisper in my ear, waking me with kisses and cuddles. Then she'd carry me, still half asleep, to the car, tucking a blanket around me to ward off the early-morning chill. We'd get to the fork in the road at the end of the town, and she'd say, 'Left or right?' and I'd choose which way to go. And then we'd be off, exploring, stopping at the side of the road to eat, pulling in if we saw something interesting, like a castle ruin, or following a signpost that promised an amazing view. We never had any idea what we were going to do, or where we would end up, but we always knew we had the whole day to do it.

'This is the life,' she'd say, as we sat on a crumbling stone wall at the side of the road, eating our sandwiches and admiring a valley laid out below us. 'Who needs routine, eh?' I'd hug myself with joy that she was there and that we were 'special together', like she used to tell me. And then I'd wake up the next morning and, more than likely, she'd be gone again and I'd go back to school.

The icy cold in the car jerks me from my reminiscing and I fiddle with the heater, trying to turn it to full blast, and failing. This car needs a service. It's so cold in here that I haven't taken off the pink sequined hat, scarf and glove set that Cat gave me last Christmas to glam me up, as she put it.

I reckon I must be near Glacken by now. Of course, I should have an iPhone and some sort of App to tell me where I'm supposed to be going. Cat has sat-nav in her car – although David always jokes that she doesn't need it because she has an internal navigation system of her

own – the Cat-nav, he calls it. I'm the complete opposite:
I have no sense of direction.

Ten minutes later, surprising myself with my rusty map-
reading skills, I'm in Glacken, wondering which turn to
take next. It seems to be a bit of a one-horse town, a single street with a few houses, a small shop and a garage
opposite that has bales of briquettes and sacks of coal
stacked outside for sale. I pull into the kerb and step out
of the car, pulling my hat down lower over my ears against
the chilly air. My legs feel wobbly beneath me. I'm really
nervous now that I'm here, so close to where Duke was
brought up. A hot coffee, that's what I need – the shop
will surely do takeaway and they can tell me where Duke
lives too, hopefully.

I push open the door, blinking in the half-light. It's like
I've stepped back in time as I cross the threshold. I look
around for the coffee machine, but there doesn't seem to
be one. Instead cans of fizzy drinks are lined up in a neat
row on a shelf beside tinned beans, a basket of rhubarb
and a selection of birthday cards with dogs driving cars
on the front.

'Hello there, can I help you?' A ruddy-faced, middle-
aged woman steps out from behind the counter, greeting
me very cheerfully. She's wearing an apron with a frill and
her hair is in tight curls. A badge that says, 'I'm sexy and
I know it,' is pinned to her large bosom. I really can't picture the moment when she saw that for sale and decided
it was perfect for her.

'Er, hello,' I say. 'Do you have coffee?'

'We do,' she confirms robustly. 'What would you like?'

'A latte?' I ask, with little confidence that I'll get it in such an old-fashioned country establishment.

'No problem,' she says. 'Skinny?'

'Er, yes, please,' I reply.

She turns her head. 'Ted!'

A man sticks his head out from behind the door. 'Yes, Peg?'

'This nice girl here would like a skinny latte,' she says.

'Coming right up!' he says, winking at me.

'Great, thanks,' I reply, smiling at him. His toothy grin is very infectious.

A silence falls between us as he disappears again and the woman surveys me, smiling broadly all the time. 'Sorry about the delay. We have to keep the coffee machine out the back – the one we had in here broke, so it did. Only ten years old it was and it just gave up the ghost. But sure, they don't make things like they used to.' She sighs heavily, although I get the impression she's not losing any sleep over it.

'That's true,' I agree.

'Did your machine break down, too?' she asks, leaning her elbows on the counter, like she's settling in for a long chat.

'Nothing like that. But I work in the antiques business. Old things are my stock in trade.' It's out of my mouth before I can stop myself. Why am I telling this woman my business? I'm not here to make friends.

'Oh, *antiques*! Do you hear that, Ted?' The man is back, with a steaming polystyrene cup in his hand.

'What's that?' he asks amiably, handing it to me.

'This girl works in antiques!'

'I don't *believe* it!' he exclaims, and she chuckles loudly, clearly getting the reaction she was looking for. 'I love antiques!'

'Glued to *Antiques Roadshow* when it's on, he is,' she explains to me. 'You can't budge him when that Fiona Bruce is on the screen.'

'I love it, so I do,' Ted says. 'It's addictive, like that crack cocaine.'

'Ted – show her the clock. Go on,' Peg says.

He looks bashful all of a sudden. 'Ah, now, Peg, I couldn't,' he says. 'That wouldn't be right.'

'Go on,' she urges him, turning to me. 'You wouldn't mind, would you? Sorry, I never caught your name – isn't that criminal? Here I am gassing away . . .'

'Er, it's Coco,' I say.

'Coco!' she says. 'Isn't that terrible romantic all the same? Like Coco Chanel, is it?'

'Yes,' I reply, smiling at her. She's a bundle of energy and good humour – they both are.

'Oh, I loved that film – did you?' She keeps talking, not giving me the chance to reply. 'Such an independent woman she was.'

'Er, yes, she was,' I agree.

'Will I tell you something silly? I always fancied getting one of her bags. They're so stylish those Chanel bags.'

'Well, now, Peg, I never knew that,' Ted says, looking surprised.

'There might be a lot about me that you wouldn't know, Ted,' she replies, winking at me. 'Now, Coco, you're the very woman to ask.'

'I am?' I can barely keep up, they're talking so rapidly.

'Yes, the very woman! Ted here has a clock, passed down the generations from father to son. I've been telling him he should get it valued. But will he listen to me, Coco? Indeedin' he won't.'

'Ah, it's probably not worth anything,' Ted says, waving her away.

'I saw one just like it on the Internet, Coco,' Peg says. 'It was worth thousands.'

'It wasn't the same,' he disagrees.

'It was close to no difference,' she argues. 'Even Maggie said so.'

'Maggie?' I ask. Who's Maggie when she's at home – their daughter?

'Maggie is a friend of ours,' Ted explains. 'Lovely girl – married to Edward in the livery up the road.'

'She knows a thing or two about that sort of thing – she used to work in property before she started concentrating on her art,' Peg explains.

'And looking after the girls, of course,' Ted interjects. 'Edward's daughters – of course, they're her daughters too now. She's a great mum to them.'

'Oh, yes, she idolizes those girls – and they idolize her. Although it wasn't that way when she came here first,' Peg says.

'Just the opposite,' Ted says gravely.

'But all's well that ends well,' Peg finishes.

'I see,' I say, although I don't see at all – in fact, I'm completely lost. I have no clue who these people are or why they're telling me about them.

'So, anyway, Maggie thinks the clock might be valuable – not that Ted would ever sell it, would you?'

Ted shakes his head vehemently, as if the very idea offends him.

'But you'd like to know if it's worth anything?' I ask. That's reasonable – lots of people feel the same way. They wouldn't be parted from their prized possessions, but they still like to know their value.

'Well, yes.' Peg looks a little uncomfortable now. 'You see, the thing is I have a bet on with Jimmy. He thinks it's not worth a red cent, but I disagree.'

'And Jimmy is?'

'The local guard. Bit of a knowledge about these things,' Ted explains.

'Or likes to think he is,' Peg mutters, and they glance knowingly at each other.

'Well, I'd be happy to look at the clock, if you like,' I say. 'It's not my speciality, but I could give an opinion.'

'What's your speciality then?' Peg asks, full of curiosity. 'No, don't tell me – let me guess . . . Eighteenth-century ceramics?'

'Er, no.'

'Dutch furniture?' Ted pipes up. 'Silverware?'

'Well, actually, I don't have a speciality as such.'

'Ah – you're more broad-stroke knowledge, is that it?' Ted says, nodding.

'Yes, er, something like that. So, would you like me to look at the clock?'

Ted shakes his head firmly. 'No, thanks, Coco,' he says. 'I'm sticking to my guns on this one. Peg knows how I feel about it – she never should have brought it up to you.'

'But, Ted!' Peg howls, clearly very disappointed. 'This could be the perfect opportunity to know how much it's worth!'

'Er, I'm not sure I could give you an exact figure – maybe just a rough guess,' I say. But neither of them is listening to me now.

'There's no point arguing with me, woman,' Ted says. 'I'm not getting it valued and that's that.'

'You're no fun,' she grumbles, scowling at him. 'Honestly. You'd think you'd do it just to keep me happy . . . I don't ask for much.'

'Well, I'd better be off, then,' I say, glancing at my watch. I've been in here for almost ten minutes – and I certainly don't want to get caught up in a domestic argument between these two.

'Of course you should!' Peg exclaims, coming to from her sulk about the clock.

'It was very nice to meet you, Coco,' Ted says.

'Yes, it was,' Peg agrees. 'Lovely to see a new face come through the door, so it was. We never see anyone new, so we don't, Ted?'

'Indeedin' we don't. Sure we're like a pair of old dinosaurs, so we are,' he says. Again, I get the definite impression he's not losing any sleep over it.

'I don't suppose you know where Glacken House is, do you?' I ask, giving over the money for the coffee, then taking the change that Peg offers me and slipping it into my pocket.

'Of course we do!' Peg says. 'Now, drive straight up the road –'

'– past the church –'

'– past the graveyard –'

'– keep going until you get to the crossroads –'

'– and if you get to a double-storey house with ugly pillars, then you've gone too far.'

'That's Paddy Moran's house – built the pillars himself, God love him, and he blind in one eye –'

'– terrible shame, the poor cratur.'

'Go past Edward and Maggie's –'

'– the livery stables, like we said –'

'– round the bend –'

'– and Glacken House is on the left-hand side.'

'Will I write it down for you?' Ted asks, blinking at me.

'No, thanks, I think I have it,' I say, hoping I do. I'm not the least bit convinced I got even a quarter of it, but I'll take my chances.

'Good girl yourself.' Ted smiles at me.

'Sure we might see you again,' Peg says.

'Yes, you might,' I agree, a little doubtfully.

'If you think of it, will you Like our Facebook page, Coco?' Peg calls, as I leave. 'We're trying to get ten thousand Likes – and we're not far off it now!'

'You have a Facebook page?' I ask, pausing in the doorway. This tiny shop in the middle of nowhere is on Facebook?

'Of course! You can follow us on Twitter too, if you like – Ted loves a good tweet, don't you, Ted?'

'I do!' he agrees wholeheartedly.

'Jay Z tweeted him the other day,' she goes on proudly.

'Jay Z? The rapper?'

'The very same. Even re-tweeted one of your tweets, didn't he, Ted?'

'Ah, 'twas probably a mistake.' Ted is blushing now.

''Twas no mistake,' she insists stoutly. 'And he got a load of new followers after it too. Anyway, here, take our card and keep in touch.' She bounds out from behind the counter and thrusts a business card into my hand. There's a nice logo and a hand-drawn picture of the shop on the front.

'I love the drawing,' I say, turning the card over in my hands.

'Our friend Maggie did that,' Peg says proudly. 'She's a very talented artist. She could do one for your shop if you wanted – she takes commissions. Very reasonable she is.'

'You could Google her,' Ted says. 'You can see her work on-line – she has a great website.'

'Thanks. I'll think about it,' I say.

'See you soon!' Peg says, waving.

'Don't be a stranger!' Ted grins. 'And don't forget to Like us, so you won't? You could win a six-month supply of crisps!'

I really need to get my act in gear, I think, as I move out from the parking space and drive up the hill. If that tiny shop in the middle of nowhere can be so clued in, I have to pull up my socks. They have a Facebook page with almost ten thousand Likes! Wait until I tell Mark – if he ever talks to me again, that is.

I drive past the church, then the graveyard, until I come to a sign for the stables. I'm almost there. I round the final corner and there's a sign for Glacken House on the left-hand side, just like Peg and Ted said.

It's a large two-storey grey house, set back from the road up a long, tree-lined avenue. Red ivy creeps up its walls and its white sash windows are large and imposing. There are three chimney stacks that I can count and a fleet of granite steps to the grand entrance door. It seems that Glacken House is a proper country manor. As I drive up the avenue, bordered on both sides by green pasture, frosted white, I try to decide what I'm going to say.

I'll have to be sensitive – I can't just barge in, show Duke the letter and tell him I believe it's meant for him. That could give the poor man a heart attack if he doesn't know about his past. No, I have to find a way around it. Break it to him gently.

I'm pulling up the car's handbrake when I spot a man. He's standing in the distance, his back to me, and there are several dogs at his feet. My heart leaps. If this is Duke, I'm going to change his life for ever.

'This is it, Mum. Wish me luck,' I whisper. Then, before I can change my mind, I open the door and step out.

18

I walk towards the man, who hasn't noticed me yet. A dozen dogs, all different shapes and sizes, surround him, yapping and pushing their noses against his legs. I can't see his face as he's bent over, scooping dry dog food into an array of bowls for them, talking to them all the time.

'Now, boys, behave,' I hear him say, in a deep voice. 'If there's any messing like yesterday, there'll be trouble, right?'

The dogs yap at him as if they understand every word.

'Ah, yeah, you all say that now,' he replies, as if he understands them too, 'but actions speak louder than words.'

I take a deep, steadying breath. This could be it – I could be about to meet Duke and slot the final piece into this puzzle. My knees are knocking at the prospect.

He turns and our eyes lock. My heart sinks. He can't be Duke – this man is far too young. Duke has to be in his fifties, but this guy is only in his thirties, like me. He's tall, at least six foot two, with very broad shoulders, thick, dark brown hair and a tanned, almost weather-beaten face. His nose has clearly been broken more than once – it's even wonkier than mine. He's wearing a shabby red-and-navy checked shirt, worn blue jeans and rugged tan work boots, covered with muck, laces missing. He's not wearing a coat, but he looks the hardy sort who doesn't feel the cold, like a big grizzly bear. But it's his eyes I notice most of all. They're the darkest brown I've ever seen, almost black.

All in all, he's not who, or what, I'd been expecting.

'Hello,' he says. 'Sorry, I didn't hear you arrive.' There's a friendly smile as he rubs the head of a dog that's already finished eating and is looking for attention. He wipes a hand on his grubby jeans and reaches to shake mine, smiling inquisitively at me.

'No problem. You look pretty busy there,' I say. My hand, which I usually think is so large and unfeminine, feels like a child's in his.

'Never a dull moment with these boys and girls.' He laughs ruefully, rubbing his chin as all around him the dogs guzzle food, tails wagging.

A black Labrador, coat as glossy as paint, trots over to me and licks my hand. 'Hello, boy,' I say, bending down to rub his head. His big brown eyes look up at me and I could swear he's smiling.

'That's Horatio,' the man explains. 'He's our meet-and-greet.'

'He's lovely.'

'And he knows it.' The man laughs heartily. 'So . . .' he peers behind me '. . . where's the pup?'

'Pup?' What's he talking about? I look behind me, as a puppy might appear out of thin air.

'Aren't you the lady who rang me about the pup found on the motorway?' he goes on, cocking his head to one side.

'No, sorry, I'm not,' I reply.

'Oh, I see. Crossed wires,' he says, dipping and petting

a long-eared spaniel. 'I had a call earlier – some moron had thrown a pup out of a moving car on the motorway.'

'That's awful!' I say, feeling instantly sick that someone would be so vicious. 'How could anyone do something like that?'

He sighs. 'I ask myself that sort of question every single day. Some people think animals are disposable, I guess.'

'I hope they're prosecuted!' I'm enraged at the thought of someone being so mindlessly cruel to an innocent, defenceless puppy.

'Well, the problem is catching them at it. Even then, animal cruelty can be tough to prove.' He bends to scoop up a yapping Yorkshire terrier that's already finished its food. 'You're such a greedy guts, Pudding,' he says affectionately, tickling its ears as he talks. 'This one would eat me out of house and home if she got a chance. Not that I blame her – the poor little thing was starved for the first few months of her life.'

I watch as the Yorkie snuggles contentedly into his arms. 'Deliberately?' I ask, not wanting to believe it. How could anyone starve such a gorgeous little dog?

'Yes. She was left outside in all weathers, not even a dog box for shelter. She was a quivering wreck by the time we got her. She's making progress though, little by little. Aren't you, Pudding?'

'She's really cute,' I say, as the little dog wriggles about, making happy little noises. 'So, this is a dog shelter?' I ask, looking around. The couple in the shop hadn't mentioned it, but maybe they presumed I already knew.

'That's right.' He laughs ruefully. 'I run it for my sins.'

'It must be such hard work.' I love animals, but I can't imagine being responsible for all these dogs.

'Yep, it is,' he says. 'Worth it, though. A lot of these would be on Death Row if they couldn't come here. Horatio included.'

Horatio is now busy licking the inside of his bowl as if his life depended on it.

'So if you're not the puppy lady, who are you?' he asks, regarding me curiously now.

I come to with a little start. I've been so caught up in all the dog stories that I've almost forgotten why I'm here.

'Sorry. My name is Coco Swan. I was looking for Glacken House – the couple in the village shop said this was the place.' I gesture to the big house. Maybe Duke is inside somewhere. My stomach flutters when I think of it.

'Ah, so you met Peg and Ted, did you?' He grins at me. 'They're legends round here.'

'I bet.' I smile back at him.

'So, how can I help you?'

'Well, I'm looking for Mr Flynn. Is he around?' I ask.

'James Flynn?'

So, his adoptive parents called him James, not Duke. Poor Tatty, her wish about his name was obviously ignored.

'Yes,' I reply.

'I'm afraid you've come to the wrong place, sorry. He doesn't live here any more.'

'He doesn't?' My face falls.

'I bought this house from him more than three years ago. I'm Mac Gilmartin. Am I any good to you?' He grins at me once more, the skin around his eyes crinkling deeply. He really is very attractive in a Grizzly Adams sort of way, not that I have either the time or the inclination to notice that now.

I'm so disappointed. How stupid of me – I never thought that Duke, or James as he's now known, might have moved on from here. How naïve could I have been? Of course, it was never going to be this easy to find him. I was deluded to think otherwise.

'I'm taking your silence as a no, then?' Mac Gilmartin says.

'Sorry, yes, that's a no.'

'Was it important?'

'Um, yes, sort of,' I reply.

'Hmm . . . You don't give much away, do you?' He cocks his head to the side again.

'What do you mean?'

'Do you always do that?'

'Do what?'

'Answer a question with a question?'

'Do I?'

He laughs. 'Yes – you've just done it again, in fact. It's a classic avoidance tactic. And I still don't know any more about you. You're very good, I must say.'

'I don't suppose you know where he went, do you?' I ask, my mind clicking into gear. OK, so Duke/James isn't here, but maybe he didn't move far. Maybe I could still find him. All hope isn't lost – this could be just a blip. He might be up the road, or in the next parish.

Around us, the dogs are getting restless. They've all fin-ished eating now and are sniffing the ground feverishly, trying to figure out if we have anything else interesting to offer.

'Can we walk and talk?' Mac says, gesturing across the yard to the field beyond. 'These guys need a run.'

'Er, yes, OK,' I reply. If I want to get any more information, it looks like I don't have a choice. Luckily, I'm wearing my trusty boots, so tramping through mucky fields won't be a problem.

'Right, come with me, everyone, time to let your hair down,' he says, picking up the empty bowls and piling them on a high wall out of reach.

The dogs bound off before us, scrabbling across the lawn, skidding sideways as they round a corner. It seems they know where they're going and they can't wait to get there.

'Sorry about this, but they like their routine,' he explains. 'They go a bit bananas if they don't get at least two walks a day. And, believe me, it's not pretty if that happens.'

We both laugh as Horatio leaps over the gate at the end of the garden and a tiny white ball of fluff behind tries to copy him and fails.

'Blondie, when will you ever learn?' Mac says, opening the gate so she can scramble through.

'She's so sweet,' I say.

'She thinks she's a Dobermann trapped in the body of a shih-tzu.'

'I can see that.' I giggle.

'Still, at least she's come out of herself. She was terrified of everything when she came here first.'

'What happened to her?' I ask, watching as the little dog flings herself into a mucky patch and rolls ecstatically, grinding her shoulder into the mud and wriggling with happy abandon.

'She was in a puppy farm – she had untold litters in three years. The poor girl was exhausted when she came to us. Plus she had mange and all her teeth were rotten. But she's getting there.'

'That's awful.' I wince as I listen to this tale of woe.

'So, anyway, enough about this crowd. You're looking for James, yeah?' he asks. 'Are you a relative? Or a friend?'

He's studying me discreetly now, clearly sizing me up, trying to decide if I'm some sort of lunatic.

'No, I'm not,' I reply carefully. 'I just have . . . something I think belongs to him.'

'Ah, you're definitely the mysterious type! Still no details.' He raises his eyebrows.

'Well, it's kind of a long story,' I say, not sure where to start.

He says nothing, just waits for me to begin.

'How well do you know Duke – I mean James?' I ask.

'Not at all. I only ever dealt with the estate agent.'

I'm weighing up in my mind how much to reveal. If he and James aren't friends, I'm safe enough to tell him the story surely. He's a stranger, yes, but he has the sort of open face that makes the idea of confiding in him very appealing. I've nothing to lose by telling him the story, either way.

'Well, here's the thing. I have an antiques shop in Dronmore,' I say. 'I bought a handbag at an auction and there was a letter inside . . .'

'A letter?'

'Yes, a very personal letter. I think it might be meant for James.'

'You only think? You're not sure?' He half smiles at me, almost teasing.

'Yes, that's the thing. I'm not sure of anything.'

'I see. Well, what does this letter say, or are you not going to tell me that?' he asks.

Ahead of us, the dogs are scattered, gleefully sniffing and exploring every corner of the field.

'The letter was written by a mother to the child she had to give up for adoption. I think that child was James.'

'Wow – that *is* personal,' he says, giving a low whistle.

'I know. The woman who wrote it passed away recently so I can't give it back to her.'

'So you felt you had to try to reunite it with the person it was written to instead, is that it?'

'Well, yes.'

'It could be for anyone, though. Why do you think it's for James?' he asks.

'Because I've done some research and it's led me here,' I reply.

'Research?'

'Yes. I tracked down the woman's nurse and that led me to London and then to a convent and then here . . .'

His eyes are wide as he looks at me. He thinks I'm nuts. Telling him was the wrong thing to do.

'Can I ask why you've gone to all this trouble? I mean, it's nothing to do with you really, right?' he asks.

'Well, I thought the letter should be reunited with the person it was intended for. And I was . . . curious.' I'm not going to tell him about Mum. That would definitely sound crazy, and I don't need any help in that department.

He looks at me, as if weighing up the situation. 'Yeah, I can relate to that,' he says at last. 'It is pretty compelling. I mean, if I'd been adopted, I'd want to see a letter my mother had written to me.'

'That's what I think,' I reply, relieved, and strangely pleased, that we agree.

'And I guess you sort of feel responsible, huh? Seeing as you found the bag.'

'Yeah, that's it. I feel it's my duty to find this man. It probably sounds stupid . . .'

'No, not at all. It's lovely.'

He grins at me again and I feel another surge of pleasure. He understands where I'm coming from – he doesn't think I'm a lunatic. He seems to think that what I'm doing is completely logical.

'So, James moved away from here about three years ago?' I ask, dragging my eyes away from his. The more I talk to him, the more I realize that he really is incredibly attractive.

'Yeah, that's about right – maybe a little more.'

'And that's when you moved in?'

'Yep. I was looking for somewhere with space and this place fitted the bill.' He gestures to the expansive grounds – there must be at least a few sprawling acres of land attached to the house and gardens.

'It's beautiful here,' I say. Ahead of us, wide-open space stretches as far as the eye can see.

'Yeah, we like it, don't we, guys?' he says, to the dogs.

Something about the way he says that makes me wonder

if he lives here alone. Hardly: the house is enormous. He probably has a glamorous wife and a clatter of perfect children. I can just imagine them now – like something in a Boden ad, all wearing matching polka-dot wellies, surrounded by their devoted animals. With difficulty, I pull myself back to our conversation.

'And you've no idea where James went after he left here?' I ask.

'I –'

He doesn't get a chance to finish because a voice calls, 'Hello? Are you Mac?' A distressed-looking woman, with a puppy in her arms, is hurrying towards us. This is obviously the lady he was expecting, with the pup that was thrown from the car.

'Will you excuse me for a second?' he says, glancing at me. 'I just need to sort out this pup and I'll be right back, OK?'

He strides towards the woman and they walk quickly towards the house, talking animatedly, heads close together. As I watch them go, I suddenly feel a little foolish. What must this guy think of me? Probably that I'm one sandwich short of a picnic. OK, so he's pretending otherwise – he even said he thought what I was doing was lovely – but he seems like a polite person. He's probably laughing at me on the inside. If someone turned up on the doorstep of Swan's with a long-winded story like this, I'm not sure I'd be as accommodating. I'd probably try to get rid of them as fast as possible. Mac Gilmartin has been as helpful as he can be, but the trail has gone cold. If Duke/James moved away from here three years ago, he could now be anywhere.

The best thing to do is to leave before Mac Gilmartin comes back. We really have nothing left to talk about, and I'll be twice as embarrassed if we have to make chit-chat again. I feel more than a little foolish now – coming all the way here on a whim wasn't brave, just silly.

'It was very nice to meet you,' I say to Horatio, who trots behind me, escorting me to my car, as I make a quiet getaway. Wrenching the car door open, I give him a piece of biscuit I find in the side compartment and he gobbles it, licking my hand once it's gone, looking for more.

'Sorry, buddy, that's all I have.' I know by the expression on his face that he understands. He really is the most intelligent-looking dog I've ever met – something in his eyes tells me he's seen more than most people ever have.

'How could anyone have been cruel to you?' I ask, giving him a final pat and he thumps his tail on the ground. As my car bumps back down the gravel driveway I see him trotting away and out of view, his tail still waving happily, and I feel a pang of regret that I'll never see him – or Mac Gilmartin – again.

19

'What a pity Mac Gilmartin couldn't tell you more,' Ruth says, as we head up the main street of Dronmore together mid-afternoon.

I link my arm through hers as we go. A walk was the last thing I wanted when I got back, but Ruth insisted that we both needed some fresh air after I'd regaled her with the story of my visit to Glacken. I'd resisted initially, but she practically frogmarched me out of the door and now I'm enjoying it, even though it's bitterly cold, with more than a hint of ice in the air.

'Isn't it lovely and crisp?' Ruth says, like she can read my mind. 'I always think a walk can cure almost anything. It blows all the cobwebs away.'

'Yeah,' I agree distractedly, my mind a million miles away.

'Stop beating yourself up, Coco,' she says, out of nowhere.

'What do you mean?' I ask, even though I already suspect I know what she's referring to.

'You're annoyed with yourself because you didn't stay and dig a bit deeper, aren't you? You think Mac Gilmartin might have been able to give you more information about Duke.'

'James,' I correct her.

'Sorry, James. But I'm right, aren't I?'

I nod. 'I could kick myself,' I admit. 'I should have stayed and tried to find out if he knew anything else, but I got cold feet.'

That's exactly what happened – I got the wobbles. Ruth squeezes my arm sympathetically. 'I think Mac Gilmartin spooked you,' she says. 'He seems to have had quite the effect.'

'No, he didn't,' I say, automatically denying this although she's right. He did have an effect, one I haven't felt in quite some time. And it threw me, more than a little.

'OK, maybe not. Anyway, there must be some other way we can track down James Flynn. He can't just have disappeared off the face of the Earth.'

'I dunno, Ruth. I think I've come to the end of the line. Maybe I should just give up.'

'You can't give up now,' she says, nodding to a passer-by. 'Not when you've come so far.'

I don't answer. Right now, giving up seems the right thing to do. Maybe I was mistaken, thinking that all this had something to do with Mum. I felt so sure when we were in London that I had to reunite the letter with Tatty's son. Now I don't know. Maybe the smart thing to do would be to forget about it – enjoy the handbag and relegate the letter to the past. But that's easier said than done because I can't stop thinking about it: Tatty, her lost baby and their sad story. If he's out there, shouldn't he know how his mother felt? Shouldn't he have this piece of his history? She loved him so much and was devastated to let him go. Doesn't he deserve to know that?

My heart tells me yes, but my head tells me it might be wiser to leave well enough alone. After all, I followed the story where it led me, and I hit a dead end. Maybe I should take it as a sign that now is the time to walk away.

The trouble is, though, that a nagging voice in my head is telling me I didn't tie up all the loose ends. I left before Mac Gilmartin could tell me anything else he might have known, any other clues to help me find Tatty's son, and I can't help thinking I bottled it. Isn't that what Cat said about me not going to New Zealand with Tom, that I backed out at the last second because I was frightened? Maybe I've just done the same thing with the letter: I went so far and then, just on the edge of a breakthrough, I ran.

Ruth squeezes my arm again as if she knows the turmoil that's going on inside me. 'Tell me, how are those adorable twins of Cat's? Aren't you babysitting them tonight?' she asks, deliberately changing the subject.

'Yeah, I am,' I reply. 'I just hope they behave!'

Despite how I joked with Cat earlier, I'm looking forward to babysitting.

'I'm sure they will,' she reassures me. 'You're great with kids.'

'I dunno about that,' I say, thinking how I screwed up my chat with Mark.

'And how's Mark doing?' she goes on, like she's reading my mind again. 'Cat must be worried about him, getting suspended from school like that?'

'Definitely,' I say. 'They're at loggerheads. She doesn't know what to do about it. I've been trying to talk to him, you know, see what's going on, but he just won't open up.'

'Ah, yes, the dreaded teenage years. We skipped all that angst with you,' Ruth says, smiling at me, her cheeks dimpling.

'Did you?' I ask.

'Yes. I'd been preparing myself for it because your mother was such a minx, but you were so well behaved.'

'Boring, you mean.' I sigh. I was far too quiet to engage in teenage rebellion.

'No, darling, you were never boring. Anyway, Mark will be fine, trust me. I got suspended from boarding school once and I turned out relatively OK.'

'You got suspended?' I laugh with disbelief. 'What for?'

'For fighting – what else?' she replies, a glint in her eye.

'What did you do?'

'I wrestled a girl to the floor – I even pulled out some of her hair.'

'You didn't!'

'I did. It was quite the cat fight. Everyone was talking about it for months afterwards. The nuns nearly had nervous breakdowns over it, of course.'

'And what about the other girl? Was she suspended too?'

'Oh, no. Anna played the victim – she was such a clever clogs.'

'*Anna?*' I squeak. 'You had a brawl with your *sister*?'

'Yes. She deserved it.' Ruth's eyes twinkle.

'What had she done?' I ask, laughing at her mischievous tone.

'She told the nuns I'd crept out after dark to meet my boyfriend.'

'And you hadn't?'

'Oh, yes, I had. But she was such a Goody Two Shoes, she couldn't bear not to sneak. I think she was jealous, actually.'

'Wow! How long were you suspended for?'

'A week. I was sent home. Our parents weren't too pleased, I can tell you.'

'Did they ever find out what it was about?'

'No – I threatened Anna that if she told them I'd rip her eyes out. And she believed me!' She throws her head back and roars with laughter, her silver curls shaking under her red woollen hat.

'Ruth! That's terrible.'

'I know – I was awful. Poor Anna . . .' she's lost in thought suddenly '. . . she was always a bit intense.'

'Maybe she's loosening up a bit?' I say. 'We had fun on our road trip, didn't we?'

Ruth nods. 'Yes, that was good for her – she needs to do a lot more of that sort of thing. She's been like a coiled spring for years now. Lying about Colin has really damaged her.'

'Do you think she'll ever forgive him?' I ask. Anna hasn't mentioned him since our trip, but he must still be on her mind.

'I wish she'd consider it, for her own sake. But I don't think it will happen, no. She's hardened her heart to him. Not that I blame her.'

'I can't believe she went through so much and I never knew,' I muse, shoving my hands into my coat pockets to keep them warm.

'Yes, she had a lot to carry all right. That's why she created that hard shell of hers, to protect herself.'

'You're a good sister, Ruth,' I blurt out. I want her to know this.

'Am I?' Ruth says, her face twisting. 'I'm not sure about

that. I feel she judges me so sometimes I deliberately press her buttons.'

'Nobody's perfect,' I say.

'Don't I know it!' She laughs. 'Even if Karl thinks I am.'

'Things are going well between the two of you, aren't they?' I smile at her.

'Yes, I guess they are,' she replies. 'There's just one bone of contention. He wants me to tell Anna about us.'

'And are you going to?'

'I don't know. If I do . . .'

'. . . it means you're moving on and it's getting serious between you two,' I finish for her.

'Exactly,' she says, glancing at me in surprise. 'When did you get so wise?'

We lapse into silence as we go on up the hill, away from the town. The cool air feels good in my lungs, the wind against my face as we stride out, falling into companionable silence. The fresh air is clearing my head. Ruth was right – getting out and walking is making me feel better.

'Here we are,' Ruth announces, coming to a stop all of a sudden. I realize we're at the gates of the graveyard and my heart drops. Is this what the walk has been about? She wants to go to Mum and Granddad's grave? I haven't been here for quite some time – it's just too painful a reminder of everything we've lost. I say nothing as Ruth pushes through the gate and walks down the narrow path to their resting place. I just follow her. If she wants to visit, I'll go with her. I owe it to her to keep her company, after everything she's done for me.

'It's so peaceful here, isn't it?' she says, as we reach their graveside, then stoops to pluck a stray weed from the mixed stone. 'I always think they have one of the best plots because the view is so good.'

We look across to the rolling hills in the distance, the winter sun now just setting behind them. The grey sky is streaked with pink as the light disappears beyond the horizon. Ruth is right: the view from here is spectacular. If Granddad can see it, wherever he is, he'll certainly be enjoying it. I close my eyes and try to remember him as he was before he got sick and the mischievous light in his eyes dimmed until it was eventually extinguished for good. He liked nothing better than a good view on a nice evening. He always maintained that the simple pleasures were the best. As for Mum, I don't know if she'd like the thought of being here or not. She spent so much of her life wandering the globe, following some faraway star. I can't help thinking, as I look around me, that this quiet spot in a small local graveyard might not be her idea of Heaven.

'I miss them,' Ruth says simply.

'Me too,' I reply. Sometimes I find it hard to imagine Mum: it's so long since she died. I have photos, of course, some video of us together too, but she still seems almost like a figment of my imagination. Maybe that's why I look for messages from her so much, to have that connection with her.

Ruth's face is sombre, pale in the fading light. 'He wasn't my first love, you know,' she says, out of nowhere. 'Your granddad.'

'Who was, then? That boyfriend you snuck out to see when you were at school?'

'Yes, actually. That's why I hated Anna so much for telling on me. When I came back after having been suspended, I found out he'd been cheating on me with another girl.'

'No! What an arsehole!' I gasp. Poor Ruth – that must have really hurt, especially when she'd risked so much for him, then suffered the consequences.

'He sort of was, all right.' She sighs. 'He broke my heart. It took me years to get over it. But you always remember your first, don't you?'

'You weren't sleeping with him, were you?' Ruth is a passionate person but to be having sex with a boy while still at school, well, it wasn't the done thing back then.

'Yes, I was,' she admits, glancing at me to check out my reaction. 'It was all very scandalous! And quite a few others too, before I met your grandfather.'

'You Jezebel!' I burst out laughing at her knowing expression.

'Yes, I suppose I was. Granddad was fine about it, luckily.'

'So you told him?' I look at the grave where he and Mum are laid to rest. He adored her so much – no wonder he didn't care about her past.

'Oh, yes, we had no secrets. It was one of the things I loved most about him – I could be completely myself. He never judged or tried to change me.'

She moves to the headstone and caresses his name with her fingers. 'He understood me like no one else could,' she says quietly, and I hear the pain in her voice.

I'm not sure what to say to that. She looks so sad that I'm unsure what I *can* say. I thought she was happier, welcoming Karl into her life, but clearly she still feels conflicted about moving on.

'Hey, Jezebel, do you fancy a bag of chips?' I suggest. 'I think we've earned them after that monster walk, don't you?' I know I'm changing the subject but this time I don't think she'll mind.

'You're a girl after my own heart, Coco Swan,' she says, smiling. But the smile doesn't quite reach her eyes so I give her a hug, as much for me as for her. As I do, I look over her shoulder, to the two names on the head-stone. The truth is, I hate this place. I never feel close to either of them here, ever. Ruth seems to find some comfort in visiting but I don't, and I don't think I ever will. All it does is remind me of what I've lost and can never get back.

As I look at the headstone, I catch sight of a small white flower peeping out from under the stones covering the grave – a weed probably. I disentangle myself from Ruth's arms and bend to uproot it when she stops me.

'No! That's not a weed, Coco,' she says. 'It's a flower.' She bends to examine it. 'Well, I never,' she exclaims.

'What is it?' I ask.

Ruth is on her hunkers now, taking a closer look at the flower that's peeking out from among the pea gravel. 'It's incredible. That's your mum's favourite flower,' she says, looking at me with wide eyes. 'I can't imagine how it ended up here, especially at this time of year. Can you see any more anywhere?'

I look around, but there's only this one small patch, on the grave. 'No, I can't.'

'How strange. I wonder how it got here. I always meant to get around to planting some, but I never did . . .'

As she says this, goose-bumps prick my skin. Mum

loved this flower and it's somehow just appeared on her grave – that's really bizarre. Like . . . a sign.

'What's it called, Ruth?' I ask.

'It's gypsophila, but it's known as "baby's breath". Such a sweet translation, I always thought.'

I inhale sharply. This flower is called baby's breath? Can that be a coincidence?

Ruth looks at me and I can tell she knows what's going through my mind. We're both thinking the same thing: could this be another sign? A message from Mum not to give up on Tatty and her baby? 'Well, if you were looking for a sign to keep going in your search, I think you've found one,' Ruth says, shaking her head in wonder at the little white flower.

'Trust Mum to throw a spanner in the works,' I say, bending to stroke the delicate petals, so tiny and yet so exquisitely perfect.

'Maybe she doesn't want you to give up just yet,' she replies, grinning at me.

'Next you'll be telling me Granddad's in on it, too!'

'Maybe he is,' she says. 'He loved a good detective story.'

'That's right . . .' Granddad was devoted to *Inspector Morse* and *Miss Marple*.

'So, what do you say, Coco?' Ruth asks, as she stands up again. 'Will you keep going?'

I look at the flower trembling in the cold breeze, fragile but standing strong. 'Well, I suppose I'd better. I don't want all you lot ganging up on me!'

'Good girl!' She claps her hands together. 'Now, what's going to be your next move?'

'Well, my next move is going to be devouring a massive

portion of chips and cod. Then I have to get to Cat's to babysit. After that . . . who knows?'

'Oh, the unknown's always so exciting, isn't it?' Ruth says, as we traipse back up the graveyard path to the gates.

And as she says it, a very clear picture appears in my head – of a very scruffy, dark-eyed Mac Gilmartin.

20

'Jesus, he sounds like a total ride,' Cat swoons.

I'm at her kitchen table, having just described my trip to Glacken and my encounter with Mac Gilmartin. 'Yeah, he was pretty nice,' I admit. 'Pity he couldn't tell me any more about Tatty's son, though.'

'We need to find out if he's married or in a relationship,' she replies thoughtfully, her mind clearly not on Tatty at all.

'Cat!'

'What?' she says innocently. 'You're not the only one who can play detective, you know. I like the sound of this guy. I can picture the two of you together.'

'I had a ten-minute conversation with the man,' I remind her.

'Yes.' She smirks. 'Ten minutes of pure Heaven by the sound of it.'

'It was all business, believe me.' I swipe at her with a tea towel, not wanting to admit outright that she's right – I did think Mac was nice.

'Ah, come on, Coco, a little bit of romance wouldn't kill you,' she says coyly. 'It doesn't have to be love, just lust.'

'You have a dirty mind. I'm not lusting after anyone,' I retort. But a little quiver in my tummy as I think about gorgeous Mac Gilmartin tells me otherwise.

'Really?' Cat raises an eyebrow. 'So you're not fantasizing about getting down and dirty with Mr Grizzly Adams in his hay loft, then?'

'Shut up!' I squeal. 'I never should have described him to you!'

'I'm very glad you did.' She chortles. 'He sounds yummy!'

'What are you two talking about?' David ambles into the kitchen, straightening his tie.

'Oh, nothing,' Cat says airily. 'Hey, you're hot!'

David does a twirl, showing off his smart navy suit. She's right – he looks really handsome. 'I scrub up well,' he says modestly. 'And you do too.' He winks at her.

'Oh, God, get away out of that,' she moans. 'I'm a mess.'

Far from looking terrible, Cat is as gorgeous as ever. She's wearing a tight red bandage-style dress that accentuates her every petite curve, and her hair is pulled back into the sort of elegant up-do that I could never achieve, even if I worked on it for a full twenty-four hours. I peer down at my regular uniform of jeans and sweatshirt and think she might be right about me – maybe I should make more of an effort, glam myself up a bit.

'No, you're not, you're a ride,' he says, grinning at her.

'You have to say that.' She giggles. 'It's in the contract.'

'Would you ever stop fishing for compliments?' I say to her. 'You look beautiful and you know it. Now, get going or you'll be late.'

She glances at her watch. 'Are you sure you'll be all right?' she asks. 'Mark will be back at eight, OK?'

'I still think he shouldn't have been allowed out,' David says, checking his tie in the mirror.

'We can't keep him locked up, David. It's not like he was going nightclubbing, he was only calling round to a friend's.'

'Yeah, well, he'd better be back here on time, or he won't be going out again until he's an old-age pensioner,' David says grimly.

Cat glances at me and I nod in reply – our shorthand is so good that I know what she's asking me to do without her even saying a word. I have to try to talk to Mark again and gain his confidence.

'Will you two get a move on? You're going to be late.' I tut, hustling them out.

'You'll be OK, then?' Cat asks, one more time, shrugging on her black velvet coat.

'I'll be fine,' I reassure her. 'I'm quite a good babysitter, you know.'

I'm delighted to step in. Cat and David never go out together alone any more – everything revolves around the kids, their after-school activities and play dates. Cat often says the boys have much better social lives than their parents do. A night out with her husband is exactly what the doctor ordered and I'm more than happy to make sure she has one. Maybe it'll take some of the pressure off: what with work, the energy required in caring for the twins, and now Mark acting up and getting into trouble at school, I reckon she needs to let off some steam. Besides, I haven't seen the boys in ages and I love spending time with them. Yes, they can be a handful, but that's not going to last for ever. Mark used to be boisterous too, and now

I can hardly get a word out of him. I have to make the most of the twins while they still think I'm cool and have, if not all, at least some of the answers. Before I know it they'll be all but ignoring me.

Cat pauses at the door and hugs me. 'Thanks for this, Coco. I'm really looking forward to tonight.'

'Yeah,' David agrees, shrugging on his coat. 'Just you, me, a bottle of wine and a three-course meal. And no work, Cat!' He wags a finger at her.

'I promise,' she says seriously. 'Unless it's an absolute emergency.'

David makes a face at me. 'Coco, will you tell her, please? She needs to switch off for once.'

'Listen to your husband,' I instruct her sternly. 'Otherwise you'll end up a mad old spinster like me.'

'I have a feeling that might change, if the gorgeous Mac has anything to do with it.' She dances away from me as I reach out to slap her for being so bloody cheeky.

Suddenly the twins come barrelling into the hallway, flinging their chubby little arms around me. 'Coco! Coco! Can we have chocolate?' they ask.

'I didn't hear that,' Cat says, clamping her hands over her ears as she and David walk out of the door. 'Good luck, Coco!'

An hour and a half later I'm an exhausted mess. But I'm also having the time of my life.

'Just one more story, Coco? *Pleeeease?*'

Michael and Patrick are both on my lap on the small rocking chair in their bedroom. I remember Cat breast-feeding them in this chair – I used to marvel at the way she could manage it with very little fuss, holding them confidently like little rugby balls under each arm.

The chair definitely isn't built for one broad-shouldered adult and two squirming five-year-olds, though – my back is starting to ache and both twins are hanging onto me for dear life, not ready to admit defeat and slide to the floor. I shouldn't have given in to their pleading to be read a story in this thing. I should have got them both into bed first, as Cat advised. I just couldn't resist their chubby little faces, though – when they're on a charm offensive, it's really hardcore. I can only imagine what kind of tag team they're going to make years from now when they're dating. Women won't stand a chance against these two professionals.

'Aw, come on, guys. I've read you four stories already. It's time for bed,' I say, trying to stretch my cramping legs. The twins are getting heavier and bigger every day – sometimes it feels like every second. Now I know what Cat means when she says she has only to turn her back to make a ham sandwich for them to shoot up another inch.

'I don't wanna go to bed,' Michael says, truculent now.

'Me neither,' Patrick agrees, pulling his thumb out of his mouth and looking at me mournfully. His big violet eyes, the mirror image of Cat's, are huge in his face.

They're getting a little tearful, I can tell. If I don't distract them now, they might start crying for Cat – maybe even insist on phoning her. The last thing I want to do is interrupt her night out. I try to think of some way to distract them. Food or drink is out of the question at this point – I don't want any puking or bed-wetting on my watch. Then it comes to me.

'But sure if you don't go to bed, how will the tooth fairy come?' I ask, inspired.

Both boys lost a tooth today – almost within minutes of each other – and have been happily chattering about an impending visit all evening. Cat even put the teeth under their pillows earlier so they wouldn't lose them. In all the excitement of having me to babysit, they seem to have forgotten this. Maybe a reminder will convince them that climbing into bed and falling asleep immediately is a very good idea.

They look at each other now, as if they're deciding whether they should agree to snuggle down and go to sleep or not.

'Ryan Delaney said the tooth fairy isn't real,' Michael announces. 'He said it's mummies and daddies who put money under the pillows.'

'Yeah. And he's in third class,' Patrick agrees. 'So he knows stuff.'

I gulp. What do I say to this? It's like being asked if Santa is real – there's no good answer.

'Ryan Delaney is a tool,' I hear someone say. It's Mark, standing in the doorway, back on time, thankfully. He's wearing a pair of baggy jeans, slung low on his hips, and a Hollister T-shirt tucked inside. Cat went through hell to get that T-shirt for his birthday – she queued up outside to get into the store and did battle with hordes of adolescents when she eventually got in. Then, when she gave it to him, he barely grunted and said it was the wrong colour.

'How the hell was I supposed to be able to tell the difference?' she complained to me later. 'It was so damn dark in there, I couldn't see my hand before my face.'

'What's a tool, Aunty Coco?' Michael asks me now.

'A big eejit,' I reply, smiling at Mark over the twins' heads. I really hope he's not going to give me the cold shoulder. I haven't seen him since I tried to talk to him about Sean O'Malley – and I don't know what his reaction to me is going to be.

'Ryan Delaney's not a big eejit!' Patrick protests. 'He can get ten baskets in a row – with a proper basketball!'

This sounds pretty impressive, to be fair.

'Listen, I can get twenty baskets in a row, can't I?' Mark replies, cool as a breeze.

The twins look at each other. 'Yeah,' they agree reluctantly.

'Yeah. So I know way more than Ryan Delaney and I'm telling you that the tooth fairy is real, OK?'

'Are you sure?' Michael asks, doubt in his voice.

'Yes, I'm sure. I saw him.'

'You did?' the twins say together, their little faces lighting up.

'Yep,' Mark replies seriously. 'But you can't tell anyone, OK?'

'Why not?'

'Because the tooth fairy wouldn't like it, of course – he might get in trouble with his boss. Now, if I was you I'd hop into bed quick. If he comes and sees you're awake . . . well . . .'

The boys spring off my lap and dive into their beds, pulling the covers up to their chins, desperate not to have the tooth fairy see them being bold. I shoot a grateful look at Mark and he nods back – anything their older brother says goes, apparently. I only wish I had that magic touch.

'How much do you think we'll get?' Patrick asks me, as I tuck him in under his Bob the Builder duvet.

'I don't know what the tooth-fairy rate is, these days.' I smile, bending to kiss him and then his brother. 'But I'd say the quicker you go to sleep, the more it will be.'

Two pairs of eyes are already closed as I switch on a small lava lamp I brought them back from the markets in London.

'I love you, Aunty Coco,' Patrick says.

'Me too,' Michael agrees.

My heart swells. Is this what Mum used to feel when I kissed her goodnight? This surge of unconditional love? It's pretty powerful stuff.

'I love you guys, too,' I say, feeling a little teary, it has to be said. 'Now go to sleep and have sweet dreams.'

Back downstairs, Mark is sprawled on the sofa in the kitchen, laptop in front of him.

'Have a nice time at your friend's?' I ask, keeping my tone nice and neutral as I walk in. Cat has just texted to ask if he's home and thankfully I was able to tell her the truth.

'Yeah,' he replies. 'It was OK.'

'Would you like a cheese toastie?'

This is my master plan. Mark can't resist my cheese toasties. They're his favourite and have been since he was little and I used to cut them into shapes with cookie-cutters. I'm hoping the offer will restore the equilibrium between us after the up-cycling class. It can't do any harm anyway.

I wait with bated breath to see what his response will be, pasting a smile on my face to show him I'm not going to ask any more intrusive questions or get on his case. If I do, he might just retreat to his room and that would be game over.

'OK,' he says, and I exhale with relief. 'Don't forget the HP sauce.'

'How could I?' I scoff. 'I'm the *Queen* of HP sauce, remember?'

He laughs, and I know we're back on safe ground. I'll just have to bide my time and hope he might tell me what's going on when he's good and ready.

'Are you having another of those up-cycling classes soon?' he asks, as I turn on the grill and take the cheese out of the fridge.

'Why? Are you coming back?'

He grins, a little sheepishly. 'Maybe. If I'm not going to get the third degree.'

'I'm only trying to help you, Mark,' I say carefully. 'If you need help, that is.'

He pauses and our eyes meet. I'm hoping against hope that he'll open up to me, tell me what's going on. But I can't push him, much as I want to.

'Remember you saw me talking to Sean O'Malley?' he says at last.

'Yeah,' I say, my heart thumping.

'If I tell you something, will you promise not to tell Mum?' His eyes are still on mine.

'Aw, Mark, I can't promise that,' I reply. 'But I will promise that if you're in trouble I'll help you find a way to get out of it.'

He takes a deep breath. 'Sean wants me to smuggle weed into the youth disco in the hotel so he can sell it,' he says.

'The little bollix!' I gasp.

Mark laughs grimly. 'Yeah, something like that,' he says. 'He's been on my case pretty bad about it. He's not giving up.'

'What's he been saying?' I'm filled with outrage and trying to control my reaction is pretty difficult.

'He said if I didn't do it, he'd report the hotel to the police for underage drinking.'

'But your mum's really strict about that – she'd never let it happen.'

'I know. But that wouldn't stop Sean trying to make trouble for her. And she doesn't need that.' He looks down.

'Aw, Mark, you've been trying to protect her, haven't you?' The same rush of love I felt for the twins earlier is bursting in my chest. All this time, when they were at odds, Mark was trying to shield Cat from trouble, not cause it.

He shrugs, pink rising in his cheeks. 'She has enough on her plate. She doesn't need this aggro too,' he mutters.

'Is that what the fight on the plane back from Spain was about?'

'Yeah. Sean said Mum was a slag. I lost the head.'

My hand flies to my mouth. 'The little shit! And he said something on Facebook too, didn't he? That night in the shop?'

Mark nods. 'It's been getting pretty intense.'

I'm appalled. This thug is making Mark's life a misery, that's clear. 'But why didn't you say anything to your mum or dad?' I ask.

'I didn't want them to get stressed out,' he admits. 'I thought I could handle it myself.'

'Oh, Mark,' I say.

'Yeah, it was stupid. And now I sort of don't know what to do.'

He looks at me helplessly and a rush of pure anger courses through me. I'm going to sort this out, if it's the last thing I do. That little thug isn't going to get away with intimidating and bullying Mark, no way. Over my dead body.

'Don't you worry,' I say fiercely. 'I'll think of something and we'll sort it out, I promise.'

'But how, Coco? Nobody messes with Sean.'

'And nobody messes with us either, Mark,' I say firmly.

My mind is working overtime. Cat is going to hit the roof when she hears about this, so it'd be good to have a plan in place before I tell her. But how can I resolve it without making things even harder for Mark at school? I don't know yet, but there has to be a way and, come hell or high water, I'm going to figure it out.

21

A few days later, I'm in the room off the shop floor, vigorously sanding down a rocking chair and deep in thought about Mark. There's something about sanding furniture that's therapeutic. Maybe it's the rhythmic motion of sliding the roughened paper back and forth across the surface that's so soothing. You can just lose yourself in the process, let your mind clear and allow it to wander wherever it wants to. Some people think it's the most tedious task on the face of the Earth, but I love putting in the elbow grease – it's so satisfying. Today, though, I'm going at it as if the chair is Sean O'Malley's face and I'm scrubbing it out of our lives. I have to come up with a way to get rid of him, without causing him to bully Mark even more.

I'm miles away when the shop bell tinkles. Reluctantly I stand up, my knees creaking. I leave the rocking chair and go to see if a customer needs my help. I have to make a real effort to paste a smile on my face, though: the last thing I want to do is make small-talk when I'm so preoccupied, but needs must. Ruth has taught me over the years that a welcoming smile is crucial to create a warm atmosphere in which people feel relaxed enough to wander around and browse. Scowling at them isn't conducive to good business.

'Hello there,' I call, to a man who's examining a blue-and-white vase I bought at auction ages ago.

He turns to me.

With a bolt of shock, I see he's Mac Gilmartin. He looks smarter today, less scruffy, in dark jeans, a navy fleece and a checked scarf. I'm so surprised, I have to look twice to make sure it's him.

'Hi, Coco,' he says. From the way he grins at me, it's obvious he's not surprised to see me and that this is no coincidence.

'Er, hello,' I stutter, struggling to contain how flustered I am. It looks like I won't have to pluck up the courage to go back to Glacken and ask him what he knows about James because he's standing less than five feet away from me, so close I can smell his very pleasant musky after-shave.

'I remembered you said you had an antiques shop in Dronmore,' he explains, smiling again. 'I thought I'd pop in when I was passing.'

So he didn't come here to see me on purpose then. Why would he? I'm not sure why I was even thinking that.

He glances around, taking in the shop and all the paraphernalia heaped high. Then his gaze returns to me and he looks me up and down. I blush a little under his stare. I'm a mess, of course, as usual – I'm wearing my oldest working gear to sand the rocking chair and my hair is tied up in a rag to protect it. If I was trying to make a good impression, I'd be failing miserably.

'I love the display. Did you do that?' He gestures to the window.

'Thank you. Yes, I did.' I try to sound completely cool, but I'm not sure I've pulled it off.

'How long has the shop been here?' he asks.

'A long time.'

'How long is long?' His eyes twinkle at me and I remember how he teased me about not giving anything away the last time we met.

'Well,' I wipe my hands on my thighs and loosen my hair out of the rag, 'my grandfather opened it in the 1950s.'

'I see. So you run it now, do you?'

'With my grandmother, yes.'

'Who's talking about me?' I hear Ruth call. She's coming down the stairs and I haven't had a chance to warn her of who's here. This is the very person she's been telling me I need to go back and talk to, and here he is, standing in Swan's like it's nothing out of the ordinary.

'I was,' Mac replies, as she breezes in, her silver curls swinging loose around her shoulders, contrasting with the bright blue smock she has on. She looks electric.

'And you are?' She stretches out her hand to take his, her smile broad as it always is with strangers. Strangers are only friends we haven't met yet – that's her sunny outlook.

'I'm Mac Gilmartin,' he replies, shaking her hand firmly.

'From Glacken,' I add with meaning.

Ruth's eyebrows shoot into her hairline. 'Aha. I see.'

She looks at me and I shrug. I know as much – or as little – as she does about this unexpected visit. Why has he turned up out of the blue? Was he really just passing, or is there more to it?

278

'So, Mac from Glacken,' she says, 'let's have some tea, shall we?'

'I don't want to put you to any trouble,' he replies politely.

'It's no trouble. I was just about to put the kettle on, so you've come at the perfect time. How do you like it?'

'Well, if you're sure, I'd love a cup,' he says. 'Just milk, please.'

'Coco?'

'Yes, please,' I say. Although I'd rather have a very stiff drink after this shock. Ruth glances conspiratorially at me, then disappears into the back, leaving Mac and me alone again.

'You offer excellent service, I must say,' he says, smiling at me again. 'Do you give tea to everyone who comes in?'

'Not really,' I reply.

'Well, I'm honoured,' he says.

He's very good at making idle chit-chat but he still hasn't told me what he's doing here. I decide to force his hand. 'So, you were just in the area, were you?'

'Yes. I was doing some business nearby when I remembered that you said you had an antiques shop round here, so I thought I'd visit. You sort of disappeared off the face of the Earth the other day.'

'Er, yeah, sorry about that. I had to leave quickly,' I explain, deliberately keeping my reasons for scarpering as vague as possible.

'I gathered that.' He smiles. 'The puppy's making a great recovery, I'm happy to report.'

I remember the tiny puppy that had been thrown from a moving car onto the motorway. 'I'm so glad. He was really cute.'

There's a small pause while we survey each other.

'Any more news about that letter?' he asks.

'No. I haven't actually done any more about it,' I reply, feeling immediately uncomfortable.

'Why not?'

'Well, I've been busy.' I gesture vaguely around the shop. 'Plus, you know, it's nothing to do with me . . .'

'Well, I thought it was really nice, what you were doing.'

'Thanks,' I murmur.

'And I might be able to help you.'

He turns away from me, so he's looking out of the shop window. My eyes follow his and I see Karl wiping clean his specials blackboard, then beginning to write slowly. Chicken fillets are on offer today – three for the price of two. It's taking all my willpower not to demand that he tells me what he knows, how he thinks he can help.

'So, here we are.' Ruth is back with a tray of tea. 'I have some biscuits too, in case anyone would like some.'

'Thanks.' Mac smiles at her. 'I'm starving – I didn't have breakfast.'

Ruth tuts. Not having a hearty breakfast is a cardinal sin in her book. 'How did you manage that?' she asks disapprovingly, as he bites into a biscuit.

'I guess I just forgot.'

'Didn't your wife try to feed you before you left the house?' she asks, all innocence. She's digging for information, using a little flirting as her spade.

'I'm not married,' he replies easily. I can't help it – my insides do a little leap when I hear this. Stupid, but still . . .

'Aha, a lonesome bachelor. Well, we'll have to feed you up, won't we? Here, help yourself to another.' She pours him some tea and pushes the plate of biscuits towards him. 'So. Coco tells me you have a dog shelter?'

'That's right, I do.'

'How long have you been running it?' she asks.

'A few years on and off . . . I sort of fell into it, really.'

'And now it's taken over your life?'

'Something like that. Luckily I can fit it in around my other work commitments, but it's definitely a juggle.'

So he has another job, too – I wonder what he does. I'm just about to ask him when Ruth pipes up wistfully, 'I'd love a dog.'

I'm amazed. 'I didn't know that,' I say.

'Didn't you? Oh, yes, I've always wanted one, but your granddad was never much of a dog lover. And we don't have much space here . . .' She gestures to the cramped shop, piled high with stock in every corner.

'A little one might suit you,' Mac says. 'They don't need much room – just a walk or two each day.'

'Do you have anything in mind?'

I stare at her. What's she doing?

'Well, we have a lovely little Yorkie that came to us recently. We had almost rehomed her, but that fell through. Er, Coco saw her, didn't you? Pudding – do you remember?'

'Yeah, she was cute,' I reply.

'Maybe I could come and see her,' Ruth says.

'Definitely,' he replies. 'You two may be perfect for each other.'

They smile at each other like long-lost friends. It's sort of bizarre.

'So, Coco told you about the mysterious letter she found, huh?' she says, changing tack.

'Well, yes, she did. And I was just telling her that I may be able to help.'

'Really?' Ruth leans forward, her face lighting up, barely able to contain her excitement.

'Yes. Well, you see, the truth is, I wasn't exactly just passing,' he says, colouring a little around his neck.

'Oh?' I say, feeling oddly pleased. So he came here on purpose, then – my tummy does a little flip at this. Out of the corner of my eye I see Ruth look from him to me, a tiny smile on her lips, as if she's figuring it all out.

'You've found out something about James, haven't you?' she asks.

He nods at her, then turns to me. 'Yes. After you left, Coco, I became curious about him, so I called the estate agents who sold me the house, Carroll and Carroll.'

'Aha!' Ruth says, punching the air. 'And did they know anything?'

'They did, as it happens. They had an address for him in Port-on-Sea.'

Ruth claps her hands together. 'So now we know where he lives. How clever of you, Mac!' she whoops.

Mac blushes further. 'It was no trouble,' he says, almost bashfully. 'Here, I wrote it down for you.'

Ruth takes the scrap of paper from him. 'Port-on-Sea is a beautiful spot – I used to go there all the time with my late husband. You can't beat the sea air. We loved it there – we used to take picnics, when we were first married, before your mum was born, Coco . . .' She trails off, as if remembering happy times long gone with Granddad.

'Thanks for all this, Mac,' I say to him, our eyes meeting for a beat too long. 'It was very kind of you. I really appreciate it.'

'No trouble,' he replies. 'I hope you don't think I was sticking my nose in where it's not wanted.'

'Not at all. I really didn't know what I was going to do next, so you've solved that dilemma for me.'

We smile at each other.

'Do you think you could take Coco to see him, Mac?' Ruth interrupts.

'Ruth!' I protest. What's she thinking of? I'll kill her!

Mac seems a little startled by her request, but he has the good grace to agree politely. 'Em, yes, of course, if she'd like,' he replies, glancing at me.

'Perfect,' Ruth says, oozing charm. 'Coco's car is off the road for repair. It won't be out of the workshop for days yet – they still haven't found out what's wrong with it.' She gives a dramatic sigh, as if my car's mysterious ailment is keeping her up at night. It's a complete lie, of course. My car's fine. It needs a service and it's nearly out of petrol, but that's nothing new.

'I can drive you, no problem,' Mac says gallantly.

'Honestly, there's no need . . .' I'm mortified.

'Coco, don't be silly. Mac is offering. And it's not far from here, is it?' Ruth adds.

'I'm sure Mac has much better things to do with his

time,' I say, through gritted teeth, staring hard at her. 'Besides, he's already done more than enough.'

'But wouldn't it be grand if the two of you went together? In fact, you could grab the bull by the horns and go right now. We're not exactly rushed off our feet here.'

She smiles encouragingly at us both and I try not to glare at her.

'Actually, I was just working on something, Mac,' I say. 'Maybe another day.'

'Oh, nonsense,' Ruth tinkles. 'You can do that any day of the week.'

'But –'

'Coco. If James is the person you're looking for, then time is of the essence, isn't it, Mac?'

'Em, yes?' he replies uncertainly, glancing at me.

'Sensible boy.' Ruth is beaming at him now. 'And you're sure you don't mind, Mac?'

'Actually, there's a dog shelter close to Port-on-Sea that I've been meaning to drop in on. This afternoon could work . . .'

'Well, there you go. It's Fate!' Ruth claps her hands with glee. 'Now, let me get you a flask of coffee for the journey.'

She disappears at speed, probably so that I can't protest any more.

'Sorry about that,' I say to Mac. 'She's not exactly subtle.'

'Don't worry,' he says. 'She's great.'

A silence falls between us as we glance awkwardly at each other, like teenagers.

'Oh, I nearly forgot!' he exclaims. 'I brought this to show you.'

'What is it?'

He rummages in a brown-paper bag. 'An old compilation album from the fifties,' he says, pulling out an ancient vinyl record. 'I'm a bit of a music nerd, so when you mentioned Tatty Moynihan to me, the name rang a bell. She usually sang as part of a duo called the Chanelles, with another woman called –'

'Bonnie Bradbury.'

His eyes widen. 'Yes,' he says. 'Not many people know that.'

'I met Bonnie in London,' I explain, 'when I was researching Tatty's story. She did say Tatty'd made a recording once, but I never thought I'd find it.'

'Ah, I see. Well, that must be what's on here. I think it's pretty rare actually.'

He hands me the record and my hand flies involuntarily to my mouth when I see her name in print on the back.

'I can't believe it,' I whisper, overcome with emotion.

'She's singing a Duke Ellington number. I should have brought my old gramophone so you could listen to it.'

'It's OK,' I say. 'I have one right there.'

I cross the floor to where Granddad's record player sits, slip the vinyl from its cover and let the needle fall. A haunting voice fills the room. It's full of regret and longing, sorrow and melancholy, singing a song I recognize immediately. Tears spring to my eyes as I listen and I try to fight them back. This is her – my Tatty. Not only do I know what she looks like, I know now what she sounded like. Ruth reappears from the doorway, coffee flask in hand, tears in her eyes too. She doesn't need to ask, she's already guessed who is singing.

'Thank you, Mac,' I say, smiling at him. 'You don't know how much this means to me.'

And as I say it, right at that second, I know for sure how much it really does mean to me, and why. It's as if I've reached right into the past and touched Tatty, felt her spirit come alive. And not just her either, because the song she's singing, a tune of love and loss, was the one that Mum used to hum to me as I fell asleep when I was little. Why did I never know it was called 'In A Sentimental Mood'? Or that Duke Ellington recorded it? I guess because Mum died before she could tell me if it meant something special to her or was one of her favourites. This has to be a sign from her – it has to be. The song I knew as a child is the same song that Tatty and her lover called their own, the reason why Tatty named her son Duke, even. It can't be a coincidence. Hearing Tatty sing it now, it's as if my story and hers are reaching their own crescendo, joined together across the years. I can only imagine how her son would feel if he heard this.

'I'm sorry, have I upset you?' Mac asks, with concern. He has no idea why I'm reacting as I am.

'Not at all. Quite the opposite. Thank you,' I reply, wiping my eyes and trying to compose myself.

'You're welcome,' he says, smiling at me. 'Are you ready to go?'

'She was born ready!' Ruth quips.

'Give me five minutes,' I say to them, making for the stairs and my room. 'If I'm going to meet Tatty's son at last, the least I can do is dress for the occasion!'

22

We're on the road, me and Mac Gilmartin, the almost-stranger from Glacken. I'm feeling a mix of nerves and excitement at the thought that I might be about to meet Tatty's son. How will he react to the letter I have for him? I can't imagine what I would do if someone landed on my doorstep and gave me a letter from Mum, almost from beyond the grave. I'm sure I would treasure it, though, especially if it was as beautiful as the one Tatty had written. But then again, maybe the whole thing would come as such a shock that I might not want to read it. All of these jumbled thoughts are running through my mind as we drive along, leaving Swan's behind.

I'm also feeling oddly uncomfortable sitting in such close proximity to Mac in the front of his battered old van, but I'm trying to stifle that schoolgirl feeling. Mac is just being kind. There's no more to it than that. In fact, Ruth railroaded him into helping – the poor guy probably has far better things to do with his time. The only thing making me feel slightly less embarrassed about it is that he wants to visit some dog shelter close to Port-on-Sea, so it's not a totally wasted trip for him.

'I'm sorry about all the dog hair,' he says, as he shifts down a gear to round a bend. 'It's an occupational hazard, I'm afraid.'

'I hadn't noticed it,' I lie, plucking another hair from my fitted black jacket, the one I usually save for best.

I'd changed out of my old clothes into smarter jeans, a black top and jacket and my only pair of heels. Then I'd slipped on Mum's favourite pearls for luck, added Cat's pink sequined scarf and hat and grabbed Tatty's Chanel bag. Ruth raised an eyebrow as I left, noticing I had made much more of an effort than usual. But I'd felt I had to – not because I was going to spend time with Mac but because I knew this was going to be a significant moment in Tatty's story and I wanted to look the part. OK, maybe a *small* part of it was because of Mac too. He'd only ever seen me in scruffy gear and I might have wanted to impress him, just a little. But I wasn't about to admit that to Ruth – I can't even properly admit it to myself.

'I have a roll of sticky tape in here somewhere, if you want to try taking some of it off,' Mac says now, eyeing me sideways. 'I probably should have told you not to wear a dark jacket, sorry.'

'Don't worry,' I reply, wondering how I'm ever going to get it looking half decent again. It's as if the hairs are rapidly multiplying as I watch. How many dogs have sat in this front seat?

I'm just thinking this when I feel something hot and wet breathing in my ear and I jump, startled. It's the Labrador from Glacken House – right behind me in the back of Mac's van. I hadn't noticed him when I got in.

'Horatio, get down!' Mac says. 'Sorry, Coco.'

'That's OK. I remember Horatio,' I say, patting his head. He rests it on my shoulder, happily snuffling into

289

my collar, as if he remembers me too, his big brown eyes locking on mine.

'He likes to come with me when I go out,' Mac says, looking straight ahead and concentrating on the road. 'He hates being left behind, I think because of his background.'

'What's his story?' I ask.

'Horatio is sort of special,' he says. 'He was my first. I found him on the road a few years ago. He'd been dumped there. Poor guy was skin and bone and his leg was broken in three places.'

'I can't believe someone would do that to this gorgeous dog.'

'Yeah, the vet thought he was going to have to lose the leg, but miraculously, as you can see, he didn't. He still limps, but he's as fast as anything.'

I think of how he jumped over the gate when I saw him last. 'But no one wants to adopt him? He's so adorable – how could anyone resist him?'

'He's not really up for adoption,' Mac replies, a little bashfully. 'Like I said, he's special.'

'Your resident meet-and-greet?'

'Exactly.' He laughs as Horatio gives my neck a lick and I squirm.

'Why did you decide to open a dog shelter?' I ask, curious to know more about him.

'Well, I never did as such,' he replies. 'After I found Horatio, word sort of got out. Someone brought a spaniel to me. And then someone else found another dog at the far side of the village and brought him, too. It's mushroomed since then, I suppose.'

'You must love dogs.'

'Guilty.'

'What's your favourite breed?'

'I like them all,' he replies, glancing at me for a millisecond, smiling slightly.

'I love basset hounds,' I say.

'Why – their long ears?'

'I don't know, really. I had a dog book when I was a kid and there was a basset hound on the front. I guess it made a big impression on me.'

'I had that book,' he says.

'You did not!'

'I did too – *The Great Big Book of Dogs*. I got it from Santa.'

'So did I!' I gasp.

'Maybe it was on special offer somewhere,' he says, and we both laugh.

'My second favourite dog in that book was the Irish wolfhound,' I remember aloud. 'I've never seen one in real life, though.'

'I have – at an olde-worlde banquet once. He was pretty impressive I have to say, sort of regal. He ran off with a side of beef. I don't think they were very pleased with him. The jester, who was supposed to be looking after him, got a right rollicking.' He laughs again and I notice how his eyes crinkle attractively at the edges.

'I've never been to an olde-worlde banquet. Was it fun?' I ask, trying to drag my gaze away from his face.

'Not exactly. I was there for work – and all that harping gave me a headache.'

'What? Like people were fighting?'

'No, harping – as in the harpist? She was at it all night. There's only so much harping you can listen to in five hours before you start to lose your sense of humour.'

'Aha.' I giggle.

'So, I've told you my dark secrets – now you have to tell me yours.'

'I don't have any, really,' I say.

'You live with your grandmother?'

'That's not a secret.'

'Unusual, though.'

'My mother died just before I was thirteen. I never knew my father.'

'I see.' He takes his eyes off the road and they rest on mine for a second. 'Sorry.'

'It's OK. It was a long time ago. And Ruth's great.'

'Why do you call her that? Ruth?'

'She prefers it. She says it's not as ageing.'

'Ah, I can see her point. When I'm a grandfather, I'll definitely get all the grandkids to call me Mac. Mac-Daddy, maybe.' He drums his fingers on the steering wheel and I find myself staring at his hands.

'Mac-Daddy?' I ask, pulling my eyes away.

'Yeah, why not? It'd be cool, right?'

'Er, I don't think so.'

'Really?' He frowns. 'Mac-Granddaddy, then.'

'You're pretty sure you're going to be a granddad!'

'Of course!' he replies. 'Aren't you going to be a glamorous granny, like Ruth?'

'Er, I'm far from glamorous,' I say, blushing a little.

'I dunno about that. You look pretty good to me.'

There's a beat of embarrassed silence between us,

and I try desperately to think of something else to talk about.

'Do you work at the shelter full-time?' I ask. I'm itching to find out more about the other job he referred to, but I don't want to be obvious about it.

'Not exactly. I pitch in when I'm there, of course, but it's not my main work. I have a couple of helpers who volunteer.'

There it is – his mysterious work again.

'What do you do again?' I ask. 'I can't remember.'

'You probably can't remember because I never told you.' He grins, still keeping his eyes on the road ahead.

'Didn't you?' I reply, pretending to be confused.

'No, I didn't. But, since you ask, I'm a jingle writer. I write music for ads.'

'You're kidding!'

'Nope.' He shakes his head. 'It's true.'

'That's really cool. Would I know any of your jingles?' I'm fascinated.

'You might. You know that insurance one, with the guy and the guitar?'

'You wrote that?' It's one of the best-known ads on TV.

'Yep, that was me,' he confirms solemnly. 'Some of my better work, I have to say.'

'It's so catchy!' I say. 'When I get that in my head, I can never get it out again. I can be singing it for hours – it drives me mad!'

'You're just saying that to make me feel good, aren't you?' he replies drily.

'Sorry, but it's true. It drives Ruth mad, too. We sing it to each other, back and forth. "If you're broke and you can't get no quote, then just don't give up hope . . .'" I'm singing unselfconsciously at the top of my lungs when I realize that Mac is roaring laughing. I stop. 'What's wrong? Did I mix up the words?'

'No, it's just really funny to hear you sing it like that.'

I'm suddenly shy. 'I don't have a very good voice.'

'On the contrary, you have a great voice,' he says, and our eyes meet.

'So, er, would I know any of your other ads?' I ask, awkward and suddenly a bit sweaty.

'Well, I did a particularly good one for an organic haemorrhoid cream a few years ago.'

'You did not!' I snort.

'I did too,' he replies. He glances at me with a smile, then launches into a deep-voiced rendition: 'If you have an itch and you wanna scratch . . .'

'. . . and you don't wanna get a rash . . .' I join in.

'You know it?' he asks, cocking one eyebrow.

'Who doesn't?' I giggle.

'Keep going.'

'Only if you join in.'

'All right so, from the top – one, two, three, four.'

And as the miles roll by, the green fields stretching as far as the eye can see, we sing together and I can't remember being as stupidly happy in a very long time.

It seems as if we're at Port-on-Sea in no time and Mac is steering the van into the pot-holed driveway of a small, ramshackle cottage.

'This is the address the estate agent gave me,' he says, pulling up the handbrake.

We sit and look at it in silence. The pale blue paint is flaking off the wooden window frames, obviously succumbing to the salty sea air, and the climbing roses, which must have been beautiful once, hang dejectedly from the trellis, their leaves blackened and pockmarked, no chance of them flowering even when summer arrives. Weeds push their way through cracks in the gravel path and the lawn is completely overgrown. This cottage needs some tender loving care – it almost looks as if no one lives there.

'It must have been lovely in its day,' I remark.

'Yeah. It looks like it needs some work, but it's certainly the picture-perfect location,' Mac says. 'Imagine waking up to that view every morning.'

I look to where he's pointing and see a vast expanse of blue water in the distance, sparkling in the pale sunshine, the seagulls freewheeling overhead.

'Wow. No wonder he wanted to move here.'

'Shall we go and see if he's in?' Mac looks at me, a question in his eyes.

'Part of me feels like turning around and leaving,' I admit.

'And the other part?' He smiles.

'Feels like banging the door down.' I laugh.

'Let's go with that part,' he replies, winking at me. 'Be brave – isn't that right, Horatio?'

Horatio licks my neck again in response. I take a deep breath, close my eyes, think of Mum and Tatty and push myself out of the van.

I ring the doorbell and we wait. I ring again, still nothing. The third time, I'm losing hope. It looks like James isn't in.

'We might be out of luck,' Mac says.

'I can't believe it,' I say, thoroughly fed up. I stand on tiptoe and peep into the front window, but I can't see much through the shabby net curtains.

'Let me call the estate agent, see if he can get me a phone number,' Mac says. 'I'll just be a tick.'

As he strides back to the van I hear wisps of music from somewhere inside. I have to strain to catch them, but it seems they're coming from the back.

I follow the sound, round the side of the cottage, until I reach a small conservatory tacked onto the rear, looking straight out over the water. Inside, stark naked except for a straw hat and a bandanna round his neck, a man is working on a sculpture. He has his back to me, so I'm getting a panoramic view of his saggy buttocks. It's surprising enough to make me gasp. Probably sensing he's being watched, the man suddenly twirls around, treating me to a full frontal, and I fight the urge to throw my hands in front of my face. Instead I concentrate on keeping my eyes trained on his. I don't think I'll ever get rid of that particular mental image. I'll have to add it to the one of Karl in his Homer Simpson briefs. How many more ageing men will I see in the buff? I'm starting to make a habit of it.

He smiles at me, unfazed to see me peering in at him from the garden. His eyes are a bright blue and his hair a shock of white. He beckons at me to come in and, tummy somersaulting, I open the glass door and step inside.

'Hello,' he says, turning down the music with a remote control. 'Can I help you?'

'Er, hello, I'm sorry to intrude . . .' I don't know where to look.

'Don't be.' He smiles. 'I don't mind, although you might.'

I blink in the winter sunlight that bounces off the conservatory glass and into my eyes. It's so warm in here, compared to the chill outside, that it's almost tropical.

'I prefer to work in the nude,' he explains, casually reaching across and shrugging on a dressing gown, tying it at the waist. 'It clears my mind, I find. Now, how can I help you, my dear?'

He's friendly anyway. That's good. At least he's not kicking me out without giving me a chance to explain why I'm here.

'I'm not sure where to begin,' I say, trying to gather my thoughts and fight the urge to run away. Coming face to face with him like this has completely thrown me. I'm clutching Tatty's bag for courage. I'll have to hand it over to him soon. This will be the last time I'll ever have it in my hands.

'Sounds ominous. Am I in trouble?'

'No, no, nothing like that, it's just . . .' I reach for Mum's pearls automatically, fiddling with them at my neck as I search for the right words.

Looking at him now, his broad, open face, I don't know where to start. I might be about to change his life for ever, give him news about his past that he might not want to hear.

'Why don't you tell me your name?' he says, as I flounder.

'Coco Swan,' I say, offering him my hand.

'Nice to meet you, Coco Swan,' he says, shaking it. 'That's lovely. Named after Coco Chanel, are you?' He asks as if it's completely understandable and not at all unusual. It's so nice when that happens.

'Yes, I am actually.'

'Intriguing woman, Chanel,' he says. 'An icon for our times. Your parents were admirers of hers?'

'Well, my mother was sort of obsessed with France.'

'Aha, that explains it. So, Miss Coco Swan, have you plucked up the courage to tell me why you're here? You're not a wealthy city gallery owner, are you, by any chance, here to offer me a million for my latest piece?' He gestures to the clay sculpture behind him. I can't tell what it is from this angle – it could be an animal or a person, or something else entirely.

I take a deep breath. It's now or never. 'I found a letter,' I blurt out. 'From a mother to her child – the child she gave up for adoption in 1956.'

'I see. And?' He seems completely untouched by this news.

'I think you might be that child.'

I exhale, feeling as if I've been holding my breath for ever. I've finally told him and the relief is enormous. There's a second of silence as he digests this, before he breaks into helpless laughter. 'Oh, my dear, dramatic by name, dramatic by nature.' He continues to laugh uproariously.

I look at him, confused. In all my imaginings of this moment, a burst of laughter from Duke/James never appeared on my list of possible reactions.

'You don't think it's you?' I ask.

'God, no,' he says. 'Not a chance, sorry.'

'But hear me out . . .'

'Believe me, Coco, if I was adopted I would have known about it,' he says, still smiling. 'There's no chance it's me, sorry to disappoint you.'

'Not everyone knows they were adopted, though,' I say. 'Times were very different back then.'

He pauses, adjusts his hat slightly. 'Where did you say you found the letter?'

'In this Chanel bag I bought at auction. It was in a secret compartment. Look.' I open Tatty's bag and show it to him.

'How extraordinary,' he says.

'I know it sounds strange, but it's all true. I have the letter here, if you'd like to see it.'

'Why not?' He shrugs.

I hand it to him, and watch as he reads it.

'It's very moving certainly. But what makes you think this was intended for me?' he asks, giving it back.

'Well, I did some investigating that led me to Glacken. And then I met Mac.'

'Mac? Who's Mac?' He looks totally puzzled.

'Mac Gilmartin? The man who bought Glacken House from you?'

I'm a little surprised he can't remember who he sold his old house to. Perhaps he's becoming senile – that may be why he sculpts in the nude. I mean, it's only a few years since he sold his home to Mac but he looked positively blank at the mention of his name.

'I'm sorry, my dear, but you've lost me entirely,' he says now, shaking his head.

At that second Mac comes ambling round the corner, stuffing his phone into his pocket.

'Here he is now,' I say, as he steps into the conservatory.

'Mac Gilmartin, nice to meet you at long last,' he says, stretching out his hand.

'James Flynn, pleasure,' the man replies, pumping Mac's hand energetically in his.

Mac glances at me and raises an eyebrow, as if to ascertain where we are in the proceedings.

'You live in Glacken, I believe?' James says.

'Well, yes, I live in your old property,' Mac says, shooting another enquiring glance at me. 'It's a very beautiful house – I've been really happy there.'

'I'm glad to hear it.' James smiles. 'But I'm afraid there's been a misunderstanding.'

Mac looks at me, bewildered, and we both look at James.

'I'm sorry, Coco, but you've got it all wrong,' he says. 'I'm not the James Flynn you're searching for.'

'But, James, let me just explain to you from the beginning,' I start. The poor man clearly has no idea that he was ever adopted. He can't process the information.

'No, my dear, I know I'm not who you want. I've never lived in Glacken. I've never even visited.'

'But . . .' I start.

'I moved to Port-on-Sea from Cork a few years ago to work. It's the ideal spot for me to sculpt. But I'm definitely not adopted. I'm not the man you're searching for. I'm sorry. There's been a case of mistaken identity.'

'But the estate agent gave Mac this address? Carroll and Carroll?' I twirl to look at Mac, who seems just as surprised as I am.

'There must have been crossed wires,' Mac says, frowning. 'I can't understand it.'

'Carroll and Carroll? Well, my details would be on their system,' James goes on. 'I bought this place through them. But you'll likely find that there are quite a few James Flynns out there – that's the trouble with having such an unoriginal name, my dear, not like Coco.'

I smile at him out of politeness, but inside I'm crushed. I can't believe we got it wrong. I don't want to believe it. 'You're positive?' I ask.

'One hundred per cent,' he says. 'I wish I could tell you different. That's a beautiful letter, and whomever it was intended for is going to be extremely touched to receive it.'

'If he ever does.' I sigh. It seems more unlikely now than ever.

'Oh, I'm sure he will,' James replies, chuckling. 'You seem like a determined sort of girl, just like your namesake.'

'I'm sorry we wasted your time,' I say, putting Tatty's letter back in her bag and closing it. I feel I've let her down, and Mum too, by getting this wrong.

'Please don't apologize,' James says kindly. 'I just hope you find him. Now, I suppose I should get back to work while the muse still calls . . .'

He looks across to the unfinished sculpture and I realize he's politely asking us to leave.

'Well, thank you very much – sorry to intrude and sorry again for the mix-up,' I say. 'It was nice to meet you.'

'Not at all, my dear,' he replies. 'The pleasure was mine.

I'm only sorry I couldn't help you. I know you'll solve the mystery. Don't give up!'

As we walk back to the van, Mac says quietly, 'We seek him here, we seek him there . . .' no doubt in an effort to make me smile. But I can't. All this seizing of the day I've been doing, against my own better judgement, and it's got me precisely nowhere.

23

'Are you sure you're not too cold?' Mac asks, as we settle ourselves at a tiny table outside a little café called the Seagull.

'No, I'm fine,' I say, still trying to muster a genuine smile. 'It's nice to get some sea air.' In fact it's icy, but I'm wrapped up well, and sitting outside like this is very refreshing. Plus it means Horatio can join us.

'As long as you don't freeze to death,' he says.

'The chips will warm me up,' I reply, 'won't they, boy?' Under the table, Horatio licks my hand.

'They do smell good,' Mac agrees.

The unmistakable aroma of fish and chips wafting towards us from inside is making my stomach grumble. The café is sweet – small, with a real seaside theme. When I popped into the Ladies I admired the collection of shells in glass jars, and the wooden anchors attached to the walls at odd angles. It's the view from out here that's the clincher, though – from where we sit, we can see the vastness of the sea, the boats bobbing on the water, the gulls swooping overhead. Even out of season, with the chill in the air, this place is gorgeous. As I sit here, gazing out at the water, I feel oddly content, even though I'm also extremely disappointed that I've hit another dead end.

'Well, he was an interesting character,' Mac says, pulling the menu to him and examining it.

'Yeah, he was. And you didn't see the half of him . . .'

I've already told Mac that I walked in on James Flynn working in the nude and he laughed so hard I thought he might choke. He grins widely at me now across the table. 'I'm guessing you won't be forgetting him in a hurry,' he says.

'He's imprinted on my memory all right.' I giggle.

The sight of that shrivelled bottom is burned on my brain. I can't help but admire him a little, though – imagine having the confidence to work naked. I can't walk from the bathroom to my bedroom without something on. Ruth is completely comfortable with her body and doesn't give a fig about exposing it – she often sunbathes topless out the back of the shop in the summer, much to Anna's indignation. Anna is of the opinion that God gave women breasts to cover, not to expose to the world. She despises even a hint of cleavage – I've lost track of the amount of times she's scolded Ruth for flashing too much skin. Cat is pretty loose about nudity too – I've seen her naked countless times. But I like to keep covered up. I've never been happy enough with my body to show it to anyone without a lot of dim lighting and some carefully draped sheets to disguise it as much as possible.

'There must be something quite freeing about working in the buff,' Mac muses now, plucking some bread from the basket, breaking it in half and giving some to Horatio. He snaffles it immediately, then sits to attention, ready for another treat if he plays his cards right. I sneak him some more bread under the table and am rewarded with another hot, wet lick.

'Liberating, you mean?' I ask.

'Yes,' he replies. 'Not that I'm advocating we should all do it.'

'No, of course not,' I reply seriously. 'I'm not sure the world is ready for that yet. At least, not around here.'

As we watch, two little old ladies amble up the street, dressed in black, with thick tan tights, lace-up shoes, and headscarves tied underneath their chins.

'Appearances can be deceptive, though,' he replies. 'Take those two. They could be the oldest swingers in town.'

I watch as they pause to talk to an elderly man passing the other way.

'And that could be a love triangle,' Mac goes on, dead-pan.

I chuckle, and beside me Horatio thumps his tail.

'I'm telling you,' Mac raises one eyebrow, 'you never know what goes on behind closed doors.'

'Hello there, what can I get you?'

We both look up to see an ultra-glamorous waitress beside us, notepad at the ready. Her eyes are trained on Mac, as if I've somehow become invisible.

'What's the catch of the day?' he asks, smiling politely at her.

'John Dory,' she says. 'Caught this morning in the bay. Lovely, it is.'

'All right so, I'll have that,' he says, handing the menu back to her.

'Chips and mushy peas?' she asks, leaning in close to him in a way she definitely needn't. I can't help notice that her eyes are unusually bright and her smile is dazzling.

'Go on, you've twisted my arm,' he replies, smiling back at her. She gives him another megawatt grin.

Oh, right, she fancies him. Of course. That's why she's all over him like a rash. How rude. For all she knows we could be a couple. We're not, of course, but she doesn't know that. The cheek of her flirting with him!

'I like a man with a healthy appetite,' she says approvingly, her eyes now blatantly roaming over his chest. But it's like he doesn't notice how obvious she's making it that she thinks he's hot.

'The sea air always makes me really hungry,' he says politely.

'It's one way to work up an appetite all right . . .' she replies suggestively.

I get the impression that if I don't speak up, she might forget about me altogether and my stomach is starting to growl. 'Er, I'll have the seafood platter, please,' I venture.

'OK.' Her eyes flick to me for a millisecond, but she doesn't write down the order.

'Em, does that come with anything on the side?' I ask. 'Can I have some chips?'

'Are you just visiting?' she says to Mac, ignoring me again.

'Yes, passing through,' he replies.

'Oh, what a cute dog,' she purrs, stooping to pat Horatio on the head and giving us a real eyeful of her boobs. I tug at my scarf and shift a little in my seat as I watch her pert bosom heaving under her very tight T-shirt. Obviously she doesn't feel the cold. Or she doesn't believe in covering herself up, whatever the weather.

Horatio remains resolutely unmoved by her attention and I stifle a smile – he's not keen on her either.

'He's adorable!' she gushes now, completely over the top. 'What's his name?'

'Horatio,' Mac replies, tickling him under the chin.

The waitress is on her knees now, rubbing Horatio's neck like her life depends on it. It's so transparent it's staggering, but Mac doesn't appear to notice her antics. Instead he's looking across the table to me.

'Do you want to share a basket of onion rings?' he asks. 'They look great.' He gestures to a table just inside the window where a couple are digging into some with relish.

'Sounds good to me!' I reply. I haven't had onion rings in years, but they look delicious and it's not like I have to be careful what my breath smells like – neither Mac nor Horatio will care.

'Er, excuse me?' Mac addresses the waitress who's still crouched on the ground, pretending to be Horatio's number-one fan.

'Yes?' She looks up at him, eyes wide, chin tilted to show her best side. I'd bet my life she's practised that coquettish expression more than once.

'Can we get some onion rings to start, please? Garlic sauce, Coco?'

'Why not?'

'Your name is Coco?' the waitress asks disbelievingly, scrambling upright, leaning across Mac as if she'd sit on his lap, given half the chance.

'Yep,' I reply warily. I can tell by her expression that she thinks this is stupid.

'Wow – how . . . unexpected,' she says. Then, flashing a smile in Mac's direction, she totters off towards the kitchen, hips swaying double time. She's wiggling her rear as hard as she can to impress him. Mind you, she has a pretty good one, especially in those skin-tight bubblegum-pink jeans.

'Do you get that a lot?' Mac asks, as I watch her sashay inside.

'What? Being ignored by a waitress?'

'Eh?'

'She was practically giving you a lap dance,' I say. 'Don't tell me you didn't notice.'

'Em, I thought she was just being friendly,' he says, looking a little embarrassed.

'Yeah, very friendly.' I laugh. 'And no, usually I'm not invisible in restaurants, if that's what you're asking.'

'Actually, I meant do people ask you a lot about your name? It *is* unusual, isn't it?'

Under the table, Horatio is now snoring softly on my toes. His breath is hot and warm, and it's so nice that I don't move my feet away.

'Ah, I see,' I reply. 'Sorry. Yes, I suppose it is unusual, and people do ask about it.'

'So, why are you called Coco?' he says. 'Or is that top secret, too?' His eyes twinkle across the table at me, and I can sense the waitress watching us intently from inside.

'No, it's not,' I say. 'Mum called me that because she loved Coco Chanel and she loved France. It's pretty simple, really.'

'Cool. It's a great name.'

'Thanks, but I don't always think so,' I say.

'Why not?' He pours me a glass of iced water, then does the same for himself.

'I used to get teased about it – there aren't very many Cocos in small-town Ireland. And it doesn't exactly suit me . . .'

'What do you mean?'

'Well, when you have a name like Coco people expect you to be glamorous and stylish. I don't fit that bill.' I glance through the window and, sure enough, the waitress, leaning on the counter, is staring at us. 'Like the woman said,' I add drily, 'it's *unexpected*.'

An expression crosses Mac's face that tells me he hadn't caught the insult the waitress had paid me. He drinks some of his water before he replies.

'You're pretty tough on yourself, aren't you?' he asks.

'No, just realistic.'

Out of nowhere, the waitress slams the basket of fried onion rings in front of me, staring at me coldly. Then, in the blink of an eye, her expression changes utterly and she smiles sweetly at Mac. 'I've brought some water for Horatio,' she purrs, placing a bowl at his feet so we're treated to another eyeful of her chest. 'I thought he might be thirsty.'

'Er, lovely, thanks very much,' Mac replies, a hint of something like nerves in his voice.

'No problem at all, my total pleasure,' she says. 'If there's anything else I can get you, just let me know.'

She gives him a long, lingering look, then sashays away

again, even slower and more deliberately this time. She's been watching far too many Beyoncé videos – she's going to do herself damage if she keeps it up.

'See?' I say, biting into an onion ring with relish. I can't remember why I ever gave up on these – they're absolutely delicious.

'What?'

'She fancies you.'

'Well, I don't fancy her,' he replies. Something about the way he looks at me makes my insides flutter.

'It's lovely here, isn't it?' I say, dipping another onion ring into the garlic sauce.

'Yeah, it is. There are some great spots in this country. I don't know why people ever go anywhere else.'

'Me too. I'm a real home bird.'

'Snap,' he says.

'You are? I don't think people understand that instinct.'

'No?'

'No.' I remember what everyone said about me being too afraid of change to go to New Zealand.

'It sounds like there's more to this story.' He wipes his mouth with his napkin. 'Spill.'

At my feet, Horatio gives a little snort, then snuggles closer to me. I take a deep breath. 'OK, well, my boyfriend moved to New Zealand. My ex-boyfriend, I should say.'

'Ah, I see. And is he your ex-boyfriend because he moved away or in spite of it?'

'It's complicated.'

'It usually is,' he says wryly. 'But go on.'

'Well, he wanted me to go with him, yes.'

'And you didn't want to go?'

'No.'

'Why not? Don't you like the sound of New Zealand?'

'I'm sure it's lovely. But I like where I live. I didn't want to change that.'

'You didn't consider going over there and giving it a try?'

'Not really, no.'

'Was that because of your grandmother? I mean, I can tell you're very close.'

'No. She wanted me to go – she thinks I'm mad not to have tried it. And so does my friend, Cat.'

'But you wouldn't listen, eh?'

'I like things the way they are. Besides, Tom and me, we weren't exactly true love.'

'You weren't?' He raises his eyebrows.

'No. I mean, he was a nice guy. He *is* a nice guy. But . . . there was something missing – you know? Sometimes I think we were more like brother and sister than anything else.'

'Hmm . . . that's not good.'

I laugh. 'No. Definitely not.'

There was a lack of chemistry between Tom and me from the start. No heat or passion. He knew that too, I'm betting, although he never owned up to it. I can't help wondering if he's feeling it now, with his new girlfriend. I hope he is.

'So, let me get this straight,' Mac says, frowning. 'In spite of pretty high-octane pressure from friends and family to travel "out foreign", as they say, you resisted, am I right?'

'Yep, that's pretty much it.' Everyone had wanted me to go – they'd all encouraged me to spread my wings and fly.

'OK. So either you're just a seriously stubborn woman or you're one hardcore home bird.'

I burst out laughing, not knowing whether to be amused or insulted.

'How do you feel about foreign holidays?' he goes on.

I laugh out loud again. 'I quite like them.'

'Are you sure about that?' His eyes narrow. 'When was the last time you travelled abroad? I only ask so I can verify your status, you understand.'

'I was in London recently.'

'You were? You're not just saying that to get me off your case?'

'I went there to speak to one of Tatty's old friends.'

'Of your own free will?'

'Yes!'

'Any other plans to travel in the near future? To Europe, perhaps?'

'Definitely not.'

'OK.' He clasps his hands in front of his chin, his long fingers linked together. 'So, I'm thinking you're a moderate case of home-birditis.'

'I am, huh?'

'Yes. You see, the more severe cases won't even go to the airport. They get twitchy around the luggage department in shops, that sort of thing.'

'They avoid the summer-clothes aisles too?'

'Exactly!' he says. 'That's spot-on. They just don't hold any truck with travel in whatever shape or form.'

'And which sort of home bird are you? Can you self-diagnose?'

'Well, I'm a rare breed. I sometimes have to travel for work, but if I had the choice, I'd stay at home all year and never go anywhere. You're lucky you got me to come this far today.' He has that deadpan expression again, and I know he's kidding.

'Well, you can blame Ruth for that,' I tease. 'She forced you into it.'

'Did she?' He tries to pull off another innocent look, as if he doesn't know what I'm talking about.

'Stop pretending. You know she did.' I giggle.

'OK, maybe she did, but she didn't exactly have to twist my arm.' Again, something about the way he says this makes my tummy flutter.

I glance at my watch – it's even later than I thought it was. 'What about the dog shelter?' I ask.

'What dog shelter?' he replies, a flash of confusion on his face.

'Didn't you say you wanted to visit some shelter round here? Kill two birds with one stone?'

'Er, yes,' he replies, his eyes flicking away from mine. 'Well, it might be a little late to call there now. I'll come back another day.'

'But that means you drove all this way for nothing!' I feel really bad now – Ruth forced him into this good and proper.

He waves away my concern. 'Don't worry about it. It's fine.'

'Your main course.' The waitress places a plate of food

in front of me, none too carefully. She's reapplied her lip-stick and now there's a bright pink stain on her two front teeth. Usually I'd make a discreet gesture to let someone, even a stranger, know this but today I decide to let it go. And as she dangles herself over Mac again, I can't help having a little chuckle to myself. So much for the sisterhood.

Mac reaches across, robs one of my chips and pops it into his mouth.

'Hey!' I say, and pull my plate to me.

'Sorry – they just look so delicious.' He laughs. 'And sharing is caring, you know.'

'Humph,' I mutter, pretending to mind. But I can't help smiling at his cheek.

'Thanks,' he says, to the waitress, as she gives him his plate. 'This looks amazing.'

'I gave you extra chips,' she points out sulkily, as if she's annoyed that he's not responding to her charms. Then she waits for a second and walks away, a disappointed expression on her pointy face. Her over-the-top flirting has gone unnoticed. I'd say that rarely happens to her, and she looks very put out.

Mac shakes the ketchup bottle, then pours the contents all over his plate.

'Like chips with your ketchup, do you?' I ask.

'I love ketchup,' he says. 'Don't you?'

Then he looks at my plate, devoid of red sauce, and his eyes widen. 'You're not one of *them*, are you?'

'One of what?'

'The anti-ketchup police.'

'Who are they when they're at home?'

He exhales. 'Phew. Well, if you haven't even heard of

them, I'm safe,' he says. 'There are people out there who are enemies of ketchup.'

'Enemies of ketchup?' I say, laughing at his silliness.

'Yeah, they're everywhere. They go around dipping coins in ketchup to show you how it's stripping out your insides. That kind of thing.'

'I've never met one.'

'Well, thank your lucky stars,' he says. 'So, what's your plan, Coco Swan?'

'My plan?'

'To find the real James Flynn?'

'I don't know yet,' I say, swirling a chip through some salt and taking a bite.

'Well, you'd better hurry up and make one. I mean, now you've got me involved too . . .' He gives a theatrical sigh.

'You're not involved,' I reply, slipping a chip to Horatio, who gobbles it.

'Oh, yes, I am,' he says, fake-mournfully. 'I mean, how will I sleep at night, knowing there's a letter that needs to be reunited with its real owner? That's not right. I don't think I could rest easy.'

'I'm sure you'll manage,' I say.

He leans across and cheekily grabs another of my chips, even though he has a plateful of his own, popping it into his mouth again before I can protest. 'Nope. I won't. So, in the absence of you coming up with a plan, I've come up with my own.'

'You have?'

'Yep. Plan-making is my speciality. That and being an ace find-outer. I was almost awarded a Scout badge for that.'

'Oh, yeah?' I can't stop a big fat grin spreading across my face. He really is very funny. And, inexplicably, incredibly attractive.

'Yeah,' he replies confidently, nicking another chip. In his pocket, his phone rings. 'Aha!' he says. 'And so it begins.'

'Who is it?'

'The estate agent. While you were in the Ladies making yourself look pretty, I took the initiative and called them again. They're getting the address of the right James Flynn this time.'

He answers the call and I try to make out what's being said, but it's impossible. All he does is nod and mutter, 'Uh-huh.'

'Well?' I ask, as he hangs up. 'What did they say?'

'Just as we thought. They had two James Flynns on their system,' he says. 'But there's no good news about our James Flynn, I'm afraid.'

My heart is in my mouth. 'He's dead?' That would be the worst possible ending.

'No. But they don't have an address for him. After he sold Glacken House to me he moved overseas, they don't know where.'

I'll never find him now. 'They have no idea?' I ask.

'No, sorry, Coco. Apparently he's a violinist with an orchestra. He travels all over the world performing, they said. God knows where he is now.'

My mind is working overtime. 'Give me your phone,' I say.

'Sorry?' He's a little startled by my commanding tone. 'It's a smartphone, yeah?'

'Yeah,' he says, handing it over.

'What's the Wi-Fi code?' He cranes his neck to read it out from a tiny poster in the café window, and I type it in. In seconds, Google has popped up and I punch in 'James Flynn, orchestra'. Mark would be dead proud of me, I think, as I wait for the page to load. Good thing he explained how Wi-Fi works to me that night he helped me with Swan's Facebook page or I'd be clueless.

'Of course!' Mac says, watching me. 'If you can find where the orchestra is playing, it may be all you need.'

I hope so. I really hope so. It seems like it takes the page for ever to load, but then the website opens and I scan the information as fast as I can, hands trembling with anticipation.

'He's the primary violinist with the Irish String Collective Orchestra,' I read. 'And their next performance will be in . . .'

'Where?' Mac asks.

I lift my head and look at him. I can barely believe it. It's a sign, another one in a very long list. 'Paris,' I say. 'Their next performance will be in Paris.'

24

Cat and I are huddled together in a booth at the Central Hotel bar, out of earshot of everyone else. I asked her to meet me because I've come up with what I think is the perfect plan to help Mark. It came to me in a flash after Mac dropped me back at the shop yesterday evening. In fact, I don't know why I didn't think of it before. I climbed out of his van, happy and windswept after our trip, excited that I had more information about James.

As I waved him goodbye and let myself into Swan's, I saw the thug Sean O'Malley skulking past Karl's shop and it suddenly came to me. Out of nowhere, I knew exactly what to do to get Mark out of the mess he'd found himself in, and in a way that wouldn't get him into any more trouble.

'Do you think it'll work?' Cat says now, worry etched on her face.

'Yes,' I reply. 'He's the perfect man for the job.'

'But what if it goes wrong?' she says, her eyes darting to the bar entrance, waiting for him to appear.

'It won't,' I say firmly. 'I'm sure of it.'

'You're full of confidence,' she says admiringly.

I take a sip of my wine and grin at her. 'Maybe I am,' I quip.

'Hang on,' she says, her eyes narrowing in suspicion. 'Is there something you're not telling me? Have you snogged Grizzly Adams? Is that what's put pep in your step?'

Before I can answer her, we hear a deep voice. 'Hello, you two, what's the big secret?'

Karl is standing before us, an uncertain smile on his face.

'Sit down, Karl,' I say. 'I have a proposition for you. Well, more of a request, really.'

Karl slides into the seat opposite us and rests his beefy arms on the table. 'This is all very mysterious,' he says. 'I feel like some sort of secret agent.'

Cat laughs darkly.

'This is the thing, Karl,' I start, sliding the pint of Guinness I'd bought in preparation for his arrival across to him. 'Cat's son Mark is in a bit of trouble.'

Karl takes a sip of his pint and gives a satisfied sigh. 'What sort of trouble?'

'A little shit called Sean O'Malley wants to sell weed at the teenage discos here,' I explain. 'He's been trying to bully and blackmail Mark into helping him do just that.'

Karl has another sip of Guinness and surveys us both. 'I see,' he says solemnly. 'That's not good.'

Cat shakes her head. 'No, it's not,' she says. 'Mark's been behaving strangely for ages now, and I couldn't understand why. Coco got to the bottom of it.'

Karl smiles at me. 'Good woman, Coco,' he says. Beside me, Cat squeezes my hand. Since I told her what Mark had confided to me, she's been a basket of nerves. It's taken all of my persuasion to prevent her storming straight over to Sean's house and throttling him – David too, for that matter. But they had reluctantly agreed that rash action like that wouldn't help Mark. In fact it would probably make things worse.

'The thing is, Karl,' I continue, 'we have to be careful

how we deal with this. Mark doesn't want any more aggro at school. It's a tricky situation.'

'Naturally.' Karl nods.

'But Sean still needs to get a message, as such,' I add carefully.

'And you want me to help?' he asks.

'We think you're the perfect man for the job. You could go and . . . talk to Sean.'

Karl nods thoughtfully. 'I could. But how does young Mark feel about that idea?'

'He's on board with it,' I confirm. 'He just wants Sean off his case, with as little fuss as possible.' I'd called Mark about my idea before I even spoke to Cat and David and he'd sounded really relieved that someone would step in and take control.

'So, will you do it?' Cat asks, desperation in her voice.

Karl pauses. 'Course I will, love,' he says at last. 'I can give me tattoos a day out when I go to see him. I might even wear me bloodstained butcher's apron, forget to take it off, like.'

'That'll frighten the life out of him,' I say approvingly. 'Just what we want.'

Cat exhales. 'Thanks, Karl. I don't want any trouble, I just want you to . . .'

'Scare him a little?' Karl finishes. 'I can do that, don't worry.'

'You're a star,' I say, smiling at him.

'No problem. Now, I'd like you to do something for me too, a favour in return.'

I grin at him. 'I think I have that covered already,' I reply.

I indicate over his shoulder, to where Ruth and Anna are walking into the bar, arm in arm. I asked them to meet me here on purpose. Another inspired idea.

When she sees him, Ruth pales, then glances at me, knowing full well I've set her up. She's going to have to tell Anna about Karl now, just like he wants her to. There's no escape. I feel a little cruel for doing this, but it's for the best, I know. Karl and Ruth are perfect for each other, and Ruth shouldn't be ashamed for everyone to know about them, including Anna.

Karl's eyes widen as he clocks them, and I see his hands start to shake a little. For all his tough-man appearance, he's a big softie inside.

Anna doesn't bat an eyelid when she spots him. 'Hello, Karl,' she says drily, eyeing him. 'So Ruth finally let you out in public, did she?'

Beside her, Ruth gasps.

'You really didn't think you could keep a secret from me, did you?' Anna asks, arching a brow at them. 'If you scale that wall one more time, you'll do yourself an injury, Karl.'

Ruth and Karl look at each other and laugh sheepishly.

'Can I get you a drink, Anna?' Karl asks, gallantly getting to his feet.

'I'll have a small sherry, thank you,' she replies, taking his seat.

'Come on,' Cat says, rising and guiding Karl and Ruth to the bar. 'These are on the house.'

Anna and I are left sitting opposite each other.

'It's not like you to take a drink in the middle of the day,' I say fondly to her.

'I don't usually,' she says. 'But today is exceptional.'

'Why's that?' I ask.

She looks me in the eye. 'I wrote to Colin.'

'You did?' I'm shell-shocked to hear this. She'd seemed so against the idea of forgiving him.

'Yes. Well, I thought about things, and while I don't believe I'll ever be able to forgive him fully, I wanted to move on at last. That's such a modern, vulgar phrase, isn't it? But you know what I mean.'

I reach across the table and take her thin hand in mine. 'I know exactly what you mean,' I say. 'I think you're great.'

'Oh, don't be silly,' she says, colouring. 'You're the great one.'

'Me? What have I done?'

'Well, who else would have dug so deep looking for Tatty's story? You've been so determined. It's taught me a thing or two, I can tell you. And I believed I was too long in the tooth to learn anything new.'

'Well, I dunno about all that . . .' I murmur, a little bashful.

'It's true, Coco. You followed your heart and I admire you so much for that. You're brave, in more ways than one.'

'I'm not that brave,' I say.

'Yes, you are,' she says firmly. 'And I think you should be even braver.'

'What do you mean?' There's a funny look in her eye now.

'Well, what about this nice Mac that Ruth's told me so much about?'

My heart leaps at the mention of his name. 'What about him?'

'Exactly,' she says, smirking at me as Karl, Ruth and Cat arrive back at the table, drinks in hand.

'So, Coco, what are you going to do about this James bloke then, now that he's overseas?' Karl asks. Ruth has clearly filled him in on the most recent developments.

'It's such a pity.' Ruth sighs. 'I mean, it's not like she's going to fly all the way to France to talk to him.'

'Actually,' I say, relishing the moment I know is coming, 'that's exactly what I'm going to do.'

'*Whaaaaat?*' Ruth says, her jaw dropping.

'You'll be OK in the shop for a bit, won't you?' I ask, draining my wine glass and setting it back on the table decisively. I pick up my satchel and take a sheet of paper out of it. 'Would you believe,' I say, to their shocked faces, 'that this is what constitutes an airline ticket nowadays? I just bring that to the airport and apparently they'll let me on board my flight to Paris.'

There's total silence. I'm enjoying myself hugely.

Cat is the first to react. She throws her head back and laughs. 'Finally,' she wheezes, 'Coco Swan starts living the life I always knew she could! I love you for doing this!'

I grin at her.

'Oh, but, Coco . . . Paris . . .' Ruth's eyes are glistening with tears. Paris robbed her of her precious daughter, me of my beloved mum.

'I have to, Ruth,' I say simply, looking into her eyes, willing her to understand.

'Sarah would want her to, Ruth,' Anna says softly.

'I know,' Ruth says, leaning into Karl and smiling weakly at me. 'I know.'

'Well, then, now that's decided,' I say, getting to my feet, 'I'm off.'

'What? Right away?' Cat gasps, suitably shocked all over again.

'Well, I have someone to visit first,' I reply, feeling a blush creeping up my neck.

'Oh, my *God*! She's going to see Mac!' Cat whoops, clapping her hands.

'Good on you, Coco,' Anna says. 'Tell him how you feel. Ask him out on a date.'

'I'm not going to do that, Anna,' I tell her firmly.

Around the table, their faces fall a little.

'Come on, Coco,' Cat pleads. 'Why don't you just –'

I cut across her: 'I'm not going over there to ask Mac Gilmartin out for a date.' I shove the paper back into my satchel and stand up. 'I'm going over there to kiss him for all I'm worth and behave like a floozy for as long as he'll let me.'

'Oh, Coco!' Ruth almost shouts. 'That's the best thing you've said to me in a long time!'

They all burst out laughing, and I grin wickedly at them. 'Mac Gilmartin won't know what's hit him,' I announce, and march out of the bar, with their catcalls and laughter ringing in my ears.

25

The butterflies in my tummy are dancing as I shut the car door and crunch across the gravel outside Glacken House. I can hear the dogs at the back, so I know exactly where Mac is. I only hope he's alone because what I want to say to him doesn't need an audience. I round the corner and there he is, surrounded by yapping dogs, just as he was on the first day I met him.

Horatio sees me first and races across the grass, almost knocking me over with an enthusiastic leap at my chest.

'Hello.' I giggle, patting him as he licks me wherever he can reach. And then I look up – straight into Mac's eyes.

'What brings you here?' he asks, breaking into a wide smile.

'You,' I reply simply.

There's a beat as he registers what I'm saying and then I'm by his side and we're kissing hungrily, and it's like I'm submerged under water, oblivious to everything else. His arms are around me, then his hands are in my hair, and I feel as if I'm being swept away to somewhere I've never been before, somewhere I want to stay.

'Wow,' he breathes, when we finally come up for air.

'I've been wanting to do that ever since we first met,' I admit.

'Snap,' he whispers, his breath on my neck, his lips at my ear.

'Actually, if you don't mind, there's quite a bit more I'd like to do,' I say, my knees feeling weak as he goes to kiss me once more.

His face moves away a little, his eyes searching mine. 'Is that so, Ms Swan?'

'Yes, it is,' I say, staring straight back at him, drinking him in, feeling a wave of lust so intense wash over me that I'm almost breathless. 'I'm a brazen hussy, you see.'

'Aha!' he says, deadpan as always. 'And there I was thinking you were a nice girl.'

And then he sweeps me off my feet into his arms and I feel like the happiest girl alive.

'Well, that was very unexpected,' Mac says, a few hours later.

We're in his big bed, and I haven't felt as happy in a long time. Coming here and making my feelings for him plain was the best idea I ever had. I still can't believe I had the guts to make the first move, but I'm so glad I did. And now here I am, lying naked beside him and I'm not even self-conscious. It's like I'm a whole new me.

'Yes, it was,' I agree, curling my toes around his under the covers and snuggling into the crook of his arm. It's the perfect fit. 'I don't suppose you thought I was the type to turn up at your doorstep and lure you into bed.'

'I don't suppose I did,' he says, propping himself up on one elbow and gazing down at me, his almost black eyes warm. 'Not that I'm complaining.'

'I should hope not,' I say, giggling. 'Anyway, I only made my move because you were too much of a gentleman to do it.'

'Meaning?'

'Meaning that there never was any dog shelter near Port-on-Sea, was there? You made that up.'

'Rumbled,' he admits. 'A man has to do what a man has to do. So, the question is, Coco Swan, where do we go from here?'

His fingers are grazing the skin on the inside of my thigh now and I shudder with pleasure at his touch. There's electricity between us, like nothing I've ever experienced before.

'Well, I'm going to be unavailable for a day or two. I'm going to Paris,' I reply loftily.

'Oh, you are, are you?' he says. 'Now, why doesn't that surprise me?'

'I have to follow the story.' I shrug.

'Fancy some company?' he asks. 'I'm an ace find-outer, remember?'

'Thanks, Mac, but not this time, sorry,' I say regretfully. 'I'd love you to, but . . .'

'This is something you have to do on your own?'

'Yes.' I nod. 'I know it's what my mum would have wanted, you see.'

'I get it,' he replies. 'That voice inside is talking to you?'

'You have that too?' I smile at him.

'Oh, sure,' he replies. 'Everyone does, I think. The thing is to listen to it – it's rarely wrong.'

'That's what I'm hoping,' I say, stroking his cheek, relishing being there with him.

'But you'll be back, won't you? You won't disappear over the horizon?' he asks, lowering his lips to my collar bone, his eyes still locked on mine.

I lean back against the pillow and sigh with pleasure, revelling in his touch. 'Oh, yes, I'll definitely be back. You can count on it. I'm a home bird, remember?'

'That's good. Because I'll be waiting.'

And then I close my eyes, lost in his touch once more.

26

Chanel Boutique, 31 rue Cambon.

I can't believe I'm finally in Paris, standing in front of the iconic Chanel store. This was Coco Chanel's realm, her kingdom, and, strange as it may sound, I can feel her spirit in the air. This was where Tatty's beautiful bag was created. It's also where Tatty and her married lover spent a magical evening in Chanel's company, the weekend their baby was conceived. This is where James's story began.

Tonight I'm not wearing my trusty jeans and scruffy ankle boots. Instead, I'm wearing a little black dress in honour of the occasion. Mum's precious pearls are at my neck and Tatty's beloved Chanel bag is decorating my arm. It's a wondrous thing, but being here, in this exotic, incredible city, so full of light and mystery, I feel close to them both – to Tatty and to Mum. Both of them spent time here. Both of them loved Chanel. It's like a glorious circle of life, corny as it may sound.

I hate to leave this place, but it's time to go. I turn away from Coco's shop and hurry through the cobbled back-streets towards my destination. It's almost midnight and I can't be late, tonight of all nights.

The café on the corner is warm and inviting, with a seductive smell of espresso brewing. I order a coffee and sit by the window. I look around, wondering if Mum was ever here. It's very close to where she was knocked down. Maybe that's why I chose it. Being here, near to where she drew her last breath, makes me feel closer to her. No wonder she loved Paris so much: everything about the city is magical. I should have come here long before now, I know that, because I feel at peace with her death in a way I never have, just from being in her beloved City of Light. As I sip my coffee I look around. There's an old photo hanging on the wall above me that shows a baker, arms crossed, expression both arrogant and proud. He must have been the previous *boulangerie* owner, before this place became the chic little café bar it is today. For all I know, Mum could have bought her baguette in here every day – that baker might have known her, even. The idea makes me feel warm inside. I'm not at all sad to be here, as Ruth feared. I'm content. I'm doing what Mum would have wanted me to do.

Tonight has been unforgettable in many ways. The recital at La Salle Pleyel, on rue du Faubourg Saint-Honoré, was bewitching. I couldn't pick out James in the orchestra, of course, because there were so many musicians on the stage, but just sitting in the audience, soaking up the atmosphere and listening to the music, was an electrifying experience. I'd never been to an orchestral performance before and I loved it.

I cradle my demi-tasse cup and breathe in the rich aroma, closing my eyes for a second, thinking about how it felt to be lost in the moment, letting the music wash over me and take me away.

When I open my eyes again, a man is standing before

me, a violin case tucked under his arm. He's dressed in a thick black coat and formal black patent shoes. His face is partially hidden by the thick white wool scarf wrapped around his neck, but his eyes are inquisitive as he surveys me. I know in an instant that this is James Flynn, Duke Moynihan – those eyes are Tatty's, the eyes that shone with so much life from Bonnie's dressing-room wall in Farringdon.

'James?' I ask, looking up at him.

'Coco?' he replies.

I nod and invite him to sit. Incredibly, now that he's finally here, I'm totally calm. It feels like destiny.

'Thank you for coming to meet me,' I say. 'I'm sure you must have thought it a bizarre request.'

When I'd left the note for him at the stage door before the performance, I wasn't sure he would turn up to a rendezvous with a total stranger. I had just hoped that what I'd asked would be enough to pique his curiosity.

'Well, it was an intriguing note,' he replies, cocking one eyebrow. 'How could I refuse?' He catches the waiter's eye. '*Un grand café, s'il vous plaît, Monsieur.*'

'The performance was wonderful,' I say. 'I was transported.' This is nothing but the truth.

'You're very kind,' he says. 'The Salle Pleyel is one of my favourite venues in Europe, actually, because the acoustics are incredible. It's always a huge honour to perform there.'

The sallow-faced waiter places his coffee before him and backs away, as if sensing we have something important to talk about.

'So, Mademoiselle Coco,' he says. 'Do you want to tell me why I find myself sitting with a fellow Irish native in a Parisian café after midnight?'

I look into his eyes, so like Tatty's.

'It's about your mother,' I say.

His expression changes instantly, as does the very air between us. 'You mean my birth mother?' he asks. It's as if he's not in the least surprised, as if he's been waiting a very long time to hear news of her.

I nod, relieved that at least he knows this much. 'Yes.' I put Tatty's bag and the letter she wrote to him on the table. 'These were hers,' I say simply. 'I'm here to give them to you.'

He reaches for both items, caressing the bag with his slim violinist's fingers with such care and emotion I think I might cry. Then he unfolds the letter and starts to read. The space between us is still and silent as he does.

'I need to explain where I got them,' I say to him as he finishes, tears glistening in his eyes.

'There's time enough for that,' he says, his voice choked with emotion. 'I'm just so happy you made the effort to find me and give them to me.'

My heart soars with joy. I couldn't have wished for a better response. If Tatty is watching, I know that her heart will be overflowing too.

I smile gratefully at him. 'I was afraid you'd be shocked or angry or hurt by this. I'm so glad you're not.'

'I can't tell you how much it means to me,' he says, his coffee cup shaking in his hand. 'I've waited all my life to find out about my birth mother. I had given up hope that it would ever happen. I never even knew her name.'

I reach for his hand. Even though we've never met before, this powerful story and the emotions it provokes have connected us immediately.

'Your mother's name was Tatty Moynihan,' I say, 'and she carried that letter with her everywhere from the day you were born until the day she died.'

'Tatty Moynihan,' he says, as if he's trying on the name for size. 'Did you know her?'

'No.' I shake my head. 'But I've met people who did. She seemed like a wonderful woman, musical like you.'

'Really?' His eyes lift to mine. 'My adoptive parents were farmers and, you know, I always thought I must have inherited music from my birth parents.'

'Well, she had a beautiful voice,' I say. 'I have a recording of her you can listen to.'

I made a CD of Tatty's recording and have it with me. I've already mailed a copy to Mary Moore in Dublin and to Bonnie Bradbury in London, to thank them both for helping me.

'I can't believe it,' he says, shaking his head. 'I spent my life wondering about her, and now it's like she's come for me at last. Thank you, Coco.'

I look at his joy and feel it too. 'I know what you mean,' I whisper. 'Mothers have a funny knack of coming through when you need them most.'

We embrace across the table, tears streaming down both our faces now. I can sense the waiter looking at us with interest. He doesn't seem all that shocked to see two adults crying openly, but then, it is Paris after all, the city of emotion.

'We have a lot to talk about,' I say, when we pull apart. 'Maybe we should get another coffee.'

'Forget the coffee,' he says, laughing. 'I need a cognac.'

The next morning, James and I are strolling together arm in arm by the Seine. We talked late into the night, yet there still seems so much to say.

'So you'll come to Dronmore, then?' I say, leaning into him as we navigate the frosty path, our breaths in clouds before us as we walk and talk.

I've invited him to visit Swan's when he's next in Ireland. We spoke about the shop at length last night, how much I love it, my plans and dreams for it. Listening to James talk about his passion for his music reminded me of my passion for my work, and now I'm inspired to bring the unique spirit of Paris back to Swan's with me. I've already decided to visit some of the markets while I'm here, make new contacts and source new stock. I'm even thinking about setting up an on-line store, selling unusual and quirky French pieces. I suddenly feel as if anything is possible and I'm excited about what the future will bring, which direction my life may take. I may never be a true wanderer, like Mum – I'm definitely more of a home bird, like I told Mac – but I can still tap into the adventurous side of myself, especially now I know how much fun that can be.

'Just try to stop me visiting you.' James chuckles now. 'I want to meet everyone – all the lovely friends and family you've told me about.'

'And you'll play your violin for us? Perform a recital in Swan's, among the chaos?'

'Of course.' He nods gallantly. 'You have to promise to bring Mac, too. I want to meet the man who's living in Glacken House now. I have many happy memories of my years there.'

'I will, I promise,' I say, hugging the idea to myself. I can't wait to see Mac again and tell him my grand plans.

We pause and look out over the dark water together, the icy breeze on our cheeks.

'It's such a beautiful city, isn't it, James? No wonder my mum loved it.'

'It must be sad for you to be here, too,' he says quietly.

I've told him all about Mum, the accident, and how her beloved Paris finally claimed her life.

'It is, in a way, but in another it's been really . . . liberating.'

'I'm so glad you searched for me, Coco,' he says. 'I can't tell you how glad.'

'Me too.' I smile at him.

He reaches into the music satchel on his shoulder and pulls out Tatty's Chanel bag. 'This is yours,' he says, handing it to me.

'Oh, no,' I reply. 'It belongs to you, James. Your mother would want you to have it.'

'No.' He shakes his head vehemently. 'This bag has your name all over it, Coco. Tatty would want you to have it, I'm sure. Both our mothers would.'

He gives it to me and I hold it close to my chest, breathing in its special scent, the faint whiff of lavender.

'Thank you,' I say simply, too overcome with emotion to trust myself to say anything else.

'It's my pleasure,' he says, smiling warmly. 'I've been lucky enough to get a letter from my mother when I least expected it. I only wish you could have, too.'

I smile back at him, knowing in my heart that I have been blessed too. 'This bag has been my letter, James. It's given me everything I needed.'

He nods, as if he understands what I mean. 'You know how you said that you thought your mother sent it to you, Coco?'

'Yes?'

'What do you think she was trying to tell you?'

I look at the Seine, at the elegant buildings of Paris, at the bridges arching over the water, connecting the city in all its parts. I look at the curve of the street we're standing on, the promise of what might be around the corner. I'm smiling because I can't help it, because at home Mac is waiting for me. I'm smiling because I'm so happy I could burst.

'I think . . .' I say '. . . she was telling me that it was time to start living.'

Dublin, May 2012

Tatty's hand shook as she gripped the pen. Writing was more difficult, these days, but she was determined to do it, now more than ever.

It was the nurse who had made up her mind. Mary Moore. Oh, yes, she came across as a tough cookie, what with her bossy attitude, but she was as soft as butter underneath. Tatty still chuckled to herself when she remembered the interview. Mary had actually scolded her for living in such a grand house, claiming that the stairs were too much for an old dear like her. She had impressed Tatty so much that she'd hired her on the spot. She'd reminded her a little of her old friend from London, Bonnie Bradbury – she had exactly the same feisty attitude. Poor Bonnie. She felt bad for holding her at arm's length, but she couldn't take the chance that her old friend would talk her out of her final decision. Bonnie was always on her side – she always had been – and she might not think what she had planned was very bright. No, she might not understand now, but she would in the end, Tatty knew that.

Tatty also knew that she wouldn't be needing Mary for much longer. She was already wheelchair-bound. It was time to get organized.

She took up her pen again and began to write her instructions for her solicitor, Dermot Browne. He was an arrogant so-and-so, but he would follow her orders to the letter and that was all that mattered.

Half of her fortune would go to the single mothers' charity. Things were different these days, of course – lots of children were born without their parents being married and forced adoptions were unheard of, thankfully. But, still, the money would be useful to them.

The other half would go to the charity that supported those who had no record of their adoptions but were desperate to unearth their histories. There were so many people out there who had no idea where they had come from. The money would help. After all, as Mary Moore had reminded her earlier that day, material things were just that – things. She couldn't bring them with her. Instead, the house and all the contents would make a pretty penny or two for those who needed it, and that thought made Tatty very happy.

It was only her beloved Chanel handbag that she would be sad to leave behind. It had meant so much to her for so long. She had to ensure that it wasn't sold to some hot-shot collector who wouldn't value it for what it really was. She already knew what she would do with it.

Her mind was made up. She would pack it into a box of worthless trinkets and send it to a small country auction, with the marble wash-stand that reminded her of the one that had stood in Chanel's magnificent *salon* on rue Cambon. If she closed her eyes, she could still see the vase of dried lavender that had stood atop it on that unforgettable weekend, the weekend her beloved Duke had been conceived. Before they'd left the *salon*, she'd slipped a sprig into her bag, to keep for ever. It had crumbled into nothing over the years, of course, but the scent still lingered, reminding her of all she had won and lost.

She would leave the letter she had written to Duke all those years ago inside the bag. She couldn't explain that decision, even to herself, but somehow the bag and her son were so bound together in her mind that it seemed impossible to separate them.

If she told anyone what she was doing, they would call her a daft old woman – to leave a valuable bag at the bottom of a box of nothings. Tatty smiled to herself. She'd learned a couple of things in her lifetime and one of them was to trust in what was beyond you. She was going to trust this bag, this letter, to destiny. She didn't know who would find the bag or where it would eventually end up, but something told her that Coco Chanel would guide it to its rightful owner – to a woman who would treasure it as much as she always had. The bag's story was not over, even if hers almost was.

Laying down her pen, Tatty looked out of the window to the street below and remembered the way her beautiful baby boy had rested in her arms for those eight brief, exquisite, painful hours. They had been the shortest, most precious hours of her life – the centre point of her entire existence. Her son, the boy she hadn't seen grow to be a man, had known he was loved for their short time together, of that she was certain. She could only hope that her mother's love had lasted his whole life through, and that somehow he could feel it still, wherever he was.